KU-061-353

ESCAPE THE NIGHT

Richard North Patterson

ARROW

Published in the United Kingdom in 1994 by
Arrow Books

5 7 9 10 8 6 4

Copyright © Richard North Patterson, 1983

The right of Richard North Patterson to be identified as the
author of this work has been asserted by him in accordance
with the Copyright, Designs and Patents Act, 1988

First published in the United Kingdom in 1994 by Arrow

Arrow Books Limited
Random House UK Ltd
20 Vauxhall Bridge Road, London, SW1V 2SA

Random House Australia (Pty) Limited
16 Dalmore Drive, Scoresby, Victoria, 3179

Random House New Zealand Limited
18 Poland Road, Glenfield
Auckland 10, New Zealand

Random House South Africa (Pty) Limited
Endulini, 5a Jubilee Road, Parktown 2193, South Africa

Random House UK Limited Reg. No. 954009

A CIP catalogue record for this book is available from the British
Library

Papers used by Random House UK Limited are natural, recyclable
products made from wood grown in sustainable forests. The
manufacturing processes conform to the environmental regulations of
the country of origin

Printed and bound in Germany by
Elsnerdruck, Berlin

ISBN 0 09 937421 8

FOR LISA

The gods visit the sins of the fathers upon their sons.

EURIPIDES

I am thy Father's spirit,
Doom'd for a certain term to walk the night, . . .
Till the foul crimes done in my days of nature
Are burnt and purg'd away.

SHAKESPEARE,
Hamlet, Act I, Scene v

PART I

Manhattan

JUNE 1, 1952—
APRIL 19, 1959

CHAPTER 1

Alicia Carey cried out.

Snakes writhed on the bare walls of the labor room. The thin white gown became a straitjacket. The nurse holding the fetoscope was a withered hag.

She had been hallucinating for five hours.

She had lost dominion over her body. The scopolamine warping her senses left her numb. In lucid moments she recalled dimly the wetness of her water breaking and Charles rushing her into the cool dark. She remembered hating him more clearly than she remembered his face.

That had been twenty-six hours ago. Their driver had sped them to an emergency entrance framed by sickly cracks of light. Its doors slammed behind her. An attendant wheeled her alone to a narrow bed. The nurse shaving her pubic hair frowned at her slim hips. The doctor stabbed her with Nembutal.

Except for nausea that shot was the last thing she truly felt or perceived. The i.v. piercing her arm went unnoticed. The overhead light became the sun. She vomited.

Her makeup had run and her ash-blond hair was lank with sweat. Her legs thrashed beneath the hospital gown. Her mouth tasted bitter.

Only her eyes hadn't changed.

Since the moment of her debut, Alicia's eyes had excited and disturbed, their charged bright greenness promising intensity past reason to that man who could touch it. When Charles Carey first entered her, they had filled with tears. Carey felt as if he had lost his soul.

He sat in the waiting room with an ashtray stuffed with cigarette butts and a New York *Times* folded in his lap. He had shaved and changed into a windbreaker and slacks, but fatigue took the edge off his vitality. Dr. Schoenberg approached him with hesitance. This was unusual: few people had ever felt sorry for Charles Carey.

Charles rose. He seemed younger than thirty-two, a blade-slim man with an auburn shock of hair and a tactile gaze that grasped Schoenberg's pity and shot back a split second's resentment. Since childhood, Carey had hated sympathy for the fear it made him feel.

Charles Carey had seldom been afraid. He had made first-string back at Harvard by playing on an injured knee. Later, in the Air Corps, he had learned to fly and shot down twelve German planes. He took chances others would not take. When anti-aircraft fire tore through his fighter, he crash-landed in the English Channel. A cutter found Charles Carey treading water, one arm crooking the neck of the skinny tail gunner who had passed out from the cold. They gave him the Air Force Cross. The doe-eyed nurse who treated him took him home.

In bed, they laughed over his luck. Half facetiously, she asked whether he'd run for governor of New York if he managed to survive the war. Carey turned quiet, and said that he had something else to do.

Charles Carey became the only man to successfully defy his father.

In 1907, John Peter Carey had quit eighth grade to scuttle coal at Van Dreelen & Sons and take their books to the bindery in a horse-drawn wagon. When America entered World War I he was twenty-four and half the sales force had disappeared. John went to the sales manager. Thinking to discourage him, the man asked that Carey call on the firm's most recalcitrant customer. John Carey returned with a massive order. Later he took the man's job.

John Carey rose within Van Dreelen & Sons, marrying a Van Dreelen daughter and ignoring their own two sons. When there were no more Van Dreelen sons, he renamed the firm Van Dreelen & Carey and turned it into a predator. Publishing rivals called him "Black Jack," less for his saturnine looks than for the authors he stole. He fished with Hemingway for marlin, loaned Fitzgerald money, drank all night with Faulkner. By 1942 John Carey's books ruled the best-seller lists, their taloned eagle—a symbol of his own invention—staring past his shoulder from the cover of *Time* magazine, unprecedented for a publisher. "Which one is the eagle?" an assistant joked, then fretted for a week. His editors slaved in rabbit warrens, their doors left open on John Carey's order. From behind the Louis XIV desk that graced his own oak-paneled office, John Carey issued still more edicts, their reason less important than that they be obeyed. Part of this hunger for respect became dandyism, culminating in the iron rule that all male employees wear hats. Its darker side was a stifling paternalism: John Carey backed his staff until they opposed him. Those few who did were terminated.

In 1945, Charles Carey reported to his father's firm, without a hat.

The receptionist glanced up, startled. Within twenty minutes Charles sat in his father's office amidst the sweet, familiar pungency of thin cigars, ordered hand-rolled from Havana. John Carey leaned forward across his desk, barrel chest straining his three-piece suit, his anger—etched like scars running from his nostrils to the corner of his mouth and then to the square of his jaw—leaping from his black hawk's eyes. "Buy a hat," John Carey snapped. "Today. Otherwise you'll not set foot in this firm again."

Charles listened with the watchful stillness he had assumed in his father's presence since boyhood. "I've killed people," he answered. "And saved others. I didn't do those things to wear a hat."

John Carey stared through the smoke. "You think the war made you different. It didn't."

"Not the war. You." Charles's eyes riveted his father's. "I've watched you ever since Phillip and I were small and you were peddling books. You'd come in at the train station with that big trunk, trailing orders and neglect like some god that appeared and disappeared at will. Phillip never got over it. He still believes in God. *I* don't. You're just a man." Charles finished, in a soft voice, "I'm as smart as you, perhaps smarter. But if you fire me now, we'll never know."

John Carey brooded for a day, then rescinded his rule. It was the cost of learning about his own son.

Their edgy truce lasted, day by day, for seven years. Where

John Carey was shrewd, Charles had taste. His dash and nerve balanced his father's toughness. He signed young writers his father could not reach—men who had returned from the war to write of things Charles knew in his bones and marrow. John Carey learned the advantage of appearing to tolerate a son: it lent him a humanizing flaw. But Charles was useful in one other way.

His brother Phillip joined the firm in 1947. As if to counter Charles's perversity, the younger Carey willed himself into an avatar of his father, affecting dark suits and an entrepreneurial flair. As a child, Phillip had clung to his mother. In his twenties he chose to become John Carey—and to inherit his firm. Charles was his only rival; for five years John Carey teased them with his choice. He knew of Phillip's need, and that Charles's indifference was feigned.

Phillip festered, became fearful of mistakes. The defiant Charles prospered under pressure. He found new authors, made money for the firm. He grew in reputation. His friends were writers, athletes, actors and intellectuals. He took part in Democratic politics, was good copy for Leonard Lyons. Women responded to his zest. He had a bright, fantastic smile that banished the wariness from his face and made them wait for it again. For a while he was seen with Audrey Hepburn, displaying the same gallant detachment that had enabled him to enjoy other women until they wanted more and, without remorse or backward glances, he would play out the end game, and gently disengage. "I'm not the tragic lover type," he once remarked.

Then he met Allie Fairvoort . . .

"How is she now?" he demanded of Schoenberg.

The obstetrician shifted on the balls of his feet. "It's a difficult labor. She either can't help, or doesn't want to."

Carey felt hot. Acrid smoke rose from the ashtray to mingle with the smell of floor wax. The waiting room—worn green rug, cheap coffee table with tattered magazines—reminded him of a bad motel. Its foreignness chafed his nerves. "Is there some way I can be with her?"

Schoenberg turned away, shaking his head. Carey gripped his shoulder. "You see, she doesn't want this baby . . ."

* * *

· What Allie Fairvoort wanted was a perfect union with a man.

It was as if that single ambition sprang from all the others she'd never needed. Her family was wealthy and secure. She had learned to ski in St. Moritz and breezed through Wellesley without trying. She wrote poetry and burned it in tides of elation and despair. In college she had acted, living in some psychic twilight between her own life and the roles she played. But she had no desire to become more polished, and would not learn. She wanted neither career nor children. She attracted men, teasing and discarding them, and took no lovers. She was waiting to be consumed.

One cool spring evening, at a glittering East Side party, she saw Charles Carey, and learned his name.

He was standing near three other men, sipping a straight-up martini as they listened to a dark and pretty guest from Mississippi lecture on the Southern woman. "We're not like the others," she was saying. "We find our strength in submissiveness."

The three men, older than Charles, nodded and smiled. Charles watched her gravely, head slightly tilted, saying nothing. Taking in the cut-glass features and cobalt-blue eyes, Allie realized with a rush that he was more attractive than any man she'd known. But she was captured by his stillness: it was the stillness of someone in perfect control of his own thoughts.

"So," the young guest began, challenging her listeners, "how would you define the Southern woman?"

The bearded man furthest to the left gave a gallant smile and said, "Dazzling." Her head bobbed down the line as the next man announced, "Mysterious," with an air of drama, the third leaning forward to purr, "Desirable," as if hoping to top the others. Allie Fairvoort thought they were fools.

The woman turned to Charles Carey. He seemed to breathe in, as if considering whether to speak. Softly he answered, "Angry and repressed."

Ten minutes later, the woman left with him.

That night Allie twisted in her bed, hating the dark-haired woman, imagining her cries as Carey's body moved on hers, his mouth seeking her nipple . . .

Two months later, lying naked under Charles Carey, Allie cried out for him to kiss her breast.

She had planned it with care. Avoiding Charles, she quietly tracked him through a mutual friend, learned that he seemed driven by things he would not reveal, tested his nerves on polo and sports cars and Black Jack Carey, dated women who were shimmering and impermanent. Quickly, she declined the offer to arrange a meeting. Instead, with the delicacy of a finely wrought drama of which she was the protagonist, Allie crept into Charles Carey's mind. A glancing smile at a party, a chance meeting at the theater, the merest hint of interest, enough for a first evening out, then another. She was planning to surprise him, just as she was planning how he would feel inside her the first time they made love.

Sensing these things, Carey still did not grasp them. He was used to women of a blithe sophistication that never surprised him, whatever form it took. Trained to coolness, he was moved by Allie's buried passion without being sure of what it meant. Instead, he began feeling that they were linked in a subtle exchange as elaborate as a minuet, and as silent. He accorded his actions new weight: quick to sleep with women, he made no move with Allie, and received no invitation. Only once did she teasingly touch the subject: in a taxicab on the way to the Stork Club she suddenly asked, "Did you ever sleep with that silly girl from Mississippi?"

Charles leaned back, curious. "I make a point of never saying. Some of the women I've known are still speaking to me."

Allie smiled in the dark. "I wonder if *I* will," she replied, and then was silent.

They spoke nothing more of this. Public people, they dated in public—at the ballet, opera or theater—their thoughts remaining private. They were a striking couple: Charles's look of energy without waste, Allie with the provocative air of a woman who would say what she pleased, with quicksilver movements and eyes that changed like a cat's in the light. They laughed often. He was amused by her elaborate sympathies for people she hardly knew—derelicts or writers without money— and by the way she took Manhattan personally, as if its charms and defects were meant for her. "You're laughing at me," she challenged him early on.

They had been strolling past the Pulitzer Fountain after brunch at the Plaza—Charles in a pin-stripe suit cut crisp as a knife, Allie's hair bright as champagne in sunlight as it rippled in the fresh breeze—when she abruptly knelt in front of a stranger's poodle, ruffling its ears and cooing in a happy lilt that seemed their own language. Charles and the man passed bemused smiles across the rapt pair until Allie rose and caught Charles's look in the corner of her eye. "You *are* laughing," she insisted. "The others never have."

"They're too scared. Beautiful women do that."

She smiled at the compliment. "And you're not frightened?"

He appraised her with that same sideways tilt of the head she had first seen directed at the dark-haired woman. Without smiling he had answered, "Perhaps when I know you better."

The night it happened they had gone to *A Streetcar Named Desire* and then on to the upstairs bar at Sardi's, drinking cognac and talking about everything and nothing. Carey felt her tension: her gestures were broader, and her smile, too quick to flash and vanish, seemed wired to her nerve ends. On the way to her apartment Allie unexpectedly asked him in. Once there, she moved to the sofa without speaking and sat looking up at him.

He went to her. She kissed him avidly, pulling him down until they lay pressed against each other, then pushed him away. He stood by instinct, watching mutely as she raised her dress above her fine long legs, to show him. She quivered as he undressed.

Had Charles Carey known her fantasies, he would have said that no man could ever be that shining, and left. Unseeing, he tried to match them, then loved her for the tears in her eyes, not knowing feeling from imagination.

Allie Carey felt only sweat and revulsion as they put her on the delivery table and pushed her feet and ankles through metal stirrups bolted to its end, straddling her legs. Schoenberg and the anesthesiologist sat on metal stools by her head, next to a machine with tubes and a black rubber mask. To Allie they were dwarfs who had stolen her sense of her own body.

"I have to take the baby," Schoenberg said. "Put her all the way under."

Her neck twisted as the anesthesiologist pushed the mask to her nose and mouth and turned on the ether. A nurse checked the oxygen on the baby warmer and took a pack of glistening steel instruments from a bare shelf. The forceps fell clattering to the floor. As Allie passed out she could smell the faint freshness of ozone, before it rains.

It was raining when Phillip Carey reached the hospital, perfect as a male model and trailing the faintest whiff of cologne. He fished in his pocket and produced a box of English Oval cigarettes. Charles took one, snapped his lighter, had one deep drag and asked, "How's the patriarch?"

Phillip's smile was thin. "He said he's both too young and too old for this sort of thing. 'I'll wait until they produce something,' I think were his exact words."

"Ever the family man." Charles glanced at the *Times*, saw WEST BERLIN BORDER HOMES SEALED BY EAST GERMAN POLICE without interest or comprehension. "I wonder how much emotion he expended on our mother."

"He outlived her." Phillip shrugged. He inspected the waiting room with distaste. "Don't let you do this with much grace, do they?"

Charles looked up with a glimmer of amusement. Phillip had grown a clipped mustache to go with his tailored clothes and pearl cufflinks. His natural movements were willowy: Charles could see the military strut of Black Jack Carey in the way he held them in, discerned a tension running parallel to his own. "Childbirth is the great leveler," Charles answered. "Another Bolshevik plot for your friend Englehardt from HUAC: 'I have here a list of five hundred babies . . .'"

"We'll never agree on that, will we?"

"Politics, or babies?"

"Either one, I expect." Phillip carefully placed his hat on the table and sat across from Charles. "How's Allie taking to her new role? She's not generally noted for supporting parts."

Charles paled slightly: by now anger changed only the color

of his face, not its expression. Knowing that Phillip used his conceit of Allie as actress because it touched a nerve, he remained silent: to respond would be to acknowledge the unspoken war which now embraced even childbirth, but which only John Carey could end, by dying. Instead, finishing the cigarette, Charles watched the sinuous twist of smoke as it vanished, thinking of Allie's almost sensual relation to poetry, and how her moods—bright or melancholy—vibrated with the music she had heard. Pregnancy had cracked her like a glass.

Slowly, Schoenberg sliced her open: her hips were narrow and a Caesarean section too risky. But there was more blood than usual, and it took him a moment to see the head.

He opened his forceps, slid them through the incision, and clamped. His forehead glistened. Slowly, he pulled the baby from its mother. Its hair was matted with blood and its skin was blue from drugs and lack of air. The nurse cleaned mucus from its nose and mouth with quick jabs of a bulb syringe. Schoenberg spanked it.

Its head lolled. Schoenberg slapped it again. The baby neither cried nor moved nor breathed. Quickly Schoenberg cut its cord and rushed it to the baby warmer, clapping an oxygen mask on its face. "Damned Nembutal," he muttered.

The baby's leg moved. Slowly, its skin grew flushed. It squalled, then curled on its side, scarcely more conscious than its mother.

When Allie awoke several hours later she lay rigid, refusing to hold the baby or look into its face. They took it to the nursery.

Staring through the glass, Charles saw Allie Fairvoort in the blondness of its hair.

He glanced up, caught Phillip Carey's reflection as he looked down at the baby. For an instant, Charles read fear and vulnerability, felt their father pass between them like a feather in a vacuum, leaving no trace. Blindly, the baby reached toward its uncle with a tiny fist: Phillip's face softened.

"Ah," he said quietly. "The son and heir."

A nurse appeared, riffling a sheaf of forms. "Is one of you the father?"

Charles nodded. "I am."

"The mother won't give us a name."

Charles turned, hands in his pockets, watching his son as if wondering what its life might hold. Then he turned back again, facing his brother for a long, cool moment before he looked at the nurse. "John Peter Carey," he told her softly. "The second."

CHAPTER 2

Peter Carey looked nothing like his grandfather.

By the time he was four, it was clear that Peter would always be fair, that he would grow taller than Black Jack Carey, his features more fine. He had his father's cobalt-blue eyes. They were as watchful as his father's, his bearing—slim, straight back, chin tilted up—often as still. He was quiet near his mother. At other times he would careen down the grassy slopes in Central Park, arms flailing and hair bouncing in corn-blond waves as he fled the unnamed enemy he sensed that Charles watched for, until he ran out of control, stumbling and falling and rolling in a laughing frenzy of imagined terror while he looked back toward his father for help. In his fantasies, Charles Carey always rescued him.

They teased each other endlessly. One fine April Sunday Peter fell with his face pressed in the fresh-smelling grass until Charles came near, springing up with childish inspiration to shout, "Fluffy head!" and run laughing from his father's outrage.

"Peter Carey," Charles called after him, "did you call your father a 'fluffy head'?"

Peter chuckled deep in his throat as he slowed to ensure that Charles could catch him, and then charged forward as his father swooped with outstretched arms to pull him to the ground and pin his shoulders, demanding, "Did you call your father—ex–war hero, former publishing genius and onetime escort of Audrey Hepburn—a *'fluffy head'*?"

They laughed into each other's eyes. "Yes!" Peter shouted and Charles began tickling his ribcage and roaring, "Promise you'll never call me 'fluffy head' again," as Peter wriggled and squirmed until, his heart pumping, helpless from excitement, laughter and the need for a bathroom, he yelped, "I give up!" and they rose to take the winding path home, holding hands as they walked past fresh green trees and strangers who smiled at them—lean, striking man in a blazer, blond, laughing boy—until they reached their tall brick town house on East 60th, Charles sternly reminding Peter, "No more 'fluffy head,'" before dashing upstairs to change and await Adlai Stevenson, for dinner.

It was pheasant, served by candlelight in the Careys' dining room. Afterwards, they remained at the table—Stevenson and the Careys—sipping cognac beneath the crystal chandelier and watching tongues of orange and blue spit from the fireplace. Sensing his campaign was hopeless and liking Charles Carey, Stevenson gave himself up to laughter, hoping wistfully that John Foster Dulles might get caught with a chorus girl before November. "Perhaps a Russian ballerina," Charles was suggesting lazily, when Peter appeared in his wool sleepers to say goodnight. He kissed his mother's cool, turned cheek with a senatorial gravity that drew a wry smile from Stevenson, before edging from the room and Alicia's sight to where only Charles could see him. He stood motionless, head tilted in watchful replication of his father, until Charles turned. Face suddenly alight, Peter cupped his hands to his mouth and whispered sotto voce, "Fluffy head," as his father's eyes widened in mock horror and he scampered away, triumphant.

Watching the blond head disappear around the corner, Charles Carey knew at that moment that he loved his son more deeply than he had ever loved anyone, or ever would again. Remembering the crosscurrents that had seemed to flow from his conception, Charles hoped this love would be enough.

Alicia Carey turned from the softness in her husband's face.

Peter Carey first learned guilt from his mother's eyes.

Their green opacity followed him, even in his sleep; he could find neither love nor hate. Haunted by the suspension of their judgment, he came to fear his own actions for the anger they might hold.

Doubting himself, Peter became preternaturally sensitive to the moods of others. He watched his parents, divining from their silences an intricate skein of cause and effect. In his father's hugs, he felt his mother's loneliness.

He pondered how to reach her, searching for clues in his parents' barren touches. At length, deciding, he waited until she was alone.

She sat in the library, a volume of poetry unread in her lap, a champagne glass in her hand, staring into a shaft of afternoon sun which burned her fair, perfect profile to porcelain in the light. Peter approached on tiptoe, standing still and irresolute. She seemed not to notice. Hesitant, he asked, "Do you need a hug from a boy?"

She started, dropping the glass. It shattered on the parquetry. Peter flinched, reaching out to her as Alicia stared at the shards of crystal. Her eyes, rising to meet her son's, filled with hysteria and tears. "Don't you sneak up on me!" she cried. Her hand flailed at the glittering pieces. "It's *broken* now. *Look*, dammit—*look* at what you've done."

Backing from the library, from the hatred and confusion in her eyes, Peter Carey understood what he had done. He had destroyed his mother, and stolen his father's love.

In the loveless act that led to Peter's birth, Charles Carey had felt the death throes of his marriage.

The chill had touched him months before.

Tension ran through Allie's laughter, in the way she grasped at moments, inflating them with brittle gaiety. A bottle of champagne became perfect in his company, its cold tang lingering like velvet on her tongue. At the Byline Room, she sat transfixed by smoke and darkness, the pulse of jazz notes crowding, fighting, pushing one another for space as still others blew them out the door, until the night was magic. The filet at "21" was flawless, Maria Tallchief more tensile than Pavlova. She cried hearing Robert Lowell.

Charles Carey was her thrilling lover.

She writhed against him, body glistening with sweat, strain and hysteria until she lay exhausted, eyes fixed and staring as though in desperate search for what she had not found, and then in a rush of words she would describe to him the beauty of their act.

On their wedding night, she wept.

In subtle flight, for the first time in his life, Charles Carey retreated from reality.

Suppressed, doubt festered in his subconscious, leeching conviction from his laughter and the things they did in bed. Allie could not speak to him of her fantasies; Charles could confess his fears to no one. She became gayer and more desperate, drinking more champagne as she organized vast parties, placing new friends or entertainments as barriers between them, flirting carelessly with Phillip. Bereft of real intimacy, Charles's lovemaking turned mechanical, brain cooling to an eerie detachment in which he came full circle to the truth: his wife was an actress in bed.

He began to contemplate divorce.

The last time they made love was in the morning. Fall sunlight through their window seemed to etch his life with crystalline clarity. Coolly, deliberately, he began stroking her arm until it prickled with goosebumps, then turned her face toward his and kissed her neck, his mouth and tongue running toward her nipple, lingering there to raise it as he slid two fingers between her thighs. His tongue moved downward across her stomach to where his fingers had been, and slipped into her moistness. Her hips thrust upward. She screamed when he entered her.

As she called his name again and again, he knew that the sounds came from her throat and not her body. He made love to her for over an hour, driving, pounding, moving slow and then fast, sliding and teasing, back glistening with sweat, jaw and sinew clenched in an agony of reaching, straining to at last wrench cries from deep inside her, until she scraped his back in a spasm of feigned climax, signaling its finish, and he looked over her shoulder, at his watch.

Two months later, Alicia Carey told him she was pregnant.

From the first weeks of her pregnancy, John Carey watched their hot, buried anger rise to split his sons. They disagreed more often; championed different books or authors; grew more caustic in debate. With mixed pleasure and concern their father guessed the reason: Phillip feared that the unborn child which now trapped his brother might become the grandson that John Carey wished.

But the strain seemed worst in Charles. In Alicia Carey's eyes—which glinted but could not connect—John Carey saw the anguish of his son reflected. Charles's confidence as a lover, unspoken and unflaunted, had fed his confidence as a man. A child bound him to the woman who had stolen it.

Curiously, this time of unhappiness became in other ways Charles's best. Finding a new black writer of rare eloquence and talent, Charles insisted that they publish his first novel, which now rode a crest of fine reviews. Three more of his young authors already had best sellers; now he acquired a novel of a Roman slave rebellion, which might become one more. Yet too often he was moody and distracted: with each month that his child's birth drew closer, his judgment frayed . . .

All at once, facing a stranger too rife with potential menace for the Careys to mishandle, John Carey saw how swiftly Charles's nerve and courage might turn back upon them.

The curiously unsettling Englehardt came from Washington, as emissary of the House Un-American Activities Committee's literary witch hunt, to warn that those who published Charles's slave novel were tools of Joseph Stalin.

"Does Stalin read much?" Charles asked him politely.

They sat in the conference room at Van Dreelen & Carey—John Carey flanked by his sons—facing a crew-cut man with gray, lynx's eyes and no taste for irony. Dressed in a bow tie and black bargain-basement suit, he seemed colorless, odorless and tasteless, like poison gas. By his lack of facial lines Englehardt could not be over thirty, yet his youth seemed long dead, and his strange, relentless monotone had become as excruciating as the repeated drip of water. John Carey, who feared little, instinctively feared this man. He leaned back, closely watching both Charles and Phillip.

"You fail to amuse," the man replied to Charles. He had a cruel slash of a mouth and a bleak, level stare that took in the leather books and polished mahogany as though he wished them his. "Your list is riddled with left-wing writers . . ."

"Such as . . . ?"

"Aside from this one?" Methodically and without inflection, the man named seventeen books by author, title and date of publication, specifying the reasons for their offensiveness. "You see," he finished quietly, "I'm not here by accident."

"Just by mistake," Charles shot back. "Although your memory is excellent."

"A professional requirement." A pride close to arrogance flashed through his eyes, the first true emotion John Carey could detect. "And the mistake is yours: purchasing this piece of propaganda just when its author has publicly refused to give testimony before our Committee. We're in a war of ideologies, and those of us who know this are curious as to which side you're on. I think you may recall John Garfield..."

"I recall." Charles went pale with anger. "We ate at Downey's two nights before he died, as *you* damned well know. In the eighteen months since your committee sicked the FBI on him he hadn't had a part. His marriage had broken up, and he was much too thin. You'd read his mail and rousted his friends until there weren't many left..."

"We were investigating..."

"You were sniffing through his life like a pervert through a drawerful of panties, until he had no grace or privacy—all for the crime of signing petitions. It's as sick a way to break someone as Stalin ever dreamed of—"

"I view it less emotionally—"

"I'm curious, Englehardt. How do your people like watching me? Do I keep them amused? Maybe I should join the NAACP..."

"Wait, Charles." Phillip leaned forward, holding up one hand as John Carey turned to watch him. "We're getting into personalities, to no point. We at least owe Mr. Englehardt a hearing..."

"Under HUAC rules, I hope."

"Well, I for one don't wish to publish books which aren't in the national interest..."

"As defined by whom, J. Edgar Hoover?" Charles spun on Englehardt before Phillip could respond. "He's *my* author. I speak for the firm here. Our answer is no. If it's subversive the public won't buy it, and we'll lose money. Their choice, our risk: *that's* the American Way, not snoopers destroying lives to enhance their own. You know where the door is, I imagine."

Englehardt's returning stare at Charles Carey was expressionless; once more John Carey felt fear, sensed the effort with which he masked his fury. When Englehardt turned toward Phillip Carey, appraising him as he would a slide beneath a microscope, he smiled with a curious look of comprehension that softened his face. For a long, silent moment they regarded each other, as if no one else were there. Without turning, he said to John Carey, "You might do well to listen to your *younger* son."

"Whatever differences we have do not concern you." John Carey leaned into his line of vision. "I respect your motives, if not your methods. But Van Dreelen and Carey is something other than a ward of Congress. We must make our own decisions."

Englehardt was still; only his pupils seemed to widen. He spoke with equal quiet. "Then when you make them, Mr. Carey, you should consider the scope of our investigative powers. Your decision may have great consequences—for this firm, for you, and all those who come after." He looked back at Charles. "I'll particularly expect to hear from *you.*"

"Oh you shall, Mr. Englehardt, you shall. I've been rather hoping you'd train your investigative powers on Mr. Hoover, though." He smiled faintly. "One hears distressing rumors that he likes little boys. A lot of us who know that are curious as to which side he's on."

Englehardt's gem-cutter's stare at Charles Carey was the more piercing for his stillness. Then he shook his head, and rose from the table with a faint, lingering smile at Phillip. He walked to the door, turning back once more to survey Charles as if absorbing his thoughts and features, and left, closing the door with fearful gentleness. The room sounded with its echo.

In biting tones, Charles said to his father, "I thought for a moment that you were sitting this one out."

John Carey looked at him with contempt. "I know you're spoiling for the day I'm dead and you can ruin this firm singlehanded. But that's *if*, Charles—only if *I* will it. So I find it necessary to determine just how long that job would take you."

"I appreciate your support . . ."

"My concern is to support *writers*, not you. Compare us to the film studios, or even other publishers. Not one of our authors has had a book bounced back because these fools have pilloried him in public, or blown his brains out because we've helped them choke off his livelihood. Most important, I've still got a firm to pass on, intact. I've seen to that by not begging for trouble . . ."

"This man Englehardt came *here* . . ."

"And then you gave him no way out." John Carey's voice hardened. "Never, ever, humiliate a man in front of others unless you have the power to destroy him. With this man it's the other way around: in time he may have the power to destroy *you*, and all I mean this family to keep. I watched his eyes while you were being clever. He'll remember you thirty years from now."

"I want him to—men like that only prey on weakness." Charles wheeled on his brother. "If you ever again cut me off in front of strangers, particularly someone who'll go for your throat if he sees any weakness at all, you'd better pray that it *is* you who inherits this firm. And while you're praying, pray that what happened to Garfield doesn't happen to you or anyone in this family, because there's no one who can survive that. Especially you." He rose to leave, turning in the doorway to say in a softer voice, "It's not fatal that you lack Stalin's taste, Phil. But to lack his *guts* . . ."

He turned and left.

Staring at his stricken second son, still hearing the anger of his first, John Carey felt the unborn presence of the grandson who might follow them, to sit where he now sat.

Within weeks, Phillip Carey knew that their upsetting visitor would not forget the Careys.

Their writers were abruptly hauled before the Committee; Charles's tax returns were audited; the author of the slave novel was indicted for refusing to appear. At Committee hearings, in newspapers, the name Van Dreelen & Carey was constantly repeated. One department store refused their books . . .

Phillip began hearing noises on his telephone.

He could not explain this sense of dread.

What so clearly was in progress—a carefully calibrated form of torture—was ominous enough. Yet Phillip Carey kept seeing Englehardt's strange smile reach for him across the table, felt the penetration of his eyes. In that one moment, he had

sensed this man looking back into his childhood until he saw
Phillip as the boy Phillip still despised remembering, who en-
vied Charles for his boldness, yet was fearful of offending.
The young Phillip strove to please John Carey; Charles stole
their father's gaze without bothering to notice. This injustice
fueled a smoldering adolescent envy Phillip felt too unworthy
to display; unlike the fearless Charles, he had not earned the
right to his emotions. Growing, he took refuge in fine tailoring
and a polished air, hoping that its shine would deflect deeper
glances until he became the man John Carey was, and thereby
gained his favor...

All this he had seen in one long look of infinite comprehension on the face of a total stranger.

He did not want this man to know him.

"They're watching us," he told his father. "It's been three
months now, and tomorrow HUAC's parading yet another of
our Marxist authors, with no sign of stopping."

The two brothers sat in their father's office. Looking from
Charles back to Phillip, John Carey's eyes seemed to harden.
"What is it you want?"

Phillip paused, distracted by the weary look with which
Charles had arrived from one of those mysterious appointments
to which he dragged the pregnant Allie. Perhaps there was a
problem, some chance of a miscarriage...

Hastily, he answered, "To advise Mr. Englehardt that we're
pulling the novel that offended him."

"Englehardt." Charles turned on him with a look of disgust.
"You'd trade a gifted writer for the smile of a cockroach?"

Irresolute, Phillip wavered: he could not speak his fears in
front of Charles.

"We're committed," John Carey cut in. "To which Charles
has added a HUAC problem we damned well could have
dodged."

"Too late for hindsight." Charles's tone was flat. "Two men
followed me here, the same ones I saw yesterday. It's time
that we fight back."

"With still more words?" John Carey flashed a contemptuous smile. "Without so much as calling you to testify, Mr.
Englehardt and his Committee have displayed far greater weap-
ons. Now we can only hope to bore them, Charles, until they

bore the country. That means no political controversy or cheap heroics."

"You're directing me to respond to peepers by hoping they approve of what they see? My God, that's pitiful . . ."

"You've made yourself a liability, Charles." John Carey measured his words. "It therefore falls on you to maintain a graceful silence, or to leave."

Phillip Carey felt shocked sympathy for Charles, and then a rush of anticipation made his skin tingle. Charles *gone* . . .

Charles faced his father with a faint, sardonic smile. "I can leave right now," he answered softly. "All you have to do, is ask."

His answer lay between them like a dare. Phillip turned to his father . . .

John Joseph Englehardt held his breath with Phillip Carey. "All you have to do," Charles repeated, "is ask."

In the long silence that followed, the tape clicked off.

Abruptly, Englehardt remembered that he was not sitting next to Phillip but alone in a shabby room in Georgetown, a single light bulb hanging over him.

Wind and rain spattered the window.

In anxious haste, he pushed the rewind button and turned up the volume, thinking that John Carey's answer had been swallowed by the storm . . .

The Careys had become much more than just a file; over months their lives and voices had seduced him. Slowly, inevitably, he had been drawn to their central drama, Greek in its explosive symmetry: the father was a tyrant, the sons locked in bitter contest for his place.

He was helpless to resist.

Since childhood, Englehardt had known that he was cursed with a diamond-hard brilliance he could neither turn to grace or charm, nor use to catch the pleasure of his father. But his father's eyes had fallen elsewhere: like a snake, the younger son had drawn back. Alone as any Jesuit, he had seen that he must live through indirection, manipulating others in ways they did not see . . .

Now, in subtle choreography, he was turning HUAC to a

secret purpose: the tape, silently rewinding, had been stolen from its files. Rapt, he watched it spin...

He had joined the Committee upon leaving Yale, armed with a useless doctorate and no prospects in his father's business. From the beginning he had seen the congressmen he worked for as list-waving buffoons, stringing "secrets" they already knew into jerry-built conspiracies. The secrets he was using them to learn were deeper: the hidden workings of faceless institutions and of the minds of men. Knowing the fever fueling HUAC to be transient, he gained a deeper lesson from their hearings. As witness after witness crumbled beneath their petty crimes of thought, he learned that men, and thus the governments which were simply groups of men, shared a mystic fervor to exploit the secrets that belonged to others, and to protect their own.

For two lonely, friendless years he had ferreted out the "sins" of writers for politicians to expose, hoping that their approval of this craven service would replace the affection he could never earn, and thus commend him to still others, more secret and more powerful. Inwardly, he writhed at this submissiveness, this prostitution of his brain to buy the favor of idiots. And then his fateful meeting with the Careys had driven him beyond servility, to feed his soul.

This terrible need for power with which to touch the Careys was one secret the committee must never know.

Having failed to block publication of the slave novel, he returned to Washington despising Charles Carey as the mirror of his inconsequence, the last legacy of his father. Yet the emotions that the Careys stirred were much more disturbing and profound: Englehardt felt their kinship pierce his years of solitude. He *knew* them, knew the father's fierce passion to conserve their place, saw Charles as the object of his thwarted love, felt the pain in Phillip's heart.

This once, he would use the Committee's power to gain an end which would fulfill him.

In memos and meetings he reported the Careys' defiance; finally, HUAC ordered him to probe their support of left-wing writers. Within two weeks, without any one person's knowing the scope of his invasion, Englehardt arranged through several agencies to bug the Careys' homes and offices, to open their mail and watch their every movement.

Secret parcels of reports and tapes began arriving in his office.

At night, unseen by those for whom he worked, he began retreating to his apartment to re-live the Careys' loves and hates and listen to their quicksilver rivalries, until he knew that what he had seen in them was real, and he no longer felt alone.

Englehardt had learned that men who spied on other men, out of the loneliness of such a job, came to like or dislike their chosen quarry. But, in his soul, he knew that this secret passion for the Careys grew from something stronger.

The brothers' rivalry was also his.

He sensed, with the same bone-deep affinity that had first drawn his eyes toward Phillip Carey, that there was nothing their contest did not touch: Phillip, who hoped that Charles's defiance of HUAC would prove to show poor judgment, feared that the pregnancy of Charles's wife might return him to John Carey's favor.

Englehardt began to measure the time for his allotted task by the growth of life inside Alicia Carey...

Now, his thoughts were broken by a single click, like the short electric impulse that changes the chemistry of a madman's brain.

The tape had finished rewinding.

For a final moment, Englehardt teased himself by watching the contest of raindrops skittering down the windowpane, and then he pushed the button. Once more Phillip Carey told his father: "They're watching us..."

By design, he had made the Careys feel his pervasive presence: their authors were called to testify, there were new delays in the Careys' mail and fresh problems with their tax returns; Charles was conspicuously followed. Englehardt did not care if this was of no use to HUAC: he acted only for himself, with a passion that enraged him, to persuade John Carey that Charles's defiance was the act of an unworthy son.

"*Englehardt*," Charles shot back to his brother. "You'd trade a gifted writer for the smile of a cockroach?"

Englehardt clenched his fists in helpless fury.

His father had died without a word for him, his legacy a

preference for the elder son, a smiling, careless athlete, the father of his grandson. Reaching for intimacy without this risk of pain, a one-way mirror into others' hearts, Englehardt had looked too deeply into his own.

He had seen himself in Phillip Carey.

"All you have to do," Charles said once more, "is ask."

Englehardt bent closer.

The tape reached its silent end.

Englehardt's shoulders sagged: John Carey did not have the words to ask his oldest son to leave.

With Phillip Carey, his second self, he must await the birth of Allie Fairvoort's child.

From its earliest moment, Alicia Carey disowned the child she bore.

She stopped going out. Water weight bloated her thighs and stomach, she vomited, her nipples were sore. She learned nothing about the life inside her, and took no pleasure in it. She felt awkward. Her eyes lost quickness, transfixed by some black hole between reality and imagination. She had never imagined children.

The baby was an abstraction, subverting the chemistry between her mind and body. Straining to envision herself as a mother, she was betrayed by the ugliness she saw in the mirror, and the sickness she felt. Her imagery vanished. She could not imagine her child's face or the smell of its hair. Her husband seemed a stranger; she saw with stark clarity that his body did not move her.

As months passed, she was brutalized by this destruction of her fantasies. Her manic activity ceased; she organized no parties, betrayed by the incomprehension all around her. She grew to despise the good wishes of other women, oppressed by their smug equation of motherhood with fulfillment. An only child, she had wished to be the center of her marriage. Now she felt like a stray, trapped by Charles Carey's seed in a role she did not care for. His efforts to reach her through the psychiatrist Levy insulted her: Charles did not understand that it was he who had killed her dreams. Avoiding him, she retreated, in time, toward her parents.

They had never failed her before.

Grant and Elizabeth Fairvoort had worshiped her from infancy, dressed her in the clothes she wished, taken her to Corfu and Mallorca. The world as she learned it responded to her touch. Told early of her own enchantment, she had come to believe the lives of others less bright without her presence. As she ripened into adolescence, she would make love to herself with her fingertips—brushing her cheeks or tracing the line of her hips—as if reflecting the admiration in Grant Fairvoort's glance. Later, acting, she thrilled with pain she had never felt, to be rewarded by her parents' pleasure. Even things beyond her sight or knowledge found their purpose in her happiness. She knew that her father—a ruddy, confident man with a white, perfect smile and snow-white hair—was an investment banker; she never asked what that involved. Simply and without reflection, she knew that it was done for her.

Men became a different class of being, mysterious yet powerful, to whom she owed nothing but the acceptance of their gifts. She sought in marriage the perfection of her father's love: now, sensing Charles's needs, she could feel only contempt and fear, just as she had come to fear the child that she carried. It did not matter that Charles had some new trouble with his father, or that he kept picking up the telephone to try to catch the sound of strangers. She made plans to see her parents.

As she packed to leave, six months pregnant, the Fairvoorts crashed while flying a Piper Cub to their summer home on Lake Champlain, leaving her wealthy, and without defenses.

Nothing bad had ever happened to her until she'd married Charles.

Deflecting his sympathy, she sleepwalked through the funeral—a rote Episcopalian service that deadened her emotions—as if through a role that bored her. The caskets were empty; her father would reappear, say how fine and elegant she looked. Then, returning home, she saw her pregnant body in the mirror, and knew that he was dead.

With terrible finality she passed beyond her husband's reach.

In the last month of her pregnancy, moodily drinking Scotch in the living room, Charles heard her scream.

He raced up the dark winding stairway to their bedroom.

The bed was slashed to ribbons. Alicia's shredded clothes

were strewn across it, cut with the scissors that now protruded from a portrait of Charles Carey.

He found her in the bathroom, panting as she slashed the mirror with lipstick until her naked, bloated image seemed bloody chunks of skin. He saw lipstick reflected as blood on his mouth, watched her eyes in the mirror widen with animal surprise. Then she screamed, and her fist swung forward, shattering his reflection in the glass. He grasped her wrist, felt warm blood spurting from the back of her hand. She twisted away, and then collapsed over the basin, hair falling into the broken glass, round belly heaving with her sobs.

Levy gave her Thorazine; six days later, she gave Charles Carey a son.

CHAPTER 3

Watching Charles sit restlessly in his office, William Levy felt the weight of Carey's infant son.

At Harvard, when they were freshmen, he had not imagined Charles would ever need him. Where Charles was athletic and a WASP, Levy was Jewish and awkward, envying Carey's prep-school toughness and the girls he had, the way he drew followers by not looking back. But Charles seemed to notice neither awkwardness nor envy, casually including Levy among his friends, scrounging him dates and beers and asking his opinion of their dorm-mates or the books he read, or even Judaism, with a dispassion that suggested this was just another subject on which Levy's thoughts were interesting. In turn, Levy noted that Charles, too, said little about his family, never showed surprise or hurt or anger, as if he were born a Harvard athlete, unscarred by any past and utterly self-possessed. As months passed, Levy sensed that this unruffled *persona*—even Carey's flat, sardonic speech—was a cover for a vulnerability that Carey could not admit. With a shock of recognition, Levy saw his own loneliness in Charles Carey.

One night, in a waterfront Boston bar filled with smoke and sailors and the stale smell of beer drying on the floor, the two sophomores got very drunk. At a point Levy could no longer remember or define, they passed beyond mere palship amidst the noise and haze, and became friends.

"Why do you hang out with me?" Levy had asked. "I've been thinking maybe you were hard up for Jews."

Charles shrugged. "If you didn't study so fucking much, you'd probably notice you're one of the few people around here worth talking with."

"It's premed—the worst grind there is." Levy drained the

Scotch, smoky on his tongue and throat. "Frog-cutter to the world, that's me. I want to be a halfback."

"It's an overrated thrill. Besides, you wouldn't do all that if you didn't want to." Carey peered at him with exaggerated concentration. "Would you?"

"I don't know." Levy stared at his empty glass. "My father thinks I've got 'surgeon' stamped on my genetic code. *My Son the Doctor*, a Martin Levy Production. God help my sister—he's got *her* cast as Lillian Hellman."

"Can she write?"

"Not a lick," Levy said mournfully. "But she can read."

Carey grinned. "Then we'll make her an editor. How old is she, anyhow?"

"Thirteen?"

"Well, when she grows up send her around to Van Dreelen and Carey. 'Literacy and Loyalty,' that's my father's watchword." In a different voice—low and intense—Charles finished, "You don't have to do what he wants, Bill."

Levy caught himself smoothing his cowlick, a habit born of confusion. "What else would I do?"

Charles called for another round.

The din grew louder. A sailor next to them pitched from a sitting position face forward onto the table, as two others talked over him without missing a beat. The barman brought their drinks. Charles raised his in a mock salute and said, "Become a psychiatrist."

Levy tingled with surprise. "A shrink?"

Carey's eyes locked with his. "I've watched you. You see people—look, I know you're on to me." His gaze broke. In one quick motion he snapped a lighter at his cigarette: drunk, he had the trick of doing small things perfectly, seeming suddenly sober. "The point is that you've got the insight to help people, maybe even the need. Think of this business with your father. He wants a chest-cutter, so you wear yourself out over whether to be one. What psychiatry says is that people can escape the ambush of their own childhood." Charles stopped as if embarrassed, then began laughing. "Besides, think of all the great cocktail-party stuff you'll have: football molesters, guys who are fixated on Eleanor Roosevelt, frigid women..."

Now, treating Alicia Carey, Levy recalled with double poignancy that Charles had helped him to do so.

After that drunken night in Boston, Levy took his first psychology course. It was Charles who had queried him about it, smiling at his increased animation.

Levy took a second course, then a third, and excelled.

He told his father of this new ambition at lunch in Cambridge, with Charles present. With all the passion he could muster, he explained that he wished to treat the human mind, not the body.

Martin Levy leaned over the table. In a torrent of words he rasped that this would be a waste of his money, that psychiatrists were charlatans and that screwed-up people were born that way, beyond anyone's redemption. Levy felt himself shriveling inside; Charles, who knew that the suicide of Levy's mother was the unspoken subtext to this tirade, fixed Martin Levy with an icy stare. When the speech was finished, it was Charles who answered softly, "But suppose you're wrong."

Martin Levy's head jerked toward Charles. They stared at each other; Levy saw in his father's shocked face that he felt the thrust of Charles's meaning, and knew it was intended.

Martin Levy did not answer.

The lunch had two results. The first was that Martin Levy no longer admitted Charles Carey to his home. When his son apologized for this, over a late-night beer, Charles only smiled. "Well," he said, shrugging, "it was never kismet, anyhow."

At that moment, sensing a cool determination his smile could not hide, Levy knew suddenly that Charles meant *him* to escape a tie: the ambition of a father, with which Charles himself might have to grapple all his life.

The second result was that Martin Levy still sent him money.

In medical school, when his father could no longer help him, Charles lent him some of his own savings from the war, to help him over a few tough months. Later, at the times in Levy's internship when he felt most down and tired, Charles would call to suggest dinner, diverting him with chat of publishing or satiric imitations of bizarre imaginary patients. "I just *love* wet suits," Charles would tease, until Levy began to laugh. And so it went, through dinners and periodic evenings out, until the two men became pillars of each other's reality, making their separate worlds seem better than they were.

And then Charles had married Allie Fairvoort. . . .

"She refuses electroshock," Levy told him now.

"I don't really blame her." Charles Carey cast an ironic eye at the diploma on Levy's wall. "I thought you'd learned to cure these things without witchcraft."

"What I learned is that you don't revamp personality, only modify it by a few degrees. *If* the patient wants to."

Charles lit a cigarette. "And Allie doesn't."

"She won't talk to me as a real person." To Levy, Alicia Carey seemed impaled on her inner life, like a butterfly in a box. "Most of us consign our fantasies to daydreams, and peek at them every so often to help us get through the day. Others, like writers or actors—remember, she used to act—try to live off their imaginings, and are sometimes driven crazy by it. She's moved one step past that. Reality is poison to her, and this new baby is its symbol." Levy scowled. "I know all this sounds like such crap."

"At least your metaphors are improving." A smile flickered at the corner of Charles's mouth without changing his eyes. "You were never long on metaphor."

"She calls for it." Alicia Carey made him feel poetic and impotent, like the tall, cool women he had dreamt of in school, and could not touch. Now it was Charles Carey's wife he could not touch, even through his profession: eight months had accomplished only his own immersion in her flight. He wished he could protect her, or perhaps use his gifts to give a woman back to Charles, but he had no means. He could stir in her no interest for her infant son; she would not stay in analysis, and Thorazine—an alternative he despised—depressed her further. Finally, he had received a late-night call. Charles had found Alicia in their garden, dressed in her debutante's gown, its silk glistening in the thin silver moonlight. Levy felt a chill at the image, and at the flatness in Charles's tone as he said now:

"Well, no point in being sentimental. HUAC nips at my heels while the patriarch sits on his hands; I've got Zelda for a wife, a four-month-old son, and my sex life is giving me hairy palms." He rose, shrugging on his coat. "I'd better think of what to do."

"I suppose so." Hesitant, Levy added, "Look, I know my timing's awful, but you remember me telling you about Ruth, my sister?"

Charles looked curious. "That imminent threat to Maxwell Perkins? Has she passed puberty?"

Levy nodded, uncomfortable. "She's copy-editing at *Time* now. But she wants to work with fiction."

"She could always write their editorials."

Levy looked away. "I'm sorry, Charles. I'd promised to say something next time I saw you."

Charles waved a hand as he moved toward the door. "Oh, send her in, Sigmund, send her in. I made a dubious shrink out of you, I can surely make a bad editor of her. It's probably stamped on her genetic code." He turned in the doorway to catch Levy's smile of surprise. "You're still liking this work, I take it."

"Sometimes it's hard. It's hard now. But yes, I like it."

Charles smiled, the ghost of his college grin. "Well, I suppose that's something." He gave the coat a final shrug, squared his shoulders, and then paused. "You know, it's funny, Bill— this time *I'm* the father."

For a moment the two friends, first sons of their fathers, smiled at each other. And then Charles Carey turned and left, closing the door behind him.

As it shut, Levy remembered Charles, driven by some solitary winter mood, slipping from their dormitory into the cool night. It was late; only Levy saw him. Snow had fallen, gray as ashes, and swirled at Carey's feet. He moved into the shadows, lean and graceful and alone, until he became one of them. Levy had felt a momentary fear, was captured by the image: one lone man watching through his window as the other, merging with the unknown dark, steals his imagination. For that brief instant, Levy had believed that Charles Carey's fate would also be his own.

Watching the infant Peter sleep, Charles tried remembering his own father.

The five-year-old Charles had stood stiffly in Penn Station,

waiting with Phillip and their mother for John Carey to return
from weeks of selling, toting his black trunk. It had held few
presents, even for Ellen Carey. Her hand was cool and dry,
the face she wore for her sons still expectant and serene amidst
the rush of passengers and porters with luggage, the litany of
trains leaving for strange places, gasping steam as they de-
parted. Next to her, Charles would close his eyes and try recalling his father's face. He could never quite remember. Then
his mother would squeeze his hand, saying, "Here he is," and
Charles would strain once more to absorb John Carey's features
as he strode toward them: black, bushy eyebrows, fierce black
eyes snapping from granite planes all surfaces and angles, jaw
jutting like a prow. Three-year-old Phillip would hide behind
his mother.

John Carey would shake each son's hand and kiss his wife
once, on the cheek. She had died from cancer when Charles
was fifteen. In Charles's mind she had died from lack of love.

Undemonstrative with women, he began holding Peter often,
smelling the newness of his skin. But, looking for some change
in Allie, he saw only jealousy. He spent more time with Peter.

That Thanksgiving, Peter learned to crawl.

Charles had been playing with him after dinner, in Peter's
room. Allie looked in on them; suddenly, as if hurt by Charles's
absorption, she left. Charles rose to bring her back.

At that moment, Peter began moving.

The process seemed to enthrall him. At first he ignored his
father, inching forward one knee at a time, the bottom of his
corduroy overalls wriggling. Charles stopped, then knelt to
watch. Peter moved faster, got to his crib and turned. More
confident, he set out toward the fireplace. Suddenly he stopped,
turning toward his father with bright pumpkin eyes. He moved
two feet further and looked back again, waiting. Charles fell
to his knees. Peter went one more foot, and turned. Charles
began crawling after him. Peter's face lit up. He scurried away,
pivoting to see Charles's pursuit, scurried again. For the first
time, from over Peter's shoulder, Charles heard his son's throaty
laugh.

Charles grinned.

Abruptly, Peter curled on his side, and yawned.

A smiling Charles changed his clothes and then deposited

him in the crib, bunching blankets over his shoulders as Peter yawned and squirmed in the last resistance to sleep. Bending to kiss his son, Charles Carey felt a surge of real happiness . . .

Then Allie called to Charles from their bedroom.

It was lit by one lone candle on each night stand.

She lay on the bed, wearing the black silk dress she had worn the first night they made love. Her arms and legs were outflung. She was half smiling. The strange glint was back in her eyes.

Charles gazed down at her. Slowly she reached to the hem of her dress and pulled it above her waist.

She wore nothing else.

Candlelight cast shadows on her face and the hollows of her thighs. Charles felt excitement brush his skin. She opened her legs.

He undressed without speaking.

She looked into his eyes, and then at his erection. He reached for her . . .

She began laughing.

He froze, arms extended, shrill laughter in his ears. Unconsciously, he touched himself.

She stared at the erection in his hand. "Oh God, Charles, oh my God . . ."

She turned on her side and started weeping, hands covering her face, racking sobs coming from deep within her. For the first time, Charles saw the half-empty bottle of Chivas Regal on her night stand.

Then he heard the sound of Peter crying.

Charles looked down at his naked, sobbing wife, candlelight moving on her body, curled in an awful parody of childhood.

Turning away, Charles dressed and walked slowly to Peter's crib, to hold him. "It's okay, honey," he kept murmuring, "it's all right," until Peter fell asleep.

Carefully, he put his son back in the crib, and went downstairs.

With painful intensity, Charles Carey sat in the library and looked backwards, at his life.

He started with the past year: the birth of his son and the failure of his marriage, this nagging erosion of his privacy his father would not permit him to resist.

Until close to dawn, he weighed his lifelong conflict with John Carey, and the childhood that caused it. In their clashes, even in the hated image of his brother's triumph at what he now must do, Charles saw the need of his own son.

The next day, Charles Carey resigned.

Looking at Charles—pale but contained, staring coldly back—John Carey could not accept what he had heard.

"It's final," Charles was answering. "Besides, I thought you wanted this to pacify HUAC."

"After what it took for me to get you here? *That's* what 'pacifying HUAC' was about." John Carey pointed at the floor. "I used to stoke coal down below in a stinking furnace room you've never even *seen*, while Van Dreelen's blank-eyed sons sat in this very office you now say you don't want, all because they were *born* to it." He stood, leaning toward Charles with his palms flat on the desk. "Those pathetic cretins reached their height as *sperm*, Charles, and so did you. If I weren't your father, you'd be stoking their furnace."

Charles sat very still. In a low, sardonic voice, he said, "Some men are born right. Others marry well."

John Carey stared at his son. "Do you think that's why . . . ?"

"I don't have to see the furnace room, Father. After all, I saw your bedroom."

John Carey's face stiffened. Into a silence like a caught breath he hissed, "If you weren't my son . . ."

"I'm sure the time involved was minimal." Charles paused to catch himself, finishing softly, "As it was until the day she died."

Charles's eyes were chips of ice in an aquiline mask; a vein throbbed at John Carey's temple. "You *blame* me for that, damn you—you always have." His breathing felt ragged. "I did what I had to do, and by marrying her I also saved this firm. She knew that, and if it meant she couldn't always have my attention at least she could say she slept with a man." He paused to steady his voice, then added with silken cruelty, "Which is more than *your* vain and neurasthenic wife will ever say, isn't it?"

For a minute Charles's look was open, surprised, like that of the boy John Carey remembered waiting at the train, before his face would close. Charles lit a cigarette. "I was fifteen, Father, and I was all she had." He looked up at John Carey, face set once more. "And as she died I knew she was all *we* had."

John Carey remembered coming home too late: emaciated in death, Ellen already seemed a skeleton. "I built this firm for you."

"You built it for yourself. I won't put Peter at risk for your obsession."

"*Your* obsession."

Charles paused. In a level voice he said, "It isn't, now."

"Then you're a fool. A man needs something that belongs to him, or he's no man at all—or father." John Carey plucked a cigar from his pocket, carefully unwrapping it to steady himself. "Do you remember Clayton Barth?"

"One of our salesmen." Charles's look turned wary. "He used to cover Texas."

"And Oklahoma." John Carey waved his unlit cigar. "Sit down."

"What does Barth . . . ?"

"Sit down, dammit. I won't have you hovering like that."

Charles hesitated, then stubbed his cigarette and sat. John Carey lit the cigar, eyes narrow with concentration, letting the silence and the things in the room—fine Chinese vases, his smiling picture with Winston Churchill—work on his son. He emitted a long stream of cigar smoke. "It's quite pathetic, really. He'd been with us fifteen years. The spring of the sixteenth year Barth approached me at our sales conference at the Biltmore and said he needed to talk."

Even now, John Carey could see the man as clearly as in a photograph . . .

"He was short, with frog's eyes and a pouch for a stomach that made him wear his pants too high, and the room—the smoke and noise and larger men acting confident—seemed to shrink him even more. 'Mr. Carey,' he croaks, 'I'd like a chance at that sales manager's position that's opened up.'

"He stood there holding his overcoat and hat in front of him, as if he were ready to leave should the idea bore me. There was no point mincing words: everything about him whispered, 'Keep me where I am.' 'I'm sorry, Clayton,' I say, 'but you're fine where you are. I've got someone for the other.'

"His shoulders slump. 'Well, sir'"—John Carey's voice rose in savage mimicry—"'then I'd like permission to resign at year's end...'

"I couldn't believe the *servility* of the man. Finally, I say, 'Resign?' and let him dangle there awhile. For the first time he *interests* me—I want to see what he'll say.

"His eyes are begging me for help. 'It's Clayton, Jr.,' he stammers. 'With that sales manager's job I would travel less. What I mean, Mr. Carey, is the boy needs me now his mother's dead...'

"'My wife died, too,' I tell him. 'I haven't quit yet.'

"'I know, sir. I hope you got my letter...'

"'So what do you propose to do?'

"He looks embarrassed. 'There's a bookstore in Stillwater. I can buy half an interest if I manage it, too. I could see Clayton, Jr., at night, and I know the business...'

"'Then you know how bad a business that can be.'

"'Yessir.' I can smell liquor through the Sen-Sen he'd been chewing and realize he's shakier than last year. All at once it strikes me that he thinks the road is making him a drunk, when having a job he could halfway do was what held him together. 'But I'm worried about little Clayton,' he's saying. 'He's gotten too inward. Spending that much time alone will twist a man...'

"His voice trails off and I wonder if he's talking about himself. 'You're all right in this job,' I tell him. 'The boy can respect that, and you'll make a living.'

"He keeps shaking his head with that weak man's stubbornness. 'It's for the best, Mr. Carey.'

"'Then you'd better resign now,' I say. 'I don't want you selling with your mind somewhere else.'

"He looks pale, as if it shocks him that anything he says or does has consequences. 'But my security...I need time to arrange things.'

"I wave a hand. 'You'll get half a year's severance pay and I'll carry your life insurance for the next eighteen months. Anything else?'

"He just stares at me. Finally, he shakes his head and turns away. I watched him walk into the crowd of salesmen, looking smaller with each moment. Never saw him again." John Carey put down his cigar, watched it burning slowly in the ashtray. "Fourteen months later the salesman's job in Barth's old territory opens up again and who should call me begging it back but Clayton. Even long distance his voice was slurry. His bookstore had failed, he needed a job—to support 'little Clayton,' of course. 'Please,' he kept saying, 'I know the territory. Not just the cities, but the stores in Ardmore and Wichita Falls. I know their names . . .'

"I cut him off. He'd lacked the sense to know the job was more than money to him, and called his stupidity love for a son.

"Three weeks later to the day, my secretary brought in a copy of the life insurance policy I'd extended with a two-sentence letter signed Clayton Barth, Jr. I remember it—tight, coiled handwriting. The letter said his father had put a revolver to his forehead and pulled the trigger. I guess the boy thought I should feel guilty." John Carey's voice became an angry blast. "Why should I, when his own father never cared enough to show his son a man, even at the end." The wintry smile John Carey gave was no smile at all. "Our policy excluded suicides."

Charles studied his father. Quietly, he asked, "Why are you telling me this?"

John Carey stared at his cigar; it was no longer lit. "Because I don't relish Peter having a eunuch for a father."

Charles looked steadily at John Carey, as if debating whether to say more. Then he shrugged. "I don't equate leaving here with suicide."

"There are different ways to kill yourself."

"Then think how much closer you'll feel to Phillip."

The room was very still. John Carey asked, "So you no longer care whom I choose."

Charles's eyes closed for a moment. "Not anymore." His eyes opened. "Cheer up, Father—I may even take HUAC with me."

Watching Charles's expressionless face, John Carey realized with a stab of fear that his son's passion had fled, that they were no longer joined even in anger or ambition. He felt suddenly tired. "Well," he said dismissively, "I can't force manhood on you. But you're still responsible for editing the manuscripts you've started. Those can be done at home—after that, we'll discuss what else you might do. Considering his mother, it might be good if at least Peter saw *you* work at something useful."

"As you like." Charles stood, reaching for his coat. He walked to the door, then turned. "Clayton Barth still troubles you, doesn't he. You gave him no way out."

It took John Carey by surprise. "Why should I have," he snapped. "The only person Clayton Barth had the power to destroy was his own son."

Charles's slight smile in the doorway seemed almost pitying. "Sweet Jesus Christ," he murmured, and was gone.

CHAPTER 4

In the months that followed Charles's leaving, for the first time in his life, John Carey felt alone.

For seven years, his sons had circled him like strange dogs, bound by their hungers and the scent of his will. Neither Charles nor Phillip knew its terms, how often it had been changed, even whether it existed. Neither asked. Yet its gift of power had drawn the two competing brothers to his side in a subtle alchemy that took the place of love. Feeling the ruin of a chemistry which had relied on Charles's need, Black Jack Carey slapped at the knowledge as though it were a cobweb, denying what he could not face.

One gray and gloomy Tuesday, shortly after Peter's third birthday, John Carey called his chauffeur and left the office early, appearing at Charles's in his long black Lincoln to announce: "It's time I knew my grandson."

He gave no reason: John Carey could not explain his need for Peter, even to himself. Charles, regarding him with cool blue eyes, said, "He's playing upstairs," and John Carey's time with Peter began.

Peter knew nothing of the black-haired dandy who had terrified his sons. To him, his grandfather was a florid, soft-spoken man with shrewd black eyes and a white mane of hair, whose callused hands gripped him tightly as they crossed the street.

"Grandpa, how did your hands get so rough?"

They were waiting in line at the Hayden Planetarium, shortly after Peter's fourth birthday. John Carey smiled ruefully down, eyes penetrating and a little sad. "Do you really want to know?"

Peter nodded.

"Then the stars can wait."

The chauffeur drove them through the Holland Tunnel and into New Jersey, to the bindery.

Peter looked at the long, gray building. "What is it?"

"They make books from sheets of paper. I would bring the sheets here in a wagon drawn by horses."

"Horses? Are you very old?"

John Carey frowned. "I never think about it. Would you like to see inside?"

It was dark and hot and smelled like glue. The man in charge treated John Carey like someone special. "I want Peter to know how books are made," he said. The man stopped what he was doing to show them: at the end, he gave to Peter a finished book, its spine stamped with fine gold print, which his grandfather read aloud, "Van Dreelen and *Carey*."

"Is that our name?"

John Carey nodded. "These are our books."

"Do you still drive them?"

"No. Not anymore."

"Because the horses are all dead?"

"They don't use horses anymore—we have trucks. Other men drive them for me."

"Then what do *you* do?"

John Carey tucked the book back under Peter's arm. "I decide what books will have our name on them."

"So other people can see it?"

John Carey didn't answer: Peter felt consumed by the blackness of his stare. Then a small smile crossed his face. "We'll come again. There's something else I want to show you."

They went to the car. John Carey nodded curtly at the chauffeur. "Drive us to the firm."

An hour later they stopped in front of a twenty-story building of slate-gray stone jutting upward from the corner of Fifth Avenue and 42nd Street. On its exposed side, towering over the ruckus of Fifth Avenue, "Van Dreelen & Carey" was lettered in outsized gold script, glistening in the late afternoon sunlight. The building's front was of an elaborate French design, with a mansard roof and black wrought-iron railings around the upper office windows, its elegant glass doorway—surrounded by more windows filled with John Carey's hardback books—topped by ornate gold-painted filigree and the same gold lettering, "Van Dreelen & Carey," that Peter recognized from the book he held. "Is that our name, too?"

"Yes."

They stared up at it from the sidewalk. Chill fall winds brushed Peter's face. "Do we own this building, Grandpa?"

"Yes."

"Did we always?"

"No—not always. Men named Van Dreelen owned it once— your Grandmother Carey's family." John Carey turned, palms extended toward Peter. "I got these calluses shoveling coal into their furnace."

"Then you bought it."

"Yes—a long time later."

Peter thought of his father, the way he had of sometimes looking over his shoulder, as if someone were pursuing him. "Do other people want it, too?"

"Yes." John Carey's face was hard. "But I won't ever let them take it from us."

Peter looked back at the lettering above the door. "How come my daddy never brought me here before?"

John Carey did not answer.

Peter felt puzzled. "Does he love this building, too, Grandpa?"

For a long, silent moment, John Carey turned to stare at it. "I don't know."

"Then why do *you?*"

John Carey kept staring at the building, motionless, gripping Peter's hand. In a fierce near-whisper, he said, "Because it's *ours.*"

The hoarseness in his grandfather's voice made Peter some-how afraid. Timidly, he asked, "Are you much older than my daddy?"

"Yes, John Peter, I am." John Carey's eyes were still fixed on the building. "Why?"

Peter could not say what he knew only by instinct: that no one had driven horses or stoked furnaces for a long time, that his grandfather moved more slowly now, as if the movements were from memory and the memory was failing, that his face became redder when they had to hurry across a street, that it was autumn and leaves fell from their trees, that there was no

Grandmother Carey and no one ever spoke of her, that *old* voices sounded lonely. "Don't worry, Grandpa. I'll take care of your building for you."

John Carey knelt abruptly on the sidewalk, clasping Peter's shoulders and staring into his eyes. "What made you say that?"

"I *will*."

"Then why did you ask about your father?"

Still Peter couldn't say. He touched the lines on his grandfather's face. "Because you have *cracks*. Daddy only has little cracks near his eyes."

John Carey was silent. Then he smiled. "What does your Daddy play with you?"

"Sometimes he chases me, in the park."

It frightened Peter when John Carey started trying to chase him like his father: Peter saw that it was much too late.

His grandfather would run and then pull up, wheezing and red-faced. A worried Peter stopped asking if they could run; disappointed, his grandfather would challenge him. "I'll catch you this time, Peter." Peter learned to run less quickly, allowing his grandfather to catch up. After a time, Peter would say, "Let's talk about our building," and then John Carey would stop, and they would sit, Peter facing him, as he explained about books and authors and money, about the low cost of paperbacks and how touchy John O'Hara was—the things he no longer told his son.

Phillip Carey watched his father fall in love with Peter.

It puzzled and disturbed him, eroding his sense of place: the grandfather Phillip saw was the father he had only fantasized. Knowing too well the void which Allie left, Phillip sought to help ease Peter's hurt by re-creating moments of the childhood John Carey had denied him. Yet he was awkward with Peter—remote or overeager—the timing of his approaches subtly wrong. Hating his own childhood, he had no sense of children.

"Hey, Prince Charming, want to play catch?"

He had found Peter stretched on the floor of his bedroom, raptly arranging green plastic soldiers in close-order drill.

"Peter?"

His nephew glanced up. Phillip plucked a red handball from

his pocket and began tossing it in front of him. "I just bought this for you—let's go out back and break it in."

Peter looked uncertain. "I promised Grandpa I'd play these with him."

"Just for a minute—your grandfather's not here yet." Phillip smiled awkwardly. "Maybe you'll grow up to be like Lou Gehrig, okay?"

"Who's that?"

"My favorite baseball player—he played first base for the Yankees."

"Did you see him?"

Phillip nodded. "That was before they had television. But your grandfather took me to see him once."

"Grandpa did?"

"Yes."

"Is he dead now—the man?"

"Lou Gehrig? Yes, he's dead now."

Peter edged closer to his toys. "I'd better wait for Grandpa."

"Maybe he won't come . . ."

"John Peter Carey!" John Carey burst through the door and past Phillip, trailing Bushmills and tobacco. "You've started without me."

Peter's eyes crinkled in a great smile. He reached to hug his grandfather, face buried in his neck.

Staring down at the rubber ball in his hand, Phillip felt once more the solitude of childhood. He left unnoticed.

Alone in his office, Phillip Carey began pondering the meaning of his nephew.

He had been fiercely glad at Charles's leaving. As if on cue, HUAC's unnerving presence had diminished with Charles's own. Now their authors were less often called to hearings, Van Dreelen & Carey seldom mentioned. Only Charles was followed by strangers: to Phillip's relief, the unsettling Englehardt had not called on him again. For a while his fears diminished, too: now heir-apparent to John Carey, he plunged into the vacuum with new decisiveness, claiming power and responsibility. Less often bypassed, he felt himself grow: writers, producers, agents and paperback publishers—the men who had called Charles—now looked to him for answers.

John Carey did not seem to notice.

Unable to divine his father's feelings, Phillip wavered in his own, haunted by Charles's unspoken presence. At times, emerging from his office, he would find himself staring down the familiar corridors—cubbyholes filled with white-shirted editors, money-green rugs, walls lined with literary awards set between photographs of now-dead employees once favored by John Carey—as if he were a stranger. Finally, he asked his father whether he, who had served the firm when Charles left, would receive it when his father died. John Carey's face went cold. "I'd like to feel that you're here because you wish to be," he answered stiffly. "A thing belongs to those who love it most."

He made no further answer.

Phillip's attempts to gain his father's favor redoubled until he grew exhausted; his tiredness resulted in a heedlessness in things outside John Carey's reach. He drank too much, spent more money than he had, slept with hat-check girls and actresses until he forgot their names. He liked to dominate them, using his money as leverage to make them do as he wished, sometimes in pairs or to each other. As they performed, eyes blank and joyless, Phillip would fantasize the hurt faces of abandoned boyfriends—hicks from Kansas or Ohio who had begged their favors in the dark and hoped for marriage—witnessing their debasement at his hands. Afterwards he would shower and leave, trembling at his needs and the memory of his mother, rising in porcelain perfection from the grave of his subconscious.

He began imagining Alicia Carey.

He had mounted a stringy modeling student on a mattress in a dingy four-story walk-up in the East Village, face averted from his own act. As she moaned he could not recall her features, felt his erection die of guilt inside her, cold fear crawl across his stomach. His mind could stir no images, no act or woman which could save him. Then he thought of Allie Fairvoort.

He swelled inside the thin woman as she became his brother's wife, her arrogant disdain turning to desire, the imagined boyfriend of his fantasies now Charles, staring in stunned humiliation as Alicia Carey cried for Phillip to take her and his rhythm became a mindless pounding and he came, screaming. As the woman dressed he saw she had green eyes.

He paid her to rinse her hair ash-blonde.

She would dress in heels and black stockings, begging Phillip to do anything he wished. She banked the money he gave her. He paid her more for sodomy. When she took her savings and went back to marry her boyfriend in Texas, he wept.

He felt utterly alone.

In this despairing void, Phillip grew superstitious, until he felt the absent Charles in the silence of his father. Peter was the symbol of Charles's succession.

Slowly, against his will, Phillip Carey began to fantasize his brother's death.

It would be an accident; Phillip would be sad. Twinned with his surviving son by mourning, his father would reach out to him...

Phillip recoiled from himself in horror.

He went to a psychiatrist.

Repeating his fantasies aloud, he heard the man's pencil scratch across his notepad: in his mind the daydreams, written, became the forecast of his brother's death. The pencil kept on scratching...

Phillip Carey bolted from the office.

His mind festered with apologies he could not speak: to Charles for the deathly images dancing in his brain, to Peter for the heartache they would bring. Remembering Englehardt, he tried hoping that the clicking sounds he still heard on his telephone issued not from men, but from the reprimand of conscience against his fevered imaginings. In his guilt, from a feeling of unworthiness too deep to express, loneliness became a self-protection.

No person could be allowed too close, for the evil he might see.

Caught between self-loathing and the perfect image of his mother, he could not unmask himself to women who were peers, or reach for one to marry. Ruth Levy, in bed with Charles shortly after his return to work, called it "Phillip's prostitute-madonna complex."

Charles Carey had found sweeter consolation.

* * *

When Charles first met Ruth Levy, shortly before he left Van Dreelen & Carey, he would have laughed at the idea of sleeping with her: he did not then know that John Carey would use her to lure him closer to the forsaken conflict with his brother.

Hostage to his love for Peter, he had been discreet in finding women, worrying about Phillip or the men who followed him, and the poison they might plant with Allie. He was fearful of divorce: perhaps when Peter was older, less victim to his mother's moods. And he found that there were women—editors and actresses, writers and bored wives—who would take him on his own terms.

Ruth Levy had not been one of them.

She had come to his office that first day, severely dressed and still clutching her résumé, his friend's sister: thin-faced like Levy, with those same marmoset eyes that seemed to look through him. She covered their intensity with staccato speech and quick, birdlike gestures that betrayed the cigarettes hidden in her purse and a metabolic rate so high that she could burn off calories while perched at a desk. She had black unruly hair, long legs and no breasts to speak of. Her nose was thin, her skin ivory, and her eyes shone with an intelligence that made her seem terribly serious, yet oddly pretty. She had graduated *summa* from CCNY: Carey figured she was a Spartacist, at least, furious about the Rosenbergs and Sacco and Vanzetti and never smiled. When he told her that, in bed two years later, she laughed until her small breasts shook.

"Jesus, Carey, you are such a *smug* bastard!"

He smiled as she rifled her purse for a cigarette. "Well, most of it was true." Mocking her nasal cadences, he began, "'Harry Luce is *such* a fascist—I just couldn't stand it over at *Time*. And those *maps*, those silly, fucking right-wing maps: Italy carved up like a pizza, with the Christian Democrats getting a thirty-two percent wedge and the Communists nineteen and all the pepperoni, painted red and located near Milan, where your fucking friend *Clare* would never go because the workers smell bad and speak no English...'"

"*I* never said that."

"You were going to—next week."

She smothered him with a pillow.

From behind it came his muffled sounds of gagging. "Do you give up?" Ruth demanded.

"Christ, yes," he gasped. "I thought you didn't believe in capital punishment."

"Only for sexual purposes." Abruptly, she drew the pillow down over his chest and lay across it, holding his bemused face in her hands. "Did you know that I loved you before we ever met? From your picture in Bill's yearbook, when I was fourteen."

She kissed his forehead.

It had happened by degrees. Hiring her, Charles watched as she took on the thankless piecework of editorial assistants, screening calls for Phillip, arranging Black Jack Carey's lunches, shuttling manuscripts to Charles at his home, and writing polite turndowns to the hopeless authors of unsought masterpieces, like the widow from Kansas who, traumatized by seventeen rejections, threatened suicide should Van Dreelen & Carey refuse to publish her love poems to her dead son. "She's probably got him in the 'fridge,'" she shuddered to Charles. "Jesus, the *pain* out there."

"It's scary," he agreed and then, remembering Levy's mother, he added softly, "But these people never do, you know."

"What?"

"Kill themselves."

Her mouth curled downward: for an instant she looked almost forlorn. "Why did you hire me?" she asked. "Was it my brother?"

"No." He smiled. "It was because I figured you were either a genius or a tower sniper. I was curious which."

"And what do you think now?"

"That I hired a good editor by accident."

Assigned to Phillip, she could not find a novel that would please him. Gradually, she turned to Charles for encouragement as she battled the mind-numbing avalanche of manuscripts, winnowing, sorting, stacking and restacking, carting more stacks home on the subway to read at night until her nerves jangled with bad coffee and she realized that the page swimming in front of her had been there for an hour. "Don't worry," he told her. "Some night you'll open something wonderful by a writer no one's ever heard of, and by next year everyone else will know it's wonderful, too—even Phil."

Seven months later, from yet more memoirs of beagles and beastly parents, she pulled the sad, achingly beautiful novel of a young girl's coming of age in a harsh Georgia town. She read it twice and took it to Charles, hugging the manuscript in front of her. "It's so *good*. It's been turned down five places, and this lady is *so* good."

Standing in his library, she seemed almost to quiver with love for the book. "What's it about?" Charles asked. He frowned as she told him. "Tough to sell, I'm afraid. Who've you shown this to?"

She flushed. "No one."

"Not Phillip?"

She looked away, body taut and strained, holding the manuscript like a baby. "I thought it had a better chance with you."

He stared at her. "That isn't very smart, you know."

She nodded, still looking down. "I know."

"Then you also know that for me to intercede would make life difficult for you."

Her eyes flashed back to him. "I don't care about that."

"Don't you? I thought you wanted a *career* in publishing, not a coffee break."

Her eyes held his. Softly, uncharacteristically, she asked, "Please?"

Six days later Charles went to John Carey's office. Ruth's manuscript sat on his father's desk, Phillip at his side. "We've read the novel," John Carey told him.

"Then you must know that it's too fine to ignore."

"It won't sell," Phillip cut in. "And I don't appreciate that Miss Levy didn't clear this with me. Frankly, I'm for unloading both of them."

Charles turned on Phillip. "Ruth Levy has the sense to let us know what's good, instead of trying to tell us what we want to hear. You'd be foolish not to keep her."

Phillip eyed him curiously. "What does she . . ."

John Carey raised his hand, still watching Charles. "Does this mean you wish to resume taking some responsibility for what we publish?" he asked softly. "Because you can't just come and go, meddling as you please."

Charles hesitated. "Exactly what do you propose?"

"I won't have you throwing notes over the fence. Instead, you're going to do something that's never been done. You'll have your own imprint—the authority to choose and edit five books a year with 'A Charles Carey Book' printed under the firm name, so that you can succeed or fail in front of God and everyone. *That* is my condition for publishing every single book you want." John Carey thrust Ruth Levy's manuscript across the desk. "Including this one."

Charles read the hurt and surprise on Phillip's face, the determination on John Carey's. "You forget I'm Typhoid Mary," he answered. "You and Phil may bore them, but HUAC's still trailing me around."

John Carey shrugged. "McCarthy went too far—these people can't do much now, beyond getting on your nerves." His voice grew harsh. "You still can work at home, Charles. But unless you work on this for *me*, Miss Levy no longer works for anyone."

Charles stared back at his father, measuring the force of his intentions. In a low voice, he said at last, "Have it your way."

Silently, he took the manuscript from his father's hand. Phillip turned away.

The next day Ruth Levy asked Charles to come home with her.

"Look," he told her. "I didn't . . ."

She put her finger to his lips. "I know."

It was sweet and intense.

The voice of Charles Carey broke the silence.

"Have it your way . . ."

On a drizzly December night, in his rented room on R Street, Englehardt winced with the hurt he knew was Phillip's.

The tape clicked off. Abruptly, he felt pain becoming anger.

His deep absorption in the Careys had not yet filled the emptiness inside him: he wished to be the unseen hand, felt but not discerned, that would make Phillip Carey's future different from his past.

Remembering the notes of Phillip's fantasies, stolen from his analyst, his flesh tingled with their closeness.

The Careys were his secret life. For four years, he had done the flagging work of HUAC, returning at night to the reports and photographs and soft, taped voices of his borrowed family, to love and hate and take pride and pity, safe behind a screen. He did not find this odd: he knew that most men were at heart voyeurs, who felt seeing women's bodies in a magazine the same quick, guilty thrill of peering through a window. He simply had what his solitude made him need: a place inside the window, where voices could be heard.

The voice he heard was Phillip Carey's.

With Phillip, he had delighted in Charles's departure: the public lessening of HUAC's interest in the firm had been his private signal to John Carey that this son was better gone. Now he let his presence show only in the men who still watched Charles, to mark him a pariah. But his secret bugs and wiretaps remained: he watched John Carey's love for Peter grow, heard the murmured telephone calls that signaled Charles's adulteries, felt the doubt and loneliness that haunted Phillip's days and nights, increased by the women he could never love.

Like Phillip, he did not know the contents of John Carey's will.

John Carey spoke of it to no one.

Now, as the old man had predicted, HUAC's strength was fading fast: two months prior to this night, the Committee's Chief Counsel had suggested closing "some of our more tired inquiries . . ."

Atop the list was Charles Carey.

Englehardt stalled for time; his response was tortured and cerebral: he knew that he could not reach Charles Carey through his politics. Only in his personal life, as the father of a son he loved too much to abandon his brittle wife, did Charles show true weakness.

Englehardt felt his own weakness growing with each night.

The Chief Counsel had given him five more months to complete the Carey file.

Part of him knew, even as he felt the pain of separation, that this was a necessity. The Careys were too seductive and yet too distant from his true career; it was time to find a patron much more permanent and powerful than this farce of a Committee. He would close accounts with Charles, leaving Phillip to his prize of power, to seek his own.

But he recognized, on the tape which had just ended, that Charles Carey was moving closer to his father, just as this sweet, secret time of listening was drawing to a close.

Without much hope, he picked up the reports that had accompanied the tapes.

As always, they were neatly typed, a written schedule of Charles's life. But once more their gloss was fool's gold, reflecting nothing but a father's love for a small blond boy with a name too weighty for him to shoulder: John Peter Carey, the second...

Angrily, he flipped its pages.

The last page stopped him with a jolt.

As if rising from the printed word, Charles Carey turned in the doorway of the apartment building belonging to the slim, dark woman, Ruth, and kissed her.

Suddenly, Englehardt knew from months of listening to their conversations, knew before Charles Carey did, that Ruth Levy would be different. And, as he did, he saw at once that he might use this latest woman against Charles, in the way he would feel most deeply: to ensure that his father's favor, and thus his will, would settle on the younger son.

His means would be Peter Carey—the price of an adultery too humiliating for his mother to ignore.

All he needed were a few final months: enough time for Charles Carey to fall in love.

After that first night together, Charles began returning often, to be with Ruth.

She had a small apartment on Waverly Place, a few blocks from Washington Square. Sometimes he would meet her in the square at dusk; she waited beneath the ornate arch—spotlights grazing its white marble, the park and trees dim shadows—looking lonely and slight and vulnerable, until he came. She smiled and took his arm, and they would walk, talking and laughing, intoxicated by borrowed freedom, through the hustle of Macdougal Street for dinner at the Minetta Tavern, or up Cornelia to Bedford Street and Chumley's—its entrance still an unmarked door from its speakeasy days—and sit in a dark corner listening to the loud talk of poets and artists and hangers-on, or to the Lion's Head, passing Jimmy Walker's home on what Charles called "the best block in Manhattan," St. Luke's Place, a narrow, cobblestoned street flanked by gaslights and over-arching trees, its south side a row of scrubbed brick town houses from which Ruth selected favorites, all lined up in perfect symmetry, their black, wrought-iron railings rising with the steps to carved oak doors. Sometimes they might walk to the end of the Wharton Street Pier, watching the Hudson flow south toward Ellis Island, where Ruth's great-grandfather had arrived from Russia. Once, at the foot of the pier, she took his picture.

Always they would go to Ruth's.

Charles knew that they were still being followed, and resolved not to care.

He loved recapturing the feel of a single woman's apartment, the smell of perfume and candle smoke, the clutter of books, antique lamps, recordings of Beethoven and Bach and manuscripts strewn on the bed and on top of her refrigerator. Finally, against all odds and knowing their incongruity, he loved *her*.

Naked, she was comic as a child, laughing as their passion overtook them, and joyous after. "You're beautiful," she would say then, and her open, unforced wanting touched him beyond anything he'd known. Losing her awe of him, she learned something of his childhood and the humiliation of his marriage. She made love to him, and made him laugh. He grew to understand her humor and fear and radicalism, her uncanny sensitivity and the way she lectured herself aloud, "Come on, Ruthie, shape up," as if she were her own parent. She had never satisfied her father. Her mother had killed herself when Ruth was thirteen.

They could speak of this, he found, as they could speak of her brother with a shared affection that brought them closer. Levy and Charles remained warm friends, perhaps warmer for a shared affection too fraught with the possibility of sadness to be easily discussed: Charles knew that Levy, knowing, understood that Charles lived with such complexity because he truly cared for Ruth.

"What do you think?" he often asked her. He listened more than talked, smiled when she swore, saw the harshness she affected for what it was. "This city dries women out," he told her. "They fight the hustle and competition and men who only want to screw them until they turn to leather, all drive and double martinis and 'he's such a schmuck.' I suppose it has to be." He smiled a little. "You're one of the smartest people I know, Ruthie—be as tough as you like and take no shit from anyone. Just don't defend yourself so bitterly there's no softness left to defend."

She took his hand. "These men are so *afraid*," she said intently. "There's no one else like you."

He smiled at her certainty. "Then it's for me to guard the sweetness in you."

She touched his face. Abruptly, she smiled. "And listen to my shit, Carey."

He laughed out loud.

Feeling good for her, he grew better for himself. They dissected the manuscripts she worked on, sniffed out clues for helping her career, selected the first Charles Carey books. She bought Bombay gin for his martinis, insisting when he asked to pay that each drink advanced her "Zionist plot" to become editor-in-chief. He delighted in her outrage and outrageousness. She fumed about "those racist pricks in Little Rock" and the withdrawal from Suez; demanded that he tithe the ten dollars a month to orphans in Korea—"Christ," she blurted, "put your *wife* to work if you can't afford it," then clapped both hands over her mouth until she saw his laughter; raged at publishers in general—"inbred morons too stupid to work for banks"— and Phillip Carey in particular. "I'd rather ball Franco," she bristled one evening after a deliberate pass by Phillip. "*He's* the one having us followed—why else would he do that? He doesn't *like* women, I can smell it." After that, with the spooky prescience of the wounded, she dubbed him "Phillip Krafft-Ebing" and speculated on his private life. "I've got it," she told Charles over dinner at Sevilla. "At night he visits a hooker in the Bowery and then goes home, smears himself in his own shit, jumps into an ice-cold shower and slaps his hands with a rubber hose, screaming, 'Bad! bad!'" She grinned, pleased with herself. "What do you think?"

"It's just delightful. Care for dessert?"

"No, really."

He toyed with his fork. "I guess I know enough to feel sorry for him, though I manage to forget that."

"But he came on with me to hurt you, Charles."

"Then you hurt *him* worse than you'll ever know." He smiled. "Forget him, Ruthie—he'll not do that again. I expect it's HUAC still following me, hoping I'll bump into Khrushchev or Bulganin, and distressed that you're a woman. Besides," he added casually, "I love you."

Her eyes glistened. He looked at her across the table. Her hand touched his arm, then pulled back, as if from a flame. Softly and seriously, he said, "I really do."

Her mouth quivered. "And Peter."

He looked away. In a monotone, he said, "And Peter, too."

They rarely talked about his son. But the fact of Peter was like a compass, defining the boundaries of speech and possibility. "She'll do nothing as long as no one rubs her face in us," Charles once remarked of Allie; it was understood that fear of Allie's taking Peter from him imposed limits on his movements. Sometimes, with remembered youth, Charles would race his Jaguar through the rolling Connecticut countryside as she gasped her reluctant fear and admiration, at other times they ventured uptown—to see Olivier in *The Entertainer*, or Nichols and May at Down in the Depths; as months passed, and Peter or his work on Charles Carey books would keep him home at night, he missed her with more intensity. But he never stayed the night. They never talked of marriage. She never called his home.

And then, late one spring evening, when Charles was slaving over a manuscript and Allie had left for their summer home in Maine, his telephone rang. "I want to see you," Ruth said. "Please, for a minute."

Her voice jarred him from thought. "What time is it?"

"Past ten. Keep working—I'll come there." She paused. "If it's okay?"

He looked at his watch. Ten-thirty. Peter had been in bed since seven: *Wind in the Willows* was heavy going for a four-year-old, he had nearly dropped off before Charles finished. The cook and maid had long since retired.

He had not seen Ruth for ten days.

"Charles?"

"All right—yes. I'll leave the front door open."

She found him in the library. He was stretched out on the couch, wearing a tennis shirt, chinos and moccasins, blue-penciled manuscript pages scattered all around him. The light from the overhead chandelier made the circles beneath his eyes look deeper. His hair was mussed. Gently, she closed the double door behind her, walked to the couch and kissed him. "You look like hell."

He shrugged, smiling. "It's been like this since I joined the Roller Derby."

She switched off the chandelier.

A dim lamp at the end of the couch gave them light in a cocoon of darkness. She stood before him, mockery vanished. Silently, she began to undress, dropping her things behind her, one by one, until she was naked. Her thick hair fell on her shoulders.

"Peter..."

"Is sleeping." She held a finger to her lips. "Quiet, Carey. This is a house call." She knelt by the couch and began unbuttoning his shirt. "Sit up a minute."

He paused, thinking of Peter. She took his face in her hands. Her breast grazed his shirt. "I've missed you, Charles... missed you so much. Do you understand that?"

"Yes."

His back arched from the couch.

She pulled off his shirt, seeking his left nipple with her mouth. His eyes closed. "Jesus..."

"... has nothing to do with it." Her mouth slid along the thin auburn line of hair to his stomach, her hands to the buckle of his belt.

Her hair smelled like violets. "Look, let me..."

"No, love. Enjoy it." She pressed her cheek against his lap. "As I do you."

Tenderly, lips brushing the shaft of his penis, she took him into her mouth.

Upstairs, Peter awoke, rubbing his eyes. The room seemed very dark. "Daddy?..."

No one answered.

His mouth was dry. "Can I have a drink of water, Daddy?"
The silence frightened him.

He stumbled out of bed, found his red terry-cloth robe where he had thrown it on the miniature captain's chair and put it on, too sleepy to tie it. Charles had left the nightlight on in Peter's bathroom. He went in, filled the water cup, and drank in short, thirsty gulps. Putting down the cup, he looked around him, and listened.

There was still no sound.

He went back to his bed and stood beside it. On his pillow was a stuffed green elephant with shoe-button eyes that his father had brought home from F.A.O. Schwarz and named "Dewey," for reasons that Peter did not understand. "Elephants are a tad slow-thinking," his father had smiled, "but quite large and very brave, of course. So if you find yourself afraid of anything and I can't be there, just hang on to Dewey until I get back."

Peter picked up Dewey by his trunk and went into the hallway to find his father.

It was even darker. He edged past his mother's silent bedroom, clutching Dewey more tightly, to his father's.

It was empty.

His heart beat faster. He tiptoed back down the long, dark hall, pausing at his room. Then he went to the head of the circular stairway. He stood there—the belt to his robe trailing behind him, Dewey tucked under his arm—and looked down.

Nothing.

He rubbed his eyes again. "Daddy . . ."

Still nothing.

He hesitated, a tightness in his throat. Then he reached for the railing, smooth and polished under his hand, and began tottering down the stairway, stopping on each step to listen for sounds.

A crack of light came from beneath the library door.

He stopped once more, recalling how he had surprised his mother there and broken the glass, and she had shrieked at him for sneaking. Then he remembered that his mother wasn't home.

He couldn't lose his father. Not yet.

His father might be in the library.

Gingerly, he took the remaining stairs.

He paused again at the double doors to the library, heart pounding even faster. Then he reached for the round, smooth knob. He turned it slowly. Half frightened, half wanting to surprise his father, he thrust Dewey through the crack in the door, peeking from behind.

He stopped, transfixed by naked arms and legs and bodies, a slim, dark woman he had never seen. His father moaned.

Unable to move or speak, Peter watched them. Time stood still . . .

Suddenly Peter saw Charles staring at his stuffed elephant, saw his lips part but make no sound. Dewey slid to his chin; in one terrible moment Peter Carey looked into his father's stricken eyes as Charles came in his lover's mouth.

Peter saw his naked father shivering in a rictus of agony and release, saw the woman's black hair and ivory shoulders bobbing over his father's lap and then backed from the library, Dewey clutched in his hand, crying without knowing why.

A short time later, when it was still dark, Charles came to his room. Softly, he asked, "You'd been watching, then."

Shamed, Peter could only nod.

Charles knelt by the bed. "Are you angry?"

"No." Peter clung to his father.

"Because it's okay if you are."

Face buried, Peter shook his head: he knew that this was not his father's fault, but his. He had his mother to remind him.

Watching Charles's movements from a cover of indifference, John Peter Carey made a silent promise to his grandson: never would his son's affair put Peter in the care of Allie Fairvoort.

There must be no divorce.

He never told this to his son: Charles would not accept that his father had at last set detectives to watching only from his fear of those who followed him, in order to learn what they might know.

What he learned, to his astonishment and fear, was that Ruth Levy had become his son's sole lover.

The secret reports of Charles's movements confirmed that he was still closely watched: the odd clickings of the telephone, the strange delays in the Careys' mail, argued that these further spies might still be those of HUAC, and not of Alicia Carey. Yet this seemed too irrational.

He directed that these men be traced to whoever sent them.

A month later, the head of his detectives — a silent man, slate-gray as pavement — reported to his office.

Two men who followed Charles had met another at a Chinese restaurant on Mulberry Street. Frozen in dim photographs, they spoke to him.

The detective's finger pointed to his bow tie. "Know this one?"

Staring downward, John Carey nodded.

He did not tell him how, or from where.

The Committee was a dying force. That this man still persisted in watching Charles scared him with its senselessness: it was not justified by politics, or by anything else he knew of . . .

He looked back at the photograph, at the face of the watcher.

His long pursuit of Charles smelled too personal.

Dismissing his operative, John Carey began pondering how perverse a form such deviance might take. But he could think of nothing Charles should fear . . .

Except Ruth Levy, for the harm she might cause Peter.

He began reaching for his telephone, to fire her on the spot.

His arm stopped in midgrasp, at the thought of Charles's face. Firing her would estrange his son beyond all hope of his retrieval, without ending their affair: nor would it stop this strange and sallow man from working through Alicia Carey, should that be his true purpose.

His hand fell to his side.

It was better to destroy this man who threatened them.

Coolly, over days of thought, he studied each member of the Committee: at length he settled on a ranking congressman, lazy and in trouble in his district, and called him from a phone that was not tapped.

He had followed the man's fortunes, he explained, and wished to help. But first, civilly and in private, he hoped to discuss their treatment of the Careys . . .

He was certain that this shallow politician would not know what his Committee's staff was doing, and that he would instruct its Chief Counsel to find out.

Within the week, the congressman invited him to Washington.

En route, John Carey felt a fear he had not felt in years: Peter's life was more important than all the lesser ambitions that had driven him, when other men had blocked his way. He must not fail.

He found the congressman sequestered in the peculiar green mustiness common to public offices, leavened only by the smiling vanity pictures of well-known faces that seem so easily replaced by those of someone else. The congressman's smile was oily, his handshake weak; John Carey felt his own density, as if he could cause the other man to fade away. He almost smiled to himself: he had had this feeling before, with the Van Dreelens.

He did not smile at the man.

"I'm honored you could come here," the congressman was saying, "as busy as you are..."

"It was necessary we met. Cigar?"

The man shook his head; John Carey lit his own. Through the stream of cigar smoke, the man ventured, "You stated some interest in my re-election..."

Silent, John Carey let the man stare into the chasm of his enforced retirement. Finally, the man said feebly, "How might I help?"

"Simply by confirming that we share principles that I might comfortably support. On the respect due publishing, for example."

The man's gaze flickered. "There were some excesses..."

"Which have touched my family too long."

The man nodded vigorously. "I knew nothing of that, I assure you. I mean that it be stopped..."

"And?"

"Pardon me?"

John Carey blew more smoke. Softly, he said, "There is a man named Englehardt."

The congressman hesitated, surprised. "Yes, well, I'm certain that he'll understand that he went too far with you..."

"He understood that all along."

"We'll restrain his zeal." Smiling, the congressman spread

his arms in feigned bewilderment. "What more assurance can I give you? After all, he works for *me*."

"Not forever."

The man looked away, then, almost shyly, back into John Carey's eyes. In muted tones, he asked, "You wish him fired?"

"No." John Carey spoke with equal quietness. "I wish him destroyed."

The man blinked. "Destroyed?"

"Specifically, I wish to be certain that no one in this city will trust him with a mop and pail." He paused. "It merely requires the same assurance that I'll need to help your re-election—that you can back our common principles with action. That belief, I might add, is the sole prerequisite to a considerable commitment to your campaign."

The man fidgeted. "By 'considerable' . . ."

"Your Committee needs to solve its problem with the public perception of its excesses. By firing this man, you can signal that misguided zealotry will not mar the cause of anti-communism. Assuming, that is, that the public learns of his defects . . ."

The man looked almost frightened. "Isn't firing sufficient? Mr. Englehardt may be overzealous, but his diligence on our behalf has been exceptional."

"Which makes him a time bomb should he ever learn that I had caused his ruin; the Careys would acquire a lifetime enemy. It's basic that such an enemy have no power."

"That's not so easily arranged."

"Even were his presence here a threat to *your* survival?" John Carey leaned forward to grind his cigar in the congressman's ashtray, gently adding, "As perhaps it is."

The man stared at him. Tentatively, he said, "I suppose I might mention the reason for his firing to those who'd pass it on—the *Times*, for example. Not for attribution, of course, and not mentioning specific cases."

"Of course." John Carey nodded. "You might even place some calls to those who might have similarly employed him, to ensure he did no harm to them."

"He's a strange man." The congressman shifted in his chair, looking away. "I've never felt quite comfortable . . ."

"Fifty thousand dollars," John Carey said.

Twelve days later, he stopped reading that morning's New York *Times* . . .

For a moment he imagined the young man Peter, strong and unafraid, and for once it did not matter that then he would be dead.

Quietly, he wrote a check.

John Joseph Englehardt could not bear to leave his own apartment.

Gaze averted, the congressman had fired him, blathering of excesses without specific names. Feeling the man's indifference like a slap in the face, Englehardt was riven by the superstition of his childhood: unloved and unlovable, he would be forever punished for the distaste he caused in others, which he could neither change nor comprehend.

Only in the corridor did he learn who else had been his enemy.

Scarcely seeing his surroundings, he collided with the Committee's Chief Counsel. Righting himself, the man read Englehardt's expression. They stared at each other; foolishly, Englehardt blurted, "He fired me."

The Chief Counsel looked right through him; Englehardt could almost see himself receding in the other's eyes. In a low, cool voice, as if disgusted by a stupid error, the man asked, "What did Charles Carey ever do to *you*?" and walked away.

For days thereafter, like a man wasted by paralysis, Englehardt could barely move or speak.

He had been short weeks from bringing Charles Carey down, leaking his affair through gossip columns in a way that Allie could not miss, then sending her the pictures. The last photograph, of Ruth Levy entering Alicia Carey's home at night, would have offended her beyond recall . . .

Now he could not even touch the Carey file; as cruelly as he would with Phillip, Charles Carey had stripped Englehardt of his power.

At last, summoning a résumé like a phoenix rising from the ashes of his firing, he once more began to gather strength. He would find a spot in government, revive his career; then, in a way of his own choosing, he would see to Charles Carey.

The morning he was to begin his phone calls he opened the New York *Times* and read his name.

He went to the bathroom and vomited.

When he returned, the headline stared up from the floor: once more, in the shame of his humiliation, he felt the coolness of his father's eyes. He could not escape himself, and did not know the reason.

What he did know, without even picking up the telephone, was that no one now would reach out to save him.

Six months later, filled with hate for Charles Carey, he found refuge in the mausoleum of a research library, acquiring books.

CHAPTER 5

As time passed, Alicia Carey retreated from the precipice of madness, becoming a graceful shell.

The incidents that had scarred both son and husband now seemed scarcely real. She felt as if she had been caught alone by some dark, enormous nightfall, awakening to a gulf measured in their stares and silence, which she lacked the gift of closing. Before the traumas of death and failing marriage, no sadness had been allowed to touch her, no pain to shadow her delight; in all of her imaginings, she had never been asked to imagine someone else. Her parents, fashioning a flawless world, had rendered it incomprehensible.

Sensing her void without perceiving it, she felt alternating currents of hurt or anger, and had no words for either. Neither she nor Charles spoke of the past. Instead, she devoted herself to the minutiae of married life—what wines to serve with veal, the location of their box at the symphony—as if seeking absolution. From these rituals, the Careys erected a routine, safe, decorous and unreal. Unvaryingly polite, he told her of politics or the writers he saw; in turn, she would talk of *Don Giovanni*, or read the books he published. She never told him of the unknown man who called to detail, in an excruciating monotone, Charles's affair with the Levy woman and the things they did in bed. There was no way she could speak of it: she no longer had sexual thoughts about him. She could not face what she had heard.

Nor, still, could she quite believe she had a son. She sensed his fear, struggled to reach for him through her disbelief, yet could not. She *knew* that she should feel something; sometimes, watching him as he slept, she did. One chilly night, covering Peter with a wool blanket, she dared to imagine what she might say if he awoke from the innocence of his sleep, and found her changed.

But to Peter, who did not know these things and could not have understood them, she remained frightening and surreal, her touch as fleeting as the kisses she gave him before she fled to Maine.

Of course she seemed happier there, everyone did; his father, grandfather and even Uncle Phillip. The Careys' summer house near Prouts Neck was gabled and rambling, sitting proud and whitewashed in the sun, overlooking the sea. Its railed porch fronted on a wild, rocky beach; in the evenings the Careys would have drinks there, Peter sipping Coke from a bottle, cool beads of condensation grazing his hand, the day's sunlight still warm on his skin. Before that, before the afternoon sun fell behind the stand of slim, menthol-smelling pines where Peter hid from imagined Indians, his father would take him for long walks on the beach. They skipped stones on the water, rolled up their pants legs to run in its brisk iciness, looked for rocks or sand dollars worn smooth by its waves. On windy days they would fly the red cloth kite Phillip and Charles had made for him, until the soaring patch of red merged in Peter's mind with the feel of sun and wind, the flat, faintly laughing tone of his father's voice. Peter loved the breezes smelling of salt, the steady, lulling beat of the surf, the way it glinted like mica in the dying sun which struck it and spread in sudden splashes of light, the gulls frozen in their downward course like slivers of steel, the feel of his father's hand. To Peter, his father smelled like Maine.

They never talked about the dark-haired woman. Prouts Neck was unhaunted.

"I love our house," Peter told him.

Seemingly endless, it seemed everyone's house, with rooms for all of them—a cheerful country kitchen and spacious dining room; his grandfather's library with its leather chairs next to Grandmother Carey's white-wicker-furnished sunroom, where his mother now read poetry; five bedrooms with overstuffed brass beds and down quilts and windows cracked open to crisp night air in which he and Dewey would fall deeply, dreamlessly asleep. The house seemed to make his Uncle Phillip more lighthearted; sometimes he and Peter even played together, and one morning Phillip let Peter watch him shave before they all went on a picnic, squinting as he flicked shaving cream from the corner of his mustache. "It's all in the wrist, Prince Charming—someday I'll show you the ropes." His mother, tanned and girlish-looking, might describe sailing with her father at their place on Lake Champlain, suffused in a childhood where she could imagine her future without having lived it. Even his grandfather seemed less inclined to push himself or others: relaxing over drinks, he spoke little of current business, preferring long, digressive stories of his salesman days. Like Uncle Phillip, his father listened peaceably enough, and if his father's eyes would narrow at some passing mention of Grandmother Carey, or if they both seemed detached from nostalgia and still watchful of each other, there was less sharpness in their words and glances. Peter did not know that part of what the brothers felt was the shadow of surveillance passing: as the days closed behind him in the lulling sameness of surf and sunshine and easy talk, he dared to dream of a complete and loving family, until he wished it with the fierce, full heart of a young boy's imaginings.

The dream vanished in his parents' home.

It echoed with his mother's shattered crystal, its heedless luxury shadowed by the alien, dark-haired presence whose nakedness and seeking mouth had dyed him, heart and memory, with the knowledge of his own guilt.

As if to compensate for this hurt in Peter, Charles Carey taught his son to love Manhattan.

They went to Radio City Music Hall, watching the Rockettes and eating popcorn amidst its baroque and golden vastness. In December, they skated at Rockefeller Center—a picture-book rink dropped wondrously into a cement-and-glass canyon—and then shopped along Fifth Avenue, taking in the holiday wreaths and mandarin-collared policemen whistling down traffic, the brisk purposeful stride of New Yorkers marching toward Christmas. They went to F.A.O. Schwarz and bought a red kangaroo to be Dewey's friend. There were more stuffed animals when they entered Rumpelmayer's—lions, zebras, wolves, cats, dogs, bears, and horses—and the room behind that had colonnades and chandeliers, and clattering tables of people scooping ice cream from glass dishes, and someone famous named Marlon Brando who knew his father and liked Rocky Road. Next door, at the St. Moritz, his father found a special map and, buying two hot, salty pretzels from a man with a metal wagon, showed him how to ride the subways. They came into the station like metallic thunder; Peter was amazed at how long and crowded they were, and how before you knew it you were someplace you'd never been.

Weekends became an adventure. Sometimes, as summer heat bore in, they might leave the city, driving his father's sports car through the rolling lushness of Connecticut to visit Phillip's home in Greenwich, passed down by John Carey as a weekend retreat. "Go faster, Daddy," Peter would urge, and Charles, grinning, stepped on the gas. Peter enjoyed the freshness, the feeling of escape, but then would grow restless. His favorite place had become Manhattan, and Central Park.

It was green and safe and filled with people. On Sundays, they might plan brunch, the zoo, and a band concert: Charles would have two Bloody Marys at the Plaza while Peter, drinking milk and orange juice, absorbed the plaintive cry of violins, the smell of bacon and citrus and the perfume of women passing, the smooth, fresh-minted look of men with white handkerchiefs in the breast pockets of crisp, gray suits, until, a little before one, his father would say, "Time to feed the seals, Peter," and they would leave to walk through Grand Army Plaza with its iron statue of Sheridan on horseback and then down into the park along the path leading toward the zoo, the city falling behind them, to see the uniformed man throw fish to the seals. Passing through the wrought-iron gateway, they would reach what Peter thought of as a magic village: a cobblestone square dominated by an old-fashioned clock tower and the shingled roofs of low brick buildings with cages full of gorillas, monkeys, bears and lions, all surrounding a smaller square of gaslights and thick green hedges neatly trimmed and split on each side by steps down to the seal pool, the steps guarded by two fierce stone eagles, their eyes, beaks and talons perfectly defined, the seal pool inside flanked by four blue-painted aviaries shaped like giant bird cages and backed by a long cement snack bar with a red-and-white-striped awning beneath a mural of cows and elephants and buffalos and apes miraculously grazing in a single glade. At 1:15 a uniformed man would appear with a bucket of smelly fish and flip them to the yawping, leaping seals as Peter laughed from atop Charles's shoulders, and then they would buy two hot dogs and examine the zoo for changes before his father asked, "Like to hear some music, Peter?" and they would move on, toward the Band Shell.

Their path rose from the zoo and wound north to a wide cobblestone mall flanked by green benches and trees which swept in two straight rows to a large, open square, where the Band Shell was, a cement half-dome, whitewashed and immaculate, perched close to a hill on the square's eastern edge. Old people, families and nannies pushing babies in English prams strolled along the mall to cluster there on summer afternoons to hear band music or symphonies; Peter liked to listen to the "1812" Overture, which reminded him of his soldiers. After the concert, Charles would take Peter's hand and lead him across the low traverse to Bethesda Fountain, and the lake.

It was another world, one that Peter liked most of all.

A broad flight of steps fell steeply to a brick plaza marked by gaslights and inlaid with a Roman pattern of cement lines and circles. A winged, cast-iron fountain rose from the cement pool at its center, where small boys splashed and played with boats. Behind the plaza a long lake lined with dense green trees and speckled with rowboats and single sculls swept toward a green-roofed boathouse on the far side. Except for the cries of children the plaza was utterly still. Charles would let Peter wade in the fountain. The water was cool on his feet, his father's laugh bright with summer, the sculls moving on the shimmering lake so slowly that they seemed like special moments captured in a photograph. There, the summer of Peter's sixth birthday, came his special moment with Charles Carey.

Charles had just bought a red Jaguar convertible and they drove it to Sutton Square, Peter grinning at the wind in his face. Parking alongside a neat row of town houses, they walked to its end, a brick courtyard with green wooden benches that overlooked the East River. The Queensboro Bridge loomed above and to their left, bright tan in the midmorning sun, running toward Roosevelt Island. An oil tanker swept beneath it, past a long white yacht with its mainsail down, puttering from Florida to Long Island Sound, for the summer. To Peter it looked lonely without its sails. "Will it stay here?" Peter asked.

They were sitting next to each other on the bench, hands in the pockets of their windbreakers. "No," Charles answered. "It goes where the sun is."

"Doesn't it want to stay?"

"It can't. Its owner decides."

Peter watched it move away. "I wish it were mine."

"Why?"

"Because then it would have a home."

"What would you do with it?"

"I'd sail to where it was quiet." Peter felt his father's arm curl around his shoulders. He moved closer, smelling the after-shave and tobacco that would be his father anywhere. "I'd take you with me, Daddy."

Charles smiled. "Anyone else?"

Peter grew thoughtful. "Sometimes Grandpa."

"What would we do?"

"I'd let you drive the boat. Grandpa would rest so he doesn't get too old. I could read his books to him." Peter looked down at his tennis shoes. "Maybe *you* could, until I learn to read."

Charles glanced curiously at his son. "Do you think he'd like that?" he asked softly.

Peter nodded, still looking down. His father's arm closed around him. It felt warm.

They sat like that for a long time.

When Peter looked up, the yacht was gone. His throat felt tight. "Where did it go, Daddy?"

Charles watched him closely. All at once he sprang up, pulling Peter by the hand. "Come on, little guy."

Peter's eyes strained after the vanished yacht. "Come on," his father urged. "I've got something to show you."

In the window of F.A.O. Schwarz was a rubber pond filled with water and cabin cruisers and floating ducks. In the middle was a trim white yacht, fully two feet long.

Charles stood grinning by the window. "There's your boat, Peter."

They took it to the park, winding through the crowded zoo and mall and past the Band Shell, until they crossed the traverse and stood above the lake and fountain, bright with noontime sun and the noise of children playing.

Peter felt utterly free. "You can't catch me," he shouted, "I know where to hide," and ran down the steps with his boat.

Reaching the bottom, he veered left in an abrupt half-circle away from the fountain, the beat of his tennis shoes slapping in his ear as he ran toward the middle of three arched entrances to the tunnel which cut beneath the traverse, and rushed in.

All at once he was enveloped in blackness.

Peter stopped, disoriented. The tunnel was long and too dark: the row of stone arches along each wall made it seem like a ruined church. Turning, he blinked at the three semicircles behind him. The children's voices seemed to come from some great distance.

A shadow entered the tunnel.

Frightened, Peter felt suddenly cut off from his father, unsure now whose shadow he saw or whose steps were coming closer, confused as to whether Charles were pursuer or thwarted rescuer, deceived by Peter's foolishness. The shadow came nearer. Peter skirted beneath an arch, back pressed desperately to the moist stone, eyes screwed shut. His heart pounded.

Something nudged his shoulder.

Next to him, Charles Carey was leaning against the wall. "Maybe I can hide with you," he whispered. "My zipper's down."

Peter ran laughing toward the fountain.

He took off his shoes, rolling up his pants legs as Charles perched on the fountain's edge and readied the sail of the yacht. Stepping in, Peter gripped the slippery bottom with his toes. The water felt pleasantly warm on his calves. A breeze blew in from the lake.

He placed his boat in the water.

It skimmed past the fountain, sails stiff and hull glistening in the sun, cutting ripples that flowed behind it like thin ribbons. Two dark-haired boys picked up their motorboat and watched. His father smiled.

"Get in, Daddy—please. It's sailing fast."

Smiling wider, Charles Carey kicked off his loafers and stood on the edge, considering.

Peter caught the boat and held it out toward his father . . .

He slipped, heard Charles call out, felt himself pitching forward and his stomach flip as his head hit cement, and water flooded his shocked, open lungs. Then there was nothing but wet, swirling darkness, squeezing his ribcage...

He could hear Charles Carey's heartbeat, feel his chest and arms. It was still dark. His throat was raw. His shirt felt wet, or maybe his father's shirt—it had his father's smell. His eyes fluttered open.

"I decided to get in the water," his father told him.

He was cradling Peter beside the fountain, arms supporting his legs and torso. "You all right?"

Peter nodded shakily. "Where's my boat?"

Charles pointed toward the statue. "Out there."

He grasped Peter by the waist and stood him facing the direction of the boat, steadying his shoulders for balance. Peter tottered out to retrieve the boat under his father's watchful eye. "I'll sail it with you," Charles called.

He stripped off Peter's shirt, rolled up his own pants, and got in. He said nothing more about the accident.

They sailed the boat for hours.

The sun warmed them, the wind cooled their faces. Peter pretended the boat was taking the three Careys—his father, grandfather and himself—to the South Seas. The noises of reality barely sounded in his ear; he lost track of time, hardly seeing the lengthening winged shadow as it crept toward them. There was only his father's voice, his grip as they chased the buoyant yacht—a small, flawless world in which he and his father did the same things, over and over, content with their perfection.

He had forgotten the accident.

"It's about time to head home, Peter."

He looked up, startled. His father smiled. "Maybe one more time around."

Peter stretched it out, sheltering his boat from the wind, until, at last, it glided through a last swatch of sunlight into the shadow of his father's hand.

They sat by the fountain, putting on their shoes and socks as Peter watched the boats on the lake.

"Can we get a rowboat sometime?"

"Who's going to row it?"

"I'll help, I promise. Can we? Please?"

Charles grinned. "In that case, I'll give it every consideration."

They were silent for a while.

"It was dark when I fell, Daddy."

"I know."

"Is that what it's like to die?"

"I'll never let you die, Peter."

"But Grandpa will."

It was quiet. His father watched the lake. "Yes, he will. Someday."

Peter felt suddenly cold. "You'll always be my Daddy, won't you?"

Charles grasped his shoulders, a smile at one corner of his mouth, eyes grave and level. "Always."

Peter hugged his father's neck. "Your zipper's still down," he said.

They laughed and went home.

They did not go alone.

Once more, from a shelter much more secret than HUAC, John Joseph Englehardt was watching them.

It began on yet another solitary, dreary morning, as he was indexing books in the library. Abruptly, he looked up and saw one of his former professors, a man for whom he had excelled; it was like seeing the ghost of his failed promise.

They stared at each other in surprise; the man spoke, and offered him a cup of coffee. Englehardt could find no way to account for the misery of his work; sitting in the cafeteria, he admitted what had happened, omitting only his obsession with the Careys.

An odd expression crossed the man's face. As teacher and student they had not been close; Englehardt read it as distant pity and contempt, distaste for hearing failure's story. So he was surprised when the professor called two lonely evenings later, suggesting dinner.

He accepted with alacrity.

They dined at the man's apartment, alone; their talk was rambling and discursive, covering Yale and his studies. Knowing that the man had never married, Englehardt's nerves trembled at his indirection.

There was something, the professor finally confessed, that he wished to broach to Englehardt; regardless of his feelings, it must be confidential. Englehardt felt himself nod, expectant . . .

The man did not simply teach at Yale.

Occasionally, he went on, he did more confidential work, which Yale did not know. Englehardt's retentive mind, his skills in research and analysis, might appeal to his more shadowy employer. The position was modest, but . . .

That night, alone in his apartment, Englehardt wept.

He might have dignity again; in some secret way and place, perhaps years distant, he could repay Charles Carey for this time of silent agony.

When Englehardt at last joined the CIA, surviving its gauntlet of interviews and tests despite the black mark of his firing, Charles Carey was still sequestered in his brain.

At once, he saw that he was working among men much more serious than those at HUAC.

He sent for the Carey file, moldering in HUAC's records.

Settling modestly in Georgetown, he neither drank nor smoked nor entertained, ate only salads and lean meats, went over the Carey file in the solitude of night. Only the notes of Phillip's analyst, too powerful in his memory to need reviewing, remained unopened.

The agency became a monastery where he could cleanse his mind without the need for wealth, making its resources his own. He learned the techniques of assassination while others slept with women, saved the money others spent, used target practice as recreation, enthralled by the rhythm of his shooting. Thinking still of Phillip Carey, he devoted weekends to the study of psychoanalysis, new god of modern man, that he might control others through their inner lives. Free of friends or social life, his sole outward vanity a fondness for bow ties, he became so nondescript as to resemble the "flea on the wallpaper" that a colleague once labeled him. Englehardt no longer cared: after HUAC, he feared only to be known. His knowledge would be the most undetectable of assets and, therefore, the most lethal.

His newfound expertise with pistols was for sport: manipulating others to his ends, he could murder with his mind.

He saw himself the flawless desk man.

His superiors saw nothing.

Lacking charm or any flair for self-promotion, his bearing as lifeless as his monotone, he drew no notice from those who might grant power. This first humiliating year of stasis, as lesser men rose past him, shriveled his soul like the memory of his exile, the work of Charles Carey. Desperately, he searched for something which in itself would announce his talents.

In unconscious parallel with this new anguish, he began once more to watch the Careys.

He did not at first discern his real purpose.

Bit by bit, on a variety of pretexts, he stepped up this surveillance: to spy on Charles Carey was a drug which eased his impotence; the sound of Phillip's fear and hatred made him feel less alone. Imagining himself as Phillip, he idly wondered how *he* might best exploit the power to publish, could he place it at the disposal of his superiors, to their amazement and delight.

Finally, irresistibly, he once more opened his file of Phillip's innermost fantasies, and read the imagined death of Charles Carey.

When suddenly these two tracks converged, he was shaken by their synergy, so frightening was the depth of his response.

He must learn the contents of John Carey's will, before the will was opened.

Before the old man died.

Suppressing his excited nervousness, the sense of destiny discovered, he began to search for ways he could arrange this.

John Carey watched Peter count Fords and Chevrolets as Charles drove them both toward Maine.

The boy was life to him. He was quick and strong for his age, even smarter than his father. Already he had Charles's cobalt-blue gaze: John Carey felt as if Peter could look right through him, understand what he wanted or was saying. He seemed without fear, his leaps and bounds constantly reflected in skinned knees or a smudged face. He made paper airplanes, testing and refolding them until they were aerodynamically perfect, picked out words from cereal boxes and highway signs, played monster at bedtime, taking six different roles with changed voices and appearances—growling hunchback, unctuous, slithering lizard—concealing each change with his blanket until his entire repertoire appeared, serially, to shock his grandfather. Another Peter, grave and questioning, inveigled trips to the bindery and stories of how the Careys had come to own it. Sometimes he helped John Carey forget his own son...

He wished it were more often. This endless business with Ruth Levy was sheer foolishness: an employee, and Jewish at that. Jewesses and actresses. His own wife had been *real*, someone you could count on...

You could never count on Charles, teetering between Peter—at least that was his excuse—and the visceral dislike of turning Van Dreelen & Carey over to his brother. Such a spectacle: his older son playing Hamlet, with Ophelia a skinny Jewish editor. It goaded him until he in turn goaded Charles. Sometimes he needed help, dammit. Charles had been there for his *mother*, tearless through the funeral, as if she still relied on him.

He tired more easily, he knew that. The letters he dictated in the afternoon would sometimes drift; in the morning he threw them out. It happened too much, like the business of making people do what they'd already done. He wrote out lists, then would find himself stalled in midphrase, perhaps for minutes, transfixed by the way slanting sunlight would hit his desk, or some memory of the past.

Ellen's face in death...

He could see it in the way they looked at him—Phillip and Charles. They *knew*, damn them. Damn them both.

Now he imagined hearing things on the telephone.

He measured his secretary's silence, used other eyes as mirrors, replaying the sense of his own words on some inner ear. He didn't think he had slipped too badly yet; it was the tiredness that numbed his legs and sapped his concentration. But then, he told himself, you're always the last to know...

"Fly my kite, Daddy."

John Carey started.

It was Peter. "Come on, Daddy—it's windy on the beach."

Three days, gone like the most fleeting images in the window of a train. His wife and sons, waving...

"I'm busy, Peter." Responding, Charles looked up from a manuscript. Allie was in Boston; Phillip had walked to the store for gin. He drank too much...

"Please, Daddy."

John Carey stood, looking at Charles. "I have time now."

Peter glanced at his father.

"I have time," his grandfather repeated. "You don't have to wait."

Charles rose. "I suppose I need a break."

"Do your work," John Carey rasped. "There's precious little of that as it is."

Charles froze. Peter stepped between them; John Carey felt him tug his hand. In a low voice Charles said, "Don't be a fool..."

"Before you call anyone foolish, Charles, look at the difference between what *I* gave you and what little you've done."

His son's lips tightened. In a low, flat voice he told Peter, "Go with your grandfather."

John Carey saw his grandson's mouth tremble. Taking Peter's hand he said, "Don't worry, Peter, we'll get that kite up fine," and led him toward the doorway. He paused there, looking back at his son. Their eyes met above Peter's head. John Carey's mouth opened, and then Charles turned away.

John Carey left with Peter.

It was late afternoon; pale sun grazed the rocks and water through wisps of cirrus cloud. He hadn't remembered that Maine was so cold. But of course it was August already, and soon it would be fall, and the leaves would tumble, burnt-orange and brilliant, crunching beneath his feet.

"Where's the kite, Peter?"

With swollen fingers, he unknotted Peter's red kite from the porch rail and then stepped down along the beach, suddenly tired.

"We can just talk, Grandpa..."

The wind in his face and lungs was harsher than he'd thought. Defiantly, he said, "We'll fly this kite higher than your father ever did," and broke into a run.

"Grandpa!"

He turned, saw Peter scrambling after him, arms pumping and hair blowing in the wind. "Come on," he shouted. "Catch up with me, Peter." His chest and legs felt numb. Over his shoulder, the kite caught a gust of wind, taut string running through his fingertips as it swept straight up in a sudden draft and sailed into the air . . .

"Stop, Grandpa . . ."

John Carey ran harder, feeling a fierce, surging joy, hearing the small boy's footsteps behind him, straining to catch up. He would let him, he knew — this time he would stop, and look into his face. He turned, grinning, to call back . . .

"Charles!"

Peter saw his grandfather straighten spastically, head snapping. For a long moment he stood bolt upright, grin frozen on his face, eyes wide with terrible surprise. Then he collapsed like a heap of rags.

Peter stopped in his tracks. John Carey shuddered once, and was still. His fingers loosened. The ball of string escaped his outflung hand and skittered along the beach, unraveling as the red kite swept crazily upwards, became small and alone, disappeared . . .

The rest was nightmare fragments. Running to get his father. The ambulance coming in a wail of sirens. Two men getting out, placing his grandfather on a stretcher, one arm falling over the side as they put him in the back of the ambulance. Uncle Phillip started to climb in behind it. His father grabbed his wrist, saying in a tight voice, "Stay with Peter. This is mine to do." Then he got into the ambulance next to John Carey. Two doors slammed behind them. They disappeared with the ambulance . . .

Phillip stared after them, hands in his pockets, shivering in the wind. Then he walked toward Peter.

It felt strange; Peter had never been left alone with Phillip. They sat together on the porch as dusk began falling. Peter cried. Phillip could not speak. He looked at Peter as if he were some frightening stranger.

It was dark when Charles returned. He was pale. "He's completely paralyzed," he said to Phillip. Then he walked into the library alone, and shut the door.

* * *

That fall, Peter Carey entered Collegiate School.

His world expanded. Each day John Carey's chauffeur drove him across Central Park, passing Bethesda Fountain on the way to the Gothic church where school was. He wore a blue blazer and tie, had classmates and teachers and games to play. He made a best friend, sometimes went home with him. Learning to count and read, he traced the box scores in the *Times* with his finger, tracking Mickey Mantle's hits. On the weekend, Charles took him to Bethesda Fountain or the zoo. Caught in this quicker rhythm, sometimes he forgot that his grandfather was a still, ruined shell, gutted by Peter and a kite.

He begged until Charles took him to see John Peter Carey, once. They went to his apartment. Charles grasped his hand. John Carey sat in darkness, a male nurse hovering behind him. His neck looked shriveled in his white, starched collar. He could not speak or move or smile.

"Does he understand, Daddy?"

"No one knows."

Peter touched his face. His skin felt cold.

"I love you, Grandpa."

Outside, his father said softly, "It was good that you could tell him that, before he dies . . ."

"He hangs between death and vegetation," Peter heard Phillip snap months later, "draining the firm with each breath."

Phillip sat in the library with Charles, drinking cocktails. Coming to say goodnight, Peter stopped at the tone of their voices; from the hallway, he saw his father's eyes narrow. "You're getting poetic, Phil—it must be nerves."

"I can't make any *decisions*, dammit. Banks, agents— everyone he's dealt with—they're all waiting for a miracle."

"No," Charles said quietly. "They're waiting for the will. As you are."

"Damn you for accusing *me*." Phillip's face twisted as though he had been stabbed. "All my life you've cut me down in front of him . . ."

"Then maybe *I* should have a stroke." Abruptly, Charles spotted Peter in the doorway; in a soft voice he told him, "Sometimes even brothers need their privacy, all right?"

Recalling the naked woman, Peter looked away. "I'm sorry, Daddy."

"It's just a good thing to remember." When Peter looked up, the coolness had left his father's face. "Anyhow, it's bedtime at the zoo. Say goodnight to your Uncle Phillip, okay?"

Phillip gave Peter the same look of frightened unrecognition he had given on the day of his grandfather's ruin. "Goodnight, Prince Charming," he managed. But his arms around Peter were limp.

Peter kissed his father and rushed upstairs to his room, sensing the two angry brothers turn to face each other...

"They're waiting for the will," Charles repeated softly. "As you are..."

Englehardt sat in his bedroom with the tape, staring at the manila envelope, stolen from a bank vault, which a courier had just delivered.

Once more, he, Phillip Carey's secret friend, held his breath.

"Damn you for accusing *me*." Phillip's voice crackled in the small, spartan room. "All my life you've cut me down in front of him..."

Prisoner to their tension, Englehardt could not yet bring himself to touch the envelope: with Phillip Carey, the firm might give him the power he so craved.

Only an old man's will, unopened and immutable, could turn their hopes to ashes.

"Then maybe," Charles snapped at his brother, "*I* should have a stroke."

With fumbling hands, Englehardt reached to open the envelope...

From the tape, ghostlike, Charles Carey's voice reproached him, "Sometimes even brothers need their privacy."

Englehardt paused.

Slowly, he began to read John Carey's will.

Staring through his window, Englehardt felt the will become his future.

Like dead leaves to be raked, its pages lay behind him, strewn on the bed.

He had known its contents for an hour, and still he could not move.

Georgetown was dark; one by one, the scattered lights of neighbors vanished. But his thoughts were not of Washington, or anyone who lived there.

As if moved by another self, who knew these thoughts must now be shared, Englehardt turned at last, and walked slowly to the telephone.

His hand trembled as he reached for it; his finger dialed by rote, and yet the ringing shocked him.

It rang once, twice. With each unnerving repetition, Englehardt half-hoped for still another ring. . . .

And then, on the ninth ring, the voice he wished for, so familiar yet so strange to him, asked, "Hello?" and he no longer felt alone.

Englehardt closed his eyes. "This is John Joseph Englehardt," he began softly. "Perhaps you will remember me."

That weekend, Charles finally took Peter rowing on the lake.

It was April, and green; they faced each other, their scull skimming smooth, bright water. Peter stripped off his sweater. Charles shed his herringbone sports jacket and laid down the paddle, letting them drift through shade and sunshine, the ripple of rowboats passing . . .

"What are you thinking about, Daddy?"

Charles tilted his head. "You see into people, don't you, Peter?" He hesitated. "Actually, I need you to help me decide something."

"About Grandpa?"

"In a way—about all of us, really. You know I stopped working with your grandfather after you were born—I wanted to be with you." He paused again, folding his jacket. "Your mother . . ."

"She got sick."

Charles nodded. "She seems better to me now. What do you think?"

Peter reflected. His mother had gone out more lately, smiled more, even at him. Once she had even bought a cake from the bakery and eaten it with him in the back yard, on a day when he was lonely. "I think so, yes."

Charles seemed to weigh the meaning of his answer. "The point is that you're in school now, busy with new friends, and don't need me there so much. After all, *you're* not there either. So now I've got to decide what to do. The thing with your grandfather has been hard in more ways than you realize."

"Will he ever be better?"

Charles stared past him. "No. He won't."

Peter thought of how his grandfather, now so still and sad and lonely, had stood with him in the bustle of Fifth Avenue as they stared up at the tower with his name on it, where he had once stoked coal. "Then who owns his building now?"

"We don't know yet."

Peter's head tilted in a mirror image of his father's. "Do you want to?"

Charles took out a cigarette. "It doesn't matter. Not even your grandfather can change what will happen when he dies. Not anymore." He lit the cigarette and took one long puff, continuing in a brisker voice. "The problem is, until that happens our firm is in a terrible mess. Decisions need to be made. The people who work for us need someone they can talk to."

"What about Uncle Phillip?"

His father gave him a long, silent glance. Quietly he said, "I don't want it to just be Phillip. Can you understand that?"

Peter remembered sitting alone with Phillip on that terrible night in Maine, watching the shapeless dark. He looked away. "Yes, Daddy. I understand."

"Then can I go back to work?"

Slowly, Peter nodded.

He looked back toward his father. For a moment, Charles Carey's face was in shadow. The boat glided back into the light.

His father was smiling, his face soft. "There's something you should know, Peter, for the rest of your life. I always wanted a little boy. Even before I knew you I imagined how you'd be—smart and good at games, with laughing eyes and blond hair, like your mother's." His eyes looked into Peter's. "You're the boy I imagined, Peter. Even better."

Peter slid into his father's lap, head resting on his shoulder. They rowed like that, man and boy, through green and shadow and the cries of birds, the failing sunlight of late afternoon spreading gold upon the water.

CHAPTER 6

The weekend before Charles Carey was to return to his father's firm, Phillip invited Charles and his family to Greenwich.

"Phil probably wants to poison your potato salad," Ruth Levy jibed. "I hope you can tell 'Rough on Rats' from paprika."

Charles grinned across the pillow. "It's just Phillip's idea of *rapprochement*. Dare I assume you'd miss me?"

"I already *do*, dammit."

"Well, fear not. We've got tickets to see *Sweet Bird of Youth*, remember? I've a stake in our future."

She frowned, then leapt up, throwing the sheets back and stalking naked to the mirror atop her antique chest of drawers. Distractedly, she began brushing her hair. Only the brass lamp on her night stand lit the room: in semidarkness her back was long, slim and pale, her face grazed by shadows, her eyes in the mirror deep black. Three years, lightly touching the corners of her mouth and brightening her thick black hair with a single strand of silver, had lent a tensile poise to the way she walked and moved, a cool directness to her gaze.

"I love you, Ruthie."

She spun angrily. "Carey, that was the stupidest, the most insensitive, the most *male* remark . . ."

"I didn't mean . . ."

"Christ, I hate it when you do that—that fucking prep-school nonchalance, like there's no one home inside you." Her fists clenched with rage, her shoulders bunching inward. "It's so unbelievably shallow . . ."

He slid out of bed and reached for her. She thrust her hand between them. "Don't."

His arms fell to his sides. In a low voice, he said, "It's just that sometimes I don't know what to say."

"Then say *that*. *That* at least I can accept." She looked directly at him. "As I've accepted the way we are."

"Whatever, Ruthie, you're a bit more to me than tickets . . ."

"I'm a serviceable pit stop . . ."

"Don't cheapen yourself. Do you think I don't know that you hate making love and then waking up alone? Or that we have breakfast conversations where you imagine what I say, because you can't call me?"

"Oh, God, Charles." She turned from him. "Please, not now."

"What makes you think I don't feel these things?" He caught himself, shrugging helplessly, then finished in a near-monotone. "I've felt too guilty to say them."

She bent forward, one hand covering her face. "I'm sorry—I don't mean to make you say them now."

"Perhaps I should."

She waved the words away. "It can't be helped, Charles—I love you, regardless."

They stood facing each other, still and naked in the yellow light. Softly, he asked, "Suppose she gave me custody?"

She reached out, stopped. Tears welled in her eyes. "Let's only talk about real things, all right?"

He clasped her shoulders. "We are, now."

Turning, she shook her head. "It's enough you're finally coming back to work, Carey. Take it easy on yourself."

His smile was fleeting. "You sound like my father did."

"Then take it easy on *me*. Please."

"If you'll tell me why you still pick houses on St. Luke's Place." His voice lowered. "Can't we even talk about this?"

Gently, firmly, she broke away from him to sit on the edge of her bed. For a long time she stared out of the window, black, flat and skyless. When finally she looked up at him, her tone was level. "I just want you to think about it first. At least over the weekend."

He nodded. "Then you should, too. It's not just me, you know . . ."

"I know." She looked away. "Please, just hold me now."

He did that.

Much later, still without speaking, she stretched to turn out the brass lamp.

She reached up for him then, arm curving in a graceful arc. As if in a silent dream their mouths moved toward each other, touched, and then their hands and bodies, gently and without hurry, until at last he entered her and they moved, and then cried out, as one.

Afterwards, she lay curled in his arms, warm and drowsy in the silent dark. She turned her face to his, brushed his cheek with her fingertips. "What does Peter look like?" she asked softly.

Peter grinned in the small backseat of his father's Jaguar, watching the wind ripple his mother's champagne hair.

Once more, Peter fell in love with the convertible, enraptured by the way his father took the curves approaching Greenwich—shifting and accelerating, braking and shifting—and by its closeness to the road. Passing other cars, Peter began imagining that Charles and he were racing-car drivers in pink stucco places he'd seen pictures of, like Monaco and Nice. In his mind Phillip's drive became the finish line, where the blonde American princess with his mother's hair waited in front of the rambling white house to present a gold trophy he would show his friends at school. As they wound along North Street— passing ponds, frame houses and slim pines, white picket fences and low stone walls—Peter could see the checkered flag poised above the granite pillars flanking Phillip's drive. Then his father turned through them, and the flag fell, and a jaunty Phillip Carey trotted down the front steps to greet them.

Peter had learned the solace of fantasy: he could turn it on and off like a switch. Sensing the approach of tension, he took his toy boat from the parked car and, leaving Dewey at the wheel, wandered to the big oval birdbath set in the back garden of Phillip's house.

Noiseless save for scattered birdcalls and the soft rustling of pine boughs, the spacious grounds smelled of new-mown grass. Peter placed the boat in the water, led it in a perfect circle, felt content. Slowly, between trips inside for Coke and sandwiches and to check out the adults—Phillip too cheery

and solicitous, Charles too polite to both wife and brother—
Peter withdrew into an imagined voyage: his grandfather sat
in a deck chair with Dewey in his lap. The sun's warmth
gradually unfroze his face and limbs, and he began talking to
Peter about his building. His father smiled at them from behind
the carved wooden wheel and said that now they could sail to
Monaco . . .

When at bedtime Peter told him his imaginings, Charles
smiled again. "I'm not sure your grandfather's ever been to
Monaco," he said. "And I know Dewey hasn't. They'd like
that."

Peter remembered something. "Dewey's still in the garage—it's too dark down there for elephants, Daddy. Please,
can I go get him?"

"I'll bring him in a little bit, Peter," Charles replied. "Then
you can tell him all your plans."

"Promise?"

Lowering his face to Peter's, Charles kissed his forehead.
"Promise."

Peter closed his eyes and fell asleep.

In the morning, Peter took Dewey and his boat downstairs,
to find his father.

Phillip was up unusually early; the two brothers were in the
sunroom, with coffee and the New York *Times*. Phillip was
reading the book review section: Robert Bloch had reaped praise
for a novel called *Psycho* and Phillip was guessing that it would
make a "fantastic" film. He grinned broadly at Peter. "'Morning, Prince Charming," he called out. "The Yankees won."

Peter put down the boat and scooted with Dewey into Charles's
lap. "You promised, remember?"

His father hugged him. "I forgot to bring Dewey up, didn't
I."

"It's okay." Peter burrowed in his neck. "I went to get
him . . ."

"Listen, Peter." Phillip snatched up the sports page and
began reading, "'Yankees beat Red Sox sixteen to seven on
home runs by Bauer, Skowron and Carey.' *Carey*—someday
that'll be you, Peter."

Peter stared at him. Then he turned to his father. "What are we going to do today, Daddy?"

"I don't know. Maybe your Uncle Phillip has some ideas."

Reluctantly, Peter looked back at his uncle.

"A little bored, Prince Charming?"

Peter shook his head.

"Don't worry, you won't hurt my feelings."

Peter squirmed in Charles's lap. "Maybe a little bit bored."

"I'll tell you what, Charles. Why don't we take our boy to the reservoir and let him sail that yacht in earnest?"

His father squeezed Peter's arm. "What about that? Or do you just want to stay here?"

Peter hesitated. Phillip spread his arms wide and smiled his most ingratiating smile. "Up to you, Peter. Whatever you want."

For a fleeting moment, Peter felt sorry for his uncle's discomfort. "We'll take Mommy, too," he said.

It was cool and gray as their convertible passed through the granite pillars and headed toward the reservoir.

Phillip's mint-green Sprite led them along steep roads winding through landscapes more rural than urban: early American farmhouses with green shingled roofs, birches and evergreens and pink blossoming dogwood, grassy fields split by crooked stone walls. Charles chased after Phillip, hugging the curves. Phillip drove faster. Allie, wearing a silk scarf, patted her hair. Behind her, Peter held Dewey in his lap. From the radio Charles Collingwood read the CBS news: John F. Kennedy had made inroads in Wisconsin; Eisenhower had picked Chester Herter to replace the ailing Dulles. Tires humming, they followed Phillip Carey along roads named with antique quaintness: North Street, Dingletown, Stanwich.

Cognewaugh.

The white wooden sign came so abruptly that Charles, hitting the brake, turned on to Cognewaugh at a forty-five-degree angle and hurled Peter against the side of the car. "Be careful," Allie warned. Charles glanced quickly over his shoulder; Peter was laughing. "Go faster, Daddy. Don't let him beat you!"

Charles grinned, accelerating to catch up with Phillip. Allie reached back to zip Peter's windbreaker. She touched his cheek. "Then at least you won't catch cold."

Peter leaned forward, wind whipping his hair. The road grew steeper, dipped into a shady hollow, rose sharply in front of them. The precipitous grade ahead, curving to the right, snapped in front of him like a photograph. Charles took the curve, sped up the grade between the green trees that dappled it with light and darkness.

At the top of the grade, almost without warning, flashed an abrupt left curve.

Phillip took it, the mint-green car vanishing. Peter's laugh grew wilder. Clutching Dewey by the trunk, he shouted, "Catch him, Daddy!"

Charles stepped on the gas. Two hundred feet, a hundred . . .

"*Charles,*" Allie entreated.

Peter grasped Dewey's trunk. "Faster, Daddy . . ."

Charles braked abruptly, crying, "I've lost control," as the steering wheel spun like a toy in his hand and their car slid toward the cliff. In sickening freeze frames, Peter saw them jump the last rocks, trees and sky appearing in the windshield, his father turning to his mother, their eyes locking for one split second before his father whirled and threw him from the car.

Peter hit dirt, still clutching Dewey, falling, tumbling, air bursting from his lungs, rocks buffeting his skull and ribs. He glimpsed his father's car plummeting next to him down a hundred-foot deadfall of jagged rock, and then lost sight of it as he spun in punishing darkness on a long strip of grass without rocks and rolled until the speed of it threw him on his stomach at the bottom of the cliff, and he saw, within ten feet of him, two red cars smashing into trees, his mother's necks snapping like two rag dolls, and then his vision fused, and a single car burst into flames, and his father screamed in animal torment as fire consumed his body and his face fell forward . . .

"Daddy!"

"Peter!" Phillip Carey stood atop the cliff . . .

"Daddy!"

"It's going to explode." Phillip began scrambling closer down the cliff. He stopped to look at the boy, then at the flames leaping toward him from the Jaguar. He stood there, face contorted; suddenly, impulsively, he rushed forward. "Peter—for God's sake, *move!*"

Peter could not. Hugging Dewey as his father's face disappeared in flames he could only cry, rhythmically, repeatedly, in a mindless chant: "Daddy . . . Daddy . . ."

Leaping, Phillip rolled him from the car . . .

It exploded.

Englehardt gazed into the rising flame.

From the tape he had just received, now cradled in his hands, his own voice whispered, "This is John Joseph Englehardt . . ."

He slid the tape from the machine.

For one final moment, he held his secret in his hand.

Then, carefully, he knelt to drop it in the fireplace.

The tape crackled, writhing as it burned, and then it was ashes, and only the will remained.

With his doctor's permission, Phillip Carey told the speechless ruin of his father that his older son could not visit anymore.

In the silence of the dark apartment, Phillip thought he saw his father crying.

He left quickly.

In the morning, rising to bathe him, the nurse found John Carey cold and pulseless, and gently closed his eyes.

They opened the will directly after the funeral, in the gray, airless conference room of a Wall Street firm, where John Carey had kept it in a vault.

The will left fifty-one percent control to Charles Carey.

Its final clause provided: "Should Charles Carey predecease me, then the aforesaid fifty-one percent interest shall be held in trust by my son Phillip, until the thirtieth birthday of my beloved grandson, John Peter Carey."

Without speaking, Phillip Carey left the room.

Peter Carey, sleeping with Dewey in a bare hospital room, knew nothing of his future.

For sleepless hours, Phillip paced outside. Limp and devastated, he watched and listened to his nephew's breathing, rising and falling in a drugged, unbroken rhythm. He shivered at the thought of Peter's waking to his memories.

But Peter Carey had no memories.

He could remember nothing. Nothing about the birdbath or his boat. Nothing about looking for Dewey, the drive, the plummeting car, his father burning. Nothing past entering the driveway, Phillip stepping down to greet them . . .

In his sleep, remembering only his father's love, Peter Carey cried out.

PART II

Manhattan

JANUARY–MARCH 1982

CHAPTER 1

Noelle Ciano cried out.

Dawn flashed through her lover's apartment; a streak of winter sun lit her thick black hair, falling across his face. Her eyes shut as his torso, thrusting upwards, drew from her a last convulsive shudder, running the length of her body. Her face softened; the shudder, dying, became a slow and gliding movement of her hips. She threw her head back. Her rhythm turned fierce, yet controlled; sweat glistened on the cords of her neck as she strained to draw the nightmare from his body. She felt him grow inside her. When at last he came, soundless, her eyes opened again, and searched his face.

Peter Carey grinned up at her.

An hour before, he had cried out in fear, awakening from his dream.

It was that last moment before daybreak; the night was like thin smoke. Charles Carey stole through his brain in the nightmare of his childhood, relentless and unpitying. They were hiding in the tunnel near the Bethesda Fountain. It was a game; his father smiled at him, and then his mouth opened in a tortured scream and his face turned to ash and bone before Peter could pull him from the tunnel. Peter held the empty sleeve of his father's windbreaker, crying out as the faceless man began stabbing his eyes with garden shears. As Peter went blind, blood spurting from the sockets of his eyes, he heard laughter echo through the tunnel, and screamed aloud...

Noelle had wiped Carey's forehead with a cool cloth; he had foreseen their loving in the blackness of her eyes.

Carey sensed this, his prescience of sex in her glance and gestures, the first time they made love. Over eight months it had grown stronger. Now her body moved in his mind. He saw, even before her key clicked in the dead bolt, Noelle stalking from the elevator, camera slung on her shoulder, hair bouncing as she walked. Inside, she would reach to turn the latch; in Carey's mind her breast arched to his lips. Skin to skin, they were like lovers in a dream . . .

"It was the same dream, wasn't it—about your father."

She still looked down at him; the sun grazed her shoulders now, turning her skin a rich olive. Carey could smell their lovemaking. Nodding, he said, "You'd think I could do better."

She touched his face. "Why can't you tell me what it is?"

"Because then *you* might begin having it." He kissed her forehead and got up.

Noelle waited for a few moments before she put on the terry-cloth robe, knowing where she would find him.

Passing through the apartment, she recalled her initial impressions. The rooms were light and sparsely furnished; noting the elaborate deadbolts and alarm system, she at first had thought him haunted by some past robbery. In the living room— a tan sectional couch, a desk with laser lamp, two silver-framed originals by Kandinsky and Klee—she had noticed the low redwood shelf of books he had edited, stamped with the eagle of Van Dreelen & Carey. None of them was autographed. After Noelle had slept with him, climaxing for the first time in her life, she had re-examined the room for hints about his past. Only later did she understand their absence.

She knew now, although she did not know why, that his nightmare drove him to the window. Her keenest sense was visual, even in memory: it was not the first shock of his screaming she remembered, but his profile, perfect as a photograph, staring down into Central Park.

Peter Carey watched snow clouds darken the distant towers of the East Side, casting thin shadows across the park. In winter, stripped of grass and people, Central Park became a moonscape, the lake an icy mirror, reflecting the frozen branches of naked trees. A few strays—dogs, deviates and early runners—wandered past Bethesda Fountain . . .

He felt her behind him, even before she spoke.

"What was he like, Peter?"

He didn't move. "It's hard for me to remember, really. I guess it's hard to even talk about."

"Don't you think you should talk to someone?"

Carey could not shake this feeling of helplessness, the residue of his nightmare. "You still think I need a psychiatrist."

"The dream's happening more often." She hesitated. "You can't remember anything about the accident, can you?"

He closed his eyes. "Only what Phillip told me."

They sat drinking Italian roast at Peter's kitchen table and riffling the New York *Times*.

The Russians had loosed germ warfare on the Afghans, the Saudis had raised the price of oil, the forty-third postwar government seemed about to fall in Italy. A kidnapping had been solved: inside was a photograph, stark and flawless, of police removing a young girl's body from a car near the East River. Peter winced. "Pretty grim."

Noelle turned from the picture. "I know."

As Peter reached for another section, Noelle stopped to watch him: she valued those unguarded moments when his face, eased of nightmares, turned soft as a child's. Now his blond hair curled uncombed at his neck and his blue eyes seemed guileless. His full mouth turned up a little at its right corner: when she had first photographed him, for an article in the *Times*, she saw that he favored his left profile, which was colder and more angular, concealing this trace of humor. Later, when he would not give reasons, she tried seeing his past in this asymmetry. The right side became Peter as a child, waiting for his father. He had turned the left to Phillip Carey.

Now his head angled to the left, eyes narrowing at something on the page until all softness vanished. The look was distinctive; Noelle knew, without being told, that what he read threatened him. She had seen that same expression—head tilted, eyes cold and piercing—trained on a well-known writer who had confronted him at a cocktail party, over money, until the writer had apologized; Peter had said not a word. Thinking the trick deliberate, Noelle had asked him where he had learned it. He replied that he didn't know; it was a mannerism he had always had, without intending it. "I don't plan everything," he said.

Noelle had smiled in disbelief: more than anyone she'd known, Peter Carey let no surprise invade his life, left no opening for weakness or mischance. Only sleep, spawning images which made him cry out like a child, escaped his grasp. In New Hampshire once, after making love beneath a grove of trees which echoed with the spill of a nearby brook, swollen with spring, Noelle had asked what he would wish for were his life to start again. Softly, he had answered, "To never dream."

"What's so awful?" she asked him now.

He looked up from the pages with a look of strained amusement. "I should probably just read aloud," he jibed, and then pushed the business section across the table. "Rumor has it that a charming little predator called Barth Industries—net worth, thirty billion, number forty-one on the Fortune Five Hundred— wishes to swallow a publishing house."

"Could Barth swallow you?"

"Only if Phillip helped them." Peter frowned at his coffee. "What's peculiar is that Phil insisted we have lunch today— alone. You know how seldom he does that."

Noelle smiled faintly. "Maybe he's hungry."

Peter glanced up, annoyed; Noelle held up one palm. "Does sleeping with you mean I have to share your obsession with your uncle? What good would I be for you, then, when you're not inside me?" Her hand reached out for his. "I just want you free of this constant need to watch him."

Peter seemed to retreat within himself, searching for reasons, and then finally shrugged. "It's built into our situation – the will asks him to preserve for me the thing that he most wants, and this Clayton Barth is noted for exploiting weaknesses." His face hardened. "In five more months *I'll* own Van Dreelen and Carey, and then Barth can come to me."

"And you won't sell?"

Peter shook his head; almost playfully, he answered, "I promised my grandfather I'd hang on to it."

Noelle sensed that she was being told the literal truth, passed off as an absurdity. "But what makes *you* so committed?"

For a moment Peter's eyes were hooded, as if he were reaching to retrieve some distant memory. Falling like a shadow, this look belied the quiet laughter in his words: "Because it's *ours ...*"

Martin watched Peter Carey's apartment.

Soon Carey and the woman would go running.

He fidgeted; for now he must repress the way she made him feel. Carey was the target.

He leaned on the low wall surrounding the park, a half-block up and across the street from the Aristocrat, collar raised against the cold. There were six butts at his feet; as a distraction from the woman, he had counted them. It was his habit to count things.

He had been watching Peter Carey for thirteen days.

Dressed to run, Carey and Noelle rode the elevator ten flights down, passed two guards patrolling the lobby, and took the revolving door out. The doorman, a friendly, half-tough-looking man with thick hands and gestures, smiled. "'Morning, Mr. Carey, Miss Ciano." He jabbed a finger toward the park. "Fit for Eskimos today, nine degrees. Don't know how you stand it, smart people like you."

Carey grinned: when first he had moved in, annoyed at the imperiousness of other tenants, he had made a point of being friendly. Now the weather report was a daily ritual, as was his flippant reply. "It's Ciano's weight problem again—she's getting too fat to work."

"Hell, *I* wouldn't be working if I had the money. Florida, that's the place—my brother-in-law has a condo there." He turned to Noelle. "Was that your picture this morning—the cops pulling that little girl from the trunk?" When Noelle nodded, the doorman's low whistle turned to mist in the cold. "Jeezus—you two watch it out there."

"Always," Carey said. "And you, Art."

They hurried along Central Park West, with its phalanx of taxis and limousines, toward the crosswalk leading from the corner of West 72nd Street to the park itself. The wind stung Carey's face. He moved closer to Noelle. "You didn't tell me about the girl."

"I would have. Last night—that wasn't just for you."

"Was it bad?"

"The way it always is. Her mother began calling me a ghoul. I must have taken fourteen shots by the time she broke down."

"And that was all?"

"The cops took her away. I got that picture, too."

Noelle brushed the black bangs from her eyes. Knowing the gesture, Carey stopped her. "Sorry to have been so obtuse."

Noelle touched his elbow. "I chose this job," she said softly. "You didn't choose your dreams."

They began moving.

On the corner, they met Carey's two elderly neighbors, husband and wife, crossing with the small yipping poodle they walked each morning, and spoke to as if it were their child. Noelle knelt to ruffle the fur at its ears, smiling for the first time that morning. Carey smiled also. He liked the Krantzes, who seemed so devoted and whose stooped frames and bright blue eyes were so much alike that he thought of them as an entity that would die as one, alone in the apartment where they had lived for forty years, with no company save poodles. The woman nodded and smiled back: each day her husband spoke for both of them. "Good morning, Mr. Carey."

"Good morning, Mr. Krantz." Teasingly, because they were so shy, Carey had once suggested that they call him Peter, "at least until I turn thirty." Neither had been able to: Noelle would always smile at the way Mrs. Krantz, who said nothing for herself, called him "Peter" through her dog.

"Say hello to Peter," she said now. The dog yipped at Noelle.

"Hello, Abner," she said.

The four humans smiled at the dog. Then the Krantzes turned back toward the building. Noelle and Carey crossed the street, to run.

Martin did not follow their running; he knew their route, and that it took them twenty-six minutes to return. Peter Carey was the slave of habit; his relation to the woman imposed patterns on her. Her work was the only professional complication: it lent her unpredictability and a sense of danger. She walked looking to the left and right, for the movement which did not quite fit. But there were always trade-offs: that walk, lithe and tensile, made her distinctive anywhere. He liked to watch it.

He stubbed out the cigarette, counting to seven.

Once more he forced himself to inventory Carey's set routine. The doorman was important: sometimes only humans, and not keys, could strip his targets of their privacy. Even Carey's elderly neighbors, so benign in their appearance, might become his weapon. And then, watching Peter Carey, he might also watch the woman...

Already she was part of the drama growing in his mind, a teasing focus of the special way he needed women, so long suppressed. Her parents had no money. Ciano was their fifth daughter. She had won a Pulitzer Prize for a picture taken in Cambodia, of a starving child watching over the body of his sister, curled as in sleep. She had worked her way through Boston University.

Martin wondered what she did with Peter Carey.

He would learn that, if the small man let him. He would learn everything—Carey's passions and ambitions, what frightened him in the stillness of the night—and then use the information to control him. Peter Carey's sanity had no more meaning than his life; both now depended on the small man's wish.

Up to a point.

Martin reached into his pocket, touching the tape cassette and then the revolver.

The small man did not wish him to carry these, the tools of his profession, for fear they might be turned against him. But his mentor needed him more now than in the past, and so the balance of their mutual needs was subtly shifting in his favor. He could be more discerning about the orders he received, hearing best those which gave him pleasure.

Martin took pleasure in having tapes of his own, which the small man did not control.

He might sit near lovers in a restaurant, using his delicate instrument to record their conversation: afterwards, listening in his room, he would enter the lives of those who would have shunned him, alone no more, the ostracism of his youth and childhood redeemed. On quiet nights, imagining what things they said in private, he might imitate their voices...

He had found the profession, and the man, to meet his needs.

Once more he touched the revolver, beguiling time. The gun reminded him of the most intense professional experience of his life, which had grown from a surveillance as obscure as this...

It was the last time he had killed.

He had been in Corfu then, six years prior; the rains had stopped, and it was whitewashed spring. He had watched the foreigner for eight days. On the afternoon of the ninth, riding a rented Vespa, he followed the man along a trail twisting up through the hills behind the white marble palace, where once the Hohenzollerns had lived. Seeing him, the man had panicked and abandoned his motorized bicycle, scrambling up and over a cliff. Martin dismounted and began tracking him. Night was falling on the green rugged hills and whitewashed stucco, on the trim sailboats moored in the natural bays and harbor, so blue and yet so clear: Martin knew that the man would never look on them again.

He had been watching the man, and now, like an animal hunting in the darkness, could sense where he would go.

His heart pounded as he climbed the hill.

He made no sound. Hearing none, he knew the man's time was running quickly. He paused, letting his eyes adjust to nightfall with its thin crescent moon, and then began stalking him through the stone and underbrush, softly as a cat.

He found the man two hours later, cowering in a tiny cave, and shot him through the head. He left him there. The man was Turkish; no one in the town would bother with him.

Finding the motorcycle, he drove slowly down the trail to a dark taverna where a woman sang and the *syrtaki* dancers still broke crockery, defying the colonels who sent decrees from Athens. Martin had ordered souvlaki and a bottle of retsina: now the memory of murder was the feel of a revolver in his palm, the taste of resin, the animal sense of tracking in the dark.

He had not known why he killed the Turk, and did not care.

He did not know now why he was tracking Peter Carey. He had not asked, and would not be told. Carey's amnesia was his only clue, and only from the small man's eyes did Martin sense this was important. This obscurity was better. He would learn it gradually, this play of his own construction, from the orders he received . . .

Looking at his watch, Martin began to count the minutes until the woman would return.

Noelle and Carey jogged down a macadam path which passed from 72nd Street through a bower covered with dead vines and then wound between gaslights and low green benches, over a crosswalk and along the traverse jammed with crosstown traffic running past Bethesda Fountain and the lake. Reaching the steps to the fountain, they turned toward the Band Shell: though the tunnel's image drew him like a flame, not since the nightmare started had Carey stood inside it, refusing even as a child to take his uncle to the lake or fountain. Those places were the province of his father, and his dreams.

The plaza they crossed was empty save for a few bare trees rising from circles of brown grass. Ahead, Noelle ran lightly, easily; Carey trailed a moment longer, content to feel her long, coltish strides become another portrait in his memory.

To Carey, she always looked full of energy, even when still: he had long since pried from her that—before she grew discernible breasts and hips—the boys in her Providence neighborhood had called her "Cricket," after a day spent jumping rooftops and daring them to follow. She had broken both arms and legs as a girl; as a woman, she had covered a revolt and two famines in Southeast Asia and the Horn of Africa, once taking a bullet through her shoulder. The scar, white and pinched, was still there: now Carey saw her bunch the shoulder and swing her right arm, to shake off stiffness. He moved next to her. "Time to retire, Ciano—you're brittle as a bullfighter."

"When I'm thirty." Quickly turning, Noelle flashed a smile over one shoulder; it was the first portrait she had left him . . .

Carey had been giving an interview for the *Times Book Review*, answering questions about his father and uncle, and what he recalled of Black Jack Carey. He could already see the lead sentence—"Twenty-two years after the deaths of his legendary grandfather and dashing father, the latter in an automobile accident which he miraculously survived, John Peter Carey II stands poised to take control of the firm which bears their name"—and so was saying less than he remembered: what memories he had were his own, and the interviewer, a sleek Princetonian in tortoise-shell glasses, asked too much.

"As I recall," Carey told him, "my grandfather was a kindly man who liked children's books and never raised his voice."

The man blinked, irritated. Carey didn't give a damn: that morning he had been jarred awake early, in the West End apartment of a woman he hardly knew, by the metallic clatter of garbage trucks. Glad not to have dreamed, Carey took that as his cue to leave; the woman—a young commercial artist new to the joys of Manhattan—had wanted to make love again. Carey had obliged; now he felt tired, with an odd tinge of melancholy.

"Mr. Carey," the man was saying, "I sense these questions annoy you."

Carey shrugged. "You're asking me to remember what my memory has chosen to forget."

"And you have no idea of how you survived the accident."

"None." Carey hesitated. "My uncle rescued me—perhaps you should ask him."

"Yes, your uncle. Will that be difficult, taking over when he's run the firm so long?"

"We've both had twenty years to get used to it. My grandfather left it to me."

The man gave him a sidelong glance. "Still, it's an interesting arrangement. I wonder why he set it up that way."

"Because we talked about books." Carey smiled faintly. "When I was five."

Giving up, the man shepherded Carey to the conference room to wait for the photographer, who was a half hour late. They were trading lame chitchat when a dark young woman burst through the door and shook Carey's hand before he even got her name. All energy and movement, she looked around the book-lined conference room. "This is boring," she told Carey. "Let's try the sidewalk."

"Why?"

She waved at the shelves. "You're too young to sit here pretending you've read all this, much less understood it. Come on."

They were on the elevator before he'd really taken her in. Her hair and eyes were black and she was quite slim, with sharp, specific gestures; each word and movement seemed to have a Mediterranean intensity. "Are you Greek?" he asked.

"Italian." She marched him to the sidewalk.

"What's your name?"

"Ciano. And you're Peter Carey, right?"

"As best I recall."

She looked past him at the ornate entrance to Van Dreelen & Carey. "Let me check the shadow." She handed him the camera and stood in the doorway. "How's my face?"

"Terrific."

She gave him a quick, level glance. "I mean the shadow."

"Perfect," he assured her. "You look just like Lena Horne."

Frowning, she took the camera, backed far enough toward the street to capture "Van Dreelen & Carey" in gold script above Carey's head, and began shooting. Cars rushed behind her, pedestrians in front. A small blonde girl and her mother froze next to Carey at the sound of the camera; the mother began apologizing. Ciano grinned. "Don't worry," she told the woman. "I like people in my pictures."

The girl stared at her. "Is this your job?"

"Uh-huh." Ciano knelt, snapped a photo of the girl, and said, "I'll send this to you, okay?" She looked up at her mother. "What's your address?" The woman gave her an address in New Jersey; Ciano scrawled it down and sent them smiling on their way. Then she shook back her hair, said, "Next," and popped three more shots of Carey.

"Do you always work this fast?"

She took four more pictures, moving to her left. "When I know what I'm after."

"How long have you been doing this?"

"Since college." She snapped another picture. "Like you."

"How do you know that?"

"I know a lot about you." She took one last picture and began putting her camera back in its case. "It helps my work." Finishing, she gave a quick mock bow. "Well, that's it. Thanks." She looked around, checking the cars and traffic light, and started crossing the street.

All at once Carey had to say something, do something. "Hang on," he called after her. "I'd like to see you again."

She turned, smile snapping over her shoulder, quick as a

photograph. "Then it'll happen," she said carelessly, and disappeared into the crowd.

The next morning, Carey called her...

"When you took my picture," he asked as they ran back along the Mall, "did you expect I'd ask you out?"

Noelle looked across at him. "What made you think of that?"

"Running's dull."

She smiled. "Yes. I thought you'd ask me."

"Why?"

"Because of how you looked when I talked to the little girl. Hey, did I tell you I'm shooting Doug Sutcliffe?"

"The lead singer for Lethal? I thought he was still in the woods somewhere, doing drugs and statutory."

"Developing social consciousness, his publicist claims. Anyhow, he's coming here to put on a concert for Haitians and boat people sometime in March—it's been six years since anyone's even seen his face." She tapped her chest. "That's where I come in."

Carey felt threatened, without knowing the reason. "Why you?" he asked, and then disliked himself.

"Because I like faces." Noelle grinned across at him. "Look, Peter, they didn't retire my uniform when I took your picture. *I* just retired my body."

Carey laughed. They ran in companionable silence, all the way to his apartment.

Carey and the woman disappeared.

Inside, Martin knew, she would peel off her sweatsuit...

He knew this from the way she would reappear, fresh and clean and lithe. But for the next forty minutes, he must wait alone, to see her...

Slowly, he raised his eyes to the tenth-floor window.

For now, he would imagine himself hidden in their apartment, hoping that, if the small man wished, he no longer need imagine her undressing, but watch.

He hoped it would be soon.

He hoped the small man did not know this.

In his reports, he made no special mention of the woman, kept his voice and language neutral. But he knew that the man for whom he watched, watched him, turned on him the eerie sensitivity with which he twisted others to his will. The man still frightened him; he alone knew Martin's weakness...

Martin's orders were to cover Peter Carey.

This afternoon was special, the small man warned: for the first time Carey might feel his life begin to change, and his reactions must be closely watched. But it was morning yet, Martin mentally replied; it would be easy to catch up...

In his mind, Noelle Ciano stepped into the shower.

Carey stripped and ran the water; Noelle followed, to his low whistle of admiration.

"Nothing you haven't seen before." She tossed her hair, arching backwards to rinse it under the nozzle.

"That doesn't mean I've gotten used to it."

She squeezed out shampoo and began scrubbing. "Then why"—she stopped to rub soap from her eyes—"do you never come first."

"Because all the manuals say I shouldn't." He reached for a bar of soap. "Was that a serious question?"

"I guess so. Yes."

"Okay. I've never been able to let go. Is it really that important?"

"It's just not that flattering to fuck the 'Man of Steel.'" She opened her eyes to look at him. "One time, Peter, I'd like to feel as though it really mattered who you were inside."

Like the other fears he could not define, Carey could not explain this fear of needing her. "It *does* matter," he finally answered. "Maybe that's the problem."

"Not for me." She shot him a querying look, and then gave up. Turning, she asked, "Think you can get me in back?"

"With soap, you mean?"

They got out, laughing.

Carey dressed; Noelle dried her hair, put on jeans and a white wool sweater, and packed her overnight bag. "Meet me at the Lion's Head, okay? We can do dinner in the Village."

"Sure." He reached for a sports coat. "You know, it *is* good about Sutcliffe."

"It's not for a couple of months yet—I just hope he shows." Carey walked her to the door, unlocking it. She paused in the doorway. "About six, then?"

"Make it six-thirty." He touched her hair. "If I ever *were* to lose myself, Ciano, it would be with you. I knew that the first time we made love."

She smiled. "You forgot to tell me."

Noelle took the steps at the corner of West 72nd Street down into the subway, fished a token from her purse, and stuck it in the slot. She moved down the ramp amidst jostling commuters, one hand on the strap of her camera, body relaxing to move with the flow, face and mind becoming blank. Her watch and jewelry were in the flight bag; two months earlier a gang kid had ripped the gold chain off her neck. A dark man rushed past, snarling "Fucker" at no one in particular; she looked up at the billboard clock advertising Merit cigarettes above the waiting herd of passengers, learning that it was 9:25 and that, according to the Surgeon General, half the commuters were dying of cancer.

Stopping at the platform, she leaned slightly forward, half listening for the roar of incoming trains. The tunnel was dark and grimy: Noelle, who had once visited a coal mine to photograph the women there, recalled the loss of space and light. An express thundered past, lights flickering like a silent film; when the second train ground screeching to a stop, Noelle moved for its sliding door. Half the door was jammed. She turned sideways, and found a seat between two women who looked neither up nor down. She placed the overnight bag between her feet; without seeming to, she quickly noted the near-cadaver sitting down across from her. He wore a black leather jacket and boots; his rouge, penciled eyebrows and bleached-blond hair gave him the spoiled, sadistic look of a decadent Weimar German in a bad cabaret. The man's head was framed by illiterate graffiti, scrawled in red like the inarticulate warning of some roiling urban underclass. The train rocked; she leaned back, moving with its rhythm, and thought of Peter Carey.

Slowly, over time, she had fallen in love with him.

She had not been surprised when he had called her. What surprised her that first evening, when they had eaten by candlelight at La Chaumière, was the sense that he could slip into her skin, feeling what she felt. His blue eyes seemed to penetrate without threat. Speaking little of himself, he preferred to ask questions and hear her answers. The questions seemed to have no pattern: suddenly she could see her past constructed in his mind from the pieces she had thrown him, as historians project epochs from the bones of animals. He grasped her moods before she did, left when it was good to leave, knew the grace of silence. He touched her. When it was time, they slipped from the restaurant, leaving too much money on the table, and walked to her apartment on West 12th Street, to make love.

She began to undress; he had stopped her, gently grasping both wrists. "Let's not do this," he said, "as if it were just another thing." Kissing her mouth, he unbuttoned her without hurry until, their mouths still touching, her blouse lay on the floor, and she felt the front of his shirt grazing her nipples. A chill excitement brushed her skin. Turning, she flicked off the lamp, lit the candle on her bureau. He was naked when she turned again. Candlelight danced on the sinew of his stomach. Looking into his face, she slid out of her jeans. She had been three weeks in Asia, where children starved, and had had no sexual thoughts: now she wanted to feel his life inside her. He reached both hands toward her. She took them. They lay down on the bed. His skin smelled fresh.

He touched her with his mouth and fingertips, so slowly that she felt no invasion when his hand slipped between her legs, but wanted more, hoping fiercely that Peter Carey could do what the others had not done, drive the tension from her body. Entering, he filled her. She grasped him with her arms and legs, began moving . . .

Afterwards they lay next to each other, fingers touching; Noelle waited, for his questions or his hurt. He had none. Instead they talked of small things until she curled in his arms, and the quiet of his voice, his hand stroking her spine, made her want him again.

She stiffened when he entered her. Peter smiled into her eyes. "This doesn't bear thinking about, Noelle—not that way." He kissed her neck; his hips began moving, coiling and un-coiling, utterly controlled. She felt the weight of him, gently at first, his slow, insistent rhythm growing in intensity until she became part of it, urgent and demanding. Blood rushed to her womb, tightening . . .

When she came, body quivering from deep inside her, she cried out her celebration.

"You'll wake the neighbors," Peter laughed afterwards.

She burrowed next to him. Only later, falling asleep as he held her, did she remember that he had made no sound . . .

That night he woke up screaming.

She bolted upright, clutching him by instinct. "Is someone here?"

His body felt taut and damp. He stared at her in seeming unrecognition; then his shoulders slumped. "Only my father." He broke away from her and walked to the window.

"God," he said, "I hate staring out of strange windows."

"What is it?"

For ten minutes he said nothing. Then he sat on the end of the bed and, without emphasis or inflection, told her that his father, dying on a weekend he could not remember, had reappeared in nightmares he could not understand. They always ended in his screaming. "In prep school Phillip paid to have me room alone," he said. "I told the others I had insomnia."

He would not describe the dream.

Yet as weeks passed, and she trembled beneath his soundless loving, awakening to his screams, Noelle felt that this nightmare was the key to Peter Carey. She knew that, for the first time in his life, he slept only with one woman. But he could not lose himself in passion or say he cared. In her mind, the dream connected this silence to his cries: Peter Carey feared to love her for the hurt that it might cause.

He spoke little of his past. Yet, in that part which remained blank to him, he had been somehow terribly damaged: cool and polished on the surface, Peter awakened from his nightmare a deeply frightened man. Not remembering the crucial two days of his life, he seemed unable to trust the rest of it.

Noelle grew restive: these inhibitions became hers. She knew a life of drugged emotions to be impossible for her, yet pieces of the life they led were the richest she had known. He was sensitive; Noelle guessed that his grasp of nuance, in glance and tone, was the fossil of a childhood to which he gave only clues. One fresh spring day, strolling near the Wollman rink,

Peter surprised her by stopping at a sight of increased rarity: a small, brown-haired boy, tended by his nanny, sailing a boat on a pond. Its string had tangled on a branch, and the boy was frustrated. Suddenly Peter moved toward him; he nodded to the nanny, as if to ask, "Is this okay?" and when she smiled, knelt.

"Here." Peter took the string from the boy's hand; deftly, he worked it free. "Nice boat."

The boy looked at him. "What's your name?"

"Peter."

"Do you know Steven Birnbaum?"

Peter considered this. "I don't think so. What does Steven do?"

"We're friends sometimes, and sometimes we fight." The boy's brow knitted. "But Steven can't come here."

Noelle had never seen Peter with a child before, and yet he was perfect, quiet and attentive, as if he knew this from some memory. Now he offered, "I guess you're lucky, huh?"

The boy thought. "I *am,*" he decided. "I get to sail my boat. Do you think *you* could sail it?"

"I think so." Peter's head tilted. "Is there anyone on it?"

The boy looked puzzled for a moment, and then smiled. "Me, and Steven Birnbaum. And my mom." He thought further. "And maybe Marty—sometimes he stays with her."

Behind them, Noelle suppressed a smile. Peter received this information with fitting gravity. "Okay," he ruled, "we'll let Marty come, too."

Talking quietly, they sailed the boat; Noelle still remembered Peter's profile—perfect as that on a Roman coin, blond hair glinting in the sun—as he knelt next to the boy. "I have to get back to my friend Noelle. Can I tell her your name?"

"Jeffrey."

Peter smiled. "You're a good sailor, Jeffrey." Rising, he touched the boy's shoulder, nodded to the nanny, and walked off. When they turned to wave, the boy was smiling after him.

Peter put his arm around her waist. "A kid's world is funny," he remarked. "To Jeffrey, it was perfectly reasonable that I know Steven Birnbaum."

"That's 'cause you were good with him."

"He wanted to talk." Carey's eyes grew distant. "I wonder where the old man is—split, dead . . ."

"Maybe just not much of one." To break his mood, she added, teasing, "Although *you're* certainly prime material."

"Epic," he said dryly. He looked at her with an affectionate sideways grin. "I don't mind practice, though. You free?"

"If there's a boat in the bathtub."

They had walked back to his apartment, laughing.

More than anything it was this sweetness that kept her with him, for what it was and what it promised. As months passed, despite a job that disrupted the flow of her friendships, Peter became her closest friend. Her passport was always ready: she might disappear for two weeks, on two hours' notice, yet Peter met her smiling at the airport. He would nurse his two martinis when she was hours late for dinner, and still be curious about the assignment that had kept her. They had fun. They drank Cinzano at the Museum Café, watching passers-by from its glassed-in porch; drifting through Zabar's, they would smell the aromas changing with each section, buying Gruyère, salami and chilled white wine to spread on the floor of his apartment and eat by candlelight, or with the *Times*, on Sunday. They gallery-hopped in SoHo after brunch, choosing prints for her apartment. They listened to rock on his stereo, then took picnics to Sutton Square and watched the river. That summer they drove Peter's Jaguar to Long Island Sound, and sailed; they skied Mount Snow in winter. Noelle enjoyed these luxuries; Peter, who took them for granted, scoured Manhattan for neighborhood restaurants and good cheap wines from Hungary or Spain, free from the taint of chic. They composed mental lists of things they "didn't get": Noelle's included Bloomingdale's, so Peter bought her a hat there. They went to concerts of Baroque music, and old Garbo films. He looked at each photo she had, asking how she felt when she had taken it; she read the manuscripts he edited. They walked the city for blocks, went to jazz and after-hours clubs, to see who came there. She taught him to develop pictures: one fall weekend they drove to New Hampshire to photograph leaves and churches, and make love. They moved by subway between their two apartments. Each morning they ran. At night Peter would enter her, tenderly and without haste, until she came, shuddering, and then he cried out in his sleep.

The train screeched to a stop beneath 42nd Street, jolting her from thought.

Noelle stepped off, mind on autopilot, and moved up the ramp and steps to emerge at the corner of Eighth Avenue. Horns blasted. She took the sidewalk toward Times Square, weaving through dull-eyed men and beneath bright billboards touting sadism on film and sex organs that ran on batteries, imagining Peter's day. For Phillip's sake, she hoped that Peter would not lash out at him: whatever Phillip wanted, he had already paid too high a price for not being Charles Carey.

For herself, and for their future, she hoped that Peter would decide to face his memory.

He could not do this by himself. Against his nature, he would have to trust a stranger; only a psychiatrist could restore a sleeping memory or dispel a dream. But the dreams grew more frequent with every month they stayed together, and his defenses were a wall between them. She knew that the memory might be searing; yet only that, she was somehow certain, could give him peace with Phillip, and with himself.

Then he might cease at last to fear the gentleness which made her love him, and she could tell him how she felt. Walking amidst the noise and neon, she smiled, alone within her secret.

Following, Martin lit a cigarette.

Eight.

Peter Carey sat by the telephone, staring at the number Ruth Levy had slipped into his hand.

In his mind, Charles Carey still raced after him . . .

Central Park was green with spring; he was a six-year-old boy, running with a toy yacht in his hand, laughing as his father fell behind. Once more he felt his heart pump with the excitement and security of knowing that Charles Carey would catch up to him, hold him in his arms . . .

And then he ran into the tunnel of his nightmares, where his memory went black.

He stared down at the number.

He could not understand the nightmare; its terror had grasped him first when he was seven, asleep in Phillip's home. But its constant repetition argued that his memory, shrouding the weekend of his parents' death in darkness, had done so out of mercy.

He feared to see his father die.

For all his conscious life he had run from this. But the dream pursued him; angry, he would climb, or sky dive or drive at insane speeds, as though straining to outrun it. His memory stayed buried with his childhood; at night the dream caught up with him.

Defenseless, he blamed Phillip Carey.

The possible reasons made him squirm: that Phillip did not save his brother; that Phillip did not die with him . . .

That Phillip was not Charles Carey.

His sense of this unfairness made his response to Phillip erratic and irrational, alternating currents of dislike and self-contempt, of rudeness trailing into mumbles of apology—a distrust for which he found no reason, and yet could not prevent.

Sometimes Carey suspected that Phillip had not rescued him, but exploited his amnesia to tell lies . . .

Carey shook his head.

He despised his own suspicions; he could not imagine parading them for a psychiatrist, dependent and revealed. Ruth had looked at him so strangely.

Paranoid.

He read it in each probing of Noelle's dark eyes: at his distrust of Phillip; at his fear of her affection; at the sense she would abandon him . . .

And at the way he would reach out to her in the middle of the night, and then freeze at the faint tinkling sound of crystal shattering, in a memory he could not place . . .

He closed his eyes, and the tinkling sound receded.

Noelle must never know what he feared most.

Carey had known since their first trip together. They had driven through Vermont; returning, on the afternoon when they had made love in the grass, his contentment felt like music. He had dropped her in the Village, and driven home; he was sitting on the sofa with a brandy, savoring his thoughts, when the phone rang.

At that instant, Carey knew that Noelle Ciano had been killed.

The call was a wrong number; from that moment, the fear had never left him.

That night his dream had come once more.

Carey could not explain this fear for her, any more than he could explain the dream. He was not sure he wished to try. He had not let his nights control his days; on the sense that his life since six had been an accident, he imposed a rigid order. He tried to see the child Peter as someone else, whose pain could not be his; often, he succeeded. Over time, he had adjusted to his scars, as other people adjust to theirs.

He thought of Noelle Ciano, and knew that this was wrong.

His bed was hollow with the imprint of her body; the borrowed shirt still lay beside it.

Carey liked the smell of her hair when they awakened in the morning; the lean, smooth feel of her skin, the tenderness obscured by her quick, impatient movements, until he saw it in her eyes; the way each room in his apartment seemed stamped with the slant of her head, or the skillfulness of her hands. He admired her sheer nerve: Noelle had learned to walk among people maddened by death or famine, knowing she might be killed, without apology for the work she'd come to do. The work made her curious. She could prowl the city for hours, charming strangers, then sit cross-legged in Carey's living room, utterly still, and talk of the faces they had seen. She lacked pretense or any patience with it. "Liars are bores," she announced to Carey, after stalking from a cocktail party where a tiresome ad man was denouncing modern art without much knowledge. "We're both an hour closer to being dead, and for what?" Yet at other times he was sure she knew exactly how it was to be an old man, or a small child, or even Phillip Carey . . .

Noelle.

Paranoid.

Slowly, Peter Carey reached for the telephone.

CHAPTER 2

William Levy started at the jangle of his telephone, then answered: "Dr. Levy speaking."

"Hello," the flat voice said. "This is Peter Carey."

Levy stiffened. "Yes?"

"I'm Charles Carey's son."

"Yes, I know." Levy could not decide what to call this stranger, his dead friend's son; something in the voice disturbed him. "It's pleasant to hear from you," he finally added. "We haven't met since you were a child."

"I'm afraid this is professional." Now the flatness carried a faint sardonic undertone. "I have nightmares."

The voice was Charles Carey's.

"Might I ask," Levy ventured quietly, "how you came to choose me?"

"You were my father's friend." Peter Carey paused. "The nightmares concern my father."

"What kinds of nightmares?"

"Repeated, of my father's dying." The voice softened. "I can't make sense of it. You see, I remember nothing of that weekend."

"And you wish to?"

The belated answer was softer yet. "I think I'd better."

Levy stared at the empty chair where Charles Carey once had sat. At length, he said, "I can see you tomorrow—at nine if that's all right. After that we can discuss what's best. Having known your father complicates it, from the analyst's point of view."

"At least you'll remember what he looked like. In the dream . . ."

"We'll see what to do."

"Thanks." Peter's tone was once again crisp. "See you at nine," he finished, and hung up.

Levy cradled the telephone in his hand.

As Peter Carey entered the Grill Room to meet his uncle, his mind felt clear again.

Talking to his father's friend, Carey had heard the discomfort others took for arrogance; afterwards, he had wished to be alone.

He had called Phillip to explain that he would meet him at the restaurant, and then switched on his answering machine. He lay on the couch for over an hour, with Bach playing in the background, picturing a pool of bright water he had found once with Noelle, in New Hampshire. A fall leaf, crisp and scarlet, swirled in its ripples. It reminded him of his grandfather . . .

By the time he had put on a pin-striped suit and begun his forty-minute walk to the restaurant, he felt composed.

Except that all this mental preparation was for one lunch with his uncle, who dueled with Bloody Marys and *bons mots* . . .

Phillip Carey waved from a table on the main floor. "Over here, Peter."

Carey moved reluctantly forward. The Grill Room was the glamour spot for literary lunches, with twenty-foot windows, redwood walls lacquered to a fine sheen and lined with potted birches, a four-sided bar on the main floor with slim pieces of polished teak suspended overhead like the components of some third-world xylophone and, best of all, tables sufficiently separate to permit private conversations that could still be witnessed by all the other publishing types having private conversations.

Phillip grinned up at him. "Splendid, isn't it—the only restaurant in Manhattan that dares to waste space."

"Ostentation with taste." Carey slid into his chair. "If our authors saw how much advertising money was pissed away on sixty-dollar lunches, they'd tear down Van Dreelen and Carey and drag us howling to the guillotine."

"Let 'em eat cake," Phillip muttered between still smiling teeth, waving to the usual tables of agents and editors in the vanguard of publishing's brave new world, in which bad writers got rich as their betters met death in chain bookstores. Carey felt uneasy at the stares. In the chatty mini-world of publishing everyone knew everyone else or talked about them, anyhow: Black Jack Carey was legend, and the legacy of strife between his second son and his grandson was freely gossiped about by editors who changed houses like gypsies but kept the same bars. Carey, who was bored by gossip and disliked being known, half suspected that Phillip picked the Grill Room as a place sufficiently public to broach bad news.

"After all," Phillip continued sotto voce, still waving, "how can capitalism be so bad, when all these idiots can spend all this money?"

Carey's smile was thin. "That depends on who's asking the question."

Phillip gave him a quick, sharp look. "You're a bit of a Puritan, Peter. I'm constantly mystified by your appeal to someone as passionate as Noelle."

"As am I." Carey cocked his head. "So what's up, Phil?"

"Drinks, before all." Phillip's determined cheer dropped a notch. As always, he was impeccable, silvering hair trimmed perfectly to cover the tops of his ears. But years of affected languor, concealing what Carey sensed was inner turmoil, left him more spent-looking than mere dissipation would account for. His eyes were sunken, his face too thin, like that of an aging actor whose time was quickly passing. Imagining his uncle's life alone, with neither wife nor child, Carey felt a guilty flash of sympathy.

"Bloody Mary?" Phillip was asking.

"Gin martini, thanks."

Carey watched his uncle order drinks: his smile at the waiter was almost too ingratiating, as if his place in life were rented and not owned. Phillip's cologne wafted across the table like a memory of childhood.

"Cheers," Phillip was saying.

They drank. As always, his uncle watched him, while pretending not to. Imagining himself as Phillip, Carey wondered what he saw: perhaps he himself felt nervous now, Carey thought, because Phillip had been nervous with the child Peter.

"What I wanted to ask aloud," Phillip began, "is where we go from here."

"Us, or the firm?"

"Both, really." Phillip brandished his Bloody Mary. "Drink up, Peter, while I state two basic propositions. First, to buy new books we have to borrow front money from banks at increasingly outrageous interest rates, and then wait for sales a year or two down the road to generate the cash to pay them back. Second, hardbacks are becoming too expensive to publish—damn few people are willing to pay fifteen dollars for a book. It's a vicious combination." Phillip took another sip. "Your father would be facing the same squeeze if he were sitting where the old man wanted him—we've got no paperback line, and no one wants to lend us money. We're like a boutique in the garment district, ludicrous and out of place . . ."

"In other words," Carey cut in sharply, "you've found a buyer."

Surprise softened Phillip's features. "He—they—found me, actually."

Carey felt a rush of anger. "I see."

"I'm not sure you do. Look around you. *Deals* are getting made here: these are the rapt faces of happy men and women, discussing *money*. And whose money? *Corporate* money—money to buy paperback houses and best-selling books."

"You sound like *The Music Man*."

Phillip held up a hand. "Stop, right now, and count the other publishing houses still owned by families. It won't take long."

"Two."

"And those two are underpaying unknown writers for unsalable books and living on a threadbare pretense of literary taste. Soon we'll be like that: a cell of desiccated monks genuflecting before a dusty photograph of Black Jack Carey and making pilgrimages to our abandoned bindery."

"I get the point. And our putative saviors?"

"Are committed to quality publishing in a realistic framework."

"'I give you the man who . . .' Do I have to guess his/their name?"

"Barth Industries." Phillip checked his pearl cufflinks. "Clayton Barth, Jr., to be specific."

Carey smiled without humor. "Of course it is."

"Really?" Phillip looked unsettled. "Why do you say that?"

"Because it's so utterly logical: Barth Industries made its money in computers, and Clayton Barth has no known connection to publishing. Why this sudden interest in our particular boutique?"

Phillip began snapping his lighter at an English Oval, muttering, "Damned nuisance." Carey took the lighter, tapped it twice on the table and held out a flame. Leaning forward with his cigarette, Phillip shot him a quick, discomfited glance. "I was never very mechanical," he said. "About Barth: I really don't know."

"Then what in hell do we want with him?"

"It's as I've said: financing. Plus, Clayton Barth will guarantee that you take over as editor-in-chief on your thirtieth birthday." Phillip pocketed the lighter. His tone grew pointed. "As I am sure you planned . . ."

"So you've met with him already."

"Yes."

"You've moved quite fast. Frankly, I find it odd that he didn't approach *me*—in June, I'll own fifty-one percent."

Phillip looked past him. "Perhaps your reputation precedes you."

"What reputation is that, precisely?"

"Another of my idle comments." Phillip's face was distant, abstracted. He stubbed the cigarette. "I don't know why they came to me."

Carey waited, quite still; it was his trick to go silent at a conversation's crucial moment, until the other blurted more than he'd intended. Phillip, who knew this, said nothing. Finally, Carey asked, "How long has this been going on?"

"Just within the past two weeks. I was awaiting the right time to raise it."

"No doubt. Tell me, Phil, just what's in this for you?"

Phillip faced him again. "Money," he said coolly. "Money, and a little bit of dignity. You don't intend to leave me much of that, do you, Peter."

Carey flushed. "How much money?"

"Eight million dollars for my forty-nine percent." His eyes locked with Carey's. "*If* Barth acquires at least fifty-one percent control."

Carey's smile was sardonic. "That makes me rather important, doesn't it. To you, and to Barth."

"More so to me, as usual. Barth can always buy another publishing house."

"Then why doesn't he?"

The brisk, balding waiter served two more drinks and Carey's steak tartare, followed by Phillip's shrimp Louis. Phillip tasted his drink. "I don't know," he mused. "He's so steeped in the myth of Black Jack Carey that he knows more about the old man's career than *I* do, and takes considerably more relish in it." He looked back at Carey. "It's always strange to meet a person who reminds you of someone dead . . ."

His grandfather's grip as they looked up at the building was rough as his near-whisper, "It's ours . . ."

"Barth reminds you of Grandfather?"

"Somewhat." Phillip's gaze across the table was cool and clear. "But not as much as everything about you, right down to your Jaguar and martinis, reminds me of my brother. Someday you'll have to tell me, Peter, how hard you've worked at that."

"How could I," Carey answered in a low voice, "when I've no memory to do it with."

"I *rescued* you." There was sudden pain in Phillip's voice. He caught himself glancing around as if worried that they had been overheard. When he spoke again, his voice was low and even. "I can understand the loss you felt at six, Peter. But to be so paranoid now is crippling."

His father's laugh was bright as sunlight dancing on the ocean . . .

Once more Carey was driven by a debt cited with evident emotion that he himself did not remember and could not be sure he owed. "I must be confused," he parried. "I thought I'd heard you say you'd been meeting with Barth behind my back."

Phillip straightened, himself again. "Only until we could talk rationally. Ever since that curious business of the picture, I've known that the relationship I'd hoped we'd have can never be—that you're obsessed with being Charles Carey's representative on earth. But despite our sad divergence, I remain legally and morally obligated to act in your best interests as trustee of your fifty-one percent. So I met with Barth, and now

I'm setting forth your options in a reasonably calm environment." Phillip rested his chin on folded hands. "As is my obligation as long as you're of sound mind."

"What's that supposed to mean?"

Phillip looked away. "Perhaps that's a bit unfair, Peter. I suppose I'm somewhat wounded by your inexhaustible mistrust."

Phillip had read him stories . . .

Carey tasted his lunch. Finally, he said, "Tell me about Barth, Phil."

"He's forceful, and seemingly quite interested in Van Dreelen and Carey for its own sake: he knows our bottom line, but also our history. I find it quite encouraging that he seems driven not just to acquire a publishing house, but *our* firm. And he seems genuinely intrigued by the notion of having the old man's namesake running it for him."

Carey frowned. "What are my options?"

"As I see them?"

"Yes."

"To get bogged down in a twilight struggle where sentiment is no collateral for bank loans, or to do what your grandfather and father would have done: sell, yet keep your title with enough financing to make it mean something."

"As you retire with eight million dollars."

"I'm sixty years old." Phillip's voice grew very quiet, his stare direct. "For me, there *is* no other option—you've made that clear, in every way but speech. So now I'm asking that you consider this for me—and for yourself."

Their eyes met again; in that moment, Carey felt himself as Phillip's burden. Finally, he said, "Then I can do that much."

"Is this merely *politesse?*"

"No. Noelle and I . . ." Carey's gaze dropped. "It might be easier if I backed off a little, got some distance. I suppose I should consider what you say." He smiled. "If I do end up with any interest, perhaps we can use my reputation—as you so tactfully put it—to jack up the price."

Phillip's returning smile was his least strained of the lunch. He raised his drink. "Some days, Peter, I'm not so sorry that I saved you."

"Then you can order me dessert." Carey excused himself, still smiling.

Watching Peter Carey from the bar, Martin guessed that his sudden leaving owed little to the urgings of his kidneys.

He had ordered a Bloody Mary when they did; with Phillip Carey, he had tasted it. Like the playwright Martin felt himself to be, he enjoyed borrowing the sensations of others.

Now the drink felt queasy in his stomach: the two men were frightened of each other.

Phillip Carey's eyes were those of a cornered animal; his nephew's stillness was so unnatural that Martin's muscles felt its strain. As their bodies leaned forward across the table, their dialogue took on the sinewy tension of some martial art which pitted nerve against reflex. When Carey rose abruptly, Martin sensed that he should follow.

Lingering for discretion's sake, Martin surveyed Phillip Carey in his moment of aloneness. His eyes on Peter's back held fear as naked as the Turk's, in that instant before dying . . .

Martin waited until Phillip pasted on a smile for the nearest table, and then slipped downstairs.

Peter Carey was leaning in a telephone booth.

Martin decided to wait outside.

Twenty minutes later, he saw Peter and his uncle trade brisk farewells through the window of a cab, before Phillip drove away. His nephew stared after him, unmoving. Then, as if on impulse, Peter Carey began walking.

Martin followed: his orders were to observe how Peter received his uncle's news. He did not mind this. For six years Martin had kept himself in peak condition, awaiting the chance to track again. . . .

Carey turned down Park Avenue. Ahead, the silver mass of the Pan Am Building formed a background to the venerable tower jutting from Grand Central Station, gold-brown with winter sun and shadow. Martin kept pace: the block letters "Pan Am" loomed higher and closer, and still Carey walked with obsessive haste past pedestrians hunched against the wind and cold, never looking back until he rushed through the haze and echo of the station itself and out the other side, entering the marble lobby of the Pan Am Building. Martin watched him through the windows of the main floor, breathing easily.

Carey disappeared into an elevator.

For an instant Martin felt his disappointment: unless one killed, tracking had its limits. But there were other methods. He went inside and watched the light above Carey's elevator move from number to number, until it stopped.

Fourteen.

"What's so urgent?" Benevides asked.

Carey took a chair in front of his desk. "Phil wants to sell out."

"So you were right after all." Benevides grinned at the thought of human greed. "He's a fool to have waited this long."

"I'm not sure why he did. Do you still have those papers we drafted?"

"Locked in a safe, per your instructions. All we do if he tries selling your stock is fill in the blanks and dash down to Superior Court for an injunction."

Carey nodded. Dark and highly charged, Benevides exuded the distrustful brilliance that had drawn Peter Carey to him when, at twenty-six, Peter left the Wall Street firm which represented the Careys to find a lawyer who would maintain his confidences inviolate. Wary of Phillip, Carey decided his first need was a trial lawyer; in Benevides, a quick-tongued ex-prosecutor whose midtown firm could provide the other services Carey required, he found one so inherently suspicious that he could speak his fears without embarrassment. "What are my chances?"

"Tell me your story. It depends a little on the resources of our buyer."

"It's Clayton Barth."

"*Barth?*" Benevides scowled in disbelief. "What's a man like Barth want with a publisher?"

"That's the second thing I don't get."

Benevides picked up a pencil and legal pad and began scribbling notes. "Maybe it's the building. I'll try and find out if he's into real estate." He looked up. "You know, Clayton Barth makes old Black Jack look like Mother Teresa. He took over a client of ours three years ago—a computer software outfit.

In twenty-four hours he'd given each employee the choice of signing the most preposterous dress code and loyalty oath this side of the McCarthy era or immediate termination. I was spared the sight of all those white shirts and crew cuts when Barth posted guards to keep visitors out of the building." Benevides smiled. "The ruthlessness of the 'truly needy,' I suppose—his father was some sort of menial. So where did you leave it with Phillip?"

"That he won't try selling without my approval."

"Do you believe him?"

Phillip had burnt the pictures . . .

"No."

"Why not, exactly?"

Carey shrugged. "It's a feeling."

Benevides looked at him askance. "One you've had for years, Peter, with nothing to back it up. We've watched Phillip like hawks and he's yet to take one step out of line. *I'm* the one who's stealing your money."

"This is different." Carey paused, trying to phrase the instinct of the child Peter in the linear facts of trial lawyers. "Phil stands to make eight million dollars, and he knows I really don't want him there when I take over. Our interests aren't the same."

"I trust you restrained yourself from saying that."

"He knows it well enough. I stalled by mumbling that I'd think about it."

Benevides considered him. "With all that money, and no firm to worry about . . ."

"I just can't do that, George."

Benevides shrugged. "Then string him along awhile, and see what happens."

His smiling uncle held out the red rubber ball to ask if he would play . . .

"Phil's not that much of a fool. Oh, maybe a week or two— I showed him enough skepticism to seem like myself."

"I can imagine." The grin flashed again. "I'm glad you're not *my* nephew, Peter—you're mean as a snake. To be strung out between you and Barth . . ."

Phillip had saved him.

Carey examined his shoes. "Well, that's Phil's misfortune, isn't it. What weaknesses do we have?"

"Not many. As a trustee, Phillip's bound to act in your interests; as an adult five months from taking over, you're presumed to know what they are. Assuming you're not crazy, it would be tough for Phil to sell the firm out from under you, unless Barth backs you off somehow. Now *if* they could show that you were loony tunes . . ."

Carey looked up sharply. "What do you mean?"

"Simply this: Barth spies on people. It's pop psychology, but maybe it *does* make sense that Clayton Barth would want your firm. Publishing may not be a big moneymaker, but it adds a sort of intellectual and social sheen." Again, Carey saw the quick flash of teeth. "Barth's a little low on sheen."

"I still don't get how *his* toads and snakes relate to mine."

"There's a story, Peter." Benevides leaned forward. "Barth wanted an oil company that its owner needed to sell. Barth found out the man had acrophobia—unreasoning fear of heights—by somehow getting to his psychiatrist. He insisted on conducting negotiations on the forty-fourth floor of the Gulf & Western Building, in an all-glass conference room. It was winter, and wind and rain kept battering the window. Barth refused to take any breaks. After two hours, the other guy was sweating and nauseated. Barth bought his company for a song." Benevides paused for emphasis. "If you *do* have any weaknesses, Peter, Barth will try to use them—in or out of court. So when you finally meet him, you'd best not even blink."

"I'm fine."

"I never said you weren't." Once more Benevides looked at him slantwise. "It might help getting some rest, though. You'd probably be less scared of Phillip."

Carey was nettled. "I never said that, George."

"Didn't you?" Abruptly, Benevides decided to ease the tension. "Then don't let me scare you about Barth, either. After all, you've got youth, money, a good-looking girl friend and, even better, *me* to represent you. Christ, you're on a roll." He stood, grin abruptly wide and cocky, and spread his arms in a parody of Lady Justice. "The *law* is on your side, Peter. All you have to do is keep being yourself."

* * *

A moment after Peter Carey ducked into the Lion's Head, Noelle Ciano knew that they would not be making love: Carey stared at her through the crush of drinkers as if she were not there.

She had been hunched at the end of the bar, drawing warmth from Irish coffee and smiles that did not threaten. Outside it was cold; she had stepped quickly from the subway, looking to the right and left, yet meeting no eyes. Here no one tried to hustle her, or force conversation. She felt her body relax, its easy balance on the barstool, and realized that the city, which assaulted her nerves and heightened her sense of danger, also made her sensual. Her legs had absorbed the metallic clatter of the train, bitter wind had stung her face as she hurried across Sheridan Square, a snowflake, falling in darkness, had melted on her lips. Now the coffee was a centrifuge of warmth in her hand, the bar a cocoon of smoke and beer and argument, the press of known faces and bodies. The conversation swirling around her had begun long ago, its ends and pieces, beery contentions and outrageous Irishisms, all tended by the same crowd of writers and reporters and those who wished to be, or might be again, seeing their lives in one another's faces and in the dust jackets of their own half-forgotten books, still framed and hanging on the wall, the scraps of dreams.

The regulars packed the dark, wooden bar, facing a brick wall fronted by a shelf of liquor bottles: in caps or peacoats or rimless glasses, contrasting with the suits and skirts of patrons returning from midtown, they looked faintly proletarian, or vaguely Irish. Some were Socialists who know no more of revolution than of exercise; others, like Noelle, had seen wars, cowardice and murder. A few men and women had slept together so long ago that they were friends again, each finding dates for the other. Fewer still were strangers. Three weeks earlier, one had come in from the street looking for a woman to kill and stabbed a cub reporter for the *Daily News* as she reached for her second gimlet; two editors and a composer from NYU had interrupted their argument long enough to chase him down. They had pinned him to the sidewalk until the police came; the woman had recovered and now sat buying them drinks as she explained her assailant's insanity plea, something about necrophilia. Listening, Noelle felt glad of Peter, and of living in a neighborhood . . .

She had fallen in love with both of them at about the same time, and by accident. At twenty-two—just out of college and looking for a job—she moved from Boston into a walk-up in the West Sixties with a shower in the living room; within six months the building went co-op and Noelle, still repaying student loans, became a refugee. In the West Seventies this happened twice more; Noelle saw Brooklyn yawning before her when a colleague at the *Times* decided to move in with his boyfriend, abandoning a three-room apartment on West 12th Street. He confessed this one afternoon, over drinks; at nine the next morning Noelle appeared at the rental office with his written notice and a certified check, insisting that they accept her application. Only later did she see the apartment.

It, and the West Village, were pleasant changes. She liked returning to a neighborhood of town houses and crooked cobblestone streets, far from the midtown hassle. The apartment on West 12th Street was clean and bright, with a retractable metal screen on the window nearest the fire escape—instead of iron bars—and a closet she used as a darkroom. She met Peter Carey two weeks after moving in; he was the only man who had slept there. Sometimes she would watch him in the mirror, as he dressed . . .

The coffee warmed her; whiskey coursed through her limbs until she felt each part of her body. She took another sip and knew, with the certainty that grows unexamined in the mind until one knows it all at once, that she was happier than she had ever been. Her photographs were nearer to what she saw and felt; she felt more when Peter touched her. The thought of Peter was like sun on her skin. Her thighs felt warm . . .

Then Peter Carey entered the bar.

He knifed toward her through the crush, graceful and controlled; the daily gauntlet of exercise that burned all fat from his body made him stand out in the crowd of drinkers. She grinned.

His cobalt eyes were opaque as a cat's. "Long day, Ciano," he said, easing in next to her.

She knew the look; Peter seemed absent from his body more than any man she knew. Sometimes it amused her; one night at her apartment, where there was no dishwasher, he had wiped the same glass for minutes. "In June," he had joked when she questioned him, "we can hire Phil to do this . . ."

"Phillip?" she asked now.

"And Clayton Barth." He looked around. "I don't much feel like this tonight."

"A drink, or the Village?"

"Both, I guess."

Her warmth vanished. "There's a place in SoHo." She shrugged. "We can eat there."

They left.

Slipping out, the woman left Clayton Barth to brood in the silent blackness of his office, waiting . . .

The luminous dial of his wristwatch read 7:04.

Twenty-six minutes left.

Restless, Barth turned to the window: the view was now part of the fantasy which had brought him to this moment. His suite of offices towered above Fifth Avenue: thick panes of glass reduced the skyline to dim, silent rectangles rising from nowhere, etched with patchwork squares of yellow where unseen people worked late at unknown jobs. It had no sound or smell or feel; the only motion was in the headlights of distant cars moving like soldier ants above the black rivers of the city; the sole odd colors the pale-green dome of the RCA Building and a script "Coca-Cola" reflected backwards as a streak of red fluorescence on the dark glass of a high-rise. In Barth's mind, the city became a switchboard to which he held the circuits; he could string the yellow squares together in a pattern, or plunge it into darkness.

Turning from the window, he pulled up his pants and smiled; as always, the choice belonged to the woman.

That was part of its symmetry.

She had come to him through the personnel manager of a brokerage house he'd acquired: her broker husband had deserted her and then disappeared, leaving her to support three daughters with no assets save poise and the rudiments of typing. Barth was drawn by her air of refinement and the slender grace of her movements, the haunted, late-thirtyish good looks that suggested a frightened resolve to overcome difficulties for which she had not planned. Her eyes still betrayed the self-doubt of her abandonment . . .

To her audible surprise, he called to offer the job of receptionist for his Manhattan office; she did not know that he had fired the incumbent. He set the salary high enough to spare her the most scarifying hardships, calculating that she would know that it was more than she would find elsewhere but that inexperience and gratitude might keep her from guessing . . .

Someday he would force her to admit that she had known what he would ask.

He waited until she took her house back off the market and returned her daughters to parochial school, and then called her in, alone.

Her eyes grew moist as he explained what she must do.

He knew her pride, he told her softly, and so had invented rules. She need perform only once a week while he was in Manhattan and only during business hours; the choice of time and date was his. No one would witness their acts; he would give no hints in front of others. Answering his call, she would lock the door, then stand before him . . .

Her mouth had trembled as he named the three acts she could choose from.

Any one would please him, he explained; he only asked that she perform them all within each two-month period. Perhaps if she kept a notebook?

Of course, first she must undress.

Right now.

Looking down, he touched the first silver hairs crossing the crown of her head.

Afterwards, she wept at his feet.

It was all right, he soothed her, merely symbolic of the lives of all those helpless strivers clinging with their lips and bodies to the windows of faceless buildings, for the pension plans inside. Her debasement was no less civilized than those of others whose coinage had been devalued by modern life: he would pay her a bonus for each act, scaled in order of his preferences and the ability of her performances. He would not hurt her physically or demand that she scream . . .

Now his smile returned.

There was so much she did not know.

She had dressed in front of him, squaring her shoulders to retrieve some replica of self as he watched her set mental limits to her humiliation. Her co-workers would not guess . . .

Barth took to calling her in when they were gathered at her desk, imagining their smiles at the turning of his lock. Humiliated before the others, she still believed his grasp ended at the elevator.

In less than three months she would understand.

Even now, hair combed and lipstick reapplied, she was dining with the man she never spoke of, believing that Barth knew no more of his existence than he did of the services she performed at Barth's demand. She would smile through the candlelight of their favorite restaurant, waiting for the night when he would set her free.

Barth laughed aloud.

The man's name was David Pryor.

He was so perfect it was comic: a wealthy widower so Catholic—so concerned for her children and respectful of her hurt—that he would not touch her body before marriage. He had confided to friends that he would propose on her birthday.

March thirtieth.

Zipping his fly, Barth pondered how tauntingly close to that date he should learn of her debasement, and how . .

Suddenly, he remembered for whom he waited: unwelcome and unbidden, the image flashed before his eyes.

He would use the telephone, of course.

When he had found his father lying in a pool of blood, the telephone still dangled above his shattered skull, like a revolver dropping from John Carey's hand.

His voice had been the bullet.

The first thing he had seen was blood and bone and brains spattered on the screen door to the kitchen.

He had walked two miles from school on a sweltering Texas afternoon so airless that he could think of nothing but sweat dripping down an ice-cold bottle of Coca-Cola. Since the bookstore had failed, his father kept two Cokes in the refrigerator for them to drink at the kitchen table after school: his father would joke feebly, "See, Clayton, no whiskey for *me*, either," and then—the only friend of his only son—he would ask the story of his day. But this day his father had planned to call Mr. Carey in faraway New York; finally he might have a job to talk about again. Clayton crossed the burnt-out lawn...

His mind absorbed the ghastly still life in slow motion: blood caked on the screen, a bourbon bottle next to his father's black notebook of telephone numbers. On the hanging calendar a freckled boy chased a dog with a baseball in its mouth toward a wall telephone with no mouthpiece. Its black horn dangled one foot above his father's staring eyes. His face now stopped at his forehead: the rest was blown off. A fly droned lazily above.

Clayton stepped inside. The Montgomery Ward catalog lay atop the refrigerator where his father kept it; the sampler still asked God's blessing.

His father's notebook was open to John Carey's name.

He turned.

Staring down into the dead face, he saw with pain and loathing that he looked no more pathetic than he had for the last two years. Greyhound eyes, a smile so eager it was craven...

As they took him away, Clayton began imagining John Carey's face.

Ten people had come to his father's funeral.

Afterwards, he packed his clothes and his father's notebook and drove to Oklahoma to live with an uncle he despised. That night, alone in a strange room, he wrote John Peter Carey.

For three weeks he had gone to the mailbox. The day he found the envelope inside he stared for a long moment at the "Van Dreelen & Carey" printed in gold leaf in the upper left-hand corner above an address on Fifth Avenue, mysterious yet potent. Carefully, he opened it with a penknife: the terse letter inside—denying coverage for his father's suicide—ended, "dictated, but not read, by Mr. Carey," and had no signature.

He stood by the mailbox, quivering with rage at his father's impotence, too filled with shame to tell his uncle.

Two days later he walked to a small, dusty library in the treeless town and found John Carey's name in the index to periodicals. He went to the shelves...

John Carey's eagle visage stared at him from the cover of *Time* magazine.

He had found his real father.

He began reading any article that mentioned him, asked the salesman who visited the local bookstore for details of their meetings, until he knew how John Carey dressed, looked and acted. Clayton's gestures became that of a bigger and older man, his face, so hatefully like his father's, assumed a harder cast. His grades in high school rose dramatically. That he was friendless bothered him no more: John Carey was enough.

At Oklahoma he worked forty hours a week and carried a fulltime load; on nights when he felt too tired to study, he would recall that John Carey rose from nowhere...

He ran out of money his junior year; at the last moment an anonymous donor funded a new scholarship, to be granted to this promising young business major. Somewhat grandly, he entitled his senior thesis, "The Role of Autocracy in Creating Van Dreelen & Carey."

It was 1952.

Clayton Barth graduated Phi Beta Kappa, and promptly discovered computers.

In the process he began discovering his own infinite variety: Barth was forced to reinvent himself as a salesman.

His sole intention had been to raise cash to start a business; to his dismay, the quickest route was to sell computer services. Bending his festering inwardness to his will, he acquired the jokes and banter to oil a keen knowledge of the product, his borrowed patter ringing in his own ears like the banalities of a game-show host. What sustained him was the knowledge that Black Jack Carey had started out in sales. He imagined their first meeting, millionaire to millionaire: Barth would reveal who he was, smiling, and then offer his career as the sign of his forgiveness. John Carey would reach for him, tears in his eyes...

When John Carey died, Barth wept alone, as he had never done for his father.

The next week he began Barth Services.

Its business was to provide computer backup to companies too small to fund their own: Barth organized his employees into teams of crew-cut janissaries who would march into a customer's office and churn records into computer runs that exposed business structures like an X-ray. Suddenly, Barth saw that he was learning the weaknesses of others.

He began preying on his clients.

As he did so, Barth perfected Black Jack Carey's principle of corporate obedience. New employees were forced to observe strict dress and moral codes; adultery was punished by termination.

At thirty, Clayton Barth was still a virgin.

It was part of his sense of policy, he told himself: even the most visceral acts—sex or murder—should be the extension of his purposes. He began recruiting former officers of the CIA to act as his lieutenants. Barth was their commander-in-chief: their presence imbued him with *gravitas*. . . .

Now Barth's suits were pin-stripes, his movements slower and more majestic.

He began imagining himself as President.

This fantasy was the secret pleasure of his nights. Yet he did not envision the tumult of adoring crowds or the silver image of his face on television, but presiding in the White House Situation Room at midnight, surrounded by cold-eyed men whose loyalty he owned, ordering the murder of some foreign ruler . . .

He could not acknowledge his father's suicide.

The explosion of the computer industry only heated Barth's imaginings. His legions appeared throughout the Southwest; by 1965, he was many times a millionaire. The electronic map of the world hanging in his office traced a ruthless trail of acquisitions capped by a cover story in *Business Week* entitled "The Sunbelt Marches North." He designed a thousand-acre headquarters near Dallas as a snare for those who worked there: each movie or game of tennis caught them tighter in his grasp. His key executives lived on the premises in mansions modeled after Williamsburg and secretly equipped with wiretaps; all employees took a yearly lie-detector test modeled on the CIA's. Those who survived received salaries and incentives unmatched in the world: preparing to own John Carey's firm, Barth had built a conglomerate one thousand times its worth. Yet artists and statesmen and men of power and polish—those whose lives had placed them beyond the need for money—still shunned him, as if he were his father. He did not speak at Harvard, or know the President. The East did not call out for him . . .

Phillip Carey governed in his place.

Slowly adding new facets to his own uniqueness, Barth waited, the better to succeed John Carey, and at last to become himself. He listened to taped diction lessons until his accent became divorced from his father's; it now hovered between Boston and New York. He took an office on Fifth Avenue, repressed all memory of his father's weakness, the very mention of his name . . .

He began breaking his own rules.

Curiously, it was a portrait by Picasso which revealed this as a virtue. In the late 1960s he began to appreciate the symbolism of culture: he fancied those who met him discovering layer upon layer of his *persona*, astonished at his complexity, until they granted the acceptance that he craved. Purchasing for his office a rather abstract painting by Picasso, he had wondered whether this left-wing Spaniard, so revered among artists, could paint anything real. Some months later he stumbled on a very early and startlingly literal Picasso portrait of a woman. He saw at once that Picasso had first submitted to the rules of drawing so that he might later manipulate them to a purpose distinctively his own. So it was, he decided, with the morality he forced on his employees: this was another sign of his uniqueness only to the extent that he alone could violate it.

Two days later he paid the honey-haired wife of his chief computer programmer ten thousand dollars to sleep with him. Afterwards, he fired her husband. The new fear of his employees gave him more pleasure than the first woman he had ever had: taking her had served the highest policy.

There were women all around him.

From them he learned the terror of unexpectedness and the pleasure of his own anticipation. He liked teasing himself with whether he might choose one, when that might be and what rules he might impose. Soon after he had slept with the programmer's wife, an interviewer looking for an offbeat question asked whether he had ever imagined himself as some species of animal: suddenly he saw himself an eagle, omniscient and untouchable, watching above a field for mice . . .

So it became with Van Dreelen & Carey. For four long years he teased himself by watching the two remaining Careys, as foolish and unknowing as the mice in his field. He could feel the day approaching when John Carey's firm would need the money which only he could provide, and their manifest failure would at last seal his transcendence.

But when his acquisition people first approached Phillip Carey, in 1976, Phillip expressed no interest in even meeting him.

Enraged, Barth demanded reasons.

Phillip had been polite, his people reported: only forty-nine percent was his, and although there was some trouble with his nephew, that was a family matter, as the firm itself had always been. As trustee, he was flattered by Barth's interest, but Peter would not sell.

Still Barth waited: Phillip Carey, unworthy son and symbol of the East, would come to him.

His acquisition team brought him trinkets: there were other houses, perhaps even the *New Republic*, if he wished to dabble in the arts . . .

Only Barth knew what he wanted, and why.

Sometimes, at night, he stood outside Van Dreelen & Carey.

His spies, gathering bits and pieces of information, etched a portrait of the Careys ruthless in its clarity. Phillip lived too high and hard; haunted by amnesia, Peter clashed with his much older uncle as if born to replace his father: whether the battle was over writers or money or the future of the firm, they could agree on little. Where Phillip Carey affected ease, his nephew was a driven man, ice-cold on the surface, who would suddenly lash out at him in anger.

Barth saw that he might count on Peter Carey.

His uncle was boxed in, castrated by John Carey's will and running short of money: as his power slipped away, Peter Carey would at last push him too far, and then Phillip would help Barth take from Peter what was rightly his.

For six years, Barth had waited.

It became his pleasure to wait for Phillip, driven by his nephew and the cruelty of his father's will, at last to come to him . . .

The alarm buzzed on his desk. He looked at the fluorescent dial of his wristwatch, and read 7:25.

Phillip Carey had come early.

As Noelle and Carey emerged from the subway exit at Spring Street and Sixth Avenue, it was snowing more heavily: silver flakes fell through the rays of streetlights and then swirled at their feet, becoming soot and water on the cobblestones. Carey pushed up his collar. "Mind walking for a while?"

"Maybe a few blocks." She took his arm. "It's cold, you know."

Carey nodded. "Ten minutes."

They began wandering down Spring Street, past the restaurant where they would eat. Carey was not sure why he wished to walk: SoHo depressed him at night—darkness worked against it. Six-story warehouses on both sides turned its crabbed streets to canyons etched with a skeletal maze of fire escapes. The sidewalks were bare and treeless. SoHo had not been meant to live in; a few years back some artists, hoping to live cheaply, had begun converting the drafty floors of warehouses into lofts. They had succeeded too well: SoHo became chic, and developers followed, turning the dingy warehouses into co-ops which the artists could not buy. Carey, who dealt enough with writers to be embarrassed by his wealth, disliked this cycle of creativity and greed . . .

"Bastards," Noelle spat suddenly.

She had stopped to stare at a corner warehouse plastered with a peeling movie poster: the burly torso of a man dressed in jeans and work boots, brandishing a bloody butcher knife in one hand and the freshly cut scalp of a woman in the other, blood dripping from its long blond hair. The man's crotch bulged. "I warned you not to go out tonight," the artist had scrawled across his chest in the crooked letters of a maniac.

"Remind you of that reporter?" Carey asked. "The one who got stabbed?"

"Not just that." Noelle stuffed her hands in the pockets of her coat and kept staring. "It's the worst kind of pornography—this slime will end up causing the deaths of five women in Manhattan alone, count on it."

Carey found himself listening for footsteps. Looking over

his shoulder, he saw the shadow of a lone man against the window of a gallery across the street. He glanced down Wooster Street. The pavements were silent, the wind lashed his face. Across the street, the shadow had not moved. "Let's go," Carey said softly. "I'm spoiling your night."

Noelle turned to him. "It's just that sometimes I can't reach you. It gets *old*, always reacting to someone's moods. It makes me feel passive . . ."

"Like your father did?"

"All right, yes—like that. If there was some way I could help . . ." The sentence trailed off. "You caught me imagining our night, that's all. I wanted to be touched." She shivered. "It's *cold*, Peter. Let's go eat."

They headed toward the restaurant.

Moving back down Spring Street, they passed garbage bags and the corrugated doors of unloading docks, three garish posters screaming "Lethal Is Coming," a window filled with twisted sculpture next to a yellow civil defense sign that marked a bomb shelter. At night, Carey thought, SoHo had the stark, ruined quality of postwar Berlin. He said this to Noelle as they passed a jazz bar and then looked through a large window casting pale light onto the sidewalk. Inside a transvestite in a gold lamé dress glided across a vast wooden floor as a crowd of men watched avidly from folding chairs. "Maybe *pre*war Berlin," Noelle murmured.

Carey smiled. But as they crossed the street to the SoHo Charcuterie, he looked over his shoulder.

The streets were bare and dark and silent.

The restaurant was small and almost Mediterranean: the floors were a light-grained wood, the walls painted cream. Its tables, covered with white cloths, were bathed in the pale light reflected from dimmed track bulbs overhead, creating intimacy from a pleasant contrast of whites and shadows. They ordered dinner and a bottle of red wine. Carey raised his glass. "Sorry."

She sipped, looking over the rim. "I guess I'm not quite sure what's getting you. Just Phillip?"

He shrugged. "It's a hard thing to explain. With anyone else, I wouldn't even try . . ."

A heavy-set man brushed against their table and then glided away so quickly that Carey saw only his back moving toward the bar. Noelle's startled upward glance became a stare. Sharply, Carey asked, "Is something wrong?"

She shot a last quick glance toward the bar. "Poor man wasn't very attractive, that's all."

"You seemed spooked..."

"Look, Peter, if you don't *want* to talk, it's okay." Noelle stopped, softening her impatience. "It's just when you get so miserable, it's hard not to ask why."

Carey began twirling his wineglass; he finally spoke, without looking up. "Maybe part of it's that I don't know who or what I am if not a Carey, publishing like my father and grandfather. The firm is what they've left me." He hesitated. "I suppose I feel that if I lose it, I'm not anyone at all."

"But I'm not with you because you're a *Carey*, Peter—it's what we have when you're *not* living all that out that keeps me here." Noelle leaned toward him. "Okay, I understand that you need it, like I need photography to keep from waiting for some man to pull my life out for me. What you don't need is this endless shit with Phillip."

"You act as if it's voluntary."

"I'm not saying that. But you've got to ask yourself why his every breath takes so much out of you. Why blame Phil because Barth made him an offer?"

"All right, dammit." Carey looked at her; his voice was staccato. "For you, Noelle—the truth, as clear as I can make it. Ever since my father died, I've known that Phil would steal my inheritance. No matter that I feel guilty—the point is that I *believe* it, like other people believe in God or horoscopes or Sigmund Freud. Now that Barth's arrived to help him, I'm afraid, more deeply than I can ever tell you, I'll lose the firm."

"Like you lost your father?"

"Jesus Christ, Ciano, let's put on hipboots and wade in the Freudian slime. On second thoughts, *you* go." The hurt on her face stopped him; tiredly, Carey raised his glass. "Anyhow, why hassle about this when we can toast your retirement from psychiatric practice. This morning I called Ruth Levy's brother."

Noelle stared at the glass in his hand; Carey felt the sudden fear that she would leave. Then she asked, quite softly, "Did you talk about remembering?"

"Uh-huh." The thought made Carey feel vulnerable; lightly,

to cover this, he added, "Maybe I'll remember how much I owe to Phillip."

Phillip Carey stood in the semidarkness, facing Barth's desk. "Peter *did* promise me he'd think about it."

"That's hard to believe." Barth remained seated, Phillip guessed, to conceal his shortness. "Do *you* believe it?"

Phillip resolved to answer and leave quickly; he disliked this memory of darkness, being alone with another man. "I can only hope . . ."

"You should do better, Phillip. Your fate's in Peter's hands."

"As is yours. Like it or not, I've assumed the responsibility of trustee."

"No, Phillip; you foolishly saved a child. The humiliating role you're playing was John Carey's doing."

"Look, Barth . . ."

"So the only question is what you can make of it *now*, should Peter choose not to deal with me." Barth's voice grew harsh. "Time's running out. You're worthless goods in five more months."

"What's my penury to you? If Peter won't bite, you can buy another publisher."

"No." Phillip watched Barth's profile, turning toward John Carey's building. "I was meant to own Van Dreelen and Carey."

Phillip still could not grasp Barth's motives. "Manifest Destiny?" he inquired.

"Social Darwinism," Barth snapped. "I'm much more like Black Jack Carey than you or Peter or even the late, great Charles . . ."

"Stop exhuming him."

"Why?" Barth's voice softened abruptly. "Did Charles make you unhappy, Phillip?"

"That's enough." For a fearful instant, Phillip wondered what he knew, then snapped back. "I wouldn't play these games with Peter, Barth. *His* unhappiness is not a joy to live with."

Barth turned to face him. "Nor is mine."

Once more Phillip felt this strange man frighten him. Retreating, his mind fixed on the woman who was waiting for him; new and young, she still held the teasing promise that, somehow, this time, he might truly feel. More evenly, he answered Barth, "I'll keep trying to persuade him. As you point out, I need the money."

"Just bring him here."

"Give me time." Phillip looked away. "All that I suggest is that you not meet with him quite yet. It would be desirable if Peter didn't start off disliking you..."

"Three more weeks," Barth cut in, "to produce this terror in person."

"And if I can't?"

"Then you're out eight million dollars." Barth paused, dropping his voice. "Unless you sell me Peter's stock."

Phillip looked up at him. "I can't do that, I'm afraid."

In the darkness, Phillip sensed, rather than saw, Barth's slow, incredulous smile. "You're afraid of him, aren't you?"

"Shut up."

Barth gave a quick, barking laugh and then his voice went flat. "This isn't scruples at all. There's something in young Peter that scares you to your very soul." With terrible gentleness, he smiled again. "Perhaps, Phillip, I should find out what that is."

His father screamed...

Carey turned to Noelle. "Pardon?"

They stood beneath the awning of her apartment. Carey hardly remembered their subway ride, or the walk that followed; as he looked around for a man he would not recognize, his mind had been drawn into the vortex of his dream. Too late, he realized that they had not spoken until now.

"Earth to Mars," Noelle was saying. "I asked you to call me when you can handle conversation."

Her eyes were luminous and probing. Streetlights cast dark hollows beneath her cheekbones; all at once her animal presence pierced him as deeply as the night he had first entered her. Yet he knew that now she wished to sleep alone: it was the melding of thoughts, and not their bodies, that made them lovers. He touched her face. "I'll be back from Mars tomorrow."

"Okay." She kissed him; her mouth was soft and moist in the bitter night. "I'm glad about Levy, Peter." She brushed snow from her hair, and was gone.

He watched her disappear, walking quick and straight and

proud; against his will, Carey's memory snapped this like a photograph, of a lover he would never see again...

Glancing around him, Carey saw no one. He turned back toward the subway.

The wind felt colder.

Martin watched him from the shadows.

He did not follow. He did not wish to be seen; the woman had already seen his face. The small man was too anxious to hear voices; his orders had brought Martin much too close for anything but killing. Following them in SoHo had been awkward enough. Curious that it *had* been SoHo...

A coincidence, surely: Peter Carey was a rat in a maze. But that they had led him there, and she had seen him, felt like an invasion of the privacy, inviolate and intact, from which he stripped the privacy of others.

Perhaps she was undressing...

He hunched against the cold, the picture growing until it crawled across his skin. He had been angry when Carey left; imagining their sex might have salved this feeling of exposure. But their parting betrayed some fissure which the small man might yet use. And now he could imagine her, alone.

Perhaps, alone, she felt him. In SoHo, waiting for them to finish, he had drifted to the poster which had stopped her; reading it, he grew excited.

He saw litheness in her walk, in her slim hips...

Stroking the tapes still hidden in his pocket, he shivered. The Village was much colder than midtown; no giant buildings warmed the sidewalks with their heat, or cut the wind that sliced in from the Hudson.

In Corfu the breeze was warm and smelled of lemons...

She wore no bra beneath her sweater.

He looked up at the roof of the darkened warehouse across the street.

For reasons he could not yet define, he was troubled by the small man's motives; his mentor's absence of emotion, so different from Martin's own, had always made him feel safe. He was troubled by this lapse in judgment.

He needed something to appease him until the climax of his drama.

Some night he would watch her.

Alone in the darkness, he began counting windows, upwards from the first floor.

Her light went on.

Six.

Flicking on the lamp, Noelle glanced through her window. There was nothing but the warehouse...

She peeled off her sweater. Wool brushed her nipples.

Damn Peter.

Folding her sweater in the drawer, she wondered what had happened.

She knew that Peter's mood was much darker than the words he'd used. He concealed himself through acts of misdirection: tonight, merely to divert her, he had even played on a resentment of her father she had admitted to him alone. It was cheap, a betrayal of friendship—she disliked him for it. Coming home, he would not talk; she could not take him inside her with the passion so far gone, from some stubborn desire to retrieve it...

She stripped off her jeans.

His head had tilted as she said goodbye, eyes open as a child's: too late, he had seen *her*, and not his fear. Unguarded, Peter Carey was the most sensitive man she knew; his betrayal was a measure of what troubled him.

Perhaps it was his call to Levy: she had pushed him much too hard about it, and then probed and psychoanalyzed until he had withdrawn.

She frowned. She could not keep things going by rationalizing his moods, and asking too little for herself. She *did* resent her father: for the words he'd never spoken to her mother; for the things she'd never asked; for all the oppressive years of silence Noelle had witnessed in their home.

She could not live like that. Perhaps she was not right for Peter Carey...

Yet she would lie with Peter after making love, her forehead resting on his temple, limbs and bodies touching like kittens in a litter.

She thought back to waiting at the Lion's Head. It seemed days ago—feeling so many things so quickly made her tired. She was used to taking the world straight on, defining it through her own expectations and not through what others might give to her. Her father had taught her that.

She almost smiled: she did not think well when she was tired, no one could. They would talk in the morning.

Noelle slid out of the rest of her clothes; instinctively, she turned to the window . . .

She stopped, staring out at nothing until she could identify the other thought which troubled her.

The man.

She began hastily laying out her clothes for the next day, a habit left over from college, when she had risen early to work in the cafeteria before classes. After they had given her the Pulitzer, she had examined herself for changes, hoping they were not too great: that they were in fact so paltry had almost disappointed her, and she had resolved at least to end this practice of picking out her blouse and slacks, the remnant of financial desperation. To her amusement, she could not: to cast off habits which had gotten her this far made her feel as superstitious as the thought of Peter's money. The guilt of Catholics, she thought: at least her clothes were better, she could buy them just for fun. . . .

The man had turned so quickly.

There was an odd brilliance in his face, strange cravings in the too-bright eyes and pendulous underlip like those she imagined in a mother's boy festering in his room, nursing fantasies of revolvers and naked women. She had sensed this curious *intimacy* . . .

She searched her memory.

She *was* tired, she concluded, nerves taut from Peter's nerves and the stabbing of a woman and the poster of a bloody scalp, until she felt threatened by the sad ugliness of a stranger.

She drew down the blind.

Still naked, she crawled between her sheets . . .

Peter's mouth would feel warm on her nipple, his tongue moving slowly downward . . .

She drew her legs up: the bed felt empty and too cold. She wanted to feel him quiver with the sensuality coiled inside, hear him cry out.

And afterwards, know his feelings.

It was strange: she could imagine this moment no more clearly than the future they might share together.

She was not that sure they would. Peter's psyche was a tangle: a dream he would not tell her, a weekend he could not remember.

If only this man Levy could find reasons.

She tossed and twisted, too tired to sleep.

Phillip Carey stood staring into the empty room which had been the child Peter's.

"There's something in young Peter," Barth had said, "that must scare you to your very soul."

In his mind, Phillip Carey heard a seven-year-old child scream himself awake, from a nightmare of his father.

Behind him, with no goodbye, the woman left.

Peter Carey bolted upright, torn from the nightmare by his scream. He reached for Noelle.

The bed was empty.

Damp with sweat, he struggled to retrieve fragments of his return home. A collage of strobe-lit images pierced the fog of his depression—the blank faces of night prowlers and secretaries riding the subway like automatons on an endless treadmill, then the beams of passing headlights as he reached the sidewalk, two lovers kissing...

He had turned from them, like a child who was caught...

The woman's long black hair spilled into his father's lap ...

Maybe he had imagined that as well.

Night thoughts, getting worse.

Paranoid.

Perhaps he *was* insane: tonight he saw nothing but more solitude, running from the death of Charles Carey to his own. He picked up the telephone to call Noelle.

Was she safe?

Safe, and asleep.

Filled with loneliness and self-contempt, Peter Carey slammed down the phone.

The telephone rang in the seedy hotel room; Martin checked his watch, read 2:15, and answered.

"Did you follow them?" the small man asked.

"I placed a bug beneath their table. It was difficult."

"Necessary. I've played your tape of the Careys' luncheon. Based on voice analysis, Peter was lying."

"Afterwards, he went to see his lawyer."

"Then we need the notes of what was said. I must know his strategy toward Phillip."

"I understand."

"What did Peter say to his young lady?"

Martin had a sharp mental image of the woman, undressing. "He's consulting a psychiatrist. A man named Levy."

"*Levy.*" There was a long pause. "Concerning his amnesia?"

The small man's query was quite soft; only Martin could have heard the constriction he was learning to associate with the name of Peter Carey. "I think so."

"Make certain." The small man's voice rose. "This will not wait."

"It may take time," Martin answered cautiously, "to learn so much." His words were careful, correct; over years, his speech had come to parody the small man's. "After all, it took a lifetime for Peter Carey to become who and what he is..."

"No." The small man's voice was curt and chill. "It only took one weekend."

Staring into the bathroom mirror, William Levy re-lived the death of Charles Carey in his imaginings of the son.

He could still remember the book he had been reading when Ruth had called him, and how he felt. He rushed to Ruth's apartment: she wept, and he held her, so slight in his arms, as he had not done since the day their mother had slashed her wrists and bled to death on a patch of bathroom tile. Ruth never quite healed; for a time Levy could not cease imagining the pain of burning flesh. Now, twenty years later, he still grew sad at the approach of April, most beautiful of months.

He saw this sadness as the last tribute he could give to Charles Carey. The career that Charles had aided could be measured a success, its analytic process a bulwark against his bent toward mysticism, which frightened him. His own wife had died young, of leukemia, but she had loved him, he knew, and his concern for Ruth had softened his lack of children.

Now he lived through his work and patients. If his failures troubled him, he considered them more bearable than his initial response to Charles's death: that he had killed his friend by failing to free him from his wife, and then had failed to help his son . . .

Today, with sickening suddenness, his guilt rose from the past.

Searching for Peter at Charles's funeral, Levy had encountered Phillip Carey for the first time. Peter was not there, his uncle murmured, the shock had been too great. Levy nodded; the boy was no doubt traumatized. Awkwardly, he offered his assistance: if he might visit Peter as a psychiatrist, or simply as an older friend . . .

"*No*," Phillip had cut in brusquely. "I don't want him disturbed."

Shaken, Levy stared at Phillip Carey. Phillip's answering stare was coldly vacant; his brother's death seemed to have left him close to catatonic. The boy would be well tended, Phillip added stiffly, he himself would see to that. Levy had withdrawn, confused; Phillip Carey was the kind of man who made one feel ambivalent. He could not tell whether Phillip's rebuff stemmed from some stubborn paternal feeling, or in resistance to a friend of Charles becoming close to Charles's son.

Nor, Levy now admitted, did he know whether his own retreat followed from his selfish wish not to live with Charles's death, or from something more he sensed in Phillip.

Ruth had been so distressed he could not then have shared this thought with her. Better, he had told himself, to let it die.

He had not seen Peter Carey again. Nor, in all the years since Peter arrived at his grandfather's firm, startling Ruth, did he ask about his appearance: with an almost peasant superstition, he wished for Charles Carey's son to have no face.

Now, twenty-three years later, the son he had not reached for still had nightmares of the father.

CHAPTER 3

Peter Carey stepped from the Aristocrat, dressed in the same tan corduroy sportcoat he'd worn eight days earlier. He spoke briefly; the doorman smiled at him, then hailed a taxi.

Martin flagged a second cab and followed Carey to the hospital.

Carey went through a door on the side of the sprawling complex running along East 76th Street. Martin waited across the street. He knew that Carey would not see him. Like most New Yorkers, Carey sensed the closeness of strange bodies; Martin kept thirty yards away.

He decided not to smoke for one hour.

Restless, Martin reflected; he guessed from the small man's tone that this visit would be the catalyst of his drama, although he did not yet know the reason.

In his mind he followed Peter Carey to the doorway of his father's friend.

Levy's blond young secretary cracked open his door. "Mr. Carey's here."

"Step in for a moment." Levy glanced up from his desk. "Tell me, what does young Mr. Carey look like?"

She shot him a curious glance. "Why?"

"Just that he's the son of an old friend, and I've never really seen him."

"He's beautiful," she smiled. "Very blond. Was the father like that?"

"No; auburn, really." Levy felt himself relax. "You can send him in now."

A moment later there was a knock on the door. "Come in," he said.

A tall blond man leaned casually through the doorframe, head tilted to one side, and pierced him with startlingly blue eyes. "Complete with couch," the familiar voice observed, and then Peter Carey flashed a grin.

The grin, and the face it came from, were Charles Carey's.

Levy's skin went cold: in all but Allie Fairvoort's hair, Peter Carey was an eerie replica of his father. "You *are* Dr. Levy, aren't you?"

Levy kept staring. "You wish to know what your father looked like? He looked exactly like you."

"Well," Peter smiled, "if I'd known that, I wouldn't have been so interested. You don't mind if I sit, do you?"

"No—of course not." All at once Levy recalled the awkward freshman he had been. He gestured toward the chair in front of his desk. "You have photographs, surely?"

"I didn't for a long time—my uncle's not a sentimental man. But then your sister was kind enough to locate one." There was a glint of amusement in the cobalt eyes. "I've since found a spot for it."

Levy made note of the lethal flatness of Peter's last sentence. "Then you can see the resemblance."

"To a point. But photographs can deceive." Once more Peter's head tilted, as Charles's had, the smile at one corner of his mouth less than a smile. "Like memories."

Levy fought back the sense that he was being toyed with. "Is that part of why you came here, Peter—for my memories of your father?"

"No—the part concerning memory is a little different. I suppose I need my own." Peter's smile had vanished. "What happened is that I remember nothing about the weekend my parents died. All I have is the burning of my father's face, in a recurring nightmare that makes no sense."

Absorbing this, his instinctive fear of Peter's dream mingling with the sense of their shared loss, Levy knew by intuition that there was something about Phillip and the photograph to which he should return. "This nightmare," he ventured softly. "Perhaps you should describe it."

As Peter recited the sequence of the dream, the coolness vanished from his face and voice, until Levy felt his pain.

"Please," he said as Peter finished. "Let me recommend some-one." He looked away. "I knew your father far too well."

Peter waited until Levy's eyes met his again. "Then it would help for me to share that."

The man in Levy shrank from the fiery image of Charles's death; the professional, from treating his son. "But you also wish for me to help you end this dream. No analyst can simply draw that from you, like venom from a snake. He must help you understand its meaning, however taxing or unpleasant. I'm neither objective, nor young enough. The process may take years . . ."

"Twenty-two years, do you think?" Peter's smile was as bleak as the words. "I was seven when I first woke up, scream-ing."

Levy bent his forehead to his fingertips. "Then what is it that brought you to me now?"

"You were his friend." Peter's gaze dropped. "There's a woman—Noelle Ciano. I'm afraid I'll lose her."

"Because of this nightmare?"

"The accident—it seems to have had its effects." Peter paused; Levy saw that self-revelation was painful. "I'm not able to trust easily, to give or receive affection. Somehow it's all tied up with Phillip . . ." He shrugged, cutting himself off. "I can't explain what I don't remember."

"Is it so difficult to talk, Peter?"

Peter smiled faintly. "It's nothing I'm used to." He glanced around the office. "Incidentally, I assume you take notes. Where do you keep them?"

"Locked in file cabinets, with each file numerically coded to a separate index of patient's names." Watching Carey's eyes, Levy added, "What makes you ask?"

This time Peter did not smile. "Paranoia."

"Your word, not mine. I was wondering if you had some special reason."

Peter shifted in his chair. "A man named Clayton Barth wishes to buy our firm, which I don't wish to sell. He's rumored to use blackmail, psychiatric and otherwise."

"And?"

"He's in contact with my uncle." The clipped savagery of

Peter's first reference to Phillip Carey was gone; he seemed almost shy. "As I say, I don't trust readily."

Levy's memory flashed back to Phillip Carey at the funeral. "Especially Phillip?"

Peter's smile turned quirky and embarrassed. "Will you help me, then?"

Suddenly, Levy imagined Phillip, confronted with this double image, the hostile likeness of his brother. "This nightmare started when you were seven?"

"Yes."

Levy rubbed his temples. *And you were six,* he thought, *when I let Phillip turn me away.* Almost to himself, he murmured, "Then four hours a week is not too much to ask."

"Thank you." Glancing up, Levy caught Peter's complex look of worry and relief, just before he rose. "Still nine o'clock?"

"Yes. Starting tomorrow, if that's all right."

With a last, ironic smile, Peter Carey extended his hand.

As they shook hands, Levy felt for that brief instant that they were sealing some Faustian bargain. Later, when he had compromised all sense of his profession to help free Peter Carey from his past, he would learn what it was.

Fifty-five minutes after he disappeared into the hospital, Peter Carey strode out and again caught a cab. Martin caught another. As his watch hit sixty, he lit a cigarette.

The first cab careened down Fifth Avenue, taking Peter Carey to his office.

Martin touched his gun; Carey's visit to Levy stirred his imaginings, and not only of the woman. He wondered what secrets Carey left there, and how the small man, learning them, would touch the scales of Peter's life.

Stubbing out his cigarette, Martin counted the moles on the cabbie's neck.

Four.

Laughter echoed in the tunnel . . .

Carey glanced up at the knock on his door; Ruth Levy looked inside to ask, "How are you this morning?"

"Ecstatic." Carey smiled hastily. "A contented worker in

America's happiest and most successful family-owned business. I think I'll go out and have children."

"Try kittens first." Stepping in, Ruth asked more softly, "I was wondering if you'd talked to Bill."

Carey never felt quite ready for her. Framed in the doorway, she seemed dark, slim and ageless . . .

"Yes, thanks. I did."

"I hope that he can help you."

"Perhaps he can." Carey watched her face. "I suppose that depends on whether I should be tampering with my memory."

"I think it's always better to know." Ruth's eyes flickered to the picture behind him; once more, Carey sensed the wordless second conversation running beneath their first, its silences more telling than speech. Abruptly, she asked, "Have you read that manuscript Phil brought in?"

Carey shook his head. "Give me a synopsis."

"Subliminal violence." Her smile was a small twist of the mouth. "The sex is a pervert's fantasy of Gestapo officers and women prisoners. You should read it."

Inexplicably, Carey felt Ruth telling him that she did not trust his uncle. "I'll do that, Ruthie."

"Good." She gave the picture a last quick glance, and left.

It was midafternoon when Carey's overhead light went out.

He was on the telephone, negotiating with an agent. He tried his desk lamp without success; for an odd split second, he connected this with Clayton Barth. "Did your lights just go?" he asked the agent.

"Let me look across the hall—yeah, they're out."

The man was twelve blocks away; Carey knew what would be happening next. He pushed Barth from his mind. "Might as well wrap this up," he said. "We're not going anywhere."

They talked ten minutes longer, sealing the contract at Carey's price, and then he called Noelle. "Stay at my place tonight," he urged. "I don't want you alone, and the subway'll be hopeless."

"I know—I'm going out now to get some pictures. I won't be through till five or so, and by then the phones'll be tied up."

"Why not meet me around five-thirty, at the corner of Fifth and Forty-second. We'll walk."

"But will we talk?"

"Even that."

"All right, then," she said. "You've got me for the evening—metaphorically speaking."

Carey's smile became a laugh. "Just don't start without me," he answered, and hung up.

When his telephone rang, Martin was there to answer: the instant the blackout began, he knew that the small man would be calling.

"Tonight?" he asked.

"Yes." The small man's tone was so mild that only Martin could have sensed its sarcasm. "This should make things easier for you."

Martin smiled to himself: the small man hated his dependence. "Which things?" he probed casually. "Is there something you want first?"

There was silence.

"Don't toy with me." The unseen voice was soft and cool. "Not now, and not ever."

Martin waited.

"*Levy*," the small man hissed, and hung up.

By 5:10, when Peter Carey began edging nine stories down the darkened stairwell, Van Dreelen & Carey was nearly empty; only midtown had gone dark, and those with light at home were struggling to break free. He joined a file of reluctant bodies descending as if into a cave; it stopped to admit more bodies on each floor, then inched forward again. Trapped in darkness, Carey felt the loss of movement and control: it was 5:50 before he reached the sidewalk and began to search the milling throngs for Noelle. A long ten minutes later he saw her threading across the intersection through a mass of cars with their motors off, locked bumper to bumper in an immovable grid that kept even buses from running. Noelle kissed him as she reached the corner. "All the traffic lights are out," she said. "It's like this for blocks, even police cars and ambulances are stalled. The people stuck in subway trains are just sitting there like they're in some catacomb. Leaving the paper, I heard people shouting because they're trapped inside the elevator. There was nothing I could do."

"Want a drink?"

Noelle looked back toward the street; pedestrians had begun moving in silent packs among the cars. "Maybe a quick one."

Ducking into the nearest bar, they were surprised to find it empty; bars were the demilitarized zone of the city, offering safety from its normal terrors. "They just want to get out of here," Noelle suggested. "I didn't see too many cops on the street."

Carey nodded; the room was faint as dusk. "These used to be more fun."

They went to the bar and ordered two Gibsons. The bartender, a beefy man who looked glad to see them, asked, "Mind straight up? My cubes are melting."

"Sure," Carey said.

The bartender seemed relieved. Mixing the drinks, he wondered, "Think there'll be looting?"

"When it gets dark." Carey turned to Noelle. "Cheers."

They drank quickly. As they left, Carey said, "You know, it's strange how divorced we are from the things that run our lives, like some poor guy on a respirator. Food, heat, light: we don't even know where they come from anymore, but we'll pay any price to get them. And when they go, we're helpless."

Noelle pulled up her collar. "They'll have it fixed by morning."

Carey felt the chill of winter. The high-rises towering above Fifth Avenue were dark, their windows like dead cells. Noelle watched grim men and women hurry past them. "They still don't want to look at people," she remarked.

"They just want to get home. Like me."

They began to angle up Fifth Avenue toward Central Park South. The buildings of Carey's childhood—Rockefeller Center, St. Patrick's Cathedral, F.A.O. Schwarz, where his laughing father once bought him a toy yacht—were as dim as his memories, and the Plaza looked like a bank that had closed. "My father used to bring me here," he said.

Noelle nodded; he had never taken her inside.

For a moment, Carey stopped to stare at the entrance to

Central Park. It snaked and wound in darkness, toward the tunnel . . .

Noelle took his arm. "Come on."

They turned down the sidewalk of Central Park South, passing dark hotels; neither they nor anyone sane would risk crossing the park at night. The street was like a parking lot; some commuters had locked their cars and begun walking. Ahead, the Gulf & Western Building was an abandoned shell, forty-four stories of soot-colored glass. Noelle stopped to stare at it. "Imagine the neutron bomb."

"I am," Carey said.

Crossing the street, they turned beneath the shadowy glass building up Central Park West, hustling the last twelve blocks to the Aristocrat.

The doorman smiled in the dusk. "Something, isn't it."

They grinned back.

He had lit the lobby with lamps that ran on batteries. "Thanks," they called back, and then took ten pitch-black flights, stopping to see if the Krantzes were all right.

The small woman came to the door, peeking beneath the chain latch, Abner yipping at her feet. "We have candles," she explained to the dog.

Carey smiled. "Call me," he advised Abner, "if you need anything," and then they groped a few dark feet to his apartment.

Inside, Carey lit a candle and examined the wires of his useless alarm system. "It'll be like this all over midtown," he said. "Mass flight, and no alarms anywhere. Perfect for break-ins."

Noelle touched his shoulder. "Let's start a fire."

Carey locked the door behind them.

Martin opened Levy's outer door with the passkey.

Closing the door, he took a flashlight from his bag, blessing the power of uniforms. Dressed as a security guard, he had marched past the battery-lit reception desk and two nurses' stations with no questions asked, until he reached the darkened wing of offices, where there were no patients needing light.

Now he moved the beam around Levy's front room, frowning at the minimal decor, until he found the file cabinets tucked behind the receptionist's desk.

Six.

The locks were simple. Picking the nearest cabinet, he worked its lock and then carefully slid the top drawer open, taking out a file.

Levy had coded them.

Martin paused. Levy would keep an index at the office: no man could commit six cabinets of coded files to memory.

Turning off the flashlight, he sat at the desk, letting his eyes adjust to darkness. Levy must be an old man, he thought. He would hide the index in a place which did not require him to stand.

Martin edged toward the inner office.

There would be a desk inside.

He reached for Levy's doorknob . . .

Carey and Noelle lay watching the flames rise, just beyond their light. He felt her hair against his face. Softly she asked, "What was Levy like today?"

"Like a psychiatrist, I suppose." Carey stared into the fire. "He struck me as a very *sad* man, in his way."

"Sad about what?"

"About what he sees, I guess." Idly, Carey drank some of the wine they shared. "I think he's still sad about my father."

"Did you talk about that?"

"No." Carey hesitated. "I wanted to."

"What would you have asked?"

"I don't know—impossible things, really. What was he like, what would he be like now, what would *I* be like if . . ." Carey's voice trailed off. "The man's a professional. He wouldn't answer me even if he could."

"But you told him about the amnesia?"

"And the dream. Couldn't leave that out."

"Show-off."

Carey smiled absently. "That's when he really looked unhappy—guilty, almost. It's funny—I felt sorry for him. I guess it's a good trick for a psychiatrist."

"I doubt he wants your sympathy, Peter. Are you going back?"

"So it seems—although part of me keeps saying I shouldn't." He began playing with her hair. "You know I really don't remember that much about him. More a feeling..."

"Your father?"

Carey nodded. "It's just that sometimes I think—you know, if he had lived—that then I'd have his qualities." He reflected for a moment. "Did I tell you that he saved someone's life once, during the war?"

"I knew that, yes."

He looked over her shoulder at the fire. "It's something I think about, now and then. I don't know if I could do that."

Noelle was quiet. "Does it really matter?"

"I guess not." He shrugged. "At least what I have of him is good. He had this terrific smile. I remember him walking so quick and straight and proud that people must have felt lucky just to talk to him—except that he always had time for me. There was only once when he didn't, and that was when my grandfather died, flying this silly fucking kite to please me." Still Carey watched the flames. "The last thing he did was call out to my father—he'd forgotten who I was. Yet I can never forget why he died. Now I'm not so sure I want to remember my father's dying. It hardly takes a genius to see that the dream symbolizes something pretty bad."

She rolled onto her back. "But the dream *is* pretty bad, Peter. You should hear yourself screaming..."

"I have—recently." He looked down at her. "Let's skip it now, all right?"

"Okay." For a moment her eyes probed his and then they smiled. "Anyhow, what I really want to know is what you told him about me."

Carey tilted his head. "I told him that you're kinky."

"Kinky?"

"Uh-huh." He grinned at her. "You know, that you make me do things."

"That's outrageous." The smile moved to one corner of her mouth. "What things?"

Carey kissed her nose. "I'll show you."

Martin pressed the Carey folder to his face.

He did not yet know why Carey's amnesia so concerned the

small man; for a brief moment he did not care. In this pitch-dark time of his imaginings, the woman was inside...

He stopped himself: it was not yet time to read. Opening the file, he spread Levy's freshly taken notes out on the floor, counting pages.

Five.

Kneeling, he took the camera from his bag and photographed each page, then he placed the film back in the bag. Carefully, he inserted a small magnetic disk at the base of Levy's lamp, and then unscrewed the mouthpiece of the telephone.

Minutes later, Martin began reading, as though to touch Noelle Ciano.

Noelle's flesh quivered, nipples rising to harden in the palm of Carey's hand as he kissed the nape and then the hollow of her neck and, chest sliding against her back and spine and shoulder blades, entered her...

Carey felt the warmth inside her; as her knees rose, his legs curled into the back of hers, arms clasping her body. The flame spat and flickered, its light moving toward them, grazing their skin. Noelle turned her head, Carey's face bent to hers, and still their bodies moved, slowly, sinuously, together. Carey shivered with the blood rushing to his groin, the swelling tightness of it...

Suddenly, Carey felt his soul divide; his flesh still touched hers, warm dampness mingling, yet that same chill part of him, tauntingly aloof, now watched the dance of their bodies but would not, could not, join them...

Closing his eyes, he moved faster, straining to call it back. "Peter," she moaned. "Please, Peter—*be* with me."

Alone, Martin smiled in the cold.

The night was black and flat and skyless; he sensed its shapes but could not see them. The city had died around him; its people had vanished and the moon had disappeared. Only the lights of scattered cars cruised the silent dark.

All Manhattan lay before him, for he understood the night.

Hearing nothing but the sound of his own footsteps, he began to count them.

In his mind, to the pounding of each step, his body moved in rhythm with the woman.

"Not bad," Noelle murmured. "Where is it they do that?"

Carey smiled, face next to hers. "Albania," he answered idly. "Estonia. Several of the captive nations and a few of the Balkan countries . . ."

She turned her face to his. "Is that where *you* were?"

"What do you mean?"

"Just that I could feel myself losing you again." She hesitated. "It's like *you* feel it, too, and then you try to prove you're there."

Carey was stung by her uncanny sense of him. "Was it so bad, then?"

"Bad? You're the best in Manhattan, Peter."

Black hair spilled in his father's lap . . .

"Then what is it that you want?"

She waited for his eyes to open. Much more softly, she said, "To have you here, with me."

Martin stood at the base of the Pan Am Building.

Thirty feet above him the building disappeared; its lobbies were black caves. But in his memory, etched by the day he had followed Carey, Martin saw the image of a stairwell . . .

With the certainty of daylight he walked through the darkened building and took the stairs, counting fourteen floors. He stopped, opened a door, began moving again. He prowled the corridor with uncanny quickness, his flashlight moving from side to side until it caught the square gold letters he was looking for.

Ten minutes later, he stood in Benevides's office.

Kneeling, Carey spread the woolen blanket across Noelle's neck and shoulders, and then kissed her forehead.

Noelle slept evenly, like a child; as night grew deep, her lips parted, as though to smile at the coming of day.

Carey smiled at his thought.

He would not sleep.

Sleep frightened him; its first narcotic moments, drifting and seductive, were the ambush of his faceless enemy.

Tonight, his cries would not awaken her.

Staring at the fire, he imagined Charles Carey, burning in his car.

Finishing, Martin went to the telephone and dialed.

The small man answered on the second ring. "Where are you?"

"Benevides's law firm. I've used the same procedure as at both the Careys' offices."

"What about files?"

"You were right: Carey's stalling his uncle. He's preparing for court."

Martin paused, testing.

Softly, the small man asked, "Did you visit Levy?"

"Yes. Carey's being treated for amnesia."

"And he remembers?"

"Nothing."

"He's waited so long." The small man's voice sounded disembodied. "Why now does he wish to have a memory?"

"The woman."

"And the treatment?"

"Analysis. Four times a week."

"What about sodium pentothal?"

"It doesn't say."

"No, Levy's a Freudian. He wouldn't believe in that . . ." The voice drifted off.

"Is there anything else?"

Martin waited. At last, almost whispering, the small man asked, "Was there something about a nightmare?"

Carey fought the numbness spreading through his limbs, the pleasant, achy yielding. His lids fluttered, opened, closed again; his head rolled and then stilled once more, mind lulled by the rhythm of her breathing. Slowly, struggling, he felt sleep pull him toward the tunnel. It was dark . . .

He awakened to a flash of light.

Noelle slept on, untroubled; his living-room lamp had saved her.

Rising, he turned it off and walked slowly to the window.

Manhattan was itself again, a grid of black and yellow, thin silver to the east.

Soon it would be morning.

Martin opened the door to her apartment.

The living room was dark.

He shut the door behind him, chest tight with excitement: all night, he had been waiting for this time . . .

He must act like a professional, he told himself, so that the small man would not guess his reasons. Repressing his thoughts of the woman, he carefully checked each room, leaving what was needed.

Only then did he let himself sift through her drawers, imagining how he would dress her . . .

Dawn broke through her window.

Awakening, Noelle Ciano smiled over at Peter Carey. "Light back on?"

"Uh-huh."

"Too bad. It was like being on vacation." She looked at him more closely. "Sleep well?"

"Just got up." He kissed her. "Rise and shine, Ciano—I've made coffee."

CHAPTER 4

Martin inched the unmarked van north along Park Avenue, choked by still-abandoned cars.

The morning light through his windshield was pale and tired; the city had the desultory, cluttered look of a living room after a drunken party; Martin felt weariness in his eyes and back. His ashtray was jammed with cigarette butts. Fretful, he counted them.

Thirteen.

He was going to be late.

Anger rising with each new minute flashing on his watch, Martin turned east on 50th Street and headed at a crawl toward Lexington.

His watch hit 8:19.

Lingering in the woman's apartment had been a luxury; he had strayed from the small man's timetable...

A mustached black cabbie double-parked in front of him and began leaning on his hood. Mentally aiming, Martin put a bullet through his brain.

The cabbie started chewing gum.

Leaning out the window, Martin beckoned him. The black man hesitated, then walked over.

"You're blocking me," Martin said.

The cabbie shrugged. "I'm waiting on a fare to J.F.K., man—lots of bags."

Martin pointed toward the corner of Lexington, half a block away. "Park there," he suggested. "You can carry them."

"No way."

"Carry them," Martin repeated in a reasonable tone, "or I'll have to kill you."

The man blinked. He looked up at Martin, then at the corner, then back into Martin's eyes. Wordless, he walked to his cab, and moved it.

Martin drove past him and turned north on Madison.

He had been foolish to call attention to himself; the city frayed his nerves. But the man had been too stunned to check his license plate.

Martin resolved not to check his watch until he hit East 60th Street.

Surrounded by chaos and blasting horns, the van crawled north in agonizing fits and starts: by the time he reached East 60th, it was 8:49.

Eleven more minutes.

Seven more blocks.

He had selected the garage for its relative proximity to both Van Dreelen & Carey and the Aristocrat; a week earlier, the small man had ordered him to reserve a parking place. The balding attendant had been puzzled at this need for empty space; very soon, Martin answered him, he would need to store a van. The space should be kept free . . .

At 8:57, he passed East 67th Street and turned off Madison into an underground garage.

The attendant ran after him.

Martin braked on the ramp circling downward, opened the door, and stared into his reddening face. "There's someone parked there," the man blurted.

Martin's head turned slowly toward him. "I paid you . . ."

"Hey, you never said when . . ."

"Move the car," Martin said coolly, "while I'm able to forget you."

It was nine o'clock.

The man scrambled down the ramp. Martin drove three feet behind him, until he began running.

At 9:02, Martin parked the van, and jumped out; panicky, the attendant sped upstairs in the offending car.

Glancing over his shoulder, Martin opened the double doors of the van and stepped inside, pulling its curtains closed. There was sweat on his forehead.

Inside was a stereo set with a luminous dial of radio frequencies. Switching it on, Martin hastily shoved a cartridge in his tape deck as he checked his watch.

9:04.

The radio crackled: Martin flicked its dial through split seconds of rock music and babbling in English and Spanish, until it reached fourteen.

Slowly, carefully, Martin turned up the sound...

"Good morning, doctor," Peter Carey said.

"Good morning, Peter." Levy gestured at the couch. "Make yourself comfortable, and then we can begin."

"You want me to lie down?"

Levy nodded. "That *is* the procedure."

Peter Carey stared at the couch, then back at Levy. "What's the point?" he demanded. "It's like a *New Yorker* cartoon."

"Is that how you feel—comic? Somehow I don't think so."

"Do you always answer questions with questions?"

Levy took out his glasses. "Some people feel that relaxing on the couch helps free them from whatever shame they might feel."

"I feel no shame."

"But the couch alarms you?"

"Look, I simply want to talk to you as I would to anyone."

"How's that?"

"As an equal."

"Tell me, Peter, why does lying down turn you into a supplicant?"

"Jesus..." Carey stopped himself. "Because I feel as if I'm losing control."

"Perhaps it reminds you of sleeping. You lose control then, don't you?"

Carey's shoulders curled in. "That's why I'm here."

"Not Noelle?"

"Yes—Noelle, too."

"Do you think this nightmare and amnesia affect how you are with her?"

"I can't answer that."

Levy nodded. "*That's* why you're here. What I'm proposing is that your dream proceeds from your childhood and life— particularly from this weekend you can't recall. Until we start unraveling that, your future will be no different from your past. I'd appreciate it if you'd lie down on the couch."

Carey shook his head. "It's just not comfortable for me."

"Because then you've lost control."

"Something like that."

Levy began wiping his glasses. "You came here for my help. I have conditions—professional ones. Your choice is to accept them, or to explain to Noelle that your analyst went out of control."

Levy stared down at his glasses; angry and ready to leave, Carey stopped at his sense of the older man's surprise at his own sharpness. When Levy looked up, hesitant, Carey covered this confusion with a shrug. "I'll try it for a day."

Walking to the couch, Carey thought he heard the sound of exhaling. He lay there, listening to Levy's footsteps moving slowly to the worn armchair at the head of the couch, arranged so that patients could not see him. Green paint peeled from the ceiling; in one corner, Carey saw a spider working on the first strands of its web. From behind him, Levy asked, "How does that feel?"

"Lumpy."

"It's rather old."

Carey could hear Levy's pencil scratching beneath his voice. "Your index," he asked abruptly. "Is there a duplicate copy?"

"No." Levy paused. "Does it bother you if I take notes?"

"I don't like having this written down. Notes about Noelle—it's like invading our privacy."

"Well," Levy responded easily, "why don't we put Noelle aside for a while. Tell me, what do you recall about your father?"

Carey felt tension in the pit of his stomach. "That's hard . . ."

Listening, Levy nodded. "Just the good things," he suggested gently. "When he died, what did you most miss about him?"

"That we could talk." Peter hesitated. "After that, there was only Phillip."

Unbidden, once more Levy thought of the funeral. "Yes, what was *he* like?"

Peter folded his arms. "There's not that much I can tell you."

"No? Yesterday, I got the impression that Phillip's rather critical to what we're doing here."

"That may be, doctor. Back then, I didn't examine it."

"Then you had no feelings about him?"

Peter's body stiffened. "None that I remember."

Levy paused, weary; he had the brief, ironic thought that only Charles Carey, by dying, had stayed forever young. But by now Charles would have been sixty-two, like Levy himself, too old to rally from a sleepless night . . .

Instinctively, he asked, "How did your *father* feel about Phillip?"

Peter shifted on the couch. Then, in a voice too chill to be forgotten, he answered, "My father hated him."

For the next three weeks, they talked of Phillip Carey.

CHAPTER 5

In those three weeks, Peter Carey came to feel that someone was watching him.

Walking the city, he would glance swiftly over his shoulder, but see no one. Perhaps, he reasoned, what he felt was people *waiting* for him: Barth, to abandon the firm; Phillip, to make him wealthy; Noelle, to outrun the past; Levy, to escape the night which shrouded his memory. He felt them at the back of his neck...

"What is it?" Noelle asked.

One block from his apartment, Carey had spun to look behind him. "Nothing," he snapped. "Do you know how sick I am of questions?"

She went home early; that night, Carey feared for her.

Fiercely, he hurled himself at the familiar: editing and exercise, his banter with the Krantzes and the doorman—all these warmed him with their certainty. And then he would go running; repeatedly, he was seized by the impulse to sprint from his accustomed route into the tunnel of his nightmare.

His daily routine, rigidly constructed to lend order to his life, no longer seemed to serve him: its rhythms felt unconnected to some deeper pattern that ran beneath the surface. Carey wondered if this were the price of seeing Levy. Striving to recall the past, he felt like someone straining to see enemies in a pitch-black night: the more he tried and failed, the more he felt them moving toward him. He heard his tension in Levy's voice.

Emotion ran between them like a wire. Carey's nerve ends caught the passion beneath Levy's questions; as if responding, he remembered bits of Charles Carey, fleeting as vapor in the slipstream of a car. Yet with rising dread, he feared remembering his father's death. The conflict tore at him.

In this confusion, Carey's mind fixed on the image of an elephant...

"Dewey," he said aloud.

It was late at night; he had not touched Noelle. She glanced up from her book. "What?"

"Dewey was a stuffed toy elephant. My father gave him to me, and I just recalled his name."

"What made you think of that?"

"All these questions about Phillip and my father, I guess. Maybe it's a symbol of the memories I've lost." Carey shrugged. "That's probably bullshit—analysis is so self-conscious it makes my teeth ache."

Yet he thought of the elephant daily, trying to remember how it looked.

His nightmare came more often.

As it repeated, and he awakened screaming, he asked Noelle to stay less often. But the dream pursued him, even in waking: as Noelle shuddered with her climax, he felt his own embrace as that of death. He could not reach for her.

Returning from his third week of analysis, Carey glanced at his office calendar, and realized that the faceless stranger of his nightmare had stalked him six nights running.

There was a knock: Phillip Carey stood in his doorway. "'Morning, Prince Charming."

Carey was shaken: each morning he spoke of Phillip, then looked into his face...

"Have I grown a second head, Peter? They say the water's getting worse."

"So's my coffee. Come on in."

Phillip closed the door behind him. "I've been curious as to when you'll meet with Clayton Barth."

"Curious?"

Phillip gave a discomfited smile. "*Avid*, then. It's what three weeks of your evasions do to me."

His uncle stood there like a courtier: Carey's resentment began collapsing in a rush of pity.

"I'll listen to him," he answered dully.

And then Phillip smiled, and Carey knew himself a fool.

* * *

Phillip Carey picked up the telephone to call Barth.

His index finger froze on the dial.

Head tilted, he listened intently.

Nothing.

He put down the telephone, tried to stop the shaking of his hand. Guilt was his habit now, like fear.

It couldn't be: that part of his life was long since buried.

His palms were sweating.

The dull ache of too much gin pounded at the base of his neck and ran through his skull to his eyes. His mouth was dry; his legs tired; he was limp with hungover self-contempt. Last night, when again he could not perform, the blond young woman had simply stared at him.

Twenty-three years ago, he had lost his freedom: now he needed to run. Perhaps to the South of France; he remembered Nice, the slim lithe bodies of young men and women, the intensity of their gazes, so foreign to Americans . . .

Peter pitied him; this was the sum of his sad attempt to take the place of Charles.

Twenty years later, Peter's screams still rang in his ears. If only he had been left alone, their lives might have been different . . .

Self-pity, he thought savagely, for the lifetime he had earned. He cut it off, and probed for causes of this sharp new fear, focused by one click of a telephone.

Barth's obsession with Black Jack Carey.

Phillip felt the same suspicions he read in Peter: Barth could have *any* firm more easily than Peter Carey's. It was unnatural . . .

Phillip stopped himself: for once, he had no ugliness to hide. His motive was one any man could share—money. There was nothing for some listener to exploit.

The secret other half of him was surely dead.

Still perspiring, he again reached for the telephone.

The telephone rang.

On its second ring, Benevides glanced at his watch. It was 12:15; his secretary had gone to lunch and he was stuck with the telephone. He put down his dictaphone and answered crisply: "George Benevides."

"You may not be aware," the flat voice said, "that your client is meeting with Clayton Barth."

The monotone was so pronounced that Benevides assumed it a disguise. "Who is this?"

"There are certain things which might be helpful. You might ask young Mr. Carey if his *grandfather* ever spoke of a Clayton Barth. A review of John Carey's correspondence may enlighten him."

"Who *is* this?"

The line went dead.

Benevides stabbed out Peter Carey's number without putting down the phone.

Ruth Levy slid open another dusty drawer: in the airless basement of Van Dreelen & Carey, she rummaged through Black Jack's files, at Peter's request . . .

"Why me?" she had asked him.

"I'm meeting with Barth tomorrow." His voice was cool. "I don't want Phil to catch me doing anything unusual."

"Isn't that a little . . ."

"Paranoid?" Peter tilted his head. "You don't find anonymous calls unsettling?"

"I've begun to *solicit* them, to lighten up my evenings." She hesitated. "You really don't trust Phillip, do you?"

Peter looked steadily back at her. "Do you?"

Once more, Ruth sensed that they were nibbling at the edge of something neither wished to speak of, or even acknowledge . . .

"It's more that I trust *you*." Breaking the silence, Peter's voice was soft. "I've always sensed you'd help me, if I needed it."

Through the inner ear of memory, Ruth heard Charles Carey ask, "Suppose she gave me custody?" "And now you want me to help dig out files," she told his son. "Your father always said that I'd go far . . ."

She riffled another musty sheaf of papers.

There were five cabinets' worth: John Carey's business letters had been preserved since 1946, at the request of his biographer. After his death, his secretary had shipped those he deemed suitable to Boston University, which kept his papers, and left the rest sequestered here, where he once had shoveled coal. Alive, Ruth had thought him a bastard and closet anti-Semite; now, with the grudging admiration of one whose own heritage had not been easy, she acknowledged that he had left his mark.

She opened the fourth drawer. Like the others, its files were carefully labeled, including the one marked simply, "Clayton Barth."

Snatching it up, Ruth began reading.

On the third page, in an unconscious echo of Charles Carey, she murmured, *"Sweet Jesus Christ."*

Clayton Barth dismissed his secretary from the new task that he had set for her, and finished dressing. Walking to the door of his office, he locked it.

He wanted to be alone.

At last, he felt the hope that he might feel complete, the owner of John Carey's firm; Peter Carey would look him in the face, and see that he must yield.

Slowly, he unlocked the top drawer of his desk, and reached inside.

From the tattered cover of an old *Time* magazine, John Carey's face stared back at him.

Pale, Peter Carey looked up from the file. "Does Phillip know, I wonder?"

Ruth shrugged. "I doubt *Barth* knows that Black Jack paid for his education."

"He hid it well enough." Peter's face was set. "What Barth *does* know is that he sent this letter."

Once more, Ruth winced at its terse message:

Dear Clayton,

You seem to hold me responsible for your father's tragedy, the last in a series of choices made by him alone. Be assured that each choice pains me deeply, the more so for his choice of death. Regrettably, our insurance policy does not apply to suicides.

Very truly yours,

[Dictated, but not read, by Mr. Carey]

"And now Barth's on your doorstep." Ruth shook her head. "Your grandfather dies harder than any man I've known. Someone should have followed him around."

"*I* did," Peter murmured softly.

He had so little of the men he loved, she thought, and not all of that was good. "So what will you do?"

"Look for reasons." Peter kept staring at the letter. "First, who would point this out to Benevides?"

"A disgruntled employee?"

"But who could know something that far back? And what do they gain by telling me?"

"You can't know until the meeting."

"I wish there *were* no meeting—no good will come of it, not now." Abruptly, Peter looked up again. "I want you to come. Specifically, I want your impression of Barth."

"Why? You're not thinking of selling to him, are you?"

Peter's eyes went cold. "I wouldn't sell to him now," he answered, "at the point of a gun."

When the telephone rang, Noelle Ciano was cooking pasta sauce and uncorking their favorite Chianti Classico.

"I can't make it," Peter began. "I just found out something about Barth."

Mechanically, Noelle kept stirring the sauce. "Did it kill your appetite?"

"Barth blames the Careys for his father's death. It's fairly complex, but the short of it is that we're meeting tomorrow, and I have to plan how to handle him."

"Maybe a quiet dinner would help."

"I'd be no good."

Noelle heard him slipping beyond reach. "What do I do with the fucking sauce?"

"Save it for later. Look, Barth's interest in the firm makes sense only as psychodrama. I think he's unstable, maybe dangerous. Wherever you go in the next few weeks, be careful, please . . ."

"'Your mission, should you choose to accept it . . .'"

"I'm serious."

His tone was so anxious that she felt a moment's worry. "Why don't you at least sleep here?"

"And wake you up again?" He hesitated. "I'm afraid that's all that would happen."

Noelle felt her body slump. "Okay," she said casually, "talk to you later," and hung up.

Cleaning dishes, she had a few distracted tastes of the sauce. The worst kind of love affair, she thought, is one in which you didn't know whether to feel sympathy or anger, until you've given far too much for too little in return. She stalked to the bedroom.

Framed in her window, a shadow moved on the warehouse roof.

She went closer to the window, and stared.

There was only darkness.

She went to the living room, checked the screen protecting the window near the fire escape, and then came back. Hastily, she jerked down the blind.

Peter must be affecting her.

Suddenly, she felt alone. Walking to the mirror, she undressed, staring at her body.

Peter had not touched her for eight days.

Book in hand, she crawled beneath down covers, in search of warmth. She closed her eyes.

Lightly, she touched herself, as Peter would.

Crouched on the roof, Martin imagined Noelle Ciano's movements in the room behind the blinds.

She would have seen him as a shadow, to carry in the back of her mind. Still, they were connected now: she sensed him with her. He felt his groin stir.

Perhaps she was naked.

Perhaps she would call the police.

Slowly, he went limp.

The small man had demanded every tape of Peter Carey, right up to the meeting.

Martin had never seen him so compulsive. For three weeks, his mentor had retreated with each tape from the psychiatrist, to listen and to ponder: it was as though Carey's analysis threatened some delicate balance in the air he breathed.

Kneeling, Martin cat-walked toward the fire escape.

* * *

Pacing his apartment, Levy stopped abruptly; there was something missing.

He resolved to go early to the office, and review his notes on Phillip Carey.

Weary, he sat on the edge of his bed. The decision stopped his pacing, but did not truly soothe him.

Like an echo, Peter Carey kept repeating, "My father hated him..."

Levy snatched up the telephone and dialed. "How would you like to fix me dinner tomorrow?"

"How would *you* like to take me out?"

"We'll need some privacy." He paused. "I want you to tell me about Peter Carey."

"Peter? That's not so easy, Bill. Tell you *what*, exactly."

Once more, Levy hesitated. "He mentioned a photograph..."

Hanging up, Ruth wondered why she never spoke of Peter with her brother.

Perhaps it was that Peter aroused feelings both sexual and maternal: looking at his face, she would remember Charles Carey inside her body. Today this feeling had been truly painful: once more, she wondered if Peter *knew* she had been his father's lover.

Had Charles lived, Peter might have been her son.

She gulped three aspirin and went to bed.

Sleeplessly writhing, she pondered the photograph, until she faced the thing that she had never told her brother.

Fire ate the skin from Charles Carey...

In terror, his son awakened.

The man Peter Carey was alone.

His father's cry echoed in his mind; sweat mingled with tears on his face. Gripped by an impulse he could not stop, he went to the telephone and dialed.

"George?"

"Peter? What time is it?"

"I need some information, before tomorrow."

"Listen, you woke up two people, all right?" There was

quiet; finally, Benevides said, "Well, maybe *she* knows. What's so urgent?"

"I want to know where Barth was in April of 1959."

"What's so magic about . . ."

Peter Carey cut in softly, "Just find out, George. Please."

CHAPTER 6

Across from Peter Carey's apartment, Martin waited for the doorman.

The night before, after listening to the final tape, the small man had altered his instructions: when Carey left the building, Martin did not follow.

Motionless, he watched the doorman's rhythms—smiling, whistling, flagging taxis like the conductor of a symphony—until a second man relieved him for his coffee break.

The doorman started down the sidewalk; across the street, Martin moved with him, in silent tandem.

The doorman ducked into the coffee shop of a hotel.

He was munching on a roll when Martin approached his table. The doorman looked up, startled; Martin flipped open his wallet to show a typed identification card with his picture on it. "We should confer, Arthur," he said softly. "Concerning Peter Carey."

Reviewing his notes on Phillip, Levy pondered the ambivalence which tore through Peter Carey.

He heard it even in Peter's speech. His voice, when he discussed Phillip, was so toneless it seemed brutal; the same tonelessness, discussing Allie, reminded Levy of fearing his own father; as he recalled the time when John Carey first took him to the bindery, Peter's flatness hinted at amused affection, vanishing in the memory of a guilty child, watching an old man stumble, stricken, from beneath a small red kite. But only for Charles Carey did Levy hear the lyric melancholy Peter held within him.

At seven, there was only Phillip left.

Lonely, Peter had vacillated between an almost craven desire to make Phillip his new father, and an anger which even now he could not explain. Phillip could not long please the child Peter: he would smile at Phillip's presents, then abandon them, loathing his own pleasure. Imagining himself as Phillip, Levy cringed at his rejection by a nephew whose very face, so much like that of Charles. must daily have reminded him of John Carey's final judgment.

In his notes Levy had written: "Does Peter blame Phillip?" Now, staring at these four words, he saw Phillip at his brother's funeral.

Gradually, he had begun to cast the death of Charles Carey as the fault line running through the lives of Phillip and his nephew, dividing them irrevocably: the loss of all that Peter loved freed Phillip from the past he had despised. Phillip sold the Greenwich house and kept Peter from the funeral; Peter's father vanished without a trace. Phillip moved Peter from Charles Carey's home into his town house on East 61st Street: Peter would never take him to the lake or fountain. Saying that he preferred the warmer weather, Phillip auctioned their home in Maine to buy another in Palm Beach; John and Charles Carey died once more in Peter's mind. As he hastily remade John Carey's firm in his own image, Phillip took no time to discuss this change with the child; Peter saw him as a thief. Phillip spoke of his dead brother only when forced, until Peter, aching for the smell and feel of him, strained to remember . . .

But Peter could remember nothing, neither as a child, nor as an adult, for Levy . . .

His secretary opened the door. "Mr. Carey's here."

"One more minute."

The door shut; once more Levy read the penciled question, "Does Peter blame Phillip?" Next to that, underlined, he asked himself, "And for what?"

In troubled silence, Levy listened to Peter tell the story of Barth's past, revealed by an unknown caller. But it was the end which most shocked him.

"Why did you call the lawyer?"

"I'd had the dream." Peter's voice trailed off. "Now I feel like an idiot."

"But do you have some feeling that your parents' death was not an accident?"

"Oh, I don't know." Peter's tone was grudging. "I suppose it's easier for a kid to fantasize what he can't remember, like pretending you're adopted because you can't remember childbirth."

"Yes?"

"There are things I can't define, doctor. That must be true in your own life . . ."

To his own surprise, Levy interrupted. "The nightmare, Peter—*when* did you first have it?"

"When I was seven—I told you that."

"I meant precisely *when*—what day?"

"Why is that important?"

"Don't you find it strange that the nightmare started nearly one year *after* your father's death?"

Peter hesitated. "I've never thought of that."

"Well, I'm suggesting that it's *strange*, like calling your lawyer is strange, and that there's a reason for it." Levy felt his nameless worry overcome him. "People do things for a reason, Peter, even children and idiots, even if the reason is absurd. Don't blame something on coincidence unless you've nothing else to blame it on."

Peter lay quite still. "What was the question, exactly?"

"What *happened*, Peter—the day you first had the dream?"

There was a long silence, and then Peter shook his head. "I don't know, doctor. I really don't know."

Martin smiled at the old woman peering through the doorway. "Yes?" she asked timidly.

He slipped a discreet, printed card beneath the chain. "I was hoping to speak with you a moment."

As she read the card her shyness became bewilderment. "This is the Krantz residence," she explained.

Martin kept smiling at her dog. "I know."

Peter Carey stepped from the cab toward the entrance to Van Dreelen & Carey. He stopped suddenly, and turned toward the Public Library . . .

In a dark room filled with microfiche and yellowed newspapers, he sat with three newspaper indexes open to the same heading: "Charles Carey, 1920–1959."

For the first time, Peter Carey read the newspaper stories of his parents' death.

In the middle of the *Daily News* account, he stopped abruptly.

With the steps of an automaton, he went to a Xerox machine, and copied the article. Then he tucked the clipping in the breast pocket of his coat, and walked to Van Dreelen & Carey.

His assistant, a recent Hotchkiss graduate with two last names, looked up from her desk beside the door. "Your meeting's in a half hour."

"Has George Benevides called?"

"No."

"Hold my other calls."

Carey closed the door behind him, and sat.

The office, filled with the accumulations of the senior editor he had become, seemed a stranger's: the stack of half-edited manuscripts, the unreviewed contracts and pink slips of unreturned phone calls, all must belong to someone else . . .

He unfolded the article.

The *Times* had reported the facts of the accident and sketched the lives of Charles and Alicia Carey. But the *Daily News* had taken a different tack:

> While both parents were burned beyond recognition, six-year-old Peter was miraculously pitched from the car and then pulled by his uncle from within feet of its exploding wreckage. Greenwich police found the boy hysterical but virtually unharmed, clutching a stuffed toy elephant . . .

Peter Carey closed his eyes.

Strong arms pulled him from Bethesda Fountain; an oar slapped in water; a voice called after him as he ran toward the tunnel. He had watched the seals from Charles Carey's shoulders, smiled at his father's laughter as they named his new stuffed elephant . . .

"It's too dark down there for elephants, Daddy . . ."

The sliver of memory vanished.

Walking to his window, Carey stared out at the faceless glass of high-rises, dull smoke in winter. There was a knock;

his assistant warily poked her head inside. He turned, demanding, "Benevides?"

She shook her head. "Barth."

When Peter Carey entered the conference room and sat next to Ruth, she saw that the haunted look peculiar to his recent mornings had worsened, as if his fate had been settled years ago, or would be settled in some terrible future. It was strange, Ruth reflected; last evening, when she heard this same vagueness in her brother's voice, she first thought not of Peter but of her grandmother, face still young and eyes bright, babbling in the Russian she had not used since childhood. Yet Peter's stare at Barth had that same effect of vagrant memory, as if he were trying to fix this man in some other time or place.

Quickly, Ruth looked back to Barth.

His eyes, with their hard, myopic look of self-obsession, glared back at Peter. Between them, at the head of the conference table, Phillip Carey seemed almost fragile.

Peter said flatly, "You must be Clayton Barth."

"And you must be John Peter Carey." Barth's show of teeth vanished. "The second."

Peter's eyes glinted. "For these purposes, the *only*. Phillip suggests you wish to own my firm."

Barth's nod was curt. "Your uncle feels that Van Dreelen and Carey needs new management and money. I'm willing to provide them."

Peter looked down at his folded hands until Ruth felt tension in his very stillness, saw strain in the bodies of the two men watching him. This insight annoyed her: she had learned to read men's silences and gestures from a childhood fear of her father's moods . . .

"What are your terms?" Peter asked abruptly.

Ruth sensed Barth relaxing at this return to the familiar. "I have a proposal, summarizing our offer." He slid a typed document halfway across the table, so that Peter would have to reach for it. "As you can see by reading it, you are to receive eight million dollars and the position of my editor-in-chief." Barth's smile became a stretching of lips. "Go ahead—take it."

Slowly, Peter Carey reached for the letter.

As he read, Barth's peculiar agate eyes appeared never to blink. "Quite generous." Peter's voice seemed so flat that it held the barest trace of irony. "If I might ask, what has caused this kindness to descend on us?"

"The firm has a distinguished history." Beneath Barth's forced smile, his stare gauged Peter. "In fact, thirty years ago, John Carey was the subject of my senior thesis..."

Peter's eyes widened slightly. "Not John D. Rockefeller?" His voice was cool; only Ruth could feel his withheld anger. "What made you pick Grandfather?"

For the first time, Barth hesitated. "Black Jack Carey was a colorful man."

"I mean, you've no publishing background of which I'm aware."

Barth flushed. "I started in computers."

"Then I have to worry about that. My grandfather built this business by knowing it."

"And I've made billions in the most competitive business there is. There's simply no comparison..."

"I agree," Peter cut in. "I've watched conglomerates swallow publishers and then screw up trying to project profits on first novels. And in the end, more often than I'd like, they sell its wreckage to still another corporation." Much more softly, he finished, "I can't let that happen here."

"Don't *lecture* me," Barth shot back. "You sit here by inheritance..."

"By my father's death." Now Peter's tone was almost gentle. "Over twenty years ago, when he was barely thirty-nine."

"*Peter.*" Phillip's voice was strained. "This is simply morbid..."

Peter spoke through him. "By an accident," he told Barth, "I hold my father's place. That place is not for sale, not to secure the Carey fortune, and not"—his voice grew softer yet—"to salve whatever curious needs *you* might have inherited."

Barth bolted upright. "Damn you..."

"Peter, Peter." Phillip Carey thrust a placating hand between them, to cut Barth off. "You've vented your emotions here, I think unfairly to Mr. Barth. You were quite young when Charles died..."

Peter turned on him. "And now you want me to forget him?"

"That's insane."

"Is it?" Phillip half rose as Peter started toward him. "Then listen well: if you even *try* to sell my father's firm to this psychopath, I'll cut you off at the knees."

Phillip's mouth fell open; Peter stopped abruptly, as if bewildered by his own outburst. His shoulders sagged. Turning, he dropped Barth's letter in a wastebasket, and left.

CHAPTER 7

Peter Carey sat watching the lights on his telephone dance with calls he would not take. There were two quick raps on the door; Ruth Levy peered inside to ask, "Are you all right?"

She gave him a deep, black look: did she seem so vulnerable to others, he wondered, or just to him? "Sorry," he answered. "You shouldn't have had to sit through that."

Ruth gave a dismissing shrug. "Barth deserved it. As for Phillip . . ." Ruth's eyes darted to the photograph, and then she caught herself. "Phil shouldn't be playing with someone like Barth."

"He was right, though—I acted crazy." Carey had felt out of control, as if stumbling in the fountain before his father caught him. The pounding started in the back of his neck.

The woman's long black hair spilled in his father's lap . . .

"Want some aspirin?" Ruth was asking. "Tylenol, cocaine . . ."

Carey pointed to his desk drawer. "Thanks—I've got aspirin in here."

The clippings said that Phillip saved him . . .

"Sure." Ruth frowned as she reached for the door; Carey thought the effect was almost pretty.

"Ruthie."

She turned; her glance was startled, expectant: for an instant she seemed a young woman.

"About the meeting," Carey said. "I didn't want that to happen. I'm not sure why it did."

Ruth gave him a last pensive look. "I know," she said, and then closed the door behind her.

Phillip flung it open. "Are you receiving?" he asked. "Or is admission confined to Ruth?"

Peter slammed the drawer shut; oddly, Phillip remembered catching him with a flashlight under his blanket after bedtime, counting the baseball cards he had surprised him with at dinner. "I'm receiving anyone who knocks," Peter said.

Phillip forced a placating smile; the cold response turned his memory to anger. "Look, Peter, I thought we'd better have a talk."

The words sounded harsher than intended. Turning away, Peter answered woodenly, "My fault, Phil—I shouldn't have blown up."

There was little heart in the apology. For a moment, Phillip wondered if he should have shown more outrage: Peter was no more a fool than Charles, and even less predictable. "It *was* quite ugly, Peter—but not, perhaps, beyond redemption. A simple apology to Barth . . ."

Peter's eyes snapped up. "No."

"Peter, *look* at us." Phillip shook his head. "This place has turned three generations of Careys into pit dogs. You made that point today, better than I ever could."

"From which you conclude—what?"

Phillip shrugged. "What does it matter if the firm goes to Barth?"

Peter shook his head. "It does, though," he said with weary finality. "It matters to me."

Ungrateful bastard, Phillip thought, and then felt guilty. "I'll tell Barth," he answered crisply, and left.

Barth picked up his telephone.

Without preliminaries, Phillip Carey said, "There's nothing I can do with him."

Barth twisted with outrage and frustration. "You're *frightened* . . ."

"I just don't wish to push him—not when he's this volatile. Nothing's worth that."

"Not eight million dollars?"

"No." Phillip paused. "Not even that."

Instinctively, Barth probed what he could not yet define. "There *are* other means of persuasion."

There was silence. "Are you threatening me, Barth?"

Phillip's voice was tight; Barth's own grew soft. "There's a key to every man, Phillip. Where do you keep yours?"

Phillip Carey slammed down the telephone.

Eyes narrow, Barth listened to the dial tone.

Peter Carey cocked the telephone to his ear. "Yeah, George."

"First of all, don't do that again. If I'd wanted midnight calls, I'd have been a divorce lawyer."

Carey felt too tired to snap back. "I hear you. What did you find out?"

"Your parents died a few weeks before Barth even founded his business. In 1959 the man had no money or resources to speak of, and was nowhere near Connecticut." Benevides paused, asking pointedly, "I *did* catch your drift, didn't I?"

Carey stared at the wall. "Just forget it," he said tonelessly, and hung up.

Clayton Barth heard a strange voice speak his thoughts: "You wish to humble Peter Carey?"

Barth stared at the telephone. "Who *is* this?"

The voice droned on. "You mishandled him this morning, and now you will never own John Carey's firm."

For a crazy moment, Barth's fright became wonder: he could project his thoughts into the minds of others. "Look," he snapped, "I don't talk to strangers on the telephone. If you're selling information..."

"I'm selling you Van Dreelen and Carey, on terms to be negotiated." The voice turned steely. "The first is that you meet with me, alone."

"Peter was fine," Ruth finished, "and then he started talking about his father. That was when he turned on Phil."

Levy raised an eyebrow, watching her. "It seems to have made an impression."

Ruth looked down at her glass. "I thought Peter was going to kill him."

"And then?"

"It passed. Just like that."

Levy nodded. "He seems under terrible pressure—the more

I ask him to remember, the more fearful he becomes. No doubt it's coincidence, but whoever called could hardly have chosen a better time to make him explode at Barth, or a better way of doing it." He sighed. "I should have helped when he was young."

Ruth frowned. "From what little you've just told me, Phil didn't exactly give you an engraved invitation."

"No, he didn't." Levy felt a surge of anger; at whom, he was not sure. "I think now *you'd* better tell me about that photograph."

She gave him a quick, perceptive glance. "What are you up to, Bill? I thought you listened to patients, not spied on them."

"*You* sent him, Ruthie." Levy paused, defensive. "There's something he's not telling me, or perhaps doesn't realize himself. I have reason to think that you can help."

For a moment, Ruth looked trapped; Levy sensed that they had both been fencing. "Then pour me another glass of wine," she parried.

Levy hesitated. For a while, after Charles's death, she had drunk too much. Then, abruptly, she stopped drinking altogether: the next week she left the Village forever and moved to the airy walk-up on West 65th where they sat now, after dinner. As time passed, she permitted herself lovers and an occasional glass of wine; she had neither married, nor ever again been drunk. "Pour," she insisted.

Levy poured.

"All right, Bill." Glass in hand, Ruth leaned back, face troubled and reflective. "It's quite complex," she began reluctantly, "and it starts with a bad time for me, the weeks after Charles died. Phillip had hated him, of course—that old pissmire Black Jack Carey had kept them both dangling on a string too long. After the accident he should have been delighted." Ruth's smile was sour. "But Peter was the old man's final trick: Phillip found out that by saving him, he'd lost the firm. For months thereafter, he looked ghastly.

"More than that, he was *peculiar*. For days on end, he would stare into Charles's empty office: finally, in a frenzy, he ordered the office manager to get rid of everything that reminded him of Charles. There were rumors that Phil had even burnt all the pictures of him around . . ."

She stopped, sipped her wine, and looked down at the floor. "You know how I was then: drunk and crying, night after night. I hated Phil for how he acted, just as I hated him for inviting Charles to Greenwich. Thinking about it made me crazy: part of me didn't, couldn't, accept that Charles's death was an accident. I began to wonder, even, if somehow Phil had planned it." She looked up, half embarrassed. "I mean, he was dead sober on a dry road—*Charles Carey*, the best driver I had ever seen . . ."

Looking into his wineglass, Levy felt their years of silence. Tenderly, he said, "You never told me."

Ruth shook her head. "I couldn't, Bill—thinking it was hard enough. Finally, I had to tell myself that I hadn't come to terms with losing Charles. After all, Phillip *had* saved Peter—even if he didn't know what he was doing to himself." Quickly, she drank more wine, and her tone returned to normal. "In any case, there was Phil, stuck with a child who would grow up to succeed him. Their relationship never took. I'm sure Phil prayed for years that Peter would sell him his fifty-one percent; instead, Peter walked in at the ripe age of twenty and demanded a job. They weren't drafting people anymore, he told me later, and he'd gotten bored at Harvard. It was still later before I saw there was more to it . . ."

"When, exactly?"

She lit another cigarette, took a drag, and exhaled. "When I saw what he did with the picture."

Levy sensed her touchiness. Sniffing at the curl of smoke, he griped, "When will you quit smoking?"

"When you get tall." She gave him a sardonic look: he had first asked that question, and received that answer, her sophomore year in college.

Levy smiled. "Then tell me how you came to give it to him."

"I hadn't meant to, really—for a long time I avoided him. I had to go home the first time I saw his face." Lightly, she brushed her skirt with the tips of her fingers, as if cleaning imagined lint. "It was two days before I could come back to work. I was honestly thinking about changing jobs when he knocked on my door and asked if I could show him where his father's office had been. I could feel my stomach knot: he was giving me that peculiar sideways look Charles gave to people he was sizing up, and I began to feel he was playing some game—that perhaps he *knew* somehow, that maybe he'd adored his mother and was taunting me. But there was no way he *could* have known: Charles was so careful. Finally, I answered, 'Why are you asking me?'

"He just shrugged. 'Because I didn't want to ask Phillip.'

"Suddenly I felt sorry for him. I *knew* how Phillip still was about Charles—there was no portrait or even plaque there to say Charles Carey had ever existed—and I recalled the stories that Phil had burned every picture of Charles that he could find. Plus, I'd *seen* how he acted toward Peter . . ."

"How was that?"

"Creepy, yet craven—the full Freudian repertoire of ambivalent behavior. I've always thought if you gave Phil a Rorschach test he'd say everything looked like a crucifix shaped from two dildos."

Levy winced. "No wonder Peter searched you out."

"No, whatever it is, that's not it—he's edgy with me, too." She frowned. "I sometimes think the way he feels about Phillip frightens him."

Levy wondered why, in his more protective moments, he forgot Ruth's uncanny sensitivity. He examined her closely. "That's quite acute."

She looked away. "I guess I've come to understand him a little—not that he makes it easy. No, what finally drew me was that I didn't think he saw how Phil let him twist slowly in the wind. Instead of throwing Peter into the mailroom, as Black Jack Carey would have done, he waited four months and made him subsidiary-rights director. Phil's always been a clever bastard—in addition to handling book clubs, and sometimes even foreign and movie rights, the sub-rights person auctions paperback rights to everything we publish, sometimes for millions on a single book, and how we do frequently depends on how good he is. At its toughest, the job requires split-second timing and the guts of a cat burglar. It was years over Peter's head: Phillip wanted to humiliate him into quitting."

"Or," Levy suggested, "give him an opportunity."

Ruth jabbed her cigarette in the ashtray. "Yes, and Hitler was into birth control."

"It just seems to me," Levy offered mildly, "that Phillip's motives are open to interpretation. If he's that terrible, Ruthie, why did he keep you on?"

"Because I'm *good*." Ruth scowled at him. "Whatever else, Phil's not a fool. In any event, I took Peter to the office Charles had before he quit. The man who had it then was at lunch. Peter thanked me—and then went inside, closing the door behind him."

"And that's *his* office now?"

Ruth nodded. "One day he just quietly moved in—I suppose it touched me. I began thinking more about what he was up against . . ." Once more, she hesitated.

"Is that all?" Levy asked quietly.

"No, not all." Ruth reached for the pack of cigarettes, tapping it in the palm of her hand. "I began thinking about the last night I'd spent with Charles."

Oh God, Ruthie, Levy thought. But he said nothing.

"Charles had just . . ." Ruth's eyes closed. "We'd had a rather serious talk. We made love—for the last time, as it turned out—and then I asked him about Peter." She opened her eyes, giving the barest hint of a smile, still looking away. "Until that night I could never really bring myself to ask him, and suddenly it was very important that I know how Peter looked—

"I felt Charles's arms tighten around me. 'Like me,' he said, very softly in the dark. 'I look at Peter, and see myself again. But it's a different thing from vanity. What I'm feeling then is that he's a new start, my chance to change those things that made the Careys what we are. There's such sweetness in him—'

"*And in you,* I remember thinking. *Though you do your best to hide it.* But then Charles got dressed and left, and I never saw him again." Her face twisted. "I suppose I came to feel that if anyone there was to be Peter's friend, it should be me. That's when I took Charles's picture from the drawer.

"I'd taken it at the end of the Wharton Street pier on an early summer evening, with a new camera I was learning to use. You know how bad I am at pictures, and this one came out with no detail in the background—I suppose the light was too dim.

"What I got was Charles's face. He'd just reminded me to push the button, and began laughing because I couldn't find it. Then I did, and by total accident captured that smile I loved so much, the one which went with a tilt of the head, so that for a second or two his face looked utterly, carelessly happy, and I could see the boy he had been. It was so much Charles that I remembered the old superstition that a photograph could steal your soul . . .

"But that was the point. I remembered Charles as clearly as that picture. Peter needed it more than I.

"I decided to give it to him.

"After all, there was no way of telling where the picture had been taken, or by whom. So I knocked on his door and told him that I'd found it in his father's office shortly after he died, and then forgotten it, and now that his coming had reminded me of Charles, I thought it should be his.

"For a moment he just looked at me. Then, without saying anything, he stepped from behind his desk and took the picture from my hands. He stared down into his father's face as I watched the recognition growing in his eyes. When he finally looked back up at me I knew that he'd seen exactly what I did, that—except for coloring—he and Charles were identical. I almost shivered—I was that sure he was thinking the second thing that struck me when he'd looked up again: that Phillip saw it, too.

"But all he did was smile faintly, and then murmur, 'Thank you, Ruthie, very much.' It was the first time he'd called me anything at all.

"I left with nothing more being said.

"For a long time I didn't see the picture, and I guessed perhaps it was too painful for him to live with. I really had no idea what he'd do with it until the first big clash with Phillip, when he was supposed to sell paperback rights to *The End of the Tunnel*.

"That was a year or so after Phil had put him in the subrights job. I've never seen anyone work harder to learn a business—some days he looked so tired that I began to wonder about insomnia, some reason he missed sleeping through the night. He never even took time to decorate Charles's office—it was bare as a transient's room, as though he didn't expect to last. I'm sure Phillip made the connection—he kept taunting Peter about his office: 'Looks like a handball court, Prince Charming. You're a menace to our property values.' I'm sure it was Phil's slimy way of suggesting that Peter sell him his interest, on the way to some line of work for which he was more suited. But Peter gave no sign that he even heard him.

"Fortunately, Peter got through his first year without embarrassing himself. And then he passed over one hundred thousand dollars for *The End of the Tunnel*, and gave Phil a chance to force him out.

"*Tunnel* was Larry Santini's first novel. Santini was a Vietnam veteran who'd been wounded during the Tet offensive, and decided to title his novel after the 'light at the end of the tunnel' Westmoreland used to promise them. But Santini's tunnel was the progressive brutalization of a company of soldiers, ending in their destruction of an entire village and everyone who lived there. It was so harrowing that when the manuscript came in I wondered whether anyone else could stand to read it.

"Phillip didn't think the book would sell, and didn't like it either—he and Charles always used to hassle about his Fascist politics. What made this book even tougher was that Santini's agent wanted thirty-five thousand—pretty steep for a first novel—and at that price our money people were siding with Phil.

"I was sponsoring editor: I *wanted* this book, and it was my job at the board meeting to try and persuade Phillip, our treasurer, and the marketing people to pay that kind of money. I argued that we *should* publish *Tunnel*, problems or no, and then bust our asses to put it across.

"Only Peter agreed with me.

"He hadn't given me a clue he'd even read the copy I'd sent him until he spoke up and said people were *ready* for a Vietnam book if it was written by a veteran. 'It's nearly the *bicentennial*, Peter,' Phillip answered in his smoothest voice. 'Not even *Charles* would have published this thing.'

"Peter turned white: it's strange, sometimes that's the only way you can tell he's angry—just like Charles. But all he said was, 'Is your objection politics, or money?'

"I could see Phil mentally picking the safer ground. 'Money . . .'

"'If that's all,' Peter interrupted, 'let me talk to some paperback people and see what interest there is in buying rights. I can let you know by the next meeting.'

"Phillip looked amused, almost indulgent. 'Fine,' he said, and went on to the next topic, as if *Tunnel* were dead.

"Peter sprang his first surprise at the next meeting. He'd gone to Royal Books and returned with a backup offer of one hundred thousand dollars, assuming we committed thirty thousand for advertising. So Phil had to choke back his objections. He bargained Santini's agent down to thirty-two thousand, and bought the manuscript.

"The rule is to sell paperback rights to a first novel before it's even published, when bad reviews or sales may keep you from selling rights at all. We'd only bought *Tunnel* because the hundred thousand Peter'd lined up in advance was an amazingly good deal for both us and Santini—all Peter had to do was close the deal.

"He never did.

"When Phillip found out he stalked into Peter's office absolutely livid, and interrupted a conference we were having. 'Don't you understand this job at all?' he asked.

"Peter looked at him. 'I understand that you gave it to me. I'd hoped it was because you admired my talent.'

"'It was a *kindness*, Peter.'

"Peter just smiled. 'Then I certainly hope it wasn't also a mistake.'

"I couldn't believe it, and neither could Phil. He ordered Peter to call Royal while he stood there, just to make sure he got it right. Peter pushed that morning's copy of *Publishers Weekly* across the desk. Inside was the first advance review of *The End of the Tunnel*, calling it 'a first novel of astonishing power and maturity.'

"Phillip pointed at the telephone. 'Sell it.'

"Peter shook his head. 'There'll be more reviews like this. I'm going to collect them and auction *Tunnel* to the highest bidder.'

"Phillip waited until the next pub board meeting to recite, in front of everyone, Peter's handling of *Tunnel* in a way that made him sound pitifully inept.

"We were all sitting around John Carey's long mahogany conference table—Phil, the marketing director, the treasurer, three male editors, and me. Phil sat at the head, in Black Jack's leather chair, the three editors and our marketing and finance guys clustered around him, with me along the side.

"Peter faced Phillip from the other end of the conference table.

"'Royal just came back with one-fifty,' he told Phillip. 'I turned it down.'

"Phillip looked almost too amazed. 'On what basis?' he demanded. 'You're acting as if it were your *own* money at risk, not the firm's.'

"'Perhaps'—Peter faced him directly—'I have trouble seeing the difference.'

"The rest of us fell dead silent: it was the first time Peter had mentioned the old man's will, even by inference. Phillip folded his hands. 'I wonder if you'd feel quite so strongly, Peter, if your future rested on getting more for *The End of the Tunnel* than you've just rejected.'

"Peter flushed: Phillip was daring him in front of us to stake his future on Larry Santini's. Without thinking, I said, 'I'm sure that's unfair to Peter . . .'

"'It's perfectly fair,' Peter cut in. He turned to Phillip. 'We'll leave it this way: if I sell paperback rights to *Tunnel* for less than one hundred thousand dollars, I'll leave.' He smiled briefly. 'It wouldn't take much time to clear out my office, as you've suggested. All I ask is authority to sell this book as I see fit.'

"'Very well.' Phillip shrugged: Peter had walked right into his maw, smiling.

"I collared him as soon as we left the conference room and asked why he was so hellbent on reminding me of a lemming. He just laughed. 'I had to do *something* to distract Phillip. Someday it'll hit him that he's got nine more years to fire you.'

"His answer was so much like Charles, I felt twisted up inside. 'Or a lifetime,' I managed.

"He reached out to touch my shoulder, saying softly, 'I

appreciate your help.' There was still a trace of laughter in his voice. 'You know, my grandfather never told me it would be this hard. I guess he was waiting till I could read.'

"He turned and went back to his office.

"The next day he turned down the one-fifty for the second time.

"Peter's phone just stopped ringing—no one else wanted to pay that much. I was certain that he'd cut his own throat: all he could do was send the advance notices on *Tunnel* to an old professor of his who reviewed books for the *Times*, and try to interest *People* in profiling Santini.

"On the date of publication there was no *Times* review, and no article. Royal cut their offer back to one hundred thousand—Peter's last chance to win his bet.

"Peter turned it down.

"Phillip began to stop by Peter's office, very chatty, and ask how things were going. How Peter felt I couldn't even bring myself to ask." Ruth paused, smiling thinly. "I shouldn't have worried.

"Three weeks after publication the lead review in the Sunday *Times* was of *The End of the Tunnel*, by Peter's ex-professor. He called it things like 'a literary event of singular importance,' and 'the most profound war novel since *The Naked and the Dead.*' Even by the standards of literary events—in the seventies we'd begun having two or so a month—this became pretty eventful. *Newsweek* called Santini 'one of the most remarkable young writers we now have,' and strong reviews began appearing in cities like Boston and Chicago. Then *People* ran five pages on Santini...

"Peter called the Book-of-the-Month Club and gave them one week to reconsider. And then he called Royal, as he was obligated to do before announcing any auction, and received an offer of two hundred thousand.

"When Peter turned it down I was *certain* he was crazy. Phil looked *so* relieved...

"Then the Book-of-the-Month Club announced that it had chosen *Tunnel* as a featured alternate, and Peter's telephone started ringing with paperback offers.

"He stalled them for one more week to watch the *Times* best-seller list. The next week *Tunnel* appeared as number nine.

Peter sent letters to the major paperback publishers, announcing that *Tunnel* would be auctioned to the highest bidder, in two weeks.

"He set the minimum bid at half a million dollars—much too high, I thought.

"The next day *Tunnel* climbed to number seven.

"The Monday of the auction Peter came to his office with a bag lunch and a sack of oranges, to find *Tunnel* at number five. By the end of the day he was in shirtsleeves, looking exhausted.

"He'd gotten six bids over half a million.

"Tuesday morning he called the last five bidders from bottom to runner-up to tell them that the first day's high was six hundred and fifty thousand. By four o'clock only three were left: the lowest at eight-fifty, the next at eight-seventy-five and the high bid at nine hundred thousand. It *sounds* insane, but these things take on a dynamic of their own.

"Wednesday morning's high bid was nine hundred fifty thousand. 'For a million,' Peter told the others, 'you'll get more than fifty thousand dollars' worth of publicity.'

"At three-thirty Peter sold *The End of the Tunnel* to Seahawk, for one million dollars—a record sale for paperback rights to a first novel.

"Then Peter ordered two bottles of chilled champagne and invited Phillip down to celebrate.

"I saw Phillip coming down the hall toward Peter's office. His face was a study: pleased in spite of himself about the money, desolate that Peter would stay, relieved that he had decided to forget their quarrel. Then he turned through Peter's door and found Peter sitting there, the champagne already poured, grinning up at him with that slight tilt of the head—exactly like my photograph of Charles, hanging right behind him on the wall.

"Phillip stared past Peter's head at the picture of his brother, speechless. 'I thought it was time to decorate,' Peter explained blandly. He pushed a glass across the table, raising his own, and said, 'To my father.'

"Even as he drank, Phillip's eyes never left the picture." Ruth smiled without mirth. "It was sheer poetry—if Black Jack Carey had been a poet. Peter hadn't just humbled Phil—

he'd taken Charles's place. And I knew then that he'd planned that all along."

The window behind her was glazed with frost. She lit a cigarette, and looked expectantly at her brother, exhausted by her narrative. But Levy could say nothing: something in the story's end had made him close to sick.

Finally, it was Ruth who broached it. "Peter frightened me, Bill—then, and now again, today." Her voice fell. "Do you understand why?"

Their eyes met. "Yes," he answered softly. "You're afraid that, subconsciously, Peter Carey harbors the same suspicion of Phillip that you say you've abandoned."

Slowly, Ruth Levy closed her eyes, and nodded.

"But you've *never* abandoned it, Ruthie, have you? And that's why you sent Peter Carey on to me." When she did not contradict him, Levy asked her gently, "Have you ever said these things to Peter?"

"That I can't stop wondering if Phillip killed his father?" Her eyes snapped open. "How could I?"

There was silence; thinking of Phillip, Levy felt Ruth's burden pass between them, merging with his own. "Then *I* shall," he finally murmured. "In my way."

Noelle Ciano bent over her suitcase, wedging in a pair of boots. "Why El Salvador?" Carey asked. "It's the worst possible timing—a month before elections, with the war heating up."

"They've sent me places before, Peter." Noelle kept on packing. "Anyhow, it'll give us both a chance to think."

The thought of her leaving shook him. He fidgeted on the edge of her bed. "How long will you be gone, then?"

"Three weeks or so." She tossed a quick smile over her shoulder. "Got to be back in time to shoot Doug Sutcliffe. Hand me that workshirt, will you?"

Carey picked up the shirt folded next to him and stood with it. "I'll miss you, you know."

Taking the shirt, she stopped for a moment, holding it between them. "Enough to sleep over?"

"I don't know, Ciano. The dreams . . ." Carey looked away. "I haven't been much good for you, lately."

"No sweat." She shrugged. "Anyhow, I can sleep when I get to San Salvador. They say it's great."

"Yeah—air conditioned."

"Well, think about it." She turned to the suitcase; in that moment, Carey knew that she would not return.

"Noelle?"

She glanced back, a pair of jeans in her hand. "Uh-huh?"

"Come here. Please."

Her eyes seemed to widen. Then she turned, one hand on her hip, casually pointing at the half-filled suitcase. "Who's going to pack this for me?"

"I will. Later."

Her mouth curved slightly upward. "Really?"

"Really."

"Deal," she said, moving toward him. Gratefully, he reached for her . . .

Her skin felt warm.

Peter Carey felt Noelle Ciano's bare shoulders grazing his: in the twilight drift between sleep and waking, he hung suspended. Once more, Levy asked him: "Tell me, Peter, when did you first have the dream . . ."

Carey's eyes opened, closed, and then he felt himself drawn, helpless, into the vortex of sleep . . .

"Can I see a picture of Daddy?"

Uncle Phillip glanced up from the storybook. "A picture, Peter?"

"Yes." Timidly, the child Peter explained, "It's getting harder for me to see him now."

Uncle Phillip looked at him strangely. "Perhaps later. Don't you want to hear about Rumplestiltskin?"

"No." Peter's mood turned stubborn. "I want to see my Daddy."

His uncle shifted on the bed. "You can't, Prince Charming."

"Why not?"

"Because we don't have pictures." Uncle Phillip's voice sounded small to him. "It was for you, Peter—really. I thought keeping them would be too hard."

"Then where did you put Dewey."

"He was lost, Peter." His uncle reached out. *"In the accident..."*

Peter's mouth quivered. *"Leave me alone."*

Uncle Phillip hesitated, hand frozen in midair, staring at him. Then, touching Peter's shoulder, he left the room. Peter kept himself from crying until he heard the door, closing him inside.

He cried himself to sleep; suddenly, in the deep black of the night, his father came for him. They were in the tunnel...

Peter Carey awakened screaming.

Clayton Barth waited in the darkness.

"No one else must see me," the voice had said. "Leave your office dark, and the door unlocked. I'll find you there..."

Slowly, the door opened.

In the dimness, Barth saw the frail figure of a man even smaller than himself. Silently, the figure slipped inside.

Barth switched on his laser lamp and aimed it toward the room. Stabbing the darkness, its light caught an arm, then a bow tie.

The figure froze. Above the tie, Barth saw the death's-head of a man.

"Who are you?" he demanded.

The death's-head smiled. "My name," its voice said softly, "is John Joseph Englehardt."

The two men watched each other.

Slowly, Barth waved him forward. "What is it you want?"

Even in the semidark, Englehardt saw that Barth thought himself much larger than he was: the gesture had the sweep of a six-footer's, and he swayed with an imagined bulk. But he could not find this amusing: megalomaniacs too often became what they imagined, and he had too much at stake. Respectfully, he answered, "I've come to give you John Carey's firm."

"How can you?"

"May I sit?"

The squat form stared at him. Then, with a silent motion of authority, Barth waved him to his desk.

"Thank you," Englehardt said politely.

Slipping into a chair, he saw that the frog-eyes seemed

unnaturally white. "You'd better start explaining," Barth snapped. "How do you know what I want? How can *you* give me what I want?"

Englehardt kept his tone self-deprecating. "You're a man of trade, Mr. Barth. Trade secrets are what we technicians live by. Let us say that I'm somewhat of an expert on the Careys."

Barth frowned his disbelief. "Based on what?"

"It began thirty years ago, when I was sitting as close to John Peter Carey as I am to you now."

"John Carey?" Abruptly, involuntarily, Barth's voice lost its edge; his next question sounded close to childlike.

"What was he like? You see, I never actually met him."

Englehardt sat back, astonished.

His mental portrait of Barth's motives shattered like a kaleidoscopic image; the new mosaic that began forming was awesome in its pathology. Tentatively, he ventured, "Quite impressive, I'm afraid."

"How did you come to meet him?"

"I was doing security work for HUAC. We had a problem with the authors he was publishing. I was forced to call on the Careys."

"Then you also met his sons?"

Beneath the question, Englehardt heard a strange anxiety. "Yes," he replied with more assurance, "but the sons were never worthy of him." He paused. "Especially Charles . . ."

A dreamy, answering softness flickered through Barth's eyes.

The last piece of the mosaic fell abruptly into place.

Swiftly, Englehardt saw what he must do.

He could reveal to Barth that John Carey had helped finance his education. But one man could also manipulate another by withholding knowledge; he would not risk slaking the thirst for a connection to John Carey through which he could make Barth his own. "Let me explain," he broke in softly, "how I can help you own John Carey's firm . . ."

"Peter Carey's the one who's blocking me." With frightening speed, Barth became himself again. "What you may once have learned about his family is worthless to me."

Englehardt's smile was ironic. "Even if you believe that, the techniques I used for learning it are not. Without getting into detail, my background is intelligence—the CIA, to be precise. There are *ways*—costly, but achievable—and if we reach an agreement, I'll begin by having young Peter watched. After a time, I'll know so much about him that he'll no longer be a problem: given sufficient information, the resourceful operative can destroy anyone, mentally or physically. Destroying Peter Carey should be child's play." Softly, for his own amusement, he quoted Charles Carey: "'All you have to do, is ask.'"

"Why should I trust a man I don't know?"

Englehardt shrugged. "You shouldn't—until I bring results."

Barth considered this. "At what price?"

"Expenses." Englehardt smiled. "Expenses, and a position. I wish to be chief of security for Barth Industries."

Barth's voice resumed its hostile edge. "There *is* no such position . . ."

"There should be. Yours is a multinational corporation: its needs in political intelligence, personnel protection and, shall we say, extra-legal advancement of its interests, are legion. You're moving into oil, I believe?"

"Let's start more humbly," Barth cut in. "You claim you should watch Peter for me. Before I let you do that—before I even consider your proposal—I need something more than boasting to establish your credentials."

Englehardt adopted a reflective pose; almost teasingly, he touched one finger to his lips. "Would you settle for Phillip Carey?"

"Phillip?" Barth could not hide his amazement. "He can't be pried loose from Peter."

"Phillip Carey is as good as yours."

He could almost see the thoughts running in swift succession through Barth's mind: that Phillip refused eight million dollars, that Phillip was afraid . . .

"And if I wish it," he coolly interrupted, "Phillip will sell you Peter's firm. My question is, Mr. Barth: do you still want it?"

Barth stared at him. Slowly, almost involuntarily, he nodded.

Englehardt rose to leave. "Then you shall have it," he concluded. Suddenly Barth's voice stopped him.

"How?"

Turning, Englehardt looked down at the squat, suspicious figure. But it was another man he saw, slender and alone, waiting in the darkness.

"Phillip Carey," he said softly, "is my closest friend."

"Daddy . . ."

Noelle pulled Peter close. "It's all right, Peter—it's okay." She crooned gently over his shoulder, still drowsy. "That was twenty years ago, and it's only me here with you. Nothing's going to happen."

She felt him shudder.

CHAPTER 8

"It was half memory," Carey mused from the couch, "and half dream. I'm not sure which."

He could sense Levy turning this over in his mind. "But afterwards you went into the nightmare, then awoke?"

"Except that there's something else." Carey exhaled. "Yesterday I went to the library and read about my parents' death, trying to remember."

"And did you?"

"It's too dark down there for elephants, Daddy..."

"No—nothing about the accident. But the *Daily News* said I was found still holding a toy elephant." Carey's voice was low. "If what I dreamed last night really happened, why would Phillip tell me that Dewey had been lost?"

There was silence. "Let's put this in perspective," Levy answered carefully. "After that first nightmare, Peter, what was your relationship to Phillip?"

Carey closed his eyes; Phillip had dark hair then...

"Phil hired a nurse—I think we spent less time together. I remember him staring at me."

"And the dreams?"

"They just kept on."

"Did Phillip take you to a psychiatrist?"

"It's nice here, Prince Charming. Not so many memories..."

"No—he sent me to a boarding school in Boston, when I was eight. I hated it—word got around, and they'd laugh because I'd start crying in my sleep. Finally, I sneaked to a telephone booth and called Phil to take me home. He didn't, but after that he paid for me to sleep alone. The next year I

200

changed schools; Phillip told them I had insomnia, and so no one heard me screaming."

"How did you feel?"

"Alone." Carey could still feel Noelle's face against his neck. "After a while, you get used to that, like anything else."

"Did Phillip visit?"

"Not often. Sometimes he'd call, and I'd see him on vacations. As I got older he'd send money so I could go on trips, so mainly it was at Christmas."

It was late. Phillip had not stayed up to greet him. Retrieving his key from the milk-chute, Peter climbed the dark stairway to his room . . .

"How was that?"

"Awkward." Carey shrugged. "Sad, I suppose."

"Charles . . ." Quickly, Levy caught himself. "Your father—you still missed him?"

"I really couldn't remember much. But the dreams of him kept coming, more so when I went to college. It's funny; I've never really told anyone, but it was the nightmare that brought me back to New York. I'd been thinking about law school—just scrapping the whole publishing thing. Phil had offered to buy me out. My senior year, I'd come back from a weekend in Vermont, and a letter of acceptance from Harvard Law was waiting in my mailbox." Carey watched the dangling spider. "I sat on my bed, reading the letter. All at once I felt sick. What I saw was not the letter but my grandfather, a split second before the stroke, turning back and calling out to me . . ."

"Yes?"

Carey shifted. "Only it wasn't *me* he was calling."

"I understand."

"I tried to sleep." Carey's throat felt dry. "That night I had the dream again—my father's face burning, the faceless man laughing in the tunnel. I got out of bed, packed my stuff in the middle of the night, and drove to Manhattan."

"To Van Dreelen and Carey?"

"Yes." Carey's voice was low. "I hadn't been there since my father . . ."

"Since he *what*, Peter?"

"Had the accident." Carey paused. "When I asked Phillip for a job he wouldn't even look at me."

He twisted on the couch. Softly, Levy asked, "Looking back now, Peter, why did you return? Because you hated him?"

"My father hated him." Carey felt a surge of panic. "I didn't say *I*..."

"Or was it because he'd stolen Dewey?"

"I'm not that infantile," Carey snapped, and then his hour was up.

"I'd better run," Noelle told Carey.

They stood in a crowded corridor at Kennedy International; passengers jostled them, rushing for afternoon flights. He did not wish to let her go.

"It's best, Peter. Really."

Helpless, he murmured, "Be careful."

Her eyes had fixed on something past his shoulder.

"What is it?"

Noelle kept staring; Carey grasped her wrists. "Dammit, what's wrong?"

She looked at his hands. "That night in SoHo," she said evenly, "there was a man who brushed against our table, with strange eyes and a kind of hanging underlip. For just a second, I thought I saw him."

Carey wheeled; a shoulder dipped.

"Peter—there's no time."

He turned back. "Noelle..."

"I'll miss the plane." Her lips brushed his. "See you in three weeks." She turned, camera slung over one hip, and was gone.

Carey watched her go.

Hunched in a line of Rio-bound passengers, Martin watched with him.

Once more, he thought, the woman might have seen him. He felt her on his skin...

In his hand, in the camera shaped like a ballpoint pen, was the first picture he had taken of her.

He would start to keep an album.

But there was much to do before night fell. The tapes would still be spinning, and the small man would be needing them.

Slipping from the line, Martin slid the ballpoint into his pocket.

* * *

In a barren SoHo loft, John Joseph Englehardt waited.

He steeled himself: this moment, so crucial and so carefully planned, was too like that other moment, summoned from his past.

As subtly as Iago, he turned Barth's needs into fear of Peter Carey, concealing his own: with the Careys as his entrée, he might now control a multinational corporation.

The "Asian Gallery" two floors beneath him would be his cover, justifying a collection of the Chinese statuary that had first interested him at Yale, while studying the more Byzantine perplexities of the Manchu dynasty. The new treasures on the second floor, once secured from Barth, would be even more inscrutable: computers programmed so that the most sophisticated intruder could retrieve only the lists of inventory and available art, none bearing his true name, designed to conceal the secrets he would begin burying within. As for the third floor where he now sat, living bare of clues to his identity, SoHo was again the perfect choice. Were he to succeed, the barren sweep of warehouse floor—the cot, cardboard wardrobe and battered desk, the primitive bathroom in one corner—would be replaced by the loft of his imagination. In the middle he would place a platform and a walnut desk; the computer terminal hidden within would become his reference book of other people's secrets, an encyclopedia to be riffled through with care. All that he required was the resources of Barth Industries.

He might still have it, depending on Peter Carey: as he had learned so many years before, information was power. But the danger lurking in this equation had never struck him with more force than now; the *effect* of any specific piece of information could be altered by the random chemistry of human beings, acting one upon the other in a chain of fate and passion.

After so many years, fate made Charles Carey's son the last link in his chain.

For two months after the death of Charles Carey, Englehardt had wished the child Peter dead.

But Phillip Carey had saved his body; it was his memory that died.

For two months longer, Englehardt listened, to make certain. Then, without advising his superiors, he flew in secret to New York.

It was his final meeting with Phillip Carey.

The two men faced each other. "You're on top now," he told Phillip softly. "You can do anything you wish."

Slumped in his chair, Phillip Carey looked as lifeless as the marionette he had become. "On top?"

Englehardt reached out to touch his shoulder, and then stopped himself. "You're right, Phillip. There *is* Peter."

"You wouldn't . . ."

Englehardt laughed aloud. "*I* wouldn't?"

Phillip turned from his smile. "Oh, my God . . ."

"It would be a kindness for you to help him forget. A kindness," Englehardt repeated softly, "worthy of the uncle who saved his life."

Phillip stared up at him with misery and loathing. "And how much kindness do *you* require?"

Englehardt was stung by the harshness of his tone. "You're to abandon Charles's leftish writers," he answered crisply, "so that the books *I* tell you to publish—treatises on defense spending or Soviet expansion—confirm your natural preference. As for book assignments to serve as cover for our agents abroad, they will be spaced so as to avoid suspicion. In return, your new-won eminence will be exactly as you wished it, and the surveillance of your personal life will cease. Your orders will be strictly verbal." Englehardt's tone slid through hurt to irony. "You won't even have to look at me, Phillip. And if your luck holds, young Peter won't upset our new arrangement, at least until he's thirty."

Phillip looked away. "And if he does?"

"That would be unfortunate." Almost fondly, Englehardt smiled down at Phillip Carey. "You see, I own you now."

His superiors had been gratified beyond his best imagining.

Queried, he hid the secret of his power. "Phillip Carey," he had answered, "is my closest friend."

Friendless no more, he rose quickly.

He no longer felt a stray, the second son of an unloving father, but a professional. His ability to connect information in a seamless web of human motive now marked him as an instinctive intelligence analyst; his resolve to apply pure reason to his ends spurred him to plot the assassination of a nettlesome Congolese politician, secretly paid by the Soviets, with a precision that won fervent admiration. When the politician was later found stuffed in a meat locker on the outskirts of Léopoldville, Englehardt once more felt only satisfaction that *his* secrets were not known. He had purged his mind of both the acquired shackles of religion and man's instinctive fear of murder: stripped of superstition and marbled with secrets, his brain, honed on Phillip Carey, had at last brought him to power.

Phillip, and then Martin, new symbol of his willingness to kill.

They had met in 1962: for the second and last time in his life, Englehardt had the eerie sense of facing another aspect of himself.

It had been an accident; Martin's case officer caught influenza, and Englehardt was assigned to debrief this unliked field agent after a routine trip to Athens. Knowing Martin headed for the dustbin, Englehardt awaited him with mild curiosity; despite superior intelligence, Martin caused innate revulsion in those above him.

"Are you Englehardt?"

Glancing up, Englehardt recoiled inwardly: almost at once he knew that he reacted, not to the domed forehead, the splayed nose, or the grotesquely protruding underlip—although, shoved together in some brutal joke of nature, they would forever set this man apart—but to the eyes.

From the first time he had seen Phillip Carey, Englehardt knew that he could read the character of others in their eyes. In Martin's—perceptive and moistly bright—he saw the twisted sensitivity of one who spent too much time alone.

"Please sit down," he said easily. "I'd like to hear the facts, and your impressions."

For the next two hours, Englehardt listened and asked questions: underlying the man's slurred voice, he recognized Martin's molten need to touch those whom, before, he had only watched. A friend might win his unending gratitude.

"You've done well," he ventured.

Above his eerie smile, Martin's eyes met Englehardt's.

Englehardt felt a stab of fear: this ugly man had read his thoughts. But no measure of perception would ever change his needs. "Yes," he finished softly, "I see the things of which you're capable."

"Please." Martin's voice bore the hush of the confessional. "I need more freedom."

Englehardt gave it to him.

In quick succession, Martin killed three Belgian double agents; the men simply disappeared.

Englehardt found a new assignment, then a better one: two more men died. Succeeding, Martin added to his luster. Englehardt alone had seen his gifts.

Only later did he guess about the women.

It was in Germany that Englehardt first saw the pattern. Three women had been stalked and killed at random; though naked and abused, none was raped; police in Berlin, Munich and Frankfurt were at a loss. Englehardt did not point out to them that each woman died while Martin was in their city, that the work was too professional, that the victims were prostitutes, whom an ugly man could reach.

Given that they would not forget him, Englehardt reflected, it was well that they were dead.

When Martin returned to Washington, photos of three women were lying on his bed.

Their understanding was complete.

Martin would be cautious, for Englehardt had grown to need him.

No target would ever know his name, or look into his face.

As Martin grew still wiser and more polished, Englehardt grew in craft. They mastered the intricacies of surveillance, manipulating their targets until each target's death appeared an outgrowth of their lives. Teaching Martin the virtue of contingency planning to assure their own security, Englehardt learned with him the arcane art of converting murder into suicide: wherever possible, their work would leave no trace.

In this, they were assisted by Englehardt's passion for analysis.

Piece by piece, he would reconstruct his victim's inner life from every fact that Martin stole, until he saw the death suitable for each. If his understanding were exact enough, his subject might spare them any violence: an eminent British leftist, recoiling from a weakness for small children which particularly disgusted Martin, shot himself without knowing who had mailed him the pictures. At other times, he would drop clues to his victim's self-destruction stolen from a lover or psychiatrist: Martin, holding the gun so close that the entry wound seemed self-inflicted, would murder and then vanish, leaving no sign of struggle, nothing but a corpse, weary of life, which could not point to Englehardt had it risen from the dead.

Now and then, a woman died: this, too, was their unspoken secret.

But there remained one secret Martin did not share, and that was Phillip Carey.

In the middle of the night, Englehardt felt his absence like an amputated limb.

They never saw each other.

On a secure line, Englehardt would call him: briskly, he issued new instructions, then asked about Peter's memory.

Sometimes, when he could not help it, he asked how Phillip was.

He covered this with irony: he no longer *knew*, he would softly add, because he had kept his word.

For fourteen years, this bargain held: their secrecy had been so thorough that in 1974, when a wave of similar revelations forced the CIA to abandon its use of Van Dreelen & Carey, the operation never surfaced. On the telephone, he had said goodbye to Phillip Carey.

By then, John Joseph Englehardt was a powerful man, indeed.

Six years later, the last of the pitiful parade of post-Watergate CIA directors reviewed this proud career: deeming Englehardt a murderer beyond control, the director requested his retirement.

Staring into the director's blunt and stupid face, Englehardt felt a terrible panic: through the agency, and Martin, he had touched the postwar world with his mind. Now an amateur was ending this quarter century of power...

He went quickly to find Martin, and discovered that they had transferred him to Zurich.

Sequestered in his town house, Englehardt fought back a racking illness—blue and terrible as the withdrawal from a drug—and calculated his alternatives. One was to blackmail the director: he knew too much that outsiders should not know. But this would buy him only the clean desk and empty title forced on pariahs, serving out their time like the living dead. Outside, his secrets might again buy power: his only hope was to offer the keenness of his mind to those who held it.

Abruptly, he thought of Clayton Barth.

He knew Barth through his fetish for hiring ex-operatives like Martin, disaffected by the growing strictures on their work. This marked Barth as susceptible: the more his tentacles stretched worldwide, the more he could be used to gather intelligence. In an age of terrorism, industrial espionage and foreign bribery, a man like Barth, more ruthless than his government, might well come to depend on him. And then, Englehardt argued to himself, he might use the resources of Barth Industries to make the agency *his* client...

But he could not come to Barth as a mere supplicant: carefully, he must gauge his wants.

Stalking Barth in his mind, he bought drinks for former colleagues, fishing awkwardly for their gossip about Barth Industries while he tried to build a record, visiting other multinationals to suggest that his new services would be essential to their power.

But, like his superiors long before them, he found they did not know this.

From his home in Georgetown, he performed intelligence analyses for oil companies frightened of Qaddafy and surveillance sweeps for computer firms suspecting wiretaps, humiliated by the menial nature of his work and the crass successes of less gifted colleagues, who ran guns to Libya or traded secrets for the trinkets of notoriety. With chilling irony he saw that the rising desperation of his middle age was again that of his youth: he could not sell himself, and had no secrets he would sell.

Then, lunching with a former colleague at the Sans Souci, he learned of Clayton Barth's obsession with Van Dreelen & Carey.

"One two-bit publisher," the man told him in bewilderment, "and the boss turns into Captain Ahab."

A window opened in Englehardt's mind.

Thirty years before, John Carey had rasped at the arrogant Charles: "The only person Clayton Barth had the power to destroy was his own son."

Barth's father had blown his brains out with a revolver: Englehardt knew this from a tape.

He said none of this to the man across the table.

His final chance was Clayton Barth, the son.

But so much depended on Peter Carey, too hauntingly like his father . . .

This, above all, compelled him to reach out for Martin.

He knew the risk involved: as with Barth, he could control the ugly man only through his needs. But, six months after dismissing Englehardt, the agency fired Martin, fearing that no one else could hold those needs in check. Now, no one else could give this man what Englehardt might offer . . .

When at last he called Martin, there was a moment of strained silence: Englehardt sensed the ugly man was weeping. When he finally answered, it was with a muffled, "Thank you," and then Martin hung up.

The next day, he appeared at Englehardt's door.

Englehardt frowned: Martin had never visited his home. He drove him to the Ellipse. Near the Jefferson Memorial, hunched against the chill fall air, he outlined his proposal.

Martin was to strip Peter Carey of every scrap of privacy.

When Martin left to establish a base of operations in Manhattan, Englehardt reviewed his plans.

His savings were adequate: for a few months he could finance himself and Martin, securing a base and the equipment they would need. To insulate him from the surveillance of Peter Carey, Martin at first would carry it out alone; were agents needed, Martin alone would control them, so that they would never know the name John Joseph Englehardt, or look into his face. And, once Barth approached Phillip Carey, there was a sequence he could count on . . .

That Phillip Carey would not sell without the approval of his nephew.

That Peter Carey could be maneuvered into withholding this approval while enraging Barth.

That once this happened, Englehardt alone might give Barth what he then would want so desperately, by forcing Phillip to sell the firm.

The sole imponderable was Peter Carey.

More than anyone, he knew the risk of turning *this* nephew against *this* uncle. But he could no longer face his hollow joke of an existence, brain withering to a vestigial organ.

When Martin called, John Joseph Englehardt caught an airplane to New York, and slipped unseen into SoHo.

He arranged to live in secret.

He left SoHo only after dark, with Martin driving. Martin brought him food from elsewhere, acquired statuary under a name they had invented. The gallery delayed its opening; its loft contained no clothes with labels or books which bore his name. His identity lived on with his possessions, secreted in his Georgetown home, the refuge it had always been. At night, pacing the empty loft, he wiped it clean of fingerprints.

Within two weeks, Peter Carey had gone into analysis.

Alone, Englehardt listened to his agony on tape, sickened and enthralled. His nerves quivered at the sound of Peter's voice . . .

Helpless as a fly in amber, he waited for Barth and Phillip Carey to play out their first act.

At last, they did: his call to Benevides, the first showing of his hand, brought about the second act.

Now the third act was beginning.

Feeling Englehardt extend his power over others, Barth would not see his power becoming Englehardt's until he was too vulnerable to quibble at the price. The subtle art of mutual blackmail was one Englehardt had long since mastered: shunning wealth and public acclaim, he had less to lose than other men.

So many years since the eyes of two young men had locked

across the table, Phillip Carey might once more prove his resurrection. His eyes shut, and he remembered...

Footsteps echoed in the barren loft, and then Martin's slurred voice interrupted him. "Excuse me," he said softly, "but Phillip Carey is here," and in that moment, Englehardt knew at last how much he had missed him.

Silently, the two figures stepped from the dim light of the elevator, moving through the darkness toward Englehardt's desk. Their faces appeared; as if in a time warp, he had a schizoid vision of his two selves juxtaposed, one brutal and one willowy, and then Martin receded into the shadows, and he and Phillip Carey were alone.

"How are you, Phillip?" he asked softly.

Phillip Carey looked ill. "I thought you were dead."

Englehardt cocked his head, inspecting him. "You look older. But then it's been over twenty years, hasn't it."

Phillip's voice was hollow. "Twenty-three."

Slowly, Englehardt nodded. "How has it felt, then, running the firm?"

"What do you want?"

Englehardt remembered Phillip's power to wound him with no more than his voice. "You're to sell to Clayton Barth."

Phillip stiffened. "Do you have the same arrangement?"

"That's confidential, Phillip. *Your* role is quite simple."

"But I can't do that. I'm *trustee*."

Englehardt's smile was fond. "You're forgetting who to fear again. But then it's hard to break the habit of a lifetime, isn't it?"

Phillip's voice rose. "You underestimate Peter. There's a great deal of my father in him, as well as of Charles. He's incredibly complex..."

"Is that why he's started seeing Ruth Levy's brother?"

Phillip paled. From deep in his throat, he asked, "For what?"

"For his memory, Phillip." Their eyes met. "So," Englehardt finished gently, "you see how it is."

"It doesn't matter." Phillip looked away. "I don't want him harmed."

"Then he must be removed from the stress of his inheritance—hopefully, even, from analysis."

"But we're not close." Reaching for his lighter, Phillip added miserably, "He takes after his father."

"Suppose he were to fear for Miss Ciano..."

"*No.*"

Softly, like the rattling of a leaf, Englehardt laughed.

"I wouldn't be here, damn you, if..."

"*If,*" Englehardt lashed back, "you'd been John Carey's favored son. It is too bad, Phillip, that he thought so much of Charles."

Phillip's outrage faded in self-loathing. "Yes, you've been very understanding about that."

Englehardt shrugged. "There was a certain precedent in my own life. For a moment, Phillip, we were friends."

Phillip Carey shut his eyes. Trancelike, he repeated, "I thought you were dead."

"But I'm not." Englehardt watched Phillip's rigid body; almost tenderly, he told him, "I need you now to be my friend again."

Phillip's downward stare was silent and appalled.

"No, Phillip." Slowly, Englehardt shook his head. "There *is* no point in blaming me. You see, *I'm* your face in the mirror. Almost"—he searched for a word; irony mingling with affection, he finished—"a brother."

Phillip Carey shuddered; the moment passed, and then Englehardt pointed to the telephone. "It's time now," he said coldly. "Mr. Barth is waiting for your call."

Nerves shot by coffee and no sleep, Peter Carey bolted another cup and imagined Noelle, flying in the darkness toward El Salvador.

Part of him felt that he had driven her to this assignment; part, that she'd abandoned him...

"*It's* broken *now.* Look, *dammit—look at what you've done...*"

Crystal shattered in his memory; in his mind, a faceless stranger stalked Noelle.

He went to the window. In the scattered lights of Central Park, thin silver branches stabbed from a maze of black in which the tunnel waited.

He turned away.

Barth was bent on some elliptical and mad revenge; Carey had drawn him toward Noelle.

Barth; Phillip; a faceless man; an ugly stranger; a voice on the telephone.

Someone was watching him.

CHAPTER 9

"You keep remembering Dewey," Levy asked. "What do you suppose it means?"

"Nothing." Peter's voice was like piano wire. "It's nonsense..."

Englehardt forced his nerves to steady. He knew that Peter would not remember: it was the second time that he had listened to the tape...

"Let's go back to Phillip, then. Can you define why you don't trust him?"

For three weeks Englehardt had dangled Phillip in front of Barth, insinuating Martin on Barth's payroll and procuring the resources needed to strip all privacy from Peter Carey: Barth did not know that, four nights a week, Englehardt stood watch over Peter's memory.

"It's more a feeling," Peter answered. "Phillip, the call about Barth, Dewey, Noelle being followed, the nightmare—at night now, I imagine rushing into the tunnel. None of it adds up..."

As he had hoped, alerting Peter to Barth's past had heightened his sense of danger, but deflected its thrust: Peter could not possibly connect Barth to the time of his amnesia. Now he was staring at a Freudian puzzle with too many pieces missing.

"You seem edgy, Peter."

"I still haven't heard from Noelle. I keep worrying that somehow I've brought Barth down on her, but there's been nothing from *him* since that goddamned meeting. Even Phil's avoiding me, as if he's afraid."

He must keep Martin on a tight rein, Englehardt thought grimly; alive, Noelle Ciano was his second means of diverting Peter from his past. And after tomorrow, as a third, he would order Phillip to stay entirely out of Peter's sight.

"Phillip's behavior—do you relate that to your memory?"

Englehardt stared at the unwinding tape: blindfolded but persistent, Levy locked him in a race with Peter Carey.

Peter's voice rose. "How could *I* know?"

"You will, Peter. In time."

Englehardt looked up at the dirty windows of the loft, and realized it was dawn.

In the morning light, William Levy struggled to connect Peter's fears for Noelle Ciano to the death of Charles Carey.

For three days running, he had taken taxis to his office before dawn, searching for the answer in his notes. A sixth sense told him that the connection was buried with Peter's memory: that Noelle might have been followed did not account for the contradictions he heard in Peter. Under "Noelle," Levy had long since scribbled, "Afraid to love her, yet afraid she will abandon him."

Now he added, "Afraid his love will murder her."

Levy stared down at the words: as with his memory of Phillip, they drove him to uncover the hidden meaning of Peter's nightmare and amnesia, until he, too, could not sleep.

For what seemed the hundredth time he scrawled, "Who is the faceless man?" and scowled; like a medical chart, these jagged notes outlined his deterioration.

The analysis was floundering.

Obsessively, Peter worried for Noelle: on the morning that three Dutch photographers were murdered in El Salvador, he had been tormented by the thought that he had killed her. "She wouldn't have gone," he kept repeating, "if I'd just *said* something."

Now, Levy wrote: "Charles → amnesia → Noelle?"

In the last week, he had been snaking toward this question.

The trigger had been Peter's casual story of his sexual initiation with the precocious Tipsy, in the back of an empty bus used to shuttle her classmates to a prep school mixer. Peter recalled being startled by her cries. "Afterwards," he mused, "she said she'd climaxed because I could make it last. Actually, I was so scared they'd catch me that when she came I was still listening for footsteps. But later I thought maybe I'd stumbled on to something."

Levy first saw the story as symbolic: Peter could purge his sexual guilt, yet protect the imperative of his self-control, only by the postponement of his pleasure. He had speculated on some primal scene—perhaps involving Phillip, Allie and the child Peter. It would explain so much . . .

"Tell me," he asked Peter, "what are your first memories concerning sex?"

"How do you mean?"

"As a child, for example—perhaps of your mother or your father, something you might have seen . . ."

"I wasn't looking." Peter's voice was very cool. "My mother doesn't come back to me as a terribly physical person."

For an unhappy day or two, Levy had pondered the impact of Alicia Carey: he felt her madness in Peter's fear of abandonment. But when Peter at last admitted that his nightmare made him fear to touch Noelle, Levy began to see much more.

Nettled at Levy's sudden interest in his sex life, Peter snapped, "I feel like we're in a locker room."

"Then humor me," Levy answered dryly. "I'm older than you, and now *my* memory is fading."

At first, Peter would catalog only his more bizarre experiences, with the clipped voice of a scientist dismissing failed experiments. There were the English twins he'd taken turns with one night on Fire Island; the Radcliffe freshman who had slapped him when, remarking that his forehand was for tennis, he declined to strike her breasts; the radical feminist who, believing sex was politics, would come only on top; the policewoman with a revolver beneath each pillow; the rich ex-cover girl who'd married her plastic surgeon, a transvestite; the writer who'd asked to photograph his penis; an off-Broadway actress so strung out on drugs that his screams did not awaken her . . .

"But how did they make you *feel?*"

Peter hesitated. "Sad."

"Not revolted?"

"No."

"For whom were you sad, then?"

Peter hesitated. "For them, I suppose."

"Yes?"

Reluctantly, Peter wove a deeper litany of urban loneliness:

the city-worn women who, fearing equally the hostile streets and the silence of their own apartments, fled to smoke-filled bars for sanctuary, to smile at strangers. Talk was cheap, sentiment the barter of one-night stands: Peter, who had an ear for dialogue, recalled the social worker nine years past who took him back to her cramped apartment in Chelsea to say that "a little bit of me died with Robert Kennedy."

Gently, Peter had responded, "You mean you want to sleep with me."

She looked angry; then, seeing that his smile was not cruel, said, "Yes. I think I do."

They went to bed.

Peter did not call her again. He had learned to believe in truth, but not that truth mattered.

Peter Carey had remained alone.

This loneliness, Levy guessed, allowed him to feel its ravages in others. Some women had wished no more from him than pleasure; Peter knew that most, fleeing from their solitude, no longer knew what value to assign to the caresses of a stranger, or even to themselves. He learned to exit with a practiced grace, sorry for their expectations. But he, too, grew weary; weary of sex so interchangeable that it seemed accompanied by the same banal chatter of "relationships" which flowed like an endless soundtrack from night to night; of awakening in strange apartments to unfamiliar street sounds, and bathrooms he could not find; of surrogate mothers who wished to analyze his nightmare over breakfast; of the fear that he was drawing on some emotional capital which would at last be spent.

Yet his lovemaking remained chillingly detached.

He was good at casual sex, Peter knew; what he lacked in joy, he made up in sensitivity to the body of another. But he could not permit himself to feel love, or even pleasure. Listening, Levy had written: "Pattern: fear of attachments . . ."

And then Noelle Ciano, snapping the picture of a small girl, had stirred a feeling inside Peter Carey to which, because he seemed to fear it, he dared not give a name.

"What was it you first responded to?" Levy asked.

Peter stared at the ceiling. Finally, he answered, "That she could capture feelings without words."

Levy pondered this. "You fundamentally *like* women, don't you, Peter?"

"I hope so, yes."

"Do you find it curious, then, that your time with them has been so transient?"

"We printed that book last month, doctor. There *is* Noelle..." Peter's voice had abruptly fallen.

"You're still frightened for her?"

Peter twisted on the couch. "It's just that I haven't heard from her."

"You could hardly expect to, could you? Is there perhaps something else that might explain these fears?"

Peter crossed his arms. "Such as?"

"You," Levy had almost retorted; quickly, he switched subjects.

Now, waiting for Peter to arrive, Levy stared once more at "Charles → amnesia → Noelle?"

Slowly, he wrote beneath this: "Does Peter blame himself for Charles's death?"

Peter Carey watched the spider.

"Tell me," Levy began, "what words come to mind when you think of Noelle?"

Carey fell silent. "Courage," he answered finally. "Courage—and sensitivity."

"And what words do you associate with your father."

Carey felt his body stiffen. "Death, and loneliness."

"I was thinking of when Charles was alive." Levy's voice was soft; Carey sensed the analyst leaning forward. "Tell me, would you use the same words you just used for Noelle?"

"'Love'—my father loved me." Pained, Carey finished quickly. "And then he died."

"So now you believe Noelle will, also?"

Once more, Carey imagined the faceless man following Noelle. To speak this fear would make it true...

"Why did you come to me, Peter?"

Carey broke free from the image. "I told you why—amnesia, and this dream."

"Is another reason that you're in love with Noelle Ciano?"

"I don't know what that means." Carey felt harassed, cornered. "Look, dammit, the dream comes every night now."

"Perhaps your subconscious is struggling to explain it. What do you make of it, at this point?"

"I'm not sure." Relieved to have diverted Levy from Noelle, Carey decided to go on. "The one thing I've come up with is sort of shallow."

"Yes?"

"The dreams began the same night Phillip said he had no pictures of my father." Carey hesitated. *"Ergo,* the burning of my father's face is my loss of his pictures. Phillip is the faceless man who stabs out my eyes."

"Yes," Levy said carefully. "That *is* the obvious explanation. What do you make of it?"

"I don't trust easy answers."

"Sometimes they're the right ones. But are there other possibilities?"

"Such as?"

There was silence. Quietly, Levy asked, "Is there any chance, Peter, that *you* might feel guilt concerning your father's death?"

Carey's stomach constricted. "Why should I—I don't remember it."

"Suppose," Levy proposed gently, "that you sense the burning face and the faceless man are *both* Charles Carey."

Carey's knees drew up. "Why would my father blind me?"

"I'm not suggesting that it's true, Peter. I'm just wondering if you've some buried feeling that your father might be angry at you."

"I *loved* him."

"Yes, you *do* know what love means, Peter—there can be no doubt you loved Charles a great deal." Levy's tone grew cautious. "Do you think that's why you've suggested Phillip as your faceless man? Or is there something you can't yet acknowledge?"

"It's too dark down there for elephants, Daddy..."

Suddenly, Carey turned on him. "You know, I'm sick of these condescending, bullshit questions premised on my childishness. I'm sick of dreaming my father's death, night after night..."

"Then you can leave, Peter." Levy's voice was thin. "That choice has always been yours."

"I've gotten used to talking." Carey stopped, white-faced. "My father trusted you."

"But you're not Charles, Peter; that's not your burden." Levy finished in a lower voice. "This won't be easy for you, as it is."

Carey felt unspeakably tired; his mind kept drifting, seeing a lunatic collage: an elephant, a faceless man, Noelle. "No. It isn't."

"The question is, do you truly wish to remember."

"I don't know anymore." Carey stared at the floor. "I suppose I'm frightened."

"Yes, I know. What I don't know yet is why. Will you find out with me?"

Looking up into the sad furrows of Levy's face, Carey felt the ineffable kindness of this man, his father's friend.

"However hard?" Levy asked him. "Whatever the answer?"

Carey shut his eyes. Slowly, wearily, he nodded.

"Shall we continue, then?"

As if guided by an unseen hand, Carey lay back on the couch. The spider was still weaving...

Levy shuffled his notes; Carey heard their order changing, as though the analyst were striving to make sense of a senseless world. As if nothing at all had happened, Levy asked, "You feel some guilt about your grandfather's death?"

"*Charles*..."

"I suppose so."

"Do you also fear remembering your father's death?"

"Yes."

"And now you seem afraid to love Noelle—perhaps that she will die?"

There was silence, and then Peter Carey whispered, "Yes."

"Do you see some thread?"

Carey writhed; so odd, that he had always thought pain physical. "If I understood the nightmare..."

"Your problem's the faceless man, I take it?"

"Yes—him."

Softly, Levy asked, "Are you afraid he's *you*, Peter?"

Carey felt the question as shock from a sudden blow. *"Me?"*

"More exactly, are you afraid that you do harm to those you love?"

"No, dammit." In pain and anger, Carey snapped, "It must be Phillip."

"Do you remember something?"

"Peter!"

"Perhaps about Dewey?"

"It's too dark down there for elephants, Daddy . . ."

"Lay off, for Christsakes." Trapped, Carey lashed back. "Maybe Phil buried Dewey with what was left of my father. He knew I loved him . . ."

He could not finish.

In their silence, Peter Carey felt tears on his face.

"It's all right, Peter." Levy's voice was quiet and sad. "I loved him, too."

"I loved him, too . . ."

Nostrils stale with cigarette smoke and the trapped stench of his own body, Martin listened to Peter Carey's silence, and then Levy's door closed, and his hour in the van was up.

Martin slid the tape from the receiver and replaced it with another. Then, with the gooseflesh thrill that Englehardt had not yet satisfied, Martin took his secret album from beneath the stereo, and stared at his first picture of Noelle.

She was running for the airplane; he had caught her tensile body in midstride, hair rippling in a coal-black wave. Through the blouse, he imagined the silken tautness of skin stretching across her spine and shoulder blades.

More deeply than the others, he craved to touch her.

"Stay back from Miss Ciano." Englehardt's directive had borne an intimate distaste. "Once we're set up, you'll be able to see *all* of her . . ."

Reluctantly, Martin closed the album, chafing at those orders: this morning he felt the anger of a servant, aimed at Phillip Carey.

He disliked Phillip for what he saw in Englehardt: receiving him, his mentor had waved Martin away, eyes lingering on Phillip's face. He had slunk to the elevator like an errand boy: Phillip had stayed, sharing secrets Martin did not know. Now he sensed Phillip Carey in the small man's voice and nerves; their circle had been broken.

He had never seen the man so tender, so caring. Surely not of him . . .

Angrily, he interrupted his thoughts, and searched for ones more pleasing. His crosstown jaunt was overdue; Peter Carey was already driving down Fifth Avenue, carrying him like a shadow on the brain.

Noelle Ciano was returning.

Martin placed the latest tape of Carey's fear for her in his coat pocket, reaching for the door.

On the stereo behind him, Peter Carey walked into his office and demanded, "What the devil are *you* doing here?" and then the new tape started spinning.

Sitting at the desk, Phillip Carey smiled uneasily. "Out touring Bellevue?" he inquired. "You look like hell."

"What is it you want, Phil?"

"Civility, for openers."

"Then I'll see what I can do." Peter Carey sat behind his desk. Turning to face him, Phillip crossed his legs; the gesture struck Carey as more remembered than spontaneous, an act of self-impersonation. "Something wrong?"

"Does something have to be?" Phillip asked rhetorically; in the awkward silence, he followed with, "How's Noelle?"

"Noelle?" Carey's head tilted. "What about her?"

Returning Carey's stare, Phillip spoke in a second voice, older and harsher. "You're a cold bastard, aren't you, Peter?"

Off-balance, Carey stabbed at the fear he sensed. "Then perhaps you should have let me burn."

"And missed all this fun?" Phillip's quick, bitter smile worked its way through sour to wry. "You never much liked baseball, did you?"

Carey spoke to cover his surprise. "Not like you."

"Remember the last time Williams came to Yankee Stadium, with the Red Sox?"

"Someday that'll be you, *Peter . . ."*

The memory slipped away, banished from time or place, leaving only his discomfort. "I would have been around eight, Phil—just before you sent me off to school."

Phillip watched him. "Well," he said with care, "it's hard to remember one's own childhood."

"Do *you* remember Dewey, Phil?"

Phillip blinked. "Dewey?"

"Yes." Carey leaned toward him. "My elephant."

"I don't think I recall him." Phillip's look turned vague. "What made you think of that?"

"He was lost, *Peter. In the accident."*

"I've been trying to recall the accident..."

Phillip shook his head. "To what unpleasant end? Your amnesia is nature's kindness."

"Is there some reason, Peter, that you *might feel guilt concerning your father's death?"*

"My nightmares, too, Phil? Was *that* why you sent me off to boarding school?"

A second too late, it seemed to Carey, Phillip ruefully shook his head. With a thin, ironic smile, he looked at the photograph of Charles. "It's strange," he ventured, "what things we choose to remember."

"Not if you love the memory."

"I loved him, Peter. In my way."

"In *your* way." Carey felt a red, frightening anger. "That's such drivel."

Phillip shrank from his expression. "It was *hard*—you didn't know that side of him."

"I don't want it to just be Phillip. Can you understand that?"

"Yes, Daddy. I understand."

Carey's anger drained; its aftertaste was sour and sad and guilty. "Perhaps I understand more than you think."

"Then let me talk to you, Peter." Phillip leaned forward, beseeching. "Please, we won't have these chances forever."

Watching him, Carey was strangely touched. "What is it, Phil?"

"It's *you*, Peter. I wonder if you'll ever know how much you concern me."

"I saved you..."

"I've been tired, that's all."

"You've been hostile, and erratic. Oh, I know you don't much care for me..."

For a fleeting moment, Carey felt the undertow of shared affection. His uncle looked so much older, now.

"It's not that, Phil. Really."

"Isn't it?" Phillip hesitated; Carey sensed him cup their moment of near-friendship in his hands, before he broke it in a dead, flat voice: "Peter, Barth may be offensive, but..."

"Be plain, dammit. Are you planning to sell Van Dreelen and Carey out from under me?"

"I *could,* the way you're acting." Phillip's gaze broke. "And for your peace of mind, you *should.*"

"*I* won't. My question was, will *you?*"

"I don't know." Phillip looked away. "You need a rest, Peter. And now you have Noelle to think of."

"Noelle?" Carey stood abruptly. "What's happened to her?" Phillip recoiled. "I don't know..."

Suddenly Carey saw the faceless man following Noelle: with a crazy certainty, he jerked Phillip up by the lapels so that their faces were an inch apart. His uncle flinched. *"Peter!"*

"Tell me, dammit—what's Barth got on you?"

"It's not *Barth.*" Phillip stopped himself, straightening with ravaged dignity as he looked down at Peter's hands. "As I said, Peter, it's *you.* Now, will you kindly let me go..."

Carey's grip tightened. "What about Noelle?"

Carey could feel his uncle's breath. Phillip's eyes flickered. The telephone rang.

Carey turned, fearful.

Phillip managed a pallid smile. "Take a deep breath, Peter, and answer it. This outburst should remain our little secret."

Carey loosened his grasp, then slowly reached for the telephone. "Yes?"

"It's me," Noelle Ciano told him. "Still interested?"

Mute, Peter Carey watched his uncle open the door and then walk slowly back to his office, alone.

Carey held her face in his hands. "I thought you were dead."

"I sent three post cards and a grenade launcher." Her smile faded. "Was it those Dutch who were killed?"

"Is there something else that explains those fears that she *will die—something about* you?"

"Partly that..."

"And now you have Noelle to think of."

The loudspeaker announced a flight to Santiago.

"Tell me, dammit . . . What's Barth got on you?"

"Peter? Are you okay?"

"It's not Barth, Peter. It's you."

Carey searched her face. "Drive with me somewhere. Please."

"This business of the elephant . . ." There was little need to amplify, Phillip thought in despair; Englehardt would surely know. "He won't sell."

"Then I suggest becoming ill." Englehardt's telephone voice was habitually soft. "The problem of *Peter* Carey has at last fallen to me."

"I've *told* you—I don't want Peter harmed."

Englehardt laughed softly. "In that case, Phillip, you should have let him die."

The line went dead in Phillip's hand.

Carey stared at the white frame house. "This is the one."

He had driven them through the sloping Connecticut countryside, snow sparkling in the winter sun; as they moved closer to Greenwich, he had grown steadily more tight-lipped and observant. Braking suddenly, he had stopped on a road lined with low stone walls and rambling wooden houses, staring at the granite pillars of a driveway.

Noelle followed his gaze to the white wooden house beyond. "What is it?"

Carey's eyes were narrow. "Phil invited us here—the weekend of the accident. Driving through these pillars is the last thing I remember. I never came back."

"But you remember the drive?"

Peter grinned in the small backseat of his father's Jaguar.

"It's strange." Still Carey did not look at her. "The road kept unwinding in front of me, so that I remembered as I drove, not just trees and houses, but the wind in my face, even the exact way I loved my father."

"Jesus, Peter . . ."

Afraid that she could not understand, he looked into her face, and saw his answer there. "That day in New Hampshire, when we made love in the grass—afterwards you lay back in the sun and fell asleep, naked and half smiling, and when you awoke, I was still watching you. You asked why I looked so intent, and yet so sad. Do you remember what I told you?"

"Almost exactly." She touched his face. "You said, 'It's easier for me to remember moments than to believe they'll happen to me again.'"

Carey nodded. "It was important to tell the truth, as best I knew it, so you'd have some chance of understanding me." He turned to stare at the pillars. "This was the last moment where I believed that my life would be whatever my father and I could make it. After that . . ."

"And now?"

"I'm losing control—of myself, and whatever's going on around me. I have to learn whatever got me there, from here."

Noelle glanced through the windshield, at the road ahead. "We're driving to where it happened, aren't we?"

"Yes." Peter Carey gazed past her at his uncle's house. "In a moment."

They would have driven to the garage . . .

"It's too dark down there for elephants, Daddy . . ."

"What's wrong, Peter?"

"I keep saying something to my father." He shook his head. "One scrap of absolute, senseless trivia, and then nothing."

A long moment later, he pulled back onto the road.

By instinct, Carey began turning before he saw the sign marked "Cognewaugh."

The boy Peter knew the way.

The man Peter Carey accelerated.

In silence, Carey and Noelle sped along the steep and winding grade, past farmhouses and stone fences and bare trees.

The trees would have been green then, in April . . .

The road dipped suddenly.

Carey did not slow. The drive was making him sick; he imagined the boy Peter laughing . . .

Peter had asked to go to the reservoir, Phillip once told him, to sail a boat. Carey stepped on the gas.

A sudden uphill grade filled his windshield, curving to the right along a hill which grew steeper, more precipitous . . .

Carey took the curve and started up the grade. His stomach tensed.

"Faster, Daddy..."

At the top flashed an abrupt left curve, covered in ice.

"Peter!"

"Charles..."

The car began skidding; hitting the brakes, Carey jerked the wheel toward the skid. The car slid sideways...

"I'm losing control..."

Carey whipped the wheel; spitting gravel, the Jaguar lurched to a stop two feet from a hundred-foot deadfall.

"Peter..."

As if in a trance, Peter Carey glided from the car in one fluid movement and then stood, staring down the rocky cliffside.

At its bottom he saw a thick, crooked tree. Its trunk was scorched.

"Daddy..."

The man Peter Carey looked away.

Fighting back nausea, he studied the cliff.

It was close to sheer and its rocks the size of boulders; from below they would seem the menacing portent of a landslide. The field beyond, suddenly flat and grassy, stretched to a sudden cul-de-sac of houses. Somehow, Carey knew they had not been there when...

He turned back to the tree.

"I'll bring him up in a little bit, Peter..."

Its trunk was scarred and black and stripped of bark...

"Promise?"

His father lowered his face to Peter's...

Scarred and black...

"Promise..."

Stripped of bark...

"Peter!"

"Is there some reason, Peter, that you feel guilty for your father's death?"

Peter Carey sat on a rock, head between his knees, and vomited.

Gravel crunched behind him; he felt Noelle's fingertips on his shoulder.

"I'll drive," she said softly.

CHAPTER 10

"For a long time I just sat there, staring at my own vomit. On the drive home I could hardly face her: she'd been in fucking El Salvador three weeks, and this maniac takes her straight from the airport to the scene of his parents' death, almost drives her off a cliff, and then pukes."

"What made you sick, Peter—nearly duplicating the accident?"

"That, and flashbacks—I'm sleeping in a strange bed, and my father is saying goodnight. I keep telling him about Dewey."

"Yes?"

"Something like, 'It's too dark down there for elephants, Daddy.'"

"Do you know where 'there' is?"

"No—it makes no sense to me. But the faster I drove, flashes came that I'd never had before. My father says, 'Then I'll bring him up in a little bit'; I ask, 'Promise?'; he answers, 'Promise'; then I had to brake and Noelle cried out; suddenly my mother is crying, 'Charles!' and he's screaming, 'I'm losing control,' and then I got out to look down the hill and in my mind someone turned and shouted, 'Peter!'"

"And at that point you threw up?"

"Yes, but in the flashback, I don't know where I am. I don't think it's the accident—it feels more like a room, somewhere dark that I can't place."

Englehardt switched off the cassette and checked his watch. Seven P.M.

He breathed deeply: for twenty minutes he would think without emotion.

Alone in his loft, he considered killing Peter Carey.

He would be free of this mounting tension; Martin had been waiting.

But then he must also murder Phillip, for he did not know how Phillip would react.

His chest tightened.

He could not do that, he told himself—it was too soon. Phillip Carey was his key to Barth, Barth Industries *his* key to power. Barth had not commissioned murder: to murder Phillip would condemn himself to nothingness.

He must suffer what Peter was doing to him, until Barth was in his hands.

His hands were trembling; awkwardly, he turned on the tape . . .

"Tell me, Peter, *who* is it that shouts at you?"

In the silence, Englehardt stared at his hands, and then Peter answered dully, "I don't know."

"Could it be the faceless man?"

"I'm not sure—last night, after the nightmare, I called Noelle to see if she was safe. I'm losing control . . ."

"Like your father?"

"Like I'm crazy." The words were shot with pain. "Yesterday, with Phillip—for a split second I almost wanted to kill him, to end how scared I've been. It's as if *his* fear's rubbing off on me—sometimes I swear he's going to sell me out, that it's all tied in with the ugly man Noelle saw. But now I don't trust anyone: this morning the doorman wouldn't look at me—even my neighbors seem different, I say something and they stare down at their dog and then scurry off, as if I'm marked . . ."

"By Phillip?"

"Maybe in my mind: sometimes I don't know the difference between myself and the child Peter, reality or dream. For a moment this morning, I knew I should sprint into the tunnel and kill the faceless man."

"That's all, Peter." Levy's voice was taut. "We'll talk tomorrow."

The tape ended.

Englehardt stared at it.

By instinct, he replayed the last five minutes. Palms pressed tightly together in the attitude of prayer, he listened.

Levy sounded tenser now; the rhythm of his questions was intrusive and too fast . . .

Englehardt snatched up his telephone and called Martin. "I want all of Levy's notes," he ordered.

Martin seemed to reflect on this. "I can't be always going back there," he replied. "That would be dangerous."

"There's too much Levy isn't telling Peter—before I meet with Barth, I have to find out where he's going. Now is that clear, dammit?"

Softly, Martin answered, "Not quite yet." He let this linger for a moment, and then hung up.

Tight-lipped, Englehardt slammed down the telephone.

In the van, Martin turned on that day's final tape.

Lips pressed close to the bug that he had planted in her telephone, Noelle Ciano said, "It's me, Peter."

"Listen, about yesterday . . ."

"That was yesterday. Today, *I* took some liberties. We're going skiing in Vermont."

"Vermont." Carey sounded off-balance. "When?"

"This weekend. I've got Jill Thomson's cabin, near Mount Snow. You need to get away . . ."

"From myself? How will I do that?"

Martin heard Noelle breathing softly through the mouthpiece. "By taking *me*, Peter. We can ski as much or little as you want."

"Why are you doing this?"

"Because I like Vermont." Her voice softened. "Will you come?"

There was no answer. Martin waited with Noelle; then Carey murmured, "I don't want you there alone," and Martin smiled to himself.

Soon he would be watching her.

Now, at midnight, Martin watched the hospital, waiting for his time.

He hesitated, reluctant; perhaps he was becoming superstitious. He did not like breaking into buildings twice.

Five . . .

From across the street, he began counting the nurses who

arrived in taxis for the midnight shift, passing through the entrance he would take.

Six.

With the seventh, Martin started briskly toward the entrance—a doctor, going to work.

Reaching the tunnel, Charles Carey smiled.

The laughing Peter rushed in deeper; Charles chased him, footsteps echoing in the night. Peter turned, calling "Daddy!"

As Charles reached out for him, his face burst into flames.

There was laughter. The faceless man appeared at the tunnel's mouth; Peter turned but could not move. The stranger's shadow grew larger, closer. Tears streaming down his cheeks, the child Peter walked toward him. Burning, Charles's arms vainly stretched to save him, and then the stranger raised his knife . . .

As the stranger plunged the knife through Peter's heart, Levy saw his ice-blue eyes . . .

William Levy awakened screaming.

There were sharp pains in his chest; for a frightened instant he believed that Peter's dream connected the death of Charles Carey to his own. His skin went cold; in his mouth was the sour taste of fear. He fumbled in the dark for his reading lamp, clicked the switch. His breathing eased. The pain subsided: still he felt the pounding of his heart. By reflex, he rose and stumbled to the mirror, smoothing his cowlick. But the black eyes, staring from a face etched by years of thought, were as frightened as those of the freshman he had been, before Charles Carey had become his friend.

Hastily, he dressed and called a taxi.

Martin opened the inner door to Levy's office.

At least he could work quickly: he knew where to find the index.

Jimmying the drawer, he took the index to the cabinets, pried loose the drawer which held the Carey file, and returned.

The file, which had once contained five pages, now felt thick in his hand.

He turned on Levy's desk lamp and spread his notes across the floor.

Kneeling, he took the camera from his bag and methodically began photographing each page, snatching out rolls of film to jam in new ones, pressing the button on page after page until the joints of his knees hurt. Hungrily, he scanned the pages: over and over, Levy had scrawled, "Who is the faceless man?" as if tormented by the heart of Peter's drama.

Neither of them knew the answer.

When they did, Martin was sure, the drama would end swiftly.

In haste, he restored each page to its proper order, threw film and camera in the bag, returned the index to the drawer, switched off the light, and then took the bag and file to the outer office, closing the door behind him. He slid the file into its place, then froze.

There were footsteps in the corridor.

Silently, Martin moved to the outer door, to listen.

Echoing off linoleum, the steps grew louder. Martin crouched; the pounding sound came nearer, closer. They reached the door . . .

Martin raised his arm.

Like a drumroll, the steps receded down the hall, and died.

Carefully, Martin opened the door and looked out.

Nothing.

He slipped into the corridor, and marched quickly past the darkened offices. His back burned with imagined gunshots.

Sliding through the door marked "Exit," he took three dim flights to the main reception area.

A few strays loitered on hard plastic chairs like vagrants in a Hogarth print; two nurses conferred behind the reception desk; no one looked up as he passed. More confident, Martin turned, counting off twenty-seven steps, and hit the outer door. Cold air splashed his face . . .

He stumbled suddenly into a frail man climbing the last few steps. Belatedly, the man looked up; his lined face was abstracted, and when he murmured, "Pardon me," it was in a voice so indistinct that Martin hardly heard it.

Martin smiled quickly, and headed for the subway.

Levy stopped in his doorway as if it were a stranger's.

His office was meant as a cell where reason lived, unmarred

by pictures or shelves of unread books. Now its purity seemed as false as his detachment.

Slowly, he moved to the cabinet and retrieved the Carey file. Sitting, he noted the tremor of his hands: he had left the safety zone.

There were two interpretations of Peter's nightmare, he now saw, perhaps not mutually exclusive. The first was that it symbolized some outside danger: Barth's fixation on the Careys; Levy's own unease with Phillip, which paralleled his sister's; Noelle's sense that she was followed; Peter's fear, *and* Phillip's—all these argued this was so.

Yesterday, as Peter followed the story of his reckless drive with an imagined rush into the tunnel, Levy had scrawled the second interpretation . . .

"Suicide."

In his dream, the faceless man was Peter Carey.

The stabbing of Peter as a small boy, Levy feared, meant he wished to harm himself. If this was right, then Levy was morally certain of why: that buried in the weekend Peter chose to forget lurked some reason that he blamed himself for the death of Charles Carey, symbolized by the nightmare of his burning face.

In this interpretation, Noelle Ciano placed him in a tragic whipsaw: Peter Carey, who feared abandonment by those he dared to love, also feared he would destroy them.

One way out was to destroy himself . . .

Here, Levy also feared his analytic bias: he could not escape the morning he had found his mother.

He closed his eyes, remembering.

He had awakened early, to study. There was no one up yet—his father was traveling again, selling cheap watches to drugstores. Levy wandered to the bathroom in his underwear, to splash water on his face. The door was locked; blood, seeping beneath it, had stained the worn gray carpet. He tried kicking the door down, failed miserably, then remembered the key his mother kept in the linen closet. He unlocked the door. His mother lay in a crimson pool that had painted her hair and fingertips; she resembled a bird who'd crashed into a picture window. He stooped to touch her wrist, saw that it was ripped open. Bile rose to his throat. A scream echoed in the bathroom;

turning, he saw Ruth standing in the doorway. Levy was not a physical man: it was the first time he had ever held her. She wept in his arms for an hour. Only then did he call the police. He had felt his mother's death in the coldness of her wrist: her temperature had already dropped.

He was seventeen years old.

He had blamed his father, a bitter failure whose wife and children could never succeed enough to please him. Later, as he grew older, Levy saw that this anger had dulled the sense of helplessness and desertion which haunt the children of a suicide. Ruth had been less fortunate: he came to love her for the pain he had avoided, astonished that he had not loved her before. The shock of recognizing this became the guilty burden of his mother's suicide: driven by the need to please his father, he had not clearly seen his mother until, finding her dead, he realized with a sickening jolt that he was not surprised.

In mute offering to the corpse he had found on the cool white tile, Levy began watching for the smallest signs of hurt in Ruth. It was this prescience that made him see in Charles Carey the fear others missed, and which, in turn, Charles saw, that drunken, fateful night in Boston, when he suggested Levy enter psychiatry.

He could seldom speak of his mother's suicide—even to Charles Carey—outside the year of analysis which was a required Freudian rite of passage. Yet he looked for its seeds in every patient, dreading that midnight call from some ravaged spouse or child, keening their abandonment. The call had never come: perhaps, he thought, his fear had made him lucky.

Now he sensed death surrounding Peter Carey.

Once more, under "Who is the faceless man?" he wrote: "Charles → Noelle → suicide?"

He could not be certain that the destructive traits he saw in Peter portended suicide: Peter's fight against the forces which tormented him bespoke a strength that was astonishing. But the spoor of guilt was everywhere: in Peter's obsessive need for privacy; in a passion for fitness and the techniques of self-defense; in feelings of unworthiness so deep that his instinctive first reaction to the ringing of a telephone was that Noelle Ciano had been killed; in his fear that he would call death down upon her; in a hostility to Phillip so intense that it might be viewed as a projection of self-loathing; in his constant worry that John Carey's firm would somehow be snatched from him. This last made the gamble he had taken with *The End of the Tunnel*, staking his future against Phillip on his judgment of one book, reek of self-destruction: Van Dreelen & Carey was Peter's sole remaining link with the two people he could acknowledge loving, and now he could not love Noelle.

The insight frightened him.

When Levy had first entered practice, he had occasionally, out of boredom or resentment at the litany of petty troubles that sometimes filled his day, indulged himself in fantasy, imagining his power were he to use the secrets he had learned to destroy his patients instead of to help them. At first this fantasy had horrified him; later he saw it as harmless, and even instructive. To destroy Peter, he was certain, a ruthless enemy would sever him from the firm his grandfather had left him, or from Noelle Ciano—or, crueler and more certain, make him choose.

Levy feared that enemy might wear Peter Carey's face.

But he was missing the crucial piece that might save him— from others, or from himself.

The crucial piece was Peter's memory, and he could wait no longer.

Martin disappeared inside the elevator; Englehardt sat alone, with the photographs of Levy's notes.

Avidly, he read them, marking a few with paperclips.

An hour later, he stacked the notes he had marked—Carey's account of the anonymous call; his fear that Noelle Ciano had been watched; his concern about his neighbors' odd behavior; his inquiry about Barth's whereabouts in 1959; his suspicions of Phillip Carey—and locked them with his secret tapes of the analysis, in the desk drawer Clayton Barth would never see.

What remained was the blueprint of Peter Carey's destruction.

The worry he heard in Levy's voice ran like fever through his notes.

The psychiatrist was stymied; just when Carey had some flash of memory, his subconscious shrank from it. Levy sensed this guilt, but could not know its reason; amnesia barred his way. He could only fear for its results—Carey's potential for violence or for suicide, growing with his worry for the woman . . .

Englehardt felt a kind of admiration: in a bizarre way, Levy was correct, for it was this potential he would turn on Peter Carey.

He must move quickly, Englehardt knew: Carey was a human time bomb. But Carey's time was running faster; Englehardt would need him for but a few weeks now, to capture Clayton Barth.

In a calming ritual, he began arranging his files on Peter Carey, the next step in this seduction. One by one, he put them in his briefcase: Peter Carey's prep school and college transcripts, a complete medical history, Benevides's notes and papers, a report on Carey's haunts and habits and those of Noelle Ciano, and a biography of the Careys so intimate that it would never be published anywhere.

To these he added the text of stolen intelligence files, from HUAC and the CIA. Their subjects were John, Charles and Phillip Carey, Alicia Fairvoort Carey, and Ruth Levy.

All of this was gloss to the centerpiece that followed—a sheaf so thick that Englehardt had difficulty shutting the briefcase: William Levy's remaining notes.

He wondered how Barth would like the one on suicide.

Smiling, he snapped the briefcase shut, and called Martin.

The elevator creaked upwards from the second floor, and then Martin's footsteps moved toward him. Englehardt rose with the briefcase. "I'm ready."

Martin's face appeared in the light. "About Vermont . . ."

Englehardt snapped curtly, "It's perfect—all we need is for Barth to think it's his idea, and then you can start watching her."

Martin flushed; this shame, Englehardt knew, increased his hold. "Come," he said softly.

In sullen silence, Martin followed him to the elevator.

Beneath the lone light bulb of his attic, Phillip Carey stared at a dusty metal trunk.

"What's Barth got on you?" Peter had demanded; for a

reckless moment, Phillip had wanted to warn him, and then the telephone rang, and Phillip had been saved instead.

Warning Peter would be no act of reconciliation, but of self-destruction.

And yet, Phillip wondered, did this really matter? He was not whole and never had been: his women were young and wanton and greedy, but Peter had Noelle.

Perhaps Noelle would save them both; afraid for her, Peter might back off from Barth, and from his memory . . .

But Phillip Carey could not move back from the trunk.

In his mind, Peter asked once more, "Where's Dewey?"

Slowly, Phillip opened the trunk, and looked inside.

In the still of night, gazing at his notes about a stuffed elephant, Levy saw the distasteful thing he must do.

Carefully, he began arranging each day's notes in exact sequence. His hands were not yet steady; sliding the final page in the manila folder, he sliced his finger on its edge.

He stared for a moment at the thin red line. Then he placed the numbered folder in its unmarked file, locked it and returned the index to the drawer.

Next to it was a Manhattan directory.

Under the listing for "Psychologists," his finger stopped at "Pogostin, David M.," as though to mark his desperation.

He had met Pogostin at a seminar in Puerto Rico, and disliked him instinctively: he sensed that Pogostin, a cocky young man with liquid brown eyes, found analysis comic. Pogostin wore an offensive green shirt and laughed too much. Levy's hands stilled: it was good to dislike someone without worrying about the reasons.

On the flight home from San Juan, Levy had skimmed the paper that Pogostin had read to an afternoon session which Levy had skipped, not without pleasure, in order to see an old friend from medical school. Its subject was battle-stress syndrome: Pogostin claimed extraordinary success in treating Vietnam veterans suffering from traumatic amnesia. The purpose, his paper explained, was to surface repressed traumatic memories that affected conscious behavior. Frequently, the patient could not afterwards remember what he had recalled under hypnosis: in these cases, the therapist gradually presented him with pieces of the now-uncovered trauma until the patient's memory revived. Then he could confront it in therapy.

Levy had not been sure he believed any of this.

Now he had to know what Peter Carey could not remember. He put down his glasses, rehearsing the conversation. He would ask Pogostin to hypnotize Peter and then lead him, in minute detail, through the weekend when his parents died. And, of course, he must tape Peter Carey's buried memories, for Levy's use.

For a moment, Levy imagined listening to the tape. His hands started trembling.

It was four-thirty when Englehardt finished reading to Barth from the Benevides file and handed it across the desk. "Peter thinks he can outsmart you," he summarized, "then tie you up in court. Four months is all he needs, and he may well beat you outright."

Framed against the Manhattan skyline, the two men sat alone. Angrily, Barth demanded, "What do you propose?"

"We've accomplished much in the last three weeks." Englehardt adopted the pose of tutor, experienced and calm. "In my opinion, Peter Carey can be dealt with. It is here that our access to Dr. Levy's notes becomes crucial: we now know things about Peter Carey which he himself will never know— for example, that his own analyst fears him to be a potential suicide . . ." Feigning carelessness, Englehardt let the sentence drop.

Quite softly, Barth inquired, "Suicide?"

"You wished to know about Peter Carey." Englehardt's shrug was minimal. "In a nutshell, we've discovered that the last of the Careys is an emotionally scarred young man. Through increased surveillance, we could not only absolutely predict his countermoves, but exacerbate those weaknesses until he cannot move at all. A creative choice would be to manipulate those guilts and fears which make him a potential suicide, even perhaps his capacity for violence, into behavior so irrational that no court would listen to his pleas. The more direct alternative would be to destroy him through the young woman of whom he seems so fond. We could poison their relationship, for example. Or, given the fact that he already feels guilt for the death of his grandfather and father—of which his night-mares and amnesia are the evidence—he should be extremely vulnerable to any hint that his continued obstinancy with Phillip would do Miss Ciano harm. There'd be no question you could have his firm. Of course," he added pointedly, "I'll need your permission to go as much as one step further. Our surveillance is not complete, and the final steps I've outlined here may not be worth the candle. It's only a publisher, after all, and as you've learned through meeting him, Peter Carey can be quite volatile."

Barth kept staring at him as if he did not hear. "Then he might kill himself?"

Englehardt nodded. "There's that to it—you might not want Peter on your conscience." He smiled wryly. "Curious that someone with such pathetic weaknesses should label *you* a psychopath."

Turning away, Barth's eyes seemed to fix on a fluorescent Coca-Cola sign, flashing backwards on black glass. Englehardt felt his own fingernails dig into his palms.

"I want this firm," Barth said in a distant voice. "I can't let Peter Carey keep it from me."

Englehardt let his silence grow. Modestly, he murmured, "I've told you what I can do."

"Then *show* me." Frighteningly, Barth wheeled on him. "*You* wish to be chief of security—*show* me."

"Hypnosis," Carey broke in. "Some man I've never met, tampering with my subconscious."

He sat facing Levy; suddenly, his father's friend looked old.

"It suits our purposes, Peter—you should know the reason for your dream. Please, I thought you *wanted* to remember."

"Not through sorcery. I'll stick with you."

"He'd tape it for me, Peter—I'm not abandoning you."

The repeated use of his first name struck Carey as odd: there was a disturbance in Levy, as if the circuits which connected them, nerve to nerve, had suddenly worn thin.

"God, I hate surprises."

"Please, Peter." Levy leaned forward, as if to reach him.

"If I'm going to help, it's become imperative that I know what happened to you."

Carey stood, snapping, "I have to think," and then strode quickly from the office.

CHAPTER 11

Peter's Jaguar sped into the Vermont dusk.

Shadows merged with the coming darkness; snow-covered landscapes became a blanket of gray and silver pinned by straight black shards, the trees of winter. Jagged crests of mountains vanished in a lowering sky, the two-lane highway retreated toward his windshield. When night came, it would be black and sudden and unrelieved: Peter drove too fast, as if trying to escape. Noelle saw the road vanishing in front of them.

"Take it easy, Peter. Two more hours, and we'll be walking through the doors, promise."

Jaw tight, Peter eased off the accelerator. The only sound was the low, smooth snarl of his motor.

Noelle listened; the absence of sensation made her pensive. "It's funny," she observed. "I have to readjust to nightfall. Here it's so total—in the city we don't really get that."

Peter downshifted. "Except for blackouts."

Wet snow clung to the windshield. Watching it, Noelle ventured, "Last time was a little like the world ending, wasn't it?"

Peter flicked on his lights; their beams stabbed the moving darkness of Vermont. "What do you remember about it?"

"The people." Noelle leaned back. "I guess what I remember most is the doorman."

Peter turned to her. "Why?"

"I was glad to see him," she said simply.

As evening came, Carey's doorman was replaced by another. He checked his watch, to give the signal, and began walking away from the Aristocrat. His bulky frame, moving from light to darkness, became a shadow.

Martin followed like a second shadow.

* * *

Two men with backpacks moved across the clearing.

The cabin sat by itself: no one heard the dull crunch of their footsteps or saw the flashlight moving with them toward the door.

It opened with a soft, metallic click.

Ten minutes later, they left as they had come, silent and alone. Snow fell, blurring the trail of their boots.

It was snowing harder when Noelle and Peter reached the cabin. Peter left his headlights on for a moment: large, moist flakes fell into a flawless blanket of white. "This is more like the *beginning* of the world," he mused.

Noelle kissed him. "Let's go inside."

They got out; Peter stood gazing at the pine cabin etched against the light. Noelle sensed him letting his mind catch up with his body; silent, she looked with him. Framed against the sky and stars, the fieldstone chimney warmed her.

When she turned back, Peter was staring at an indentation in the snow.

"Come on," she said. "We'll build a fire."

"Hypnosis," Carey snapped. "Some man I've never met, tampering with my subconscious..."

Englehardt could scarcely see the tape in front of him. *Hypnosis,* he thought foolishly—not from a *Freudian*...

When the telephone rang, Englehardt was in shock, unable to move.

"Please, Peter," Levy was entreating. The telephone kept ringing.

Englehardt snatched at it. "Wait, dammit—I'm still listening."

"If I'm to help, Peter, I must know what happened to you."

"No," Englehardt commanded; as if on cue, Carey answered, "I have to think," and slammed the door behind him.

Englehardt placed both palms flat on the desk. He took one breath, expelled it, and took the telephone off "hold." "This tape..."

"Pogostin's a psychologist." Martin's voice betrayed a veiled amusement. "He graduated from Columbia and, according to his book, has used hypnosis to treat amnesia for the past six years. The book's called *Trance and Trauma*—I bought it this afternoon." He paused; Englehardt swore he heard muffled laughter before Martin asked respectfully, "Was there something else?"

Englehardt felt betrayal all around him. He had seduced Barth with promises; then Levy had panicked and changed his own rules; now, trapped in plans he'd set in motion, Englehardt was taunted by his tool.

He thought of killing Martin, and then saw it was too late.

"I want Pogostin covered." He pronounced each syllable as if it were a bullet.

"A second break-in?" Martin's voice was light with innocence. "I've been busy with what you promised Barth—the van's equipped; I have the key, and I've already spoken to the neighbors. Do you still want me to go through with it?"

Englehardt shut his eyes. "Yes," he said succinctly, "just add Pogostin," and then murdered Martin in his mind.

Softly, Martin hung up.

Noelle watched the fireplace: tongues of orange and blue came and went and came again, growing brighter in the darkness. When she looked up again, Peter had moved to the window, staring out.

"Is something wrong?" she asked.

"With me, I suppose." Turning, Carey glanced at the chain across the door, and then knelt beside her. "Since you came back from El Salvador, I haven't once asked how it was."

"Better late than never." Noelle smiled wryly. "Not so good, in fact. Poverty, an army that's on its own—Duarte tries, but D'Aubuisson's a killer: if *he's* elected, the electorate will start to shrink. That's one of the most closed-off faces I've ever seen, incidentally—there's no one home there except Francisco Franco."

"So what will *we* do?"

"Try working with whoever, I suppose." Reaching out, Noelle touched the hair curling at Peter's neck. "It was another trip, and now I'm here. I'm just glad to have you with me."

"I wish I were better company." He looked at his fingernails. "It's hard, right now . . ."

She watched him. "It's okay, Peter. I didn't *say* right now."

Suddenly, Peter pulled her close. "Right now," he murmured, "I just want to hold you."

The East Nineties, Martin thought, psychiatrists' heaven.

Across the street, in the pale light of an all-glass lobby, a uniformed guard paced circles around his desk.

Martin crossed the street, pushed through the glass door, and plopped his briefcase on the desk, smiling into the guard's face. "Forgot my homework," he said in embarrassment, and scribbled on the register the name of the building's only law firm. In the space for his own name, he signed, "Christopher Marlowe": security people were so stupid.

"You new here, Mr. Marlowe?"

Martin felt a moment of near-affection; the guard was opaquely earnest. "It's good you're so observant. They brought me in for securities work, just last week—stocks and bonds, you know."

"I thought I'd have remembered you." The guard nodded sagely. "Bonds—that's where the money is, all right. That, and those computer games."

"Oh, yes," Martin said softly. "Oh, yes, indeed."

Smiling, he walked to the elevator, briefcase swinging at his side.

He stepped in; quickly, he noted the emergency exit from the stairwell, fifteen feet across the lobby, and then pushed the button for the tenth floor. As the elevator rose, Martin smiled again: he could have used Tennessee Williams...

The elevator stopped at the door of the law firm. Martin got out, found the stairwell and descended two dark flights.

Pogostin's office was at the far end of the corridor, and its lock was moronically simple.

Inside, it was black.

For a moment, Martin stopped, imagining: when he turned on the light, Noelle Ciano would be waiting there, alone. Martin pulled the camera from his briefcase, hitting the button.

There were a couch, two chairs, and a desk.

Behind the desk, Martin saw the flat brown tape recorder.

He photographed it twice, thinking of Englehardt. With each

day of Carey's analysis, the small man seemed to need him more, just as he needed Noelle Ciano.

Someday, soon, they would make a trade.

Two flights of stairs, ten flights down in the elevator, were lost in mental images, until the guard's admiration broke his trance. "That was *fast*, Mr. Marlowe."

"I knew what I wanted," Martin said, smiling, and walked into the night.

Each morning, Noelle thought, should be as crystalline.

The lift took them up Mount Snow in a dizzying climb: its jagged peak as they moved closer was etched so clearly against a brilliant blue sky that it seemed more vivid. Slate-gray ridges marbled snow sparkling with sunlight; naked birch trees gleamed like polished silver from stands of pines; early skiers in bright jackets sped beneath them on the trails. When she turned to watch one, Peter asked, "Seeing photographs?"

"Some of my best." Noelle leaned against him. "I hope you're not too tired."

He kept staring forward. "Just of the dream."

Three men with packing crates and tool kits nodded to the doorman and took the elevator to Carey's apartment.

Martin was already there.

Answering the door, he said, "One thing from each room." The men disappeared inside.

Noelle raced after Peter Carey.

The trail was steep, narrow: Carey skied recklessly, throwing himself away. His skis spat white powder; pines flashed at the corner of her eyes; wind lashed her face and hair and crackled against her parka.

She strained to catch him.

All at once the trail widened and became less steep. Pushing off with her poles, Noelle curled forward and began skiing a breakneck straight line. Peter's back moved toward her . . .

She flew past him fifty feet from the bottom.

Skidding, Carey reached her in a nimbus of snow. "Enough," she told him. "You'll break your neck."

Silent, Carey knelt to check his bindings. "You're right,"

she remarked. "The problem's that fancy shit you buy. You should start renting your equipment, like I do."

The noonday sun was warm on her face. When Peter smiled up at her, it was worth a picture.

The tall man finished photographing each angle of Carey's apartment. The second took inventory; the third called to Martin from the bedroom. He touched the wall above Carey's bed with one fingertip. "This wall," he said. "Behind the rubber plant."

Martin nodded and went back to the kitchen.

The tall man had put away his camera and began unscrewing the mouthpiece of the telephone. "What kind of transmitter?" he asked Martin.

"The least conspicuous," he answered. "We won't be far away."

Above the rim of his first brandy, Carey glanced around the lodge, searching for an ugly stranger.

Their table near the fireplace had a clear view of the first floor: the bar and tables had begun to fill with twosomes and foursomes and singles looking to pair up for the night, their laughter forming a wall of noise against which Carey and Noelle were silent. He kept looking. "Ugly," she had told him, "with a kind of hanging underlip."

"See something?" she asked.

Carey shook his head; as cover, he remarked, "I was wondering how many of these couples would still be together next year," and then realized, oddly, that this was true.

Leaning toward the fire for warmth, Noelle shot him a quick look back. "What made you think of that?"

"The hustling, I suppose." Carey turned to her. "Maybe us."

Thoughtfully, Noelle gazed past him at the crowd. "We're really not doing much better than our parents, are we—any of us."

"At what?"

"At 'relationships'—that's a great eighties word, isn't it?" Her eyes were troubled. "I mean for *them* it's turned out pretty sad—women like my mother marrying 'good providers' who'd 'take care of them' and then they get to forty-five and their husband's this condescending stranger and their kids have split, and they're *no one*—no skills, no money: Mrs. John Doe, the maid-for-life. God, when I think of how my mother's lived, it's like someone's walking over my grave. But every time they visit, all she asks is when *I'm* getting married, like the Pulitzer was something I won in the Pillsbury bake-off. I don't know whether to be sad or pissed off."

Carey nodded. "Sometimes I imagine what *my* parents would be like. I guess one thing about it is that I don't have to watch them growing old."

For the first time, Noelle smiled. "Oh, I see your father as this rake—cool, and very *distingué*." The smile faded. "Only look at people *we* know, Peter: half my friends are living in and out with different guys, or getting divorced, and nothing lasts—it's just serial monogamy, that's all, with abortions instead of babies. And me—I've become so determined *not* to be my mother that I'm always checking to see whether I've got a fair deal or have started getting screwed."

"If you were that much of a hard ass, Ciano, you'd have bailed out in Greenwich."

"I'm talking *theory*." Her smile came and went. "Anyhow, I just hate to think that the only basis for people staying together was the economic slavery of women."

Carey permitted himself a quick glance around the room, saw nothing he could fix on, and finished his brandy. "Really, I don't know any more than you do." He stared into his glass. "Thinking about it, I've only seen one marriage I'd give a damn for—some college friends who married so young they didn't know any better than to just be happy—and she's with their kids so much that nothing she says now interests anyone but him. I'd go nuts listening to her, and yet they're happy, the kids are happy—you get into all those cosmic questions: the individual versus society, what debts we owe to others as opposed to ourselves, who raises children . . ."

"So where do *you* come out."

He shrugged. "Oh, I love my kids too much already to give them a father like me."

Noelle looked mildly amused. Half-seriously, half-facetiously, she asked, "But what if *your* father had felt like that?"

His father screamed.

Levy wished him to be hypnotized; he could not tell her this.

Carey forced another smile. "Then I wouldn't have all these problems," he said lightly. His father's burning face receded as he looked back into hers. "But then, neither would you."

"I don't mind." Noelle's eyes met his; softly, she added, "Let's go back to the cabin, okay?"

As they left, Carey checked the bar.

He locked their door behind them.

The three men selected one item from each of Carey's rooms, showing them to Martin for approval before they sealed them in a packing crate.

Martin nodded without comment: they were all appliances— a coffee-maker, a laser lamp, a clock-radio—and all plugged into walls.

When the packing was done, the three men carried the crate to the van they'd parked downstairs. The doorman waved taxis around it, clearing their way.

Martin stayed to dust each room for fingerprints: except for the missing appliances, all was as he'd found it.

Leaving, he smiled at Carey's silent alarm, then locked the door behind him.

Carey and Noelle lay next to each other on the rug.

The fire was orange-yellow, their wine glowed deep red in bright crystal, warmth and dark surrounded them. Their bodies were torpid, pleasantly weary. Their dishes were still on the table—the flames had drawn them like children. They smoked marijuana.

Carey passed her the joint. "Where'd you get this?" he asked.

"The guy next door—I thought maybe you could use some to unwind." She took a hit, passing it back.

"You talk to your neighbors?"

"Worse than incest, huh?"

"That's all right." Carey pulled acrid smoke deep into his lungs, held it, breathed out. "I don't think I've smoked dope since 1973. It's sort of nostalgic."

She grinned. "You're such a snob. Actually, it *is* nostalgic—it reminds me of college, when you had time to know people and even waste it with them. I miss that—things seem more superficial now."

Carey smiled into the fire. "'Ciano Looks Back—A Retrospective.'"

"Oh, come on, Peter—you remember."

"Not in the same way." He handed her the joint and drank more wine: the Cabernet tasted rich. "I pretty much kept my own company."

"Why was that?"

"The dreams, partly." His limbs felt warm as he stretched. "I suppose it was a matter of trust—maybe trusting myself."

She exhaled. "You really don't like letting go, do you. It's like someone's going to turn it on you."

He shrugged. "People do, though."

She rolled on her side, tapping ash in a tray, then looked at him. "But not me, Peter." She passed the joint again. Their fingertips brushed.

The fire spat and crackled, burning brighter. They watched it in silence, finishing the joint. "It's almost hot," she said.

He nodded. "Want to move?"

"It's okay." Sitting up, she shook back her hair, then peeled off her sweater.

She wore nothing underneath.

Carey stared at her. She sat cross-legged in blue jeans, sipping wine and watching the flame leap higher. Its glow burnished her olive skin, casting shadows beneath her breasts and cheekbones. Her hair shone black. Her nipples were deep pink.

With sudden fierceness, Carey wished to keep this moment.

He rose.

She looked up, startled. He raised his hand, signaling her to stay, then went to the kitchen and returned with her camera. He knelt beside her. "I'd like to," he said quietly.

Her eyes were dark brown. "Me?"

He nodded, mute. She hesitated. Then she took the camera from his hand, adjusted the light meter, and placed it in front of him, looking into his face. "No one's ever done this before, Peter."

"I know."

She turned toward the fire again. He watched her, unmoving, the camera still before him on the rug. "You can now," she said softly. "I fixed it."

He picked up the camera.

Flames danced on her skin. He pressed the button.

Turning, she took the camera, then his hand, rose, and led him to the bedroom door. There she turned again, without words, and placed the camera in his hands.

"Noelle . . ."

She put one finger to his lips. "It's all right, Peter. I trust you."

She closed the door gently behind them.

Martin was greeted by the security guard as he opened the glass door. "Back so *soon*, Mr. Marlowe?"

Martin felt his smile turn to rubber. The remark angered him: he did not like breaking into buildings twice. "Forgot something," he said sheepishly; signing in, he stalked to the elevator, a picture of self-disgust.

Inside Pogostin's office, he still felt edgy.

In haste, he pulled the tape recorder from his briefcase and placed it next to the recorder on Pogostin's desk—a perfect match.

Unplugging the first tape recorder from the wall, Martin put it in his briefcase; the one remaining would be used for Peter Carey. He bent by the outlet, to plug it in.

The door opened behind him.

Martin whirled. A slender Hispanic cleaning lady recoiled in the doorway, bucket swinging. He rose, smiling. "Wait . . ."

Frightened, she backed into the corridor.

Martin started for the door. He could twist her windpipe before she reached the elevator, pulse throbbing in his hands.

The door shut between them; Martin felt it interrupt the sequence of her death. Her footsteps skittered down the hall like a rabbit's.

He could not kill yet.

In moments she would warn the guard. He must move quickly.

In rapid sequence he replaced the second recorder with Pogostin's, plugged it in, and put the duplicate in his briefcase, leaving the office exactly as it was. Running to the elevator, he looked up at the red luminous numbers of its floors, and saw the light flash: one.

The maid would scamper through the lobby, to tell the guard. She would hide, and then he too would begin to watch the elevator.

Martin pressed the button marked ten; hearing the elevator begin to rise, he took the exit door and started scrambling down the pitch-black stairwell. He could see almost nothing; feel nothing but the rail in his hand, and his own sweat. Going down, he counted each new floor.

Five.

With a gun, even a fool could kill. Damn Englehardt...

Three.

As Martin counted two, he burst onto the second floor and ran to its elevator. Above it, the red number hit ten.

Martin pushed the button marked two, and sprinted back to the stairwell. If he was lucky, the guard would watch the numbers moving toward him.

He reached the first floor, skin crawling with tension. Creeping to the exit door, he peered out.

Back toward Martin, the guard pointed his revolver at the elevator. Above him, the red number turned to five.

Gently, Martin let himself out the door.

The soles of his shoes were rubber.

The guard's shoulders tensed; with each silent step closer, the elevator descended.

Four.

Martin took two more soft steps; a single sound, and the stupid guard would whirl to shoot him.

Three.

Five feet more; four feet; three.

The elevator hit two, and stuck.

Too late, the guard began turning, and then Martin's arm hooked around his windpipe.

The revolver clattered, echoing, on the floor.

The guard quivered. Martin could feel the warm pounding pulse in his throat, too tight to make a sound.

Martin wrenched his arm still tighter. Softly, just before the guard passed out, he whispered, "Back so *soon*, Mr. Marlowe?" and then the man dropped at his feet.

Noelle touched Peter's hair. "It feels blond," she whispered. "Even in the dark."

Naked, he lay holding her, head resting on the pillow. The camera sat on the night stand. She felt his warmth, the utter relaxation of his body. "I'm sorry," he murmured. "The way you were with me, how I felt—I just couldn't hold back."

She smiled, shaking her head. "I didn't want you to." He raised his face. "I didn't," she told him. "I've hoped someday it could be like that for you. I mean, you've always been so controlled with me—I wasn't sure . . ."

He put a finger to her lips. "You should be, now."

Englehardt's hand tightened around the telephone. "How did it happen?"

"You gave me one day, to bug an office in a building I didn't know." Martin's voice was slurred and insinuating. "Carey's memories were clearly more important than the arrival time of cleaning ladies."

Englehardt counted to five. Softly, he said. "If Carey agrees, this man will have a tape."

"I won't go back in there."

Englehardt paused for one last moment, marshaling his sense of command. "In that case," he answered coldly, "you'll go back into Levy's."

Carey still felt their second loving in the numb curl of his feet and fingertips, a lightness in his temples, warm lassitude spreading through his body in deep, even breaths. The night around them felt close, heavy, intimate. Her breasts were damp against his chest; silver moonlight crossed her face; her hair, thick, soft and clean-smelling, had fallen back upon the pillow. Her eyes shone with feeling. Carey had never been so close to anyone.

He cradled her face in both hands. "There's something else I have to tell you."

She smiled. "About us?"

He could not stop now.

"About Levy—he wants me to see a hypnotist." Carey looked away. "If I agree, I may remember what happened to me, very soon."

Noelle waited until he looked back at her. "You've been sitting on a lot, haven't you."

"I just don't know if I can do it." Rolling on his back, Carey spoke to the ceiling. "Ever since I met you, I've been afraid that you would die."

Her eyes widened. "Because of your father?"

"My guess is that Levy thinks so." He twisted sideways, to see her. "What he's *said* is that I may feel responsible for my father's death."

"But you were six—how could you be?"

"I don't know—I don't *want* to know. What I keep feeling is bad enough."

"That something will happen to me?"

"Yes." He looked away. "As soon as I remember..."

"Because I saw an ugly stranger? Peter, you can't live like that."

"I can't explain it," he said wearily. "It's just something I feel. Can you understand at all?"

"Of course—I'd be frightened, too." She grasped his wrist. "But I'd be more frightened of the way you're living now. Your father's death has defined half your life and will keep on defining the rest of it, and you don't even know why. What could be more frightening for either one of us?"

Carey's voice was soft. "I don't know yet."

Noelle said nothing.

For a long time they lay side by side, fingertips touching in the dark.

Finally, they slept, until his dream awakened them.

Martin had not slept in forty-eight hours, and his nerves were raw: this morning, he must take extra care.

Fighting weariness, he watched the three men dressed as movers re-enter Carey's apartment with the identical crate they had moved out earlier.

Checking their inventory, they unpacked and placed one item in each room.

Four.

The clock-radio, the coffee-maker, the lamp...

The bell to Carey's alarm system, from the dining room.

Martin smiled; the duplicates were perfect.

Taking the photographs from his pocket, he walked through each room, checking the pictures to ensure that each appliance was replaced exactly as before.

The three men returned to the van. Martin stayed, staring at the wall above the bed.

He felt less tired.

Carey felt his muscles straining as he passed Noelle and then turned at the bottom of the run just before she reached him in a powdery spray, laughing into the mist and sunlight and hanging onto his shoulders. "You finally win one, Carey."

He brushed snow from her hair. Softly and seriously he said, "Live with me."

"It seems so sad," the old woman told her dog, "not to live here anymore."

Her husband nodded to himself. "Still, I suppose it's the best thing. In our condition."

The doorman handed her a dog leash as she stared up at their window. "Dropped it," he said cheerfully. "Can't forget that."

The woman thanked him shyly, then knelt to apologize to the yipping gray poodle. Her husband watched the three movers load their couch onto the van, murmuring under his breath, "Be careful."

The man preferred watching the truck, he decided: he wished to remember their living room as it was rather than watch holes appearing, tables picked clean of vases. Strange that the things that filled their living room filled so little of the truck...

It was cold. The woman comforted her dog. "I'm sorry, Abner—the man told us we can't even say goodbye to Peter."

Her husband nodded again.

Driving into the afternoon sun, Carey pushed down the visor and slid a muted version of Vivaldi's "Four Seasons" into his tape deck, in preference to Tchaikovsky. "Bombast doesn't suit New England," he remarked to Noelle.

"What about surprises?" she asked dryly.

"It can't be that much of a shock."

"It's just that this weekend was so much more than I'd expected." She paused. "Not so long ago I was wondering whether I should call it off."

He glanced quickly over. "You're not serious?"

She nodded. "Sometimes you don't give me much to go on."

"I'm trying..."

"I know," she said quietly. "But do *you* know how frightened you looked after you asked me? Like you'd heard yourself."

For a moment he watched a distant spire peering from between pines and rolling hills, listened to the intricate, baroque violins. In a low voice, he answered, "Maybe I was afraid that you'd say no. Please, I want you somewhere safe."

"But that's not a reason, Peter. I can't be like some Ping-Pong ball, bouncing back and forth between emotions—mine *or* yours. I need to feel more substantial than that. I mean, Manhattan's where we'd be living, with Phillip and all those ghosts."

"And nightmares?"

She turned to him. "Please, let's just go with the weekend for a while. We were good there, *you* were so good with me. I want to build on that."

"But the dream's part of it, right? This hypnosis thing with Levy."

"Look, you've told me how you feel. I don't want to put that pressure on you." She stared ahead, as if torn by indecision, then looked back. "I love you," she said softly. "Okay?"

He turned to her. "Noelle..."

She held up one hand. "Don't say anything back, not now. You're too afraid yet." Quickly, she smiled. "And so am I. The road's pretty narrow."

A narrow road...

Carey forced himself to concentrate, shifting and accelerating and passing cars, letting his subconscious work on what Levy wanted, what *she* really wanted. Already he missed the cabin: he did not wish to face it.

There was a red Fiat ahead; as a distraction, Carey chased it, caught up. Passing, he took a curve.

"Faster, Daddy..."

A corner flashing in the windshield...

Dewey...

He braked abruptly.

Noelle seemed startled. "You okay?"

"Fine." He touched her hand. "Just daydreaming."

The two men glanced at the tire tracks that Carey's car had left, and then re-entered the cabin.

Within five minutes, they had removed the tapes from beneath the dinner table and under the bed.

Returning to their car, they began the long drive to Manhattan, to meet the ugly man.

Englehardt opened the textbook Martin had left for him, and began reading:

"What I propose," Pogostin wrote in his preface, "is that psychotherapy through hypnosis will in time supplant the more laborious analytic method of uncovering, and then healing, repressed traumatic memory."

In the background, from the tape spinning on his desk, Peter Carey said, "I'm talking to my father—something like, 'It's too dark down there for elephants, Daddy.'"

Englehardt turned the page.

It was past nine when Peter and Noelle drove up to the Aristocrat. Peter smiled; a shade ruefully, she thought. "You *can* stay the night, can't you?"

Resting her chin on one hand, she feigned deep thought. "That's a serious commitment. But then this is a meaningful relationship."

"Look, I'm thinking about hypnosis, all right?"

She turned, amusement gone. "Don't act picked on, Peter—it's not like you."

He shook his head. "It's been on my mind. Coming back was like facing it again."

"I was joking—to bring the hypnosis up then was like accusing me of blackmail. I'm not some emotional terrorist..."

"It wasn't meant..."

"Of course I'll stay. You knew that."

"Yeah, I did." He leaned back, exhaling. "There has to be an end to it, doesn't there."

"For *your* sake, yes." Noelle moved closer. "Look, Peter, whatever it is, I can take care of myself. I'm not pulling out on you, and I'm not going anywhere—except maybe to your place, for the night."

Carey looked from her to the Aristocrat, and then nodded. "I guess we'd better go there, then."

They both got out.

Emerging, the doorman called, "Evening Miss Ciano, Mr. Carey—nice to have you back."

Carey stopped by the trunk, watching him. The doorman's eyes darted away; quickly, he smiled at Noelle.

"I'll move this in a minute," Carey told him.

The doorman's smile faded. Still facing Noelle, he answered Carey, "I'll have someone move it for you," and then ducked back inside.

Peter Carey stared after him.

Tired, Englehardt listened to the latest tapes; without comment, Martin had laid them on the corner of his desk, and left.

Soft with lovemaking, frightened for her, Carey told Noelle, "Ever since I met you, I've been afraid that you would die..."

Carey had not decided.

For silent moments, Englehardt listened, deciding when to murder Peter Carey. All that was needed was a few more days.

Englehardt picked up the telephone and called Barth. "It's time," he told him softly, "for you to see what it is I've done for you."

"Problem?"

Peter and Noelle had been drinking Irish coffee in the kitchen, winding down and talking about everything and nothing, when he fell silent. Now he answered, "I just keep waiting for Barth to reappear. Phil's been watching me like a sentinel, still pushing a sale, but there's been not one word from Barth. It's eerie."

"Don't think too hard about it—you might materialize him." As a distraction, she stole the rest of Peter's whipped cream.

"Jesus, Ciano, you've *had* yours."

She licked her lips. "Breakfast," she explained blithely. "My Doug Sutcliffe session's first thing in the morning. But don't worry—I'll run off the whipped cream after that."

Peter stirred his coffee. "Just as long as you don't run off with Sutcliffe."

"I'll try and restrain myself." She leaned back, as if viewing him from another angle. "Why is it," she asked, "that you never mention your mother?"

"What brought that to mind?"

"Just that she's your first female prototype. I mean, you know all about my father."

"There's not much I can tell you." Peter's face clouded; Noelle felt sorry for her question. "Let's just say that I didn't turn out to be what she'd wanted from life." He shrugged. "I've never noticed that kids do much for anyone's marriage—which gets us back to our discussion at the ski lodge."

Shaking her head, Noelle said quietly, "It doesn't have to."

She put down her coffee. They rose from the table, together.

Barth turned from the window. "How did you accomplish this?" he demanded.

Englehardt hesitated; his services appeared more wondrous when unexplained. "Our usual procedures."

"Don't condescend to me." Barth glared at him, his acquired diction growing more pronounced. "I want to know what I'm paying you for, not some pretense of magic."

"Very well." If awe wouldn't do, better the professionalism of the humble servant—for now. "It's quite straightforward," he answered crisply. "Take Carey's apartment, for example. Most New Yorkers go to a great deal of trouble to feel safe in their own living space, and Peter Carey has ensured that his is one of the most secure in Manhattan: he's got a doorman, guards patrolling the corridors, and a deadbolt connected to an extremely sophisticated alarm system." Here Englehardt permitted himself a smile. "All of which fits with the deep and gnawing insecurity which his psychiatrist so graphically portrays. In this case, his fears are justified: even in a secure building, people remain the key . . ."

"Get to the point."

"The doorman. He despises New York, and wishes to live in Florida. Posing as a government agent, my operative offers him money, promising that none of Carey's things will be permanently displaced. The doorman knows we're not government, or we wouldn't be bribing him so handsomely, but if the motive isn't robbery he can tell himself there isn't really any harm. The manager has duplicate keys to all apartments, and it's no trouble for him to borrow one for the brief period we require to make a second duplicate. We don't have to break in: we simply enter the apartment as Carey would.

"Of course, we *were* quite fortunate in his former neighbors—it's not a golden era for the aging. For years the Krantzes watched maintenance fees and property taxes and simple inflation eating through a fixed income, until they were forced to secure a second mortgage in this time of high interest rates and proposed cutbacks in Social Security—quite a desperate step. Suddenly, we confront these frightened, passive people as representatives of a foreign buyer offering an undreamed-of amount of cash and a substitute apartment on the East Side, where Carey will never see them." Englehardt smiled professorially. "Our only requirement is that they vacate on request, maintaining the secrecy of our publicity-conscious principal from everyone, including Peter Carey. As reluctant as they were, they had no other choice. With that, we've secured the predicate for total surveillance."

"Yes." For the first time, Barth's face betrayed the eagerness Englehardt needed. "Let's see how that works."

In the darkness, Carey's hands were shadows moving across slim, silver ridges, Noelle's back and shoulders.

Sitting at the base of her spine, he massaged her, tenderly and without hurry, working down from her neck and the hollow between her shoulder-blades and then back up again, using the flat of both palms. Her eyes were closed, her murmurs of endearment gentle and indistinct. Carey stroked and kneaded, his expression for once soft, unguarded, almost unfocused. Raising her head, Noelle turned sideways and exposed one breast; Carey bent his mouth to hers and then to the firm pinkness of her nipple as she rolled on her back so that his knees now clasped her hips and, still kissing her breast, he slid one arm beneath her shoulders and two fingers of the other hand so delicately between her thighs that they seemed almost to rest there. She cried out; Carey's pelvis arched and her legs slid from beneath him and opened as if demanding that his lips move down her stomach to rest in the tangle of black hair. As his tongue probed deep within, her hips thrust upwards and began moving, Carey's mouth moving with them, Noelle's lips again parting to murmur an unfinished something to which he paid no heed until once more he raised his mouth to cover hers, both arms now clasping her back and, chest sliding across her breasts, slim hips between slim thighs, he entered her. Moving slowly at first, until she spoke, he then moved faster, at last moving so frenziedly that she cried out again; still Carey did not stop. Their rhythm repeated, over and over, Noelle crying out and moving with Carey, fingers now scraping his back, now grasping the pillows, her face abstracted, dreamy, lost as Carey moved, relentless, and she screamed, coming repeatedly, tears running from half-closed eyes down her face until all at once he cupped the back of her head with his hand, mouth open in an inarticulate moan as he looked into her face and his body shuddered, and then she looked back, eyes focusing again, mouth rising to his amidst the continuing shudders which slowed finally, and then stopped, and each stared at the other for a long silent moment before his head fell to her shoulder, and Englehardt snapped off the machine and the silver bodies became a silver dot shrinking in a blank screen. "As you can see," he said dryly, "it's quite effective."

Barth stared transfixed at the vanishing dot. His voice was tight. "How did you get the picture."

"Remarkable, isn't it? The camera you see on the wall above the video screen is peering at our young lovers through several pinpricks in a square-inch layer of paint which Mr. Carey's rubber plant now helps to conceal. The equipment is very light-sensitive."

"And the sound?"

"We take an appliance from each room—a coffee-maker, a lamp, the clock-radio—and replace them with exact duplicates containing undetectable electronic transmitters. You'll note the originals in the crate beneath the video machine—all that's required is that they plug into walls." Englehardt pointed to the large AM-FM stereo resting where the Krantzes' bed had been. "That's where the sound comes out."

Looking back, he saw that Barth's gaze had not moved from the screen. "So," he added smoothly, "Peter Carey has nothing he can hide from you. Of course, you can understand the uses of all we'll see here only to the extent we understand young Mr. Carey. Hence, Dr. Levy's notes, which you really must read, are as crucial as subtitles in a foreign film."

"Don't assign me homework, professor." Barth turned away from the machine. "*Your* assignment is to learn how to *explain* things to me."

"Very well." Englehardt shrugged. "As Dr. Levy has noted, Miss Ciano is the person for whom Peter cares, and fears, most deeply. By taking him to Vermont, and then drawing forth more emotion than he has ever dared to feel, she has made our work far easier. Peter is already feeling that she's the only bright spot in his fears, that he needs her desperately: this makes him more vulnerable than ever. So the woman you were just admiring becomes the weapon we will use; the more their bodies join in life, the more the image of her death will torment him."

Barth kept staring. Suddenly, Englehardt saw that, beneath his rudeness, the man was terribly shaken: he had seen this before, this shrinking from knowledge, as if confronted by one's own humanity, even inconsequence. "But perhaps," he went on easily, "we should consider this tomorrow. It may be well for you to absorb the change which has occurred." Englehardt finished with a benign smile. "After all, you're a much more powerful man than you have ever been before."

As if in contradiction, Barth pointed at the screen, asking in a dead flat voice, "This tape—what will you do with it?"

"Oh, for now, we'll keep it here. Security, you know. Besides"—now Englehardt was smiling—"one of my operatives will be watching it after you leave—a small reward for services rendered. But that's really just a loan. As you can see, this tape, and the people on it, now belong to you."

Casually, he flicked on the dial . . .

Noelle gazed up at Carey. Softly, she said, "You've never done that before."

He stroked her hair. "What's that, lover?"

She smiled. "Looked into my face."

CHAPTER 12

Carey and Noelle pushed out of the Aristocrat and were hit by the cacophony of rush hour. The sky over Central Park was lowering with the hard gray look of snow; when Carey did not remark on it, the doorman began moving from foot to foot. "You'll be wanting a cab, I bet."

"In a minute." Carey walked Noelle a few steps up the sidewalk, then touched her arm. "You'll be late."

She turned. "Then you're really going to talk to him—about hypnosis?"

Carey jammed both hands in his pockets; their breaths crossed in the air, as mist. "Yes—this morning."

Impulsively, she kissed him, then pulled back. "That wasn't for . . ."

"I know what you meant." His palm cupped her face. "Just promise me—no matter how absurd it seems—not to go anywhere you don't have to, and not to go alone."

She placed one hand over his. "Nights I'll be with you—it's work that's tricky. Things pop up . . ."

"Can you take time off?"

She shook her head. "We're short two people, and I'll have to print the pictures. But I haven't seen that man again—I'll just be extra careful, okay?"

"*Promise.*"

"Please." He kissed her. "Anyhow, enjoy your session with Sutcliffe—it isn't every day one photographs a living legend."

"No big deal—after all, I just slept with one." Her grin snapped clean and wide and sharp; turning, she tossed "See you tonight" over her shoulder, and marched off toward the Dakota.

Carey stared after her until she disappeared.

264

He walked back to the Aristocrat, glancing around him as the doorman whistled for his taxi. "Seen the Krantzes this morning?"

"Oh, they moved." The doorman kept whistling.

"Moved?" Carey turned on him. "You're not serious?"

"Just last weekend." A battered cab squealed to a stop in front of them; quickly, the doorman added, "Right here, Mr. Carey," and jerked open the door.

Carey looked from the cab to the doorman. "Let him go," he said, "I've got something else to do."

He hurried back into the building.

The doorman watched Carey disappear into the lobby, and then started inside.

"Pardon me." Blocking him was a stuffy resident with steel-gray hair that matched her fur. "I require a taxi, please."

The doorman glanced quickly at the house phone in the lobby; with the habit of years, he nodded, smiled, and opened the door for the woman.

Carey's taxi had not left; the cabbie had flipped open the *Times* and begun reading. "Here," the doorman announced, and trundled her into the cab.

"The Plaza," she ordered the cabbie, as the doorman rushed back inside.

In the silent bedroom, Noelle moved toward Peter Carey. She shrugged her shoulders, tossing back her dark hair. Her spine was silver. Carey held out his hand. She took it, turning toward the camera.

The telephone rang.

Still watching, Martin picked it up. "Mr. Carey's on his way," the doorman said, and then there were three brisk raps on the door.

"Thank you," Martin murmured, and hung up.

Above him, on the video screen, Noelle lay down on the bed. "Here," Carey said softly, "let me get your back."

Through the door, Peter Carey shouted, "Is anyone there?"

"Umm," Noelle murmured, and then she rolled over on her front and smiled at Martin.

* * *

Noelle stood beneath the Dakota's looming and dingy grandeur as a security guard returned her press card through the window of its wooden guardhouse, announcing, "Mr. Sutcliffe is expecting you."

His languid motion forward seemed to confer some transitory humanity which he might instantly repeal. Riding up the elevator, Noelle switched off her annoyance, amused at herself; she had been preparing to be unimpressed.

Peter would be seeing Levy; she had not seen the ugly man . . .

Doug Sutcliffe had not been photographed in six years: she must concentrate on that.

Two more guards were posted at his suite; finally, an effeminate man wearing short hair and beard admitted her with an air of parsimony and a total absence of warmth, whispering, "He has only a moment."

"That's all I want."

Entering the living room, an enormous art-deco nightmare containing plastic furniture and Warhol paintings, she saw that the young reporter from the *Times* sat listening intently; the Midlands accent still sounded hard to follow.

"It's quite simple," Sutcliffe's voice was saying. "I've reappeared because people are starving . . ."

Did you just find that out? Noelle wondered automatically, and then Sutcliffe leaned into her line of vision.

What had changed was Sutcliffe's face.

When Sutcliffe had abandoned Lethal at their incendiary height, retreating to an estate in the Adirondacks to compose songs no one had heard yet, he had looked mocking and superior, without the character to match. The thin face she saw now seemed closer to ascetic: gentler, but not in a soft way, with eyes like distant points of light. He looked up.

"Keep talking." Noelle unslung her camera and sat crosslegged on the floor. "I just want to get a feel for this."

"We're almost through." Sutcliffe faced the reporter. "The *impact* of me showing up again with Lethal is sheer accident." His shrug seemed to take in the apartment, the guards, the hovering major domo. "I guess that's how God made it so big—by not being seen. But I'll go with it if I can help feed some people in the third world."

The reporter adjusted his glasses with a look of bemusement. "But what did you learn by retreating."

"Musically, or philosophically?"

The reporter spread his hands. "Either."

Leaning back on the couch, Sutcliffe seemed to withdraw for a moment, his lean frame becoming still. "I had to teach myself reality—like having a stroke and learning to walk again. When I got hooked on rock I was playing at being an idol in shitty clubs, not telling people I was really a draftsman, even though that's how I kept eating, you know. And then one year you're this thing called a superstar and filling whole stadiums with screaming people who can't even see your face and other people are falling all over themselves to suspend the law of gravity for you—drugs, women, anything you like—and you're *still* not real, or afraid maybe you *won't* be if you don't keep getting seen and selling in the millions. There was someone or something different every night until it all got like a blur— you know, the *same*." Sutcliffe glanced over at Noelle. "I needed to put things back in scale—deal with people one to one, maybe even find out what I was like alone and what songs I wanted to write. You know," he finished sardonically, "look into the existential void."

"How is that?"

Sutcliffe held up one hand. "I'm a little tired, you know. It's like method acting—I have to think about how this concert's going to be until I can feel my way into it, 'cause it's been a while." To Noelle, he added, "I know you've got your job to do yet."

The reporter left. Noelle kept busy with her camera. "This won't take long," she said.

Sutcliffe looked at her keenly. "So what do *you* think?"

"About what?"

He spread his arms. "All this—coming back."

"Pretty dramatic." She adjusted her lens. "I've been to Thailand, parts of Cambodia—I like it that you're trying to help." Looking up, she beckoned with one hand. "A little more toward me, okay?"

He turned, face still slightly averted, eyes grave and contemplative. She snapped one picture, took a second, then stopped, frowning. He held his pose. "What's wrong?"

"Let me take another." She did that, exhaled, then decided to take a chance. "You, actually. You haven't quite gotten it down yet."

Sutcliffe faced her. "What down?"

"Secular sainthood." Noelle hesitated for one last moment, and then plunged ahead. "You know, the 'I've eaten so many peyote buttons and fucked so many groupies that now I see what other men cannot.' Only now you're wondering whether *this* routine is real." She picked up the camera, said, "Most people don't get six years off, okay?" and pushed the button.

It was done by instinct: in that split second, she had seen the surprised, ironic smile of a bright man caught between the self-indulgent rock star he had been and the man of contemplation he wished to be. Noelle put down the Nikon. "I'm sorry," she said, "but that last shot was the real one. You can throw me out now."

Sutcliffe stared at her. "Will you come to the concert?" he asked softly.

Noelle watched him until she was certain what he'd meant. "I have a boyfriend."

Sutcliffe looked back at her; simultaneously, they glanced up to see if the bearded major domo had witnessed his embarrassment, and laughed together. When they finished laughing, her smile was genuine. "Anyhow, it's true."

Sutcliffe reached toward a brass box on the coffee table and handed her a small envelope. "Two tickets, then."

Opening it, Noelle read the price and took forty dollars from her shoulder bag. "Please," Sutcliffe said, "that's not necessary."

She held it out, smiling again. "I've been there, remember?"

He took the money. "I'll see they get it, then. And enjoy the concert."

"Thank you—we will." She rose and shook his hand. Holding it for a moment longer, she said, "Good luck," and left.

Carey was still shaken. "You couldn't dynamite those people loose," he told Levy. "And just as I knocked, I could have sworn hearing one ring of a telephone, before it was picked up. But no one came to the door."

"And that's when you had further discussion with the door-man?"

"In which he denied knowing the Krantzes' precise where-abouts or who the buyer was. I don't believe him."

"Then help me, Peter. Let's take inventory of what threatens you, from A to Z. Tell me, how many of those fears relate to your amnesia?"

"I don't know."

"What I propose, Peter, is that they all do."

"Look, she saw the same man twice, no question—the eyes and hanging underlip she describes are not something I've made up."

"But you've feared for her long before *he* first appeared. Like your sense that Barth is using Phillip, all your instincts keep tying it to your father's death. Or is that too forward of me?"

"No." Carey exhaled. "I'm afraid that by remembering I'll harm Noelle."

"Do you know why?"

Carey shook his head. "You asked me if I might feel guilt over my father's death. If that were true, then it's hard to know how that might affect me. It's not pleasant to consider."

"And yet, in spite of all these things, you're considering my recommendation?"

"Yes."

"Because you need to know?"

"That, and because of Noelle. I want a life with her." Carey's voice was soft. "I realize I'm not whole."

"Then something's changed."

"I'm in love with her." Carey hesitated. "I guess I always have been."

"Well," Levy said dryly. "That makes two. Noelle, and your father."

"Yes." Carey twisted sideways. "I love them both."

Levy's voice softened. "I didn't mean to make light of your dilemma. Instinct tells you that by remembering you'll cause Noelle some harm—perhaps because of the man who followed her, or Phillip's odd behavior. And yet you feel the damage done to you: the nightmares, the flashbacks, this drive to Green-wich . . ."

"I'm afraid of losing her if I *don't* do this . . ."

The sentence trailed off. Quietly, Levy finished for him, "And afraid of losing Charles if you do?"

"You *knew* that?"

"Your connection to Charles Carey—through the firm and otherwise—is very precious to you." Pausing, Levy added gently, "As it was to me."

"But you . . ."

"And now you don't want to sever it by somehow feeling responsible for his death." Levy paused. "You see, Peter, I know that, too."

Carey sat upright, facing him. "Then can't *you* see the difference?"

"Yes." Levy looked away. "*My* memories of Charles are intact. It's his son I'm seeing now."

"I remember . . ."

"A demigod, as seen by a little boy. The man I knew loved his son more than his career or pride, or even his life." Levy turned at last to face him. "Nothing you can ever learn could possibly have changed that for him." Eyes wet, still Levy did not turn from him. "Nothing," he repeated. "I promise you that."

"You're the boy who I imagined, Peter."

"Doctor . . ."

Levy held up his hand. More steadily, he asked, "Will you, Peter? Will you go to this man, and try?"

Carey's throat was tight. "Yes," he answered. "I will."

Martin dialed the telephone, then turned back to the picture.

Once more, as in a dream, Noelle Ciano moved with Peter Carey . . .

"Yes?" Englehardt answered.

"I've been listening, as you asked. Carey agreed to hypnosis."

Martin watched the screen, waiting. Very softly, Englehardt asked, "Has he an appointment?"

"Not yet."

In the silence, Martin sensed resolve flowing through the small man. "Then let me know," Englehardt said tonelessly, "as soon as he has done that . . ."

Noelle gazed up at Carey. "You've never done that before."

"What's that, lover?"

She smiled. "Looked into my face..."

"I'll do that," Martin said, and hung up.

Soon, he sensed, Noelle would look into *his* face.

Developing the Sutcliffe film at the *Times*, Noelle recalled the roll hidden in her shoulder bag. She glanced at her watch, deciding to grab lunch at her apartment, and then hustled from the building, checking faces for the ugly man, to catch the IRT as it screeched up to the platform.

Now, stepping from her darkroom, she considered the photographs, destroying all but one.

She walked to her bedroom and held it to the light, thoughtful. Then she sat at her desk, writing a brief note. When she finished, she sealed the note and the photograph in a pale-blue envelope, smiling to herself, and left, looking quickly down both sides of the street.

Martin watched Noelle step into Carey's bedroom, and place an envelope on his pillow.

She vanished from the screen.

The system was established: the doorman had called from the lobby, announcing her arrival, and would call again when she left. Resealing Carey's mail, Martin heard the soft click of the deadbolt over the stereo.

He began imagining what message she might leave, should it ever be for him.

The telephone rang. He rose, key in hand.

The light flashed on Clayton Barth's private line. He hit the button, answering, "Barth," and then Englehardt said, "I wish to consult with you."

Barth's nerves picked up a faint, insistent message. "Concerning what?"

"It's rather urgent—I've been rethinking your acquisition of John Carey's firm, and I believe it's time to take a rather decisive step. I'll need your permission."

"I'm quite busy today." Barth paused, testing. "Perhaps we should do this by telephone."

"Really, I wouldn't waste your time on trivial matters, or those to which delay would do no harm."

Barth's eyes narrowed. In a private piece of play acting, he consulted his watch, delaying to make his point with Englehardt. "Between eight and eight-thirty," he said in a reluctant voice. "You'll have to do with that."

"I shall." Barth heard a quick rush of adrenaline in the words, and then Englehardt added, respectfully, "Thank you," and hung up.

Alone, Barth began searching for what troubled him until, instinctively, he turned to the Manhattan skyline, and saw John Carey's building.

"Manhattan information."

"Yes." Carey saw the first flakes of snow melting on his window. "I'd like the new listing for Alfred Krantz."

"How are you spelling that?"

"K-r-a-n-t-z."

"Just a moment." Turning from the window, Carey stared at the picture of his father, and then the operator said, "I have no new listing under Krantz. When did he . . . ?"

"This weekend."

"It takes ten days, sir. You'll have to call back then."

Charles Carey grinned down at him, frozen by the memory of a camera, alive . . .

Carey hung up, and headed for his uncle's office.

Phillip's assistant looked up from her typewriter. "Hi, Susan—Phil in?"

"He just called." She pushed her glasses back up the bridge of her nose. "This sore throat he's got is really rough. He said no one was to call him."

"What if it's an emergency?"

"I'm sorry, Peter—he's not even answering." She shifted in her chair. "Is there something I can do?"

"Yes," Carey snapped. "When he calls back, tell him I'm coming over."

Phillip Carey sat in the library of his town house, amidst his father's books.

He remembered them—the years, the authors, how they

had looked in galley proofs. On summer evenings, his window filtered the fading sunlight in golden shafts, and lent his shelves the gauzy richness of an old color photograph whose tints have blurred. Sometimes, sitting there drinking, he would forget...

The telephone rang, once, and then it was winter, and only Peter was alive.

The ring was Englehardt's signal.

Reluctant, fearful of some new demand, Phillip called him. "Yes?"

"Your nephew is coming to visit, Phillip. I suggest you go to the Museum of Modern Art—on a doctor's appointment, of course."

Phillip felt weary. "I'll simply tell him I'm sick."

"Not after your performance the other day. He's not to see you, is that clear?"

"Very well." Phillip closed his eyes. "What about this business of hypnosis?"

"We'll discuss that this evening—here, at ten o'clock."

"Why so late?"

"I have an earlier appointment," Englehardt said softly. "But I should be through by then."

Album in his lap, Martin stared at the copy he had made of the photograph, now restored to its place on Carey's pillow. Gently, he touched Noelle's body.

A telephone rang, and then a voice came from the stereo: "Peter Carey's office."

"Yes." The second voice sounded older each time Martin heard it. "Is Mr. Carey in?"

"He's stepped out for a moment. Can I take a message?"

"Yes, please. This is Dr. Levy. Tell him that I've made an appointment with Dr. Pogostin."

Martin dialed his own telephone, still listening.

"It's for nine o'clock tomorrow, at Pogostin's office. Let me give you the address..."

"Yes?" Englehardt answered.

"Carey's appointment is for nine o'clock tomorrow."

"I see." There was silence. "Then you must go back to Levy's, as soon as he receives the tape."

And just guess what you'll do for me, Martin thought to himself, and slid the picture of Noelle into his album.

For the second time, Peter Carey pounded on his uncle's door.

No one answered.

Carey jammed both hands in his coat pockets, and then remembered standing there once before, on the doorstep of a darkened house, three days before Christmas.

He bent, opening the milk-chute, and patted the top with his fingertips.

Ten years later, the green magnetic keycase was still inside.

Sliding back the lid, Carey removed the key, and placed it in the lock.

"Sometimes even brothers need their privacy..."

Carey hesitated; then he turned the key, and looked inside. "Phil?"

From the corner of the street, Phillip watched his nephew call to him.

Impulsively, Phillip started back, to see what Peter wanted; then Peter disappeared inside, reminding him to fear, and Phillip Carey turned and slowly walked toward the museum.

Barth waved Englehardt to the place he had selected for him. "You've half an hour," he said without introduction, "to tell me what you find so pressing."

Englehardt sat in an armless chair at the end of a table so polished that it reflected his face as a translucent mask. Barth had dimmed the conference room: deprived of props, Englehardt seemed less like a thief of power than an aging technocrat, strip-mined of dreams. His shoulders stooped. Imagining the comic figure he must cut in his underwear, Barth smiled inwardly at his own apprehension. The true leader brings his specialists to heel, training their pride to his ends: Roosevelt and Old Joe Kennedy, Nixon and Kissinger.

"Do you also wish my recommendations?"

Englehardt's voice was so soft Barth could barely hear. "Speak up."

Englehardt spoke to the table. "Perhaps if I moved closer?"

Barth paused, annoyed. With a show of carelessness, he said, "As you like," and waved him to a chair on his right.

"Thank you." Englehardt walked stiffly forward, pointing to his throat. "Sore, you know—Phillip Carey has it, too."

Deflecting the remark with a passing smile, indulgent and impersonal, Barth demanded, "What is it you have to say."

Englehardt looked up. "That it's time to force a sale from Phillip."

"Now?" Covering his wariness, Barth rested his chin on tented fingers. "I've been expecting some further effort to immobilize *Peter* Carey. You've taken some very intricate measures to set all that in place—"

"—which shall prove invaluable in telling you everything he does or plans to do—in or out of court—and *why* he does it. Indeed, without my operation, Peter would have remained an incomprehensible stranger, destroying your hopes through this lawsuit as you struggled vainly to stop him. But the effective use of *Phillip* requires dispatch."

The man was nervous, Barth thought suddenly, he never spoke this quickly. "We have four months yet . . ."

". . . and as Phillip is where you must start, the most effective use of our surveillance is in the context of a *fait accompli.*"

Barth stared at him, reasserting his control. "You're giving me conclusions without a plan."

"You've already thought of it, I'm sure." As he watched Barth, Englehardt's voice slid to a note of reassurance. "The surveillance is in place, and we've discovered Peter's weakness for Miss Ciano is much greater than we'd guessed. *Now* I direct Phillip to sell you *both* his forty-nine percent interest *and* two percent of Peter's, while he retains the power to do so. In one stroke Van Dreelen and Carey becomes legally yours, and Peter's options—which surveillance enables you instantly to counter—become quite limited. He can accept Phillip's sale of his controlling interest, sweetened by your generous offer to buy *his* remaining forty-nine percent, or try to undo the sale in court, in which case you will advise Peter that should his lawsuit fail you will refuse to buy this remnant at any price.

"In itself, that must make Peter stop and think. Should he lose, then he holds only a minority interest in a difficult business, worth so much less than a controlling interest that I doubt there'd be much market for it. He'll no longer be able even to set foot in Van Dreelen and Carey, and yet, unless he somehow unloads his remaining shares, no rival publisher will have him. No man, especially Peter Carey, will lightly contemplate the loss of virtually all he's got. At this moment of hesitation we may then *exploit* the torment in his psychological makeup, rather than *fear* it. Which"—Englehardt permitted himself a smile—"is why the young woman we are watching is so valuable." His eyes dropped modestly. "But then no doubt you perceived that last night, as I've said."

Barth began examining the odd brilliance of what he had just heard. "How do you propose to threaten him through the woman?"

"In ways which he could never trace to you. But the psychoanalysis reveals that she's the perfect counterforce to his passion for the firm. *That* passion stems from his terrible sense that he caused the deaths of both John and Charles Carey, whose forgiveness he can secure only by cherishing their work—even, perhaps, by pushing this worrisome potential lawsuit to the limit. Fortunately, despite this fear that he somehow murders those whom he loves, and despite a competing fear of women derived from his mother's distaste, he has fallen in love with Miss Ciano." The hint of a smile reappeared. "Now suppose I were to make him fear that clinging to his father's firm would bring terrible harm to *her?*"

"How, dammit?"

"His guilt would drive him quite mad, you see. I doubt that he could even face such a choice, let alone offer you resistance. He might well kill himself."

The man's insane, Barth thought; in that instant he saw his father's shattered skull. He leaned forward. "I want to know your *methods."*

"I simply do what is necessary." Englehardt closed his eyes. "My secrecy becomes your shield. Which is why, should you still desire to own this firm, *I* must approach Phillip Carey, alone."

"No." Barth's voice grew steely. "It's time I knew what you've got on him."

Englehardt's eyes snapped open. "That would be foolish, on both our parts. All I ask is one more day. Tomorrow, I will place in your hands the papers conveying John Carey's firm to you, signed by Phillip Carey. Then you can decide for yourself how important it is to know the *reason* for his signature."

Noelle looked from the fireplace to Peter. "What would you have said to Phillip, if you'd found him?"

"That I was undergoing hypnosis. I figured maybe by surprising him..." He shrugged. "If that's what frightens him, I thought he might tell me why."

"Maybe you should wait, Peter—at least to let Pogostin find out what it is." She edged closer to the fire. "Are you still nervous?"

"About tomorrow?" She nodded at the flame. "Yes," he answered. "After that, I don't know what happens."

She stared ahead. "The truth, Peter: is this for me?"

He hesitated. "Partly..."

"Because now *I'm* feeling guilty."

He turned to her. "Just feel guilty enough to be careful, all right?"

"Yeah, okay." Her voice lightened. "Another day, and no ugly stranger."

"In Manhattan?"

She smiled. "Well, not *that* ugly stranger."

"Good." Unsmiling, Carey looked toward the fire. "Anyhow, I guess some of it's for Levy. Today..."

"But is any part for *you?*"

"The biggest part." A faint smile appeared. "I've become afraid of being afraid."

She watched him. "I just wish I could be there."

"They don't even know if it'll work." His smile lingered. "I'd be afraid to disappoint you."

"Then at least let me give away the tickets. It's silly to drag you out."

"I'll probably need it. Besides"—he gave her a sardonic look—"it's nice of Sutcliffe to include me."

"Peter, you don't think...?"

"Not after this." He touched the photograph that lay between them, and then looked up at her. "It was beautiful, you know."

"I thought so, too." She turned back to the fire, ending a

long silence in a different voice. "You know, it *is* weird about the Krantzes. I wonder what made them move."

"I don't know." Frowning, Carey bent forward. Gently, almost reverently, he placed her photograph in the flames.

Noelle turned to him. "Why, Peter?"

He kissed her forehead. "I'll remember," he said softly. "And I'm the only one who should."

Englehardt placed the photograph in front of Phillip Carey. "All women are alike, aren't they, Phillip."

Sick, Phillip could not help staring at Noelle. "Where did you get this?"

"You'll recall that I'm rather good at such things." Smiling, Englehardt slid the photograph back into the manila folder. "I wonder how young Peter will react."

Phillip looked up, speechless.

"Oh, I *would*, Phillip—driving Peter across the line can only serve my purposes." His smile vanished. "I could do other things, far, far worse than this. I merely offer it as a reminder of what could happen should you, through yet another inexplicable outburst of self-sacrifice, leak word of this to Peter before I wish it." He pointed toward the certificates of transfer, sitting on the desk between them. "You may remember why you're here."

Phillip stared past him into the shadows of the loft. "But nothing's changed," he began, and then stopped, glancing up at Englehardt.

Englehardt nodded. "Hypnosis," he said softly. "Tomorrow."

"You *knew*?"

"That was what Peter wished to surprise you with, and why I did not wish for you to see him. The time has come for your vacation, many miles from here."

Nauseated, Phillip imagined Peter Carey, not the cold-eyed replica of Charles, but a boy in a hospital, unconscious and alone, clutching a stuffed toy elephant. Miserably, he asked, "What do you intend to do with him?"

Englehardt shrugged. "It does make sense to kill him, doesn't it?"

"*No!*"

"Don't be sentimental, Phillip—that's always hobbled you from perceiving your true self-interest." Phillip's gaze held fear and hatred; smiling faintly, Englehardt held out a placating hand. "Even *I* understand irrational attachments. Let's agree, then—if you sign these and leave for Europe, I'll try to persuade Peter that Miss Ciano's interests prevent him from acting on whatever he remembers."

Silently, he placed his hand on Phillip Carey's shoulder.

Phillip could no longer look at him.

In the pallid light, he stared at the certificates. Englehardt pointed to the signature line. "You'll receive Barth's check for ten million dollars," he said, "as soon as these are safely in his hands."

His hand did not move.

Phillip looked away, arm limp at his side. "Two contracts," Englehardt urged him gently. "For yourself, and as trustee for John Peter Carey."

Phillip reached into his pocket for a pen. Twice, he wrote his name; Englehardt removed his hand.

"Thank you." Englehardt took the certificates. Phillip reached out to him, mouth open . . .

Englehardt smiled down at him. Softly, he asked, "Yes, Phillip?"

Phillip's shoulders slumped. "The photograph." He almost whispered. "Can I see it again?"

Englehardt froze.

Pale with hurt and anger, he handed Phillip Carey the picture of Noelle.

The faceless man raised his knife.

Peter's head snapped back; the silver blade flashed by him in the darkness of the tunnel. He turned, his scream mingling with Noelle's as the knife stabbed out her eyes.

"Peter!"

"No! Oh, my God, no!"

"Peter!" She kept shaking him. "It's all *right.*"

He opened his eyes. Her hair fell into his face; he felt his sweat. *"Oh my God..."*

"Peter, what was it?"

"Nothing." Carey fell back onto the pillow; instinctively, he touched her. "Same dream, that's all."

CHAPTER 13

Pogostin's eyes, dark and perceptive, betrayed his breeziness as self-protection. "All right, Peter Carey," he began, "I guess Levy told you what my story is."

"Generally." Carey felt control slipping from him. "I'd like to hear it from you."

Pogostin cocked his head; the gesture drew attention to his round-tipped nose and the clownish cast of his face. "A little scared, huh?"

Carey fidgeted; even Pogostin's chocolate-brown shirt and outdated paisley tie irritated his nerves. "That's one way of putting it."

"Then cheer up—you may be impossible to hypnotize." He grinned. "Frankly, the tests you just finished predict you'll be a terrible subject."

Carey leaned forward on the couch. "You don't exactly sugarcoat your work, do you."

"No charm." Pogostin gave a disarming shrug. "I put my patients to sleep."

Carey kept noticing that his eyes never changed with his words. The windowless office—a rectangle with bare walls and floor—was reminding him of an interrogation room. He wondered what Noelle was doing, where she was . . .

"Of course," Pogostin went on smilingly, "we can just shoot the shit all morning. I cleared it for you."

Carey glanced sharply at him. "What did Levy say about me?"

Pogostin shrugged. "That you were a sweet, simple man with a childhood like Christopher Robin's."

"Do you always joke your way out of corners?"

Pogostin laughed; Carey saw a glint of self-recognition.

"According to *my* analyst, yes. You were asking what my rap is. It's simple: under hypnosis you'll re-live the weekend of your parents' death as a six-year-old boy." Pogostin pointed to a tape recorder next to his chair. "My questions, and everything you say, will be on this tape. Then you wake up."

"And remember?"

"All or part or nothing. But the tape preserves what your conscious memory still blocks. One iron rule: I don't Mau-Mau your sensibilities by playing back the tape." Pogostin smiled again. "Even *I've* got more finesse than to stage that kind of horror show."

"So what do you do with it?"

"We use it to ask you questions over the coming weeks and months, gradually serving up such pieces of your trauma as the psyche can digest, until your memory returns." The smile flashed. "Foreplay's another good analogy."

It struck Carey that Pogostin's quips, like his clothes, served to divert his patients from their fears. "All right," he interrupted. "Would *you* do this?"

Pogostin nodded briskly. "In a second."

"Why?"

"It's the kindest way to drain a wound. *Your* wound has been festering for years; you pay for it in everything you do." Pogostin leaned forward. "You're a control freak, Peter; it sticks out all over you, even if it weren't bristling at me from those tests. You try taking charge of everything, even your own emotions—which is funny, considering that you're defending what was lost twenty-three years ago, when your memory wasn't looking. You've *lost* control, pal—your dreams show that." He spread his hands in mock accommodation. "Of course, we can debate free will for a while—I wouldn't want you to feel coerced."

Carey gave his first, uneasy smile. "How long will it take?"

"Patience. An entire weekend is a major chunk of repression: you're making me slog through a lot of inane, boring material to get to the meat." The smile returned. "But then, I'm good—say an hour and a half."

Carey exhaled: in his mind, without knowing why, he said goodbye to Charles Carey. "Yeah," he mumbled. "All right."

"Great."

In the tension between Pogostin's smile and his eyes, Carey saw Noelle. "What do I do?"

"Oh, just lie back and relax for a while—remember, this may never happen. I'll be thinking of how to get into it..."

Lying back, Carey realized how tired he was. He checked his watch: 9:45.

"Actually, I might do better telling you some of *my* inane, boring childhood experiences."

Casually, Pogostin moved to a chair near the head of the couch.

"Not that my childhood's atypical..."

Last night he had hardly slept.

"In fact, it's all bullshit about how charming kids are..."

He had held her as if she would disappear.

"My Vietnam vets are much more interesting: *Rebecca of Sunnybrook Farm* was Right-to-Life propaganda."

Carey tried closing his eyes.

"They're boring little shits, as I was telling my two-year-old daughter just last night, at bedtime..."

Blood gushed from her eyes...

"*My* bedtime. You still with me?"

Fear crawled on Carey's skin.

"Peter?"

He was afraid to remember.

"Don't flake out, now."

"Uh-huh."

"You'd better count with me."

The tunnel was dark...

"One...two...three..."

He had lost control of time.

"Eleven..."

Dewey...

"Thirty-four..."

Desperately, Carey struggled to open his eyes. They were heavy.

"Sixty-five..."

Greenwich.

"Sixty-eight..."

Carey did not wish to go there. He tried to protest.

"Sixty-nine..."

The tape clicked on.

"Peter?"

As night fell, awesome and enormous, Phillip Carey trotted down the stairs, to greet them.

"Where is he?" Phillip demanded.

Peter's assistant squinted at her desk calendar. "He had an appointment outside the office at nine."

"It's eleven-thirty." Phillip's voice rose. "What's keeping him?"

"I really don't know . . ."

"You damned well *do* know."

Her eyes widened. "Really, Mr. Carey—this isn't like him. Something must have come up."

Phillip felt the irrational rush which had brought him here evaporate in fear: what had Peter remembered?

"Do you wish to wait here?"

"I'll call," Phillip snapped at her, and then turned quickly and left for home.

Carey jumped up, sweating.

He did not know where he was. A hand pushed against his chest.

"Hang on, man."

His eyes focused. He recognized the room, then the voice. His hair and clothes were damp, disheveled; there was bile in his mouth. "What happened to me?" he started, then moaned, "Oh God, what did I tell you?"

"The usual boring stuff."

Pogostin looked white; a pasted-on smile made his eyes seem frightened. Carey's head snapped up. "The accident?"

"Among other things."

Carey stood. "I need to know."

Pogostin thrust his palm between them. "Sit down."

"I need . . ." Carey looked around wildly. "Where's the tape?" He grasped Pogostin's shirt. "Give it to me."

"Sit down." Pogostin's voice was tight. "I told you I can't work that way. I'm not some Nazi."

"Noelle . . ." Carey stopped himself: almost whispering, he repeated, "I need to know . . ."

"You will—in time. You were a child, Peter, and this experience was as intense for you as war is to some farm boy. I'll confer with Levy as soon as possible, and we'll start to get this off your back."

Carey let go his shirt. He sat, rigid. "How bad is it?"

"To *me*?" Pogostin managed a second smile. "I've heard worse."

"My father's face—was it burning?"

"Trust me, Peter." Still smiling, Pogostin looked more frightened yet. "After all, I'm a total stranger."

Martin turned up the stereo.

"Look," the new voice—young, urbane, perhaps Jewish— was sounding urgent. "You'd better hear it yourself. I don't know the cast of characters."

"Please," Levy said. "Can he remember?"

"Oh he *remembers*, poor bastard—just not consciously." Now the voice conveyed tension, anger. "Just listen to the goddamned tape. I don't know the man, there's something I'm not getting. I think it's serious."

"But I've got hospital rounds, and tonight I have to give a speech." Levy's voice rose. "Tell me now . . ."

"You sound like Carey."

"He's *my* patient."

"I just can't characterize this. Look, I'll send it over by messenger as soon as I can get one here. You can play it first thing tomorrow, and then tell *me*."

"Have you a reliable service?"

"Just tell me who they should leave it with. It's the last thing I'd tell Peter, but I don't want this tape kicking around here—the other night some creep broke in . . ."

"My receptionist," Levy answered hastily. "She can lock it in my desk."

Touching his revolver, Martin smiled.

Carey sat at his desk, rubbing his temples with the fingers of both hands, and then dialed the familiar number. "Phil?"

"Peter?" There was silence. Softly, his uncle asked, "Are you all right?"

"You wanted to talk."

"It'll keep." His uncle's voice sounded reedy. "You know I don't like the telephone."

"Where were you yesterday? I needed to see you."

"I had to step out."

"To see Barth? Have you sold the firm, Phil? Is that it?"

There was no answer; Carey's grip tightened on the telephone. "Dammit . . ."

"All right, Peter." His uncle's voice wavered. "I'm going on vacation. That's what I came to tell you."

"I thought you were sick."

"I am, quite—I need to get away."

"What is it?"

"Nothing I wish you to be concerned with. Please, Peter, just take care of Noelle."

"Why do you keep saying that?"

"Because I never was so lucky, and I wish you to be—in spite of yourself." Phillip's tone grew taut. "Don't come looking for me—I'll be out this afternoon, seeing to my plans." His voice gave out abruptly.

"Phil?"

"Goodbye, Peter." Phillip Carey hung up.

Blindly, in his confusion, Carey called Noelle.

"Photography."

"Noelle Ciano," Carey snapped.

"Peter? It's me."

Carey slumped in his chair. "Thank God."

A lean young Puerto Rican with a mustache and visored cap knocked on the door to Pogostin's office and began speaking in a sibilant, breakneck cadence: "Sir—your lady tells me you have a package to give personally . . ."

"Yes." Quickly, Pogostin added, "You have identification, of course."

"Of course." The youth flipped open his wallet.

"Good." Pogostin scanned the card, certifying the young man as a bonded messenger, then walked to his desk and presented him with a neatly wrapped box. Levy's address was printed on two sides. "Can you read this?" Pogostin demanded, then mentally cursed himself.

The youth stiffened with offended pride. "Yessir."

"Some people have trouble with my writing." Pogostin shrugged, smiling. "My teachers hated me."

"Sure." The youth nodded. "Okay, no problem—I can make it out."

"Great. It's to go to Miss Lavin, no one else." Reaching into his wallet, Pogostin threw in an extra five dollars, wondering if he should. "That part's quite important."

"Miss Lavin," the youth repeated. His face was stone.

Pogostin smiled. "Thank you."

Leaving, the youth caught the next elevator down and then disappeared into the subway, clutching his package in both hands.

"Oh, he *remembers*, poor bastard—just not consciously . . ."

Englehardt stopped the tape.

Watching, Martin saw the stiffness of his body. "I must have Carey's tape," he said tonelessly. "And Levy must never know I have it."

Martin let him wait for a moment. "Easy as Pogostin," he said casually.

Englehardt's pupils widened. Martin knew this as a sign of tension: in earlier years, he would not have been so insolent. He kept looking down at the smaller man, impassive.

Englehardt's face went cold. "Bring it to me," he said.

It did not matter if the blond hair came from bottles, he thought; she was beautiful.

"Miss Lavin?"

"Yes." She smiled. He swelled with hope; the day might be better. Her eyes were so blue. "Are you the messenger?"

"I am José—Joseph Figueroa." Remembering the package, he thrust it out. "I have this from Dr. Pogostin."

It came out "Pogosteen." But she smiled again . . .

"Thank you so much. Dr. Levy was *very* concerned that this be here this afternoon."

"I hurried . . ." He shifted from side to side.

"Was there something for me to sign?"

"Oh, yes." He handed his clipboard across the desk, leaning forward to point out the correct line. She reached out, turquoise bracelets tinkling. Her perfume smelled like lilacs; her mouth made a bow as she signed.

"Is that all?"

"Well, yes..."

She smiled quickly. "If you'll excuse me, then," she said, and took the package into the doctor's office, locking the door behind her.

Carey scribbled on the tablecloth, in crayon. "What is it?" Noelle inquired.

"An elephant."

"With marbles for eyes?"

Carey drew a tail. "They're shoe buttons."

Noelle watched him. When Carey did not smile, she asked, "Still want to go?"

Carey shrugged. "We're here."

He looked up and around, hoping that the seven-thirty clutter of Un Deux Trois would lighten his unease. Waiters rushed among close tables jammed with pairs and foursomes animated by their sprint toward curtain time: tonight, the tony café decor—long mirrors flashing from gold walls, crystal chandeliers and ceiling fans dropping from black ceilings down into the noise and smoke, a long wooden bar flanked by palm trees—seemed like a rotogravure, redolent of someone else's dazzling past. Seeing no ugly stranger, Carey resumed drawing on the butcher-paper tablecloth, supplied with crayons by a clever management to divert the jangled nerves and stomachs of their patrons.

He could not remember tusks...

"Damn Phillip," he said aloud. "It's like he's falling apart."

Noelle flicked at her bangs. "I'm sorry you can't remember."

Carey glanced at the nearest tables, two couples close on either side; so much noise surrounded them that they were private. "There's something all around me I just can't get hold of." He looked back at Noelle. "*They* know, and won't even tell me *why* I feel this way..."

She touched his hand. "They must have reasons."

Picking up the crayon, Carey began drawing tusks.

* * *

Englehardt held out the certificates. "Van Dreelen and Carey," he said softly, "belongs to you."

Prolonging the moment, Barth continued staring at the Manhattan of light and shadow suspended silent in his window, silver rectangles without a base. With reluctant fascination, his gaze moved slowly toward the papers which would at last deliver him, after so many years of striving, his whole *persona*.

John Carey's firm . . .

Phillip Carey's signature, as trustee for Peter Carey.

Touching the papers, he felt smaller, withdrew his hand. "Why like this?" he demanded.

"Pardon?"

It was dark in his suite of offices. Englehardt's face looked yellow, their solitude was bitter in Barth's mouth. He remembered opening John Carey's letter, alone.

"Why not a press conference, something they could *see?*"

"'Work is play for mortal stakes,'" Englehardt quoted. "Robert Frost. In answer to your question, Phillip Carey is not, at the moment, fit for public display—particularly a signing ceremony which would inflame and forewarn Peter, drawing attention to his outcry before you've confronted him, quietly, with his very limited alternatives. Surely, at a later point, you will grace this acquisition with some appropriate event. But this is a *coup d'état*: it's crucial to strike quickly . . ."

The man was rambling; Barth had come to recognize his tension. "Do you *own* Phillip Carey, dammit, or just *rent* him?"

Englehardt smiled hastily. "Circumstances change," he soothed. "People lose the power to help, or even die. 'If something can go wrong—'"

"'—it will,'" Barth snapped, pointing at the certificates. "His signature isn't witnessed."

Englehardt paused. "That," he answered carefully, "is yet another bit of ceremony we can ill afford." He spread his hands. "Remember that *I* secured the signature you need, by means of certain pressures. *Your* only vulnerability becomes some public link between Phillip and me, where my prior connection to the Careys might be probed. You see," he continued smoothly, "the reason I've kept my name off both your payroll and all records for the gallery is the reason I obtained Phillip's signature without a witness. None is required; Phillip Carey is not about to assert that his own signature is forged—particularly when, as I will ensure he does, Phillip deposits *your* check in *his* account, evidencing consideration for the sale. Yet *you're* totally insulated from anything I've done." His cadence eased. "The successful aide survives only by preventing error. The moment I put you at risk, or permit *you* to do so to me, my career ends."

Barth hesitated; once more the face of his dead father flashed before him.

"Of course," Englehardt concluded, "my *job* ends when I present you with the alternatives of owning Van Dreelen and Carey or letting Peter Carey own it. The *choice* must be yours—to succeed John Carey, or turn away."

Flicking on Barth's laser lamp, he aligned both contracts neatly on Barth's green blotting pad, and turned his back.

Barth looked down.

Illuminated, the smooth white papers shone with the magic of their gift: he could take John Carey's firm, and all of its history, into his hands.

Van Dreelen & Carey . . .

Carey & Barth.

He picked up the pen. As he did so, the same shocking image of his father's face circled back, piercing his brain.

John Carey would not do this . . .

Barth looked up.

"I trust you brought the check," Englehardt said to the window. He was utterly still. "Imagine the expression on young Carey's face when you show him the certificates."

Hastily, Barth scrawled his name.

With twenty thousand other people, Carey and Noelle watched an empty stage at one end of Madison Square Garden.

"Le-e-thal . . ." Below them, the crowd had begun chanting. "Le-e-thal . . ."

They had found seats on the mezzanine, high above the vast cement floor. Carey watched the crowd; Noelle stared at the blue curtain covering the runway to the bare wooden stage. "Just letting it build, isn't he?"

"It's the second coming," Carey said. "No warm-up act." He kept scanning the faces.

"Le-e-thal . . ."

The clothes and pigment and features were unique to this city: Hispanics and aging hippies; olive-skinned Mediterraneans sharing black curly hair with Eastern Europeans; a few blacks and Asians; Barnard women in sweaters and jeans; punk rockers; the rude and abrasive shoving others as self-contained as only the drug-addled or New Yorkers in a crowd can be, some bearing candles or smoking dope, all standing, milling restlessly, watching the blue curtain, the focus of their energies.

"Le-e-e-thal . . ." The chant grew louder and more drawn out with each hypnotic repetition.

"Le-e-e-thal . . ."

The chant spread through the crowd, each roar wafting smoke and heat, the fetor of dope and sweat and bodies, up into the vast, echoing darkness of the rafters . . .

Carey's eyes narrowed.

"L-E-E-E-THAL . . ."

The silent apartment echoed with Pogostin's voice.

The six-year-old Peter had frightened him, and now Levy could not sleep.

He sat up in bed.

On a tape, locked inside his desk, Charles Carey lived again, and then died with Peter's memory.

He turned on the light.

Charles Carey could not wait.

Next to Carey, a spaced-out woman in rimless glasses began rocking to some inner rhythm. He ignored her, watching a wedge of uniformed cops with nightsticks rush into the bodies jostling on the floor to extract three men who had been fighting for a patch of cement and a woman who had fainted from drugs or the pressure around her. More cops ringed the stage, facing the tumult on the floor or in the multitiered oval of seats that rose on all sides, surrounding them with noise.

"L-E-E-THAL . . ."

"General admission," Carey muttered to Noelle. "Let 'em stomp each other for a ringside seat—it's cheaper."

She nodded. "We're better off up here."

The spaced-out woman began clapping to herself. Carey

watched the crowd pressing toward the stage, to the precipice of reason, screaming even louder...

His father screamed: "I'm losing control..."

"L-E-E-THAL..."

"Daddy..."

Levy wept alone.

A child's stricken cry rang through his office, again and again.

"Daddy... Daddy..."

"Charles!"

The tape clicked off: a trembling Levy realized that he had cried out to a dead man.

Desperately, he fought back panic.

He must warn Peter.

What he had heard, and a young boy's memory had rejected, was more terrible than his worst imaginings.

Shaking, he groped for the telephone.

Carey's telephone rang once, twice. There was a click.

"Hello," the tape began, "this is Peter Carey..."

Leaning against Noelle, Carey fought waves of nausea.

"L-E-E-THAL..."

"You okay, Peter?"

"Just hot." He tried concentrating on the press of bodies near the stage, half hysterical as some roadies made a teasing ritual of setting up the amplifiers and drums. "It's scary," he murmured, "to think how easily these people could get a gun in here."

"L-E-E-THAL..."

"See someone weird?"

The door opened...

"Nothing." In the tumult, Carey struggled to identify his flashes. "It's the Sutcliffe effect—he's certainly getting what he wants."

The lights dimmed.

"L-E-E-THAL..."

The crowd lit candles, rocking more fiercely with their rhythmic ululations, half entreaty and half animal demand.

Below, a man with purple hair was passed from shoulder to shoulder, waving wildly, toward the front.

"L-E-E-THAL..."

The man hurtled forward.

"Peter!"

Sutcliffe burst onto the stage.

Martin slid softly through the outer door.

Closing it behind him, he crept to the second door, placing his bag beside him, and put on gloves.

He slipped his key into the lock, turning it until he heard a click.

Slowly, softly, he opened the door.

An old man was sitting at his desk, holding a telephone. Tears glistened on his face.

Martin froze in startled recognition.

The old man looked up. His mouth opened, closed, opened again. "I saw you."

The familiar voice sounded thinner yet. Martin watched his pale hand reach out to grasp a tape cassette. His eyes followed Martin's. "This?"

Almost imperceptibly, Martin nodded.

Doug Sutcliffe began chanting into the tumult:

"Ride the subway...

Girls look away..."

"LE-E-THAL..."

Sutcliffe stalked to the front of the stage in a jumpsuit unzipped to the waist, twisting, undulating, waving them closer, whipping the cord of the microphone he shouted through as Lethal set down an electric pulse that filled the Garden and seized the crowd, now clapping with it and writhing on the floor, hurling the purple-haired man as their collective sacrifice ever closer to the stage until Sutcliffe waved him to the front and the man screamed to the crowd to keep him going.

"Go faster, Daddy..."

Carey clapped both palms to his head; Sutcliffe screamed his pain:

"My brain starts ticking like a bomb..."

Fighting for control, Carey saw the body of the purple-haired man flash through the flickering candles as the crowd threw him to the front.

Fifty feet, forty, thirty . . .

"*I'm lethal . . .*"

Twenty . . .

"Le-e-e-thal . . ."

"Le-e-e-thal . . ."

From the shoulders of the crowd, the purple-haired man screamed out at Sutcliffe.

"*Peter!*"

Sutcliffe looked up at him, mouth falling open.

The man pulled a long black cylinder from his coat and fired.

Kneeling, the ugly man pulled a black revolver from his bag, and smiled.

The office was dim, hushed. Levy realized that the last sound he would hear in life was the firing of a gun.

So odd, not to know what this sound was like.

He could not stop weeping: he would die feeling tears on his face.

Smiling, the man moved closer.

Charles Carey grinned through the smoke of a Boston bar.

Poor Charles.

He had failed once more.

Oh, Ruthie . . .

The man put the cold revolver to his temple.

He felt sharp pains in his chest.

"*Peter . . .*"

The last sound William Levy heard in life was his own cry.

The red streak of light hit Sutcliffe's chest.

As he fell back, his group dived through the curtain; a cop leaped on Sutcliffe's body; two more jumped at the man.

Wildly, he waved the gun.

Insane screaming filled the air; hands tore at the man. Carey clutched Noelle.

"*I'm losing control . . .*"

"Don't move," he told her.

She nodded into his shoulder. "They'll stomp us to death."

Blood gushed from her eyes . . .

Carey's arms tightened around her.

The spaced-out woman had fallen to her knees. People fled around her, boots kicking her head and chest, their arms and elbows battering Noelle and Carey, voices screaming for escape.

"Peter!"

An arm hit Carey's mouth. He spun, looked down, saw two cops pulling on the assassin's legs as part of the mindless mob yanked his arms and others beat his suspended torso. Another cop lay on top of Sutcliffe as the searing red light spat sparks into the air.

"My God," Noelle gasped. "He shot off a fucking *flare.*"

The tape clicked off.

Martin's smile was genuine. Levy had been disappointing; his tape was not.

Martin knew the meaning of his drama.

Quickly, he removed the cassette and put it in his bag, replacing the tape recorder in front of Levy.

Martin did not move him: he had known Englehardt for twenty years, and now knew what he must do. Systematically, he removed the receivers from the telephone and the base of Levy's lamp.

Only then did he stop to look at Levy.

He slumped in his chair, arms dangling, face slack and staring. The blood on his temple had dried with his tears.

Martin felt a surge of anger. To risk so much, his first killing in six years, and there had been no hunt, no echo of his stalking of the Turk except the fecal smell of death.

In death, Levy's cowlick stood up.

Martin turned from him in disgust; for this, he must answer to Englehardt.

But now he had the tape.

Martin felt a surge of adrenaline. Picking up the bag, he opened the outer door, looking up and down the corridor.

Nothing.

He closed the door behind him.

* * *

Carey and Noelle fought their way out of the Garden.

The worst panic had passed; the bodies around them shoved and snaked but did not lash out. Behind them, over the sound system, Doug Sutcliffe cried: *"I'm still alive!..."*

Carey's mouth was bleeding. His arm crooked Noelle's shoulders. They did not look back.

"I'm still *al-l-l-ive!...*"

The crowd kept moving.

The loft sounded with Peter Carey's last, repeated scream. *"Daddy..."*

Slowly, Englehardt looked up at Martin. Their eyes met. Englehardt fingered his bow tie. "Did you understand?"

Martin kept staring.

Englehardt looked away. "Damn you," he said harshly. "Now we'll have to kill them."

Martin smiled down at him. Softly, he asked, "Even Phillip?"

Carey and Noelle pushed through the front door of the Garden.

Night air chilled their faces. A phalanx of police cars, red lights swirling in the darkness, waited on the street for Sutcliffe; to the right, paramedics bore the injured to a separate line of ambulances. Above them, the Garden's electric billboard flashed L-E-E-THAL over and over, like the blinking of an eye.

Noelle stared at it. "Poor Sutcliffe."

"Peter!"

Carey tasted blood inside his mouth. He felt her shiver in the wind.

CHAPTER 14

Noelle traced abstract patterns on a pillow. "It was weird what you said last night—about a gun."

"Sometimes I sense things." Carey still saw the nightmare in her gaze. "You know what scared me? That something would happen to you."

"Or you." She touched the cut on his lip. "Anyhow, it won't."

"You'll always be my Daddy, won't you?"

Carey's eyes closed. "Just watch yourself, all right?"

"Always..."

"Peter?"

He looked at her: even in the morning, drowsy from sleep, she was beautiful.

"Make love with me, Noelle. Please."

Noelle's mouth moved closer, hair spilling across Carey's stomach.

Watching in torment and jealousy, Martin touched himself.

"It's all right," she was crooning. "This time it's all right..."

Slowly, her face bent down.

Martin's hips rose from his chair...

The telephone rang.

Florid, Martin clutched at it. "It's time now," Englehardt said softly.

Noelle no longer spoke.

"Was that okay?" She grinned at him from beneath the sheets. "Because if it was really awful..."

"Not for *me*." His head tilted in doubt. "But you don't get anything out of it..."

His father came in her mouth.

"I do, though. Different times are different—you know that."

"Like last night?"

"Uh-huh—then we were *both* scared." Leaning over the side of the bed, she retrieved the *Times,* headlined, "Mock Assassin Spurs Garden Riot," with a smaller, "Fifty Injured," above a picture of Doug Sutcliffe recoiling in horror from what seemed a child's sparkler. Noelle murmured, "He looks so pathetic," and then pity merged with muted professional envy. "Good picture, though."

Carey was silent. She turned to him. "You okay now?"

The sheet fell from her breasts. Her skin was rich olive, her hair shone in the light. But the best of her, honest and warm, showed in her eyes. Carey wished that he could have this moment, like a photograph, for the rest of his life.

"I love you," he said.

Hastily, Phillip Carey threw two bottles of men's cologne in the shoulder bag, on top of his ticket to Paris.

In a month, he told himself, it would be spring, the tables would appear in front of small cafés, crowded with faces. The city would be green, the air fresh; on the Left Bank it would smell of bread or pastry or couscous from Algeria. He would savor this, out of reach, and then train slowly through the South of France to Cannes and Monte Carlo. He had the sharp image of a palm tree, and then a second one, more poignant and recurring, of a young man and woman, bodies tan and taut and barely covered, gazing into each other's eyes as if they could not move.

Noelle and Peter.

Phillip stared at the bag.

Englehardt must keep his word, use Noelle to force Peter to forget the past: Phillip would remain in Europe, never to face him again. Peter did not yet remember; there still was time . . .

He would run to save himself, and then Peter and Noelle would live.

His door chime rang.

Phillip checked his watch. The cab was early; quickly, he

closed the shoulder bag and carried it downstairs, placing it in the alcove with his luggage. Rushing, he glanced at the library of his father's books; saw a sliver of the room, a shelf. He opened the door...

A black limousine was waiting.

Like my father's, he thought oddly, and then Englehardt leaned through its window.

Phillip stopped on the porch.

In silence, the two men stared at each other. Then, quite slowly, Phillip Carey walked to the car.

Englehardt's voice was soft. "It's time, Phillip."

He looked away. Phillip saw that the driver, a thickset man with rubbery lips, smiled to himself.

Noelle leaned in the doorway, not ready to leave. "So what will you do with Levy?"

"I'm not sure—I guess by now he'll have listened to the tapes." Carey frowned. "What'll happen, I've got no idea—him knowing, me trying to find out..."

For a moment, Noelle watched him. "Have I ever told you, Peter, what being with you means to me?" He tilted his head, puzzled; Noelle spoke softly. "It's like I step out the door with something we said or did, or the way you touched me, and it's not just me anymore, starting off to work. And if I take a picture, or meet someone, I know that I can tell you what I saw or felt, and that you'll get it—you just keep moving with me, past and future, so that whatever happens in between seems better." She smiled a little. "Funny, huh?"

He touched her face. "Not to me."

"Then you can take me along to Levy's, okay?" Still smiling, she kissed him, then started out into the hall. She froze at the Krantzes' door.

He started after her. "What is it?"

Noelle turned, grinning. "I love you, too," she called, and disappeared around the corner.

Bent over from nausea, Phillip Carey shivered in the abandoned bindery.

A rat scurried past his feet. The rubber-lipped man held a

gun to his head, and a check in front of his face. "Now will you sign?" he asked.

Englehardt could not look at him; arms folded, he spoke to the floor. "Go ahead, Phillip."

Barth's check was for ten million dollars.

The bindery was chill, dark and empty—dirty cement, no trace of his father. Phillip's hands were numb with cold. He tried speaking to Englehardt's profile. "I don't care to sign—I know what you'll do."

Englehardt turned, to face him.

Phillip Carey saw his brother's face, looked away.

Holding out a pen, Englehardt started toward him.

Suddenly, Phillip did not want him nearer. As if by reflex, he patted his empty pocket.

The ugly man laughed softly.

Englehardt's eyes flickered to the man and then back to Phillip. He kept moving forward. "Take it," he said gently. "We're almost through."

Phillip closed his eyes. Paris was so far away . . .

Englehardt's muffled footsteps came closer; Phillip heard him breathing, too near his face.

"*No* . . ."

Two fingertips grazed Phillip's arm. He flinched, opening his eyes, and then Englehardt placed the pen against his chest.

"Yes," Englehardt whispered. "If you wish to save Peter. With the firm in Barth's hands, I'll have no need to trouble him. Otherwise . . ."

Phillip saw Charles Carey grinning at him, alive; the illusion, afterwards, of tears on his father's face.

Phillip Carey took the pen.

Searching for a briefcase, Peter Carey saw the red light of his answering machine.

Last night, he had forgotten to check.

He pressed the "rewind" button, and then the one marked "message play." As if from far away, Levy pleaded, "Come to my office, Peter. Please—I've heard the tape."

Carey dropped the briefcase and ran from his apartment.

* * *

Englehardt slid the check into his pocket, and slowly backed away.

Martin placed the revolver to Phillip Carey's temple.

Phillip did not weep. There was nothing in his eyes but contempt of living.

"Wait." Englehardt's taut voice cracked the silence. "Not that close."

Martin stepped two feet back, and looked at Englehardt.

Englehardt stared past him. Phillip straightened to his full height, taking one last haunted glance around the bindery, and then stared back.

Englehardt inhaled. "I have to," he said softly.

Phillip kept staring.

Frozen, Englehardt tried instead to picture Barth's astonishment. He could not waver now; born of necessity and fate, his course must be as a surgeon's, the excisions of a cool brain.

When he had first seen Phillip Carey, his hair was black: Phillip's eyes, a clear, light blue, had met with his.

Thirty years later, across a dirty bindery, Englehardt looked away.

He nodded to Martin.

Carey's mouth opened.

In front of him, Levy's office turned to madness: door ajar; cabinets rifled; three police carrying black bags toward the inner office; flashbulbs spitting . . .

"Oh my God!"

An arm reached toward him. "You can't go in there, sir."

Carey struck out at the arm.

"I'm losing control . . ."

The policeman shoved him back: Carey saw his creased, sad face. His fist dropped to his side. "He was my psychiatrist," he mumbled.

The policeman stared at him. Carey turned, wandering down the corridor, aimless . . .

Levy's receptionist sobbed against the green wall.

Carey touched her shoulder. She whirled, eyes wild and red, bracelets jangling. "Did you find him?" he asked.

Her nod became a hiccup.

"How?"

"Shot." She pointed to her temple.

Carey stared at her finger. "The *tape*—where is it?"

Her look turned contemptuous, frightened. "What difference does it make?"

"No—you don't understand." Carey grasped her arm. "It *killed* him."

"Leave me alone." She turned back to the wall. "He's *dead*— please, leave me alone."

Footsteps pounded on the tile. Whirling, Carey saw two men carrying a stretcher. Levy's outline showed beneath the white sheet. The tips of his shoes splayed crazily. "Oh my God." Almost keening, Carey repeated it. *"Oh my God*, what have I done?"

The woman spun, gaping at him; suddenly, Carey burst toward the stairwell.

There was a phone booth in the lobby. Carey stabbed out seven numbers.

"Photography."

"Noelle Ciano, please."

"She's already gone . . ."

"Where?"

"Who is this?"

"Peter—Peter Carey."

"Larry?" The man's voice shouted at someone. "Where's Ciano?" Coming back, it said, "We don't know."

"Tell her to call me at work."

"Okay, Peter."

"Tell her they've murdered Levy."

Peter Carey felt a hand touch his shoulder.

Phillip Carey crumpled at Martin's feet.

Englehardt turned from them. "Hide him somewhere." His voice was hollow. "I don't wish him found for a while."

He walked away, a thin figure in a bare, ruined warehouse. Martin did not need to question him; he understood perfectly what Englehardt had done, and all that must now happen.

The woman would be his . . .

"I have the key." Knowing the answer, Martin held out the revolver. "What about this?"

Turning, Englehardt's eyes glinted with anger; Martin had forced him to look back.

For a long moment, as if acknowledging this in a way that they both would mark, Englehardt stared at Phillip's body. "As you well know," he said icily, "the gun now belongs to Peter."

He turned and went to the car, alone.

Gregorio watched Palmer, a crew-cut man with intense narrow eyes, sift through Levy's desk. "Is there a tape?" he asked.

"Nope, Lieutenant—pencils, pads, the index to his files, period. No sign of a break-in, either."

"What about time of death?"

Palmer closed the drawer. "Last night between eleven and one."

"Find Carey's psychiatric file." Gregorio tightened the knot of his tie. "After we question him, I may want to read it."

In slow motion, the sad-faced cop walked Carey toward an examining room with a sink and metal cot. Carey sat like a man in a catatonic trance; trapped, he could not find Noelle.

"Mr. Carey?" Carey looked up into the Italianate, too-thin face of a fortyish man with sharp features and a trim designer suit. "I'm Lieutenant Gregorio."

Carey nodded, disoriented. There were dim lights overhead and one window with Venetian blinds slicing gray light into faint gray ribbons on a gray tile floor. In the same even voice, Gregorio said, "Please explain about the tape."

"It's of me, under hypnosis." Speaking, Carey felt numb. "I have amnesia—the tape was my subconscious memory of the car wreck which killed my parents. Afterwards, I still couldn't remember it."

Gregorio leaned back against the wall. "Then how do you know that the tape killed Levy?"

Carey saw the sharp-eyed man look up from his notes. "He left a message on my answering machine asking me to come to his office, that he'd listened to the tape. He sounded frightened."

"He hadn't heard it before?"

"No. A psychologist taped me—Pogostin."

"And *he* didn't tell you?"

Carey closed the door behind him. "It's okay, Ruthie."

"I mean, he depended on the notion I depended on him." She stood, shaking her head.

Carey put his arms around her.

With sudden fierceness, Ruth hugged him close. "Oh, Peter, it's going to be *so* hard."

Carey felt her thin frame shaking. "I know."

Suddenly, Ruth's head snapped back; her eyes locked with his. "It's so much like your father."

Carey felt the words like shock. "What is?"

There was a knock on the door; Carey's assistant was staring in at them. "There's a Sergeant Palmer here, for Ruth."

The crew-cut man came through the door, softly asking, "Miss Levy?" Ruth nodded in slow motion; he took her arm, ignoring Carey. "I've come to take you home."

Carey reached out. "Wait."

Palmer turned, his eyes boring in. "*We'll* take her," he snapped, and then Ruth began sobbing.

Carey let her go.

His assistant watched from the doorway. "What happened?"

"It's so much like your father . . ."

Still staring, Carey answered, "Someone killed her brother."

Blood gushed from her eyes.

"Jesus."

Carey turned on her. "Did Noelle call?"

Martin slipped into the apartment and walked to Carey's desk. Opening the drawer, he found a cassette recorder—one that Peter used at home—with "Peter Carey" laminated to the side.

Perfect, he thought, and slipped it into the pocket of his overcoat.

He already knew how he would use Levy's message; his stereo had picked it up, and now Martin had memorized the words. Pushing the "message play" button, he heard Levy pleading, "Come to my office, Peter. Please, I've . . ."

Martin erased the rest.

Playing it back, he heard what he desired: Levy, calling in the middle of the night, his message cut off by Peter Carey, answering.

* * *

Carey dialed his telephone.

"Photography," a male voice answered.

"This is Peter Carey again—I've got to find Noelle. Do you know where she is?"

"Just a minute."

Gripping the phone, Carey heard muffled words about "police," and then the voice said, "She's kind of roaming today, picking up her own stuff. If she checks in, we'll have her call you . . ."

Carey hung up.

He called Phillip's home, then Noelle's; finding no one, he dialed again.

"Phillip Carey's office."

"Let me speak to him."

"Peter? He's still out, I guess. Hey, were you at that concert last night . . ."

"He can't just fucking vanish. Where is he?"

"I don't know." Silence. "I tried at home just now—there was a meeting on his calendar."

"Has he said anything about vacation?"

"No-o-o."

"Then send someone over there—one of the mailroom boys."

"But if he doesn't answer his telephone?"

"Just send him. The key's in the milk-chute."

Slamming down the telephone, Carey dialed once more.

"Dr. Pogostin's office."

"This is Peter Carey. May I speak to him?"

"I'm sorry." The voice abruptly cooled. "Dr. Pogostin has an appointment outside the office. I really don't know when he'll be back."

"Have him call me as soon as he comes in."

There was silence. "Is there some message?"

"Tell him that I have to know what's on that tape."

Palmer rushed into the squad room. "Pogostin's on his way."

Glancing up from Levy's notes, Gregorio eyed the metal desks and stained linoleum as if annoyed by the need to entertain there. "Call Cronin at the D.A.'s office—we may want a warrant for Carey's answering machine." He checked his cuffs. "Based on what was worrying Levy, I don't think we should wait."

Entering the Krantzes', Martin heard the voice of Carey's lawyer: "From the top, Peter—where do the police come in?"

"I said I thought someone killed him for the tape. But listen, I was with Noelle last night."

"Congratulations, then. On two counts."

"He was my *friend*."

"Okay—sorry. When we visit the police tomorrow, we'll bring Noelle with us."

"I can't find her."

"Settle down, Peter."

"Or Phillip, *or* the Krantzes."

"Who are *they*?"

"My neighbors. They disappeared the weekend I went skiing—the doorman said they'd moved. Something may have happened to them."

"Because they didn't tell you they were moving?" The inquiry was flat, incredulous. "Look, Peter, they murder people every *day* in Manhattan, not every *hour*. You're bucking the odds."

In the silence of the Krantzes' apartment, Martin laughed aloud.

"Just check who bought the Krantzes' place."

"I thought they were dead." Martin heard Benevides's incredulity becoming wariness. "For years you've suspected Phil without a concrete reason; not so long ago, you woke me from a sound sleep to inquire where *Barth* was when your parents died, which turned out to be Oklahoma. Now you . . ."

"Dammit, you're my lawyer."

"Among other people's," Benevides snapped. "I'll check when I have time. Now you do *me* two favors. First, mourn your friend quietly, with a drink. Second, when Noelle turns up, ask her to come with you to my office tomorrow, nine o'clock. *She's* your witness, not Uncle Phillip or the Krantzes. And if you don't stop acting crazy, she'll be the only thing that saves you."

Martin nodded, and then stepped from the apartment to retrieve Noelle Ciano.

* * *

Carey replaced the telephone, and then the room crashed down around him.

He could not move: were Noelle to call, he must be there to warn her.

Levy was dead.

"Tell me, Peter, is there any reason you might feel guilt concerning your father's death?"

His memory killed him.

Carey fought to remember. . . .

"It's too dark down there for elephants, Daddy . . ."

The child Peter stood in darkness, and then a door opened in his memory.

"Peter!"

The child saw the wheel of a sports car, and then nothing.

The man Peter Carey shook his head.

Levy was dead.

"Why did you return to take your father's place, Peter? Because you hated Phillip?"

Carey turned to his father's picture.

"Even brothers need their privacy, Peter."

Carey froze.

Phillip bent to kiss him.

He closed his eyes; not Phillip, his *father* . . .

"I'll bring him up in a while."

"Promise?"

"Promise."

Charles Carey's picture smiled down at him.

Levy was dead.

"You feel guilt over your grandfather's death?"

"I suppose so."

"And you also fear remembering your father's death."

"Yes."

"And now you fear that something will happen to Noelle . . ."

Carey rubbed his temples.

"Tell me, is there some thread . . ."

A dark room, a door opening, the flash of a wheel.

"Peter!"

Noelle.

"Who is the faceless man, Peter?"

Phillip was frightened; Phillip was missing.

"Now you have Noelle to think of..."

Carey picked up the telephone.

"Photography."

"Peter Carey. Is Noelle back?"

"No. Really, she'll call you when she gets here."

Carey put it down.

She was dead.

Levy was dead.

There was no one he could trust: Phillip was gone; the Krantzes were gone; Benevides would not listen; the doorman could not face him, yet smiled at Noelle.

Noelle had asked him to Vermont, and then the Krantzes disappeared...

"Why are you doing this?"

"Because I like Vermont."

Only Noelle had seen the ugly man. No, that was crazy...

"She's your witness, not Uncle Phillip or the Krantzes. And if you don't stop acting crazy, she'll be the only thing that saves you."

Noelle had deserted him....

"I love you, okay?"

She was dead.

The telephone rang.

"Noelle?"

"It's Susan, Peter. Aaron—from the mailroom—went over to the house. The key was missing, but nobody had locked the door. Mr. Carey isn't there."

"Did Aaron look inside?"

"Uh-huh—nothing but some luggage by the door. I'll call as soon as we hear from him."

"Noelle? My God, Phil...what's Barth got on you?"

Carey put down the telephone.

He sat back, straining for control.

Suddenly, he remembered a trick from his first nights in boarding school, when he could not sleep and missed his father. He would lie back in his bed: in his mind, they would start out from the Plaza and cross the street to Central Park. From scraps of memory, he wove a day for them, imagining their careless talk as they wound from zoo to Band Shell to the fountain until, with perfect logic, Peter knew this must have happened.

Now, one by one, Carey reviewed all that had occurred since waking—he had just parted with Noelle, and, in his mind, Levy still lived . . .

In his mind, he listened to Levy's message.

His memory was lethal.

Phillip was afraid of him; whomever his uncle feared used what Carey had forgotten, and now must fear the tape.

There could only be one other. A man who spied.

"It's ours," John Carey rasped; in his mind, his grandson whispered, "I'm sorry . . ."

Peter Carey picked up the telephone.

"Clayton Barth's office."

"Get him on—it's Peter Carey."

"Just a moment, sir." Carey stood, pacing.

"Clayton Barth."

"You win, Barth. I'll do what you want."

There was silence, and then Barth ventured, "So your uncle has persuaded you?"

"Just don't hurt Noelle."

At first, Barth did not answer. Very calmly, he replied, "I've no intention of hurting anyone."

"You killed Levy for the tape, you prick. What *happened* to me, why did you have to kill him?"

"I didn't murder anyone." Suddenly Barth sounded outraged. "You're *insane*—that's why Phillip sold to me."

"*It's ours . . .*"

"Sold? Where is he? Did you kill *him*, too?"

"*No.*" Abruptly, the sharpness vanished from Barth's voice; he paused, repeating softly, "*I haven't murdered anyone,*" and then hung up.

"*It's not Barth.*"

Carey's face fell in his hands.

Noelle Ciano hurried through the cluster of X-rated movie houses, headed for the *Times.*

So much of her work was in its surprises: returning from a routine jaunt to Rockefeller Center, shooting skaters for the Sunday paper, she had picked through the faces she saw to fulfill her pledge to Peter. Instead, she spotted people gathering at the foot of a seedy hotel old enough to have windows that still opened. She turned the corner; a woman teetered on the windowsill of an eighth-story room. Her hair was gray and damp with snow, her loose, flowered-print dress flapped in the biting wind. She stared into the silent crowd as if at a pack of animals.

Noelle first ducked into Nedick's and called the fire department; shooting two quick pictures, she shouldered through the curious and fearstruck and titillated, calling for the woman to wait. Legs trembling like stalks in the wind, the old woman stared down at her, eyes crazed and desperate in their sockets.

"Jump," a young voice shouted.

"Wait!" Noelle cried to her, over and over, like a mantra, until joined by scattered others. Her mouth was dry; her body felt the strain of the woman's legs.

Firemen came, trailing a wave of sirens. Noelle backed off; with a megaphone, one ordered the crowd away while four others ran forward with a canvas net and two more with axes rushed through the front of the hotel.

Noelle caught all seven with a wide-angle lens.

The last picture she took was of a hand reaching to pull the woman inside. Disappearing, the woman stared down at her.

Noelle felt cold; beyond that, she was not sure. She went to have an Irish coffee.

Now, coming down, she thought of calling Peter.

She neared the *Times* building, fighting the first wave of commuters in their winter coats, hunched against the snow. Its clock read 3:10; she would see him soon. As she left, his face had been so soft, as if to speak his love made him younger. Now she wondered how best to tell him what she had seen and done. Perhaps he might help sort out her feelings: about her work, the woman, her last wild stare, as an arm reached through the window . . .

She felt a hand on her arm.

Spinning, she looked into the grotesque rubber smile of the man from SoHo.

"Noelle." His voice was like a lover's. "I've been watching you."

She began backing away, stunned. *"No!"*

He stepped toward her. "Come with me," he said softly. "If you ever want to see Peter Carey, alive."

Noelle stopped moving.

CHAPTER 15

Clayton Barth felt smaller: as if contagious, Carey's fear eroded his sense of mastery.

He called Englehardt.

"Yes?"

"Peter Carey just phoned, babbling about a tape. He said this man Levy had been murdered for it." Barth stopped, waiting for an inquiry.

Without inflection, Englehardt said, "Meet me in an hour—here."

Barth's skin felt cold. "Tell me..."

"In person."

Englehardt hung up.

"Dr. Pogostin's office."

"This is Peter Carey. Please, I need to talk to him."

"I'm sorry—Dr. Pogostin is in conference. Perhaps tomorrow..."

"*Now.*"

The voice was cool. "It's not his practice..."

"People are *dying*. If you don't tell him that, it's on your head."

Silence. "Just a moment."

Carey waited. There's a madman on the telephone, she would say, talking about murders. Better to call the police.

"Hello, Peter." Pogostin sounded wary. "I thought you might have forgotten me."

"You have to tell me what's on that tape. Levy's dead."

"I know." Pogostin paused, then spoke more crisply. "I've been with the police, Peter. The tape is missing, and they asked that I discuss its contents with no one. They specifically mentioned avoiding you."

"Not you, too." Carey's voice rose. "Doctor, they're *wrong: Phillip* is missing; *Noelle* is missing . . ."

"You should tell that to Lieutenant Gregorio."

"Tell him what? I don't *know* why this is happening, or even what's on that tape . . ."

"Then how do you know your memories can help you?"

"Please," Carey finished, "do not do this to me."

"And how do I know to believe any of what you're telling me?"

Carey bent forward. From the depths of reason, he retrieved a memory, spoke it aloud. "'You can trust me, Peter—after all, I'm a total stranger.'"

There was a last, long silence. "Meet me at six," Pogostin said.

Carey's voice steadied. "Thank you, doctor."

Martin replayed the tape, then checked his watch.

4:55.

Englehardt had left him little time; the police would come for the answering machine, and he must keep Carey from Pogostin . . .

He took the tape of Carey's hypnosis, placed it on the stolen cassette recorder marked "Peter Carey" and began to play it. Carey started speaking as a child; Martin erased everything that followed, and stuffed both the recorder and tape in the pocket of his coat, with the key to Phillip's town house.

For the rest, he decided to time himself.

Quickly, Martin picked up the crate holding Carey's appliances, and carried it to the door.

There was no one in the hall.

Bearing the crate, he crept down twenty feet of carpet and entered Carey's apartment.

Within seven minutes he had replaced the original lamp, coffee-maker, clock-radio and alarm bell, wiped off his fingerprints, returned the four duplicates to the crate, and carried it to the Krantzes'.

The only trace of his work remaining was the tape on Carey's answering machine.

The surveillance of Peter Carey was over.

His woman was waiting.

Martin checked his pocket, touching the revolver and Carey's recorder, and left the building.

For the first time, Carey felt something like relief. He tried to sort out his thoughts and feelings.

Perhaps Noelle was fine.

He checked his watch: 5:15.

He would wait here as long as he could.

5:18.

Each minute eroded his calm.

5:23.

Phillip had not returned.

5:27–28–29 . . .

The telephone rang.

He snatched at it. "Noelle?"

"You've been wrong to worry, Peter." The voice was calm, reassuring. "You see, *I* have her now."

Carey slumped in his chair. Finally, he asked, "Where is she?"

"That's why I'm calling, Peter. To take you to her."

"Who *are* you? . . ."

"Leave casually," the voice interrupted, "as if you're returning home from work. Take your usual route up Fifth Avenue. We'll be watching. When you're far enough from the building, I'll make contact with you. And one more thing, Peter: don't even think about calling the police as you just did Pogostin, or Noelle will die." The voice paused, to deliver its frightening coda. " *'Okay?'* "

The voice, even the inflection, was Noelle's.

"You've been *listening* . . ."

The man hung up.

Quickly, Carey called the *Times*.

"Photography."

"Where's Noelle?"

"Is this Peter?" There was a pause; his tone was less hostile than before. "Honestly, we don't know where she is . . ."

Carey ran from the building.

Englehardt moved toward the incinerator.

The second floor was dark and empty, a no man's land. He looked around him, listening, careful to walk quietly. He saw the shed along the wall, the telephone, and nothing more. The shed was locked; he heard no sound.

Gently, he opened the incinerator.

The pilot light glowed. He turned on the gas and dropped each photocopy of Levy's file into the rising flame until there was only ash.

He followed with the videotape of the naked lovers, his extra clothes, then every scrap of paper which bore the name Carey, stopping only at a photograph of Phillip. As he dropped it in, he was breathing hard, and the only trace of his surveillance was one copy of a single tape.

He put on gloves, listening for sounds between labored breaths. Looking once more toward the shed, he walked softly to the freight elevator on the opposite wall, and took it to the gallery.

He preferred the gallery at night.

It was the perfect time; in the thin light from the windows, his dragons, serpents and warriors reached their fullest power, subtle sculpture merging in the shadows with the strength of his imaginings.

A shadow stared through his window.

Englehardt crept past the statuary, peering into the silent street, and quietly unlocked the door.

The shadow became Clayton Barth. "What have you *done*, dammit?"

"Inside," Englehardt answered softly. "It's time we had our talk."

Carey's doorman stopped the three uniformed men to slip their leader a key.

Swiftly, they went to the Krantzes' with packing crates and stripped the apartment bare.

The leader did not question this, or the order to abandon so much new equipment at a garbage dump in New Jersey; the ugly man had paid them well.

He began caulking the drill-hole where the camera had been.

* * *

Englehardt leaned on his desk. Softly, he said, "We had to terminate Phillip Carey."

"Terminate?" Barth's ghastly, testing smile died on his face; he felt how foolish he must look, how unlike a president...

"Phillip is dead." Englehardt began speaking faster. "Peter's come too close to discovering the means of our control. Learning this involved the unplanned death of Dr. Levy. Phillip's swiftly followed."

"Dead." Numb, Barth tried retrieving his fantasy of presidential power; keen faces listening around a conference table, bodies poised to carry out his will. But he was alone with Englehardt in an empty loft, surrounded by pipes and wires and hanging metal lamps, the surreal landscape of a madman's brain. "Phillip was no threat to me..."

"Once Peter discovered what I used to force his uncle's sale, Phillip would lose nothing by exposing your extortion."

"Your extortion—*I* can walk away." Barth stood. "I never saw Phillip after our one meeting. I can tear up those certificates and..."

"Then how will you explain the ten-million-dollar check you wrote to Phillip—particularly when you just told Peter that Phillip sold you the firm." Englehardt tented his gloved fingers. "Or did my man mishear your conversation?"

Barth felt the loss of his volition like the paralysis of a sudden stroke, terrible in its surprise. "You might well be ruined," Englehardt continued in a relentless monotone, "since Peter would surely perceive that sale as connecting the secret of his suddenly murdered uncle with the death of Dr. Levy—two murders which are otherwise unexplained." His tone became steely. "Perhaps you can tell me, Clayton, what John Carey would do."

"But no surveillance can be worth this to me. You had no reason..."

"Reasons are an invention of the mind, to justify the wishes of the heart. I've finally learned that, even about myself. I offered you Van Dreelen and Carey, using methods of my own, because *you* wished to have it." Englehardt's smile was slight and chill. "Just as you wished to spy on those few pathetic scraps of your receptionist's life that you had not yet purchased for your own perversions."

Barth could make no sound.

"Oh, yes, Clayton—I watched *you*, too."

In the starkness of this twisted man's contempt, Barth felt truth like a bullet in the brain; John Carey's scorn had killed his real father, a man so weak and friendless that Barth had fled his memory to pursue John Carey's firm, right into the arms of a maniac. Trapped, he must watch for the chance to regain control. Carefully, he asked, "What do you intend?"

Englehardt's smile became a frightening parody of beneficence. "To give you Van Dreelen and Carey, of course." The smile vanished. "Now, do you wish to hear more, or shall I proceed without you?"

Slowly, Barth sat down.

The manager opened Carey's door; Gregorio dismissed him, and walked with Palmer to the living room. Together, they stood over the answering machine.

Palmer pushed "rewind," and then "message play." From the tape, a voice said, "Come to my office, Peter. Please, I've . . ."

There was a click, and the machine went silent.

Palmer turned to Gregorio. "Levy doesn't say anything about a tape . . ."

"Not on this." Gregorio kept staring at the machine. "He couldn't—Carey picked up the telephone."

"Jesus."

"Find him." Gregorio turned, white-faced. "Find the Ciano woman, too."

"Peter Carey killed Levy and his uncle, and so must kill himself." Englehardt touched his bow tie. "I've designed for him the perfect death."

Barth could not stop watching the man's gloves. "That's impossible."

"Applying the fruits of our surveillance to the question of the murderer, we change his identity." Englehardt spoke urgently: each crisp word heightened Barth's sense of vertigo. "Dr. Levy's file is the blueprint which we alone have read. Now Levy's death will lead the police to discover his concerns—Peter's hatred of Phillip, his latent capacity for violence. They find a message on Peter's answering machine asking that he come to Levy's office just before he died; from Pogostin they learn that the stolen tape discloses Peter's reason for so hating his uncle, and so posit that an irrational Peter may have killed Levy for the tape.

"Phillip is missing. The police now fear that this deadly tape combined with Phillip's sale of the firm to cause Peter's smoldering hatred of him to break the bonds of reason. They discover that, in a tragic piece of symbolism, Peter has taken Phillip to his grandfather's abandoned bindery, and shot him." Englehardt's eyes shut for an instant, and then his voice began racing. "Phillip is found moldering amidst memories which are Peter's alone, murdered with the same revolver that killed Levy—further proof of Peter's guilt."

"But Peter *knows . . .*"

"Only Miss Ciano knows for sure that Peter did not kill Levy." Englehardt paused for effect. "And only Miss Ciano can lure him within point-blank pistol range. You see, we have her up on the second floor."

"Here?" Barth heard his father's high-pitched twang. "Carey was *right?*"

"For Peter to die at his apartment could lead to questioning of the doorman. Instead, my operative is bringing Peter to our doorstep through the threat to this young woman. Psychologically, he is far too vulnerable to his guilts and fears to abandon her now."

"You can't involve *me* in this."

"You *are* involved, Clayton. My operative is on *your* payroll." Englehardt's tone became deadly. "This surveillance has cost me far too much already to have been for nothing. We're going to be partners now, for as long as *I* wish it."

Barth thought of his fantasies, now turned to ash. "Partners," he repeated bitterly. "In insanity . . ."

"Insanity?" Englehardt stood, glowering. "I've spent too many years explaining too much to men too stupid to understand. Now *you* tell me our surveillance is insane—you're as small and foolish as the little men who fired me." His speech took on the molten cadence of dammed rage breaking. *"Because* of our surveillance, we can kill two prominent men in a way that replicates the inner life of Peter Carey as disclosed in Levy's files. *Because* of our surveillance, we can persuade the police that, in a final act of self-destruction, Peter Carey then shot Miss Ciano—his sole alibi, whose desertion the files show he feared. *Because* of our surveillance, we know to kill her after shooting *Peter* with the same revolver used to kill the others—the suicide that Levy foresaw, found with the psychiatrist's tape and Phillip's house key in the pocket of his coat." He turned on Barth, his last words hushed. *"Because* of our surveillance, we even know to dump them where only Peter Carey would ever choose to die, the center of his most haunting memories and nightmares: the tunnel at Bethesda Fountain."

"Walk casually," the voice had said. "As if you're returning home from work."

Carey slowed to a walk.

They had been watching and listening: placing the call, they knew that he would come for her.

Too late, he remembered Pogostin. A snowflake touched his face, began melting.

They knew what he had forgotten; knew what frightened him; knew his passion for Noelle.

Like their puppet, he was walking toward them.

He moved mechanically up the west side of Fifth Avenue, seeing an ice-silver city he no longer loved: the Pulitzer Fountain, the Plaza, the sudden darkness of Central Park.

Laughter rang in the tunnel . . .

Carey felt a hand on his shoulder, saw that he had reached the Pulitzer Fountain. He turned.

"An ugly man," Noelle had said, "with fishlike eyes and a kind of hanging underlip."

"Hello, Peter."

The man's smile was hideous.

"Who are you?"

"A friend of Noelle's." The man spoke softly; pedestrians weaved around them, concerned with their own thoughts. "Now, do you wish to see her?"

Blood gushed from her eyes.

"Who sent you—Barth?"

The stranger shook his head. "Another."

Someone else had told them of Barth's past...

Carey's mind reeled. "How do I know you have her?"

The man reached into his coat. Slowly, he placed something in Carey's hands. "Here," he whispered. "You see, I've been watching you, together."

Carey stared at his photograph of Noelle.

"Thank you," the man said quietly. "That's how I've wished to think of her."

Foolishly, Carey shoved it in his pocket.

"It's all right, Peter. I trust you..."

"She's waiting, Peter."

He had burned the picture.

"Because if you abandon her, I will simply take your place. And after that, he cannot allow her to live."

The laughter of the faceless man echoed in the tunnel...

In one wrenching moment, Carey believed in all that was happening. He looked into the eyes of Noelle's ugly man. "Then why," he asked, "hasn't he killed her already?"

The stranger hesitated. "He simply wishes to see you."

They were counting on him.

"Come, Peter."

Suddenly, Carey knew that Noelle would die if he obeyed.

"Come."

Peter Carey turned and ran.

Twisting, dodging, he sprinted across Central Park South, bounced off a squealing cab and then careened through Grand Army Square, breaking into a dead run down the pathway to the zoo, into the bowels of Central Park.

CHAPTER 16

Carey ran past a black metal sculpture into the sudden dark.

City lights vanished in the tangle of naked trees; he saw only a shattered gaslight, skeletal branches, the cord dangling from a vandalized emergency phone. The path kept twisting downward.

"Faster, Daddy..."

He had come here with his father...

Footsteps echoed behind him. Each breath sucked cold air deeper in his throat; the pavement was slick. He slipped, caught himself with one hand, stumbling forward with his palm scraped open as he saw the wrought-iron gate ahead.

"Time to feed the seals, Peter..."

Closed.

Footsteps pounded closer. Carey glanced back; the stranger's shadow became larger, nearer. He could not stop.

The gate loomed ahead.

Forty feet, thirty...

Twenty...

Ten feet high...

Carey leaped, catching the bars; straining, he pulled himself to the top of the fence, lost his balance...

"Peter!"

Carey jumped from a half crouch.

Hurtling down, he hit the cobblestones inside the zoo.

Pain shot through both knees: he pitched forward and smashed one shoulder, forehead striking dank stone. He began crawling; rose, stunned and disoriented, saw the shadow of a clock tower...

He turned.

Two stone eagles staring; aviaries; the empty seal pool.

"Is that what it's like to die, Daddy?"

Metal rang; the stranger, climbing. There were cages all around him.

"I would never let you die, Peter . . ."

Starting toward the pool, he heard the thud of his pursuer landing, and then footsteps slapping behind him.

"Would you like to hear some music? . . ."

Carey began running across the darkened square and up the steps on the far side, veered right and then left in a headlong rush toward the second gate—leaping, hanging on, pulling upwards as the steps came closer. He turned; the shadow ran toward him.

Reaching the top, Carey jumped as the shadow leaped for the bars.

Martin reached the top and jumped for the other side.

A kind of singing rose inside him; landing, he felt no pain, heard in Carey's stricken footsteps the rhythm of *syrtaki* dancers, beckoning from a warm taverna . . .

Carey vanished in the dark.

Eagerly, Martin started up the trail from the zoo, following the sound of Peter's footsteps.

Carey's path had no reason or design. Martin smelled his panic like lemons in the wind; the thought of his woman warmed him like retsina . . .

He need only keep Carey from reaching his apartment, and then Noelle would be his.

He would drive him to the center of the park.

Reaching the crest of the trail, he ran toward the dark expanse of Sheep Meadow without regard to Carey and then turned abruptly north along a wide swatch of cobblestoned road marked by benches, dead trees and winged statues which looked like harpies in the dark, placing himself between the meadow and the echo of Carey's footsteps, pounding senselessly along the Mall . . .

He was tracking again, and Carey was cut off.

Carey sprinted down the Mall.

Stark, parallel lines of trees moved like sentries at the corners of his eyes; their arching branches cut the sky to a sliver of purple at the line's end. From gaslight to gaslight, his shadow rushed forward, retreated, rushed forward, retreated . . .

His pursuer's footsteps hammered from his left.

Carey could not see him.

The beat of his own running sounded in his ears with the roar of his pulse and the ragged rhythm of his breathing. Sweat froze on his forehead; his coat was hot and confining; snow fell on his face and hair. He felt himself lose speed, his shoes slipping . . .

He stumbled, rushed forward again. Through the trees, he heard footsteps running with him.

The man was steering him away from his apartment . . .

"We've been watching you . . ."

Suddenly, the Mall became an open plaza.

Carey started across the sweep of cobblestones: arc lights captured each movement for the stranger; the moonlit Band Shell gave no shelter; the plaza stretched endlessly before him, bare stone longer than a football field.

The shadow ran parallel, flashing from tree to tree. Its footsteps sounded closer. In the distance Carey saw thick stone pillars, the traverse, steps falling to a pit of darkness.

The lake.

Leaves crunched beneath his feet; his side throbbed. The shadow curled thirty yards to his left, poised to cut him off. Carey slipped again, caught himself.

"It was dark when I fell, Daddy . . ."

The shadow burst toward him at an angle; twenty yards, fifteen. The pillars of the traverse grew larger: Carey saw where instinct was leading him.

Ten . . .

"I know where to hide . . ."

Carey burst between the pillars and hit the steps to Bethesda Fountain at full tilt.

He tripped, plummeting face-first down the long flight of cement, ribs cracking until he struck his head at the bottom, rolled sideways. Footsteps sounded from the top of the steps. Skull throbbing, Carey rose; his vision cleared.

The fountain was empty, its statue a winged shadow, the lake silvered obsidian. The sound of running would betray him in the dark . . .

Wheeling, Carey saw the triple archway, froze. The footsteps came closer.

"Peter!"

Carey began running toward the archway.

Laughter echoed in the tunnel . . .

He burst inside.

It was black.

Martin stopped at the edge of the fountain.

Suddenly, he heard nothing.

His heart beat faster. Staring across the lake, he listened for the thud of footfalls.

Nothing.

Carey had stopped running.

He was close now; Martin knew this.

The gift of tracking had come back to him.

He had driven Carey deep into the park, running easily and in control, just fast enough that Carey felt him ever closer, knew panic in his stomach and spine, until he ran with a mindless frenzy that would drain him now, exhausted and alone.

Martin would take him to the small man like a child, the price of his woman.

Turning, he smiled to himself, and then he saw the tunnel.

With a chill, Martin realized where Peter Carey had led *him*.

Carey stared through the darkness.

Peter stopped, disoriented. The tunnel was long and too dark: the row of stone arches along each wall made it seem like a ruined church. Turning, he blinked at the three semicircles behind him.

Once inside the tunnel, the stranger could no longer see him. Darkness was his chance.

A silhouette appeared in the archway.

Frightened, Peter felt suddenly cut off from his father, unsure now whose shadow he saw or whose steps were coming closer, confused as to whether Charles were pursuer or thwarted rescuer, deceived by Peter's foolishness. The shadow came nearer. Peter skirted beneath an arch, back pressed desperately against the moist stone, eyes screwed shut. His heart pounded . . .

Carey backed to the wall, waiting. He had all but ceased breathing. Blood pounded in his head.

Charles Carey stole through his brain in the nightmare of his childhood, relentless and unpitying. They were hiding in the tunnel near Bethesda Fountain. It was a game; his father smiled at him, and then his mouth opened in a tortured scream and his face turned to ash and bone before Peter could pull him from the tunnel. Peter held the empty sleeve of his father's windbreaker, crying out as the faceless man began stabbing at his eyes with garden shears . . .

Moving in the tunnel, the silhouette became a shadow with no face.

As Peter went blind, blood spurting from the sockets of his eyes, he heard laughter echo in the tunnel, screamed aloud.

Carey clenched his teeth. He must take him, or lose Noelle.

Blood gushed from her eyes.

The shadow vanished in blackness. Steps came closer.

"Suppose, Peter, that the burning face and the faceless man are both Charles Carey?"

The footsteps slowed. Carey sensed the shadow searching in the dark, fearful.

"It's too dark down there for elephants, Daddy . . ."

Carey saw the glint of metal, three feet in front of him. He raised his arms.

Carey's knees drew up. "Why would my father blind me?"

"I'm not suggesting it's true, Peter. I'm just wondering if you've some buried feeling that your father might be angry at you."

The shadow held a gun.

"Tell me, Peter, are you concerned that the faceless man is you?"

Carey clasped both hands above his head as the shadow began turning . . .

Phillip leaned to kiss his forehead. "I won't tell your father."

Screaming, Peter Carey swung down. . . .

Tensed to shoot, Martin thought of Noelle: he must bring Carey back alive.

In the split second of his hesitation Carey snapped his collarbone like a twig.

The revolver dropped to the cement, its echo lost in that of Carey's scream. Martin fell to his knees, groping. Carey stuck one palm in his face, lunged out for something, swung...

Martin spun reeling as the revolver cracked his jaw and white, brilliant pain shot through his face and shoulder. Carey grabbed for his legs; Martin broke free, stumbling toward the tunnel's mouth...

Carey's cry pursued him from the tunnel: *"Where is she?"*

Leaping with the cry still in his throat, Carey skidded on his side; the man broke free as Carey rose with the revolver in his other hand, all sinew and nerve and instinct.

"We've been watching you."

Carey caught him by the fountain.

Wheeling, the man swung his arm like a scythe at Carey's neck, slipped. The nails of his hand scraped Carey's face.

Carey struck at his head with the revolver.

There was a sickening thud. Shock ran through Carey's arm; the man pitched backwards into the fountain. Carey swung again, felt the gun butt hitting bone as the man fell back and momentum brought Carey down on top of him. Grasping his throat, Carey smelled sour breath, felt his knees digging into the stranger's ribs, the heartbeats that linked them like two animals.

Carey jammed the revolver against his head.

The man's eyes widened.

Her eyes gushed blood...

Carey began pounding his skull on the cement. The head lolled, made no sound.

Suddenly, Carey jerked the face toward his. The man's mouth was bleeding, his jaw grotesquely crooked.

Carey dropped him from his grasp.

The man's skull cracked on the cement. His eyes rolled and then focused; he was waiting to be killed.

Carey touched the revolver to his forehead. "Now," he said softly, "you can tell me where she is."

Barth watched the gray void of Englehardt's eyes.

The man's sudden quiet was unnerving. He kept glancing at the telephone. "Where is he?" Barth demanded.

Englehardt did not look up. "I don't know."

Barth felt a sudden, irrational rage. "Damn Phillip. What's on that tape—what did he do to Peter?"

Englehardt's pupils widened. He stared at Barth, his fingers stroking the telephone.

Barth saw the telephone dangling above his father's skull. His book was open to John Carey's name.

"You must wait for Peter Carey," Englehardt answered softly.

"And if he doesn't come?"

"That was always a contingency." Englehardt's long look at Barth made the words seem frightening. "I have another plan."

The telephone rang.

Carey watched the stranger lean into the light.

His face was swollen; his mouth still bled; one arm hung at his side. The other hand grasped a telephone.

Carey held the revolver to his head.

They stood in a phone booth near the traverse. Leaves swirled at their feet with a dry, skirling sound; the headlights of invisible cars passed thirty feet away and vanished with the snarl of their motors; an arc light cast silver into the booth. Carey and the stranger breathed together.

"If you so much as shiver," Carey whispered, "I'll kill you."

The man's eyes froze. "Yes." He spoke into the telephone; the shattered jaw made him slur each word. "Carey has me."

Carey saw the cost of failure on his face. He could not hear the voice.

Laughter echoed in the tunnel.

"Who is it?" he demanded.

The stranger shook his head. "He'll explain in person," he answered, then said into the telephone, "Carey won't come unless he hears her voice."

The stranger began listening. Carey slid one hand into his pocket, touching the cassette recorder that he had taken. He pressed the gun harder.

The stranger flinched and began speaking rapidly. "I've told him nothing—no names or reasons or where you are." His voice took on a jeering, bitter edge. "He needs the woman too much to shoot me."

"Hurry up."

The stranger turned. Through swollen lips, his smile reappeared, more terrible for the pain it cost him.

He held out the telephone.

Noelle clung desperately to who she was.

It was black; bound and blindfolded; she could not move or see. Trussed behind her, her wrists were raw from chafing against rope. Her legs were tied beneath her buttocks at both ankles; her thighs and calves had cramped with pain. She had no balance; one side of her face and shoulder was mashed against cold metal. She needed to urinate.

Peter was dead.

The ugly man would kill them both.

Reaching beneath her blouse, the ugly man had touched her shoulder.

He could not make her urinate.

She wept in hate and anger, for that part of her already dead.

Her legs screamed their pain, endless and unrelieved as the darkness that surrounded her, without time or faces or the sound of humans, save her own sobbing.

She had not been gagged; this freedom mocked her, the last measure of her hopelessness. No one could hear her.

She would not urinate; would not lose control.

It was so cruel; safe within their separate spaces, lovers smiled into each other's eyes, and neither knew nor cared.

She thought of the Village, warmth she took for granted, her apartment. Peter would dress before the mirror . . .

He cried out in the night.

There were candles at La Chaumière, flickering in the mirror.

Peter had brought her here.

She wished never to have met him.

She could not face her cowardice, her shame for not believing in his fears.

If she regretted loving him, fearing for her life, then Peter would abandon her to save his own.

He was dead.

She wished to hear his voice.

Blood stained his hair; he had died alone, knowing that his fear was real.

Her kidneys hurt.

The man had watched them together...

He would take her, and then they both would live.

She began imagining his touch.

He could not make her urinate.

He was using her as bait for Peter.

He would enter her, mouth pressed on her skin.

Her jeans were tight.

She would soon wake up.

No.

The ugly stranger wanted more from her; there were other men...

She would kill him.

Peter was dead.

He could not be dead; he must save her, she had earned this with her patience.

He would not know where to find her...

His love for her had killed him.

She could not let him die.

The ugly man would save her.

She would please him.

Peter's arms and chest were warm in the dark.

The stranger would kill them both.

Peter must come; she could not die.

She could not urinate.

The door burst open; the man jammed something cold into her face...

Urine ran down her leg.

"Noelle..."

A telephone: Peter.

"Peter!" she screamed out. *"Please don't come—he'll kill you."*

The line went dead in Carey's hand.

He stared into the stranger's eyes, gun pointed at his temple. Their faces were two feet apart.

"If you go to the police," the stranger said, "he'll kill her. You're being offered an arrangement."

Carey hesitated; seeing this, the man smiled again. "I'll die before you'll take me elsewhere," he added softly. "And then *you* will have murdered her."

Carey's mind shrank instinctively from believing that his faceless enemy would kill Noelle Ciano because he had reached to her in love; at his brain's center, he felt her death. His enemy knew him, better than he knew himself: for more reasons than Carey yet could understand, he had no other choice.

"I'll come," he answered simply.

Englehardt appeared in the elevator of the loft.

Barth watched as he moved toward him. "Young Peter's on his way," Englehardt said slowly, "with my operative and a revolver."

"How?..."

"He has more resources than I'd thought." Englehardt walked behind the desk and slid open its middle drawer. "It simply requires an adjustment."

Quickly, Barth calculated. When Peter came, he must surprise this man and kill him: no one else could prove the fact of his complicity. He would distract him, stall for time. "You said you had a plan..."

"I do." Englehardt looked down at him consideringly. "Let me instruct you further, as an intellectual proposition. Inside this drawer is the revolver used to murder both Phillip and the psychiatrist. Peter Carey is still an amateur: once he arrives, there are ways I can exploit his psychic pain to distract and then kill him. But I require his suicide to explain Phillip and Levy, and suicides don't kill themselves at a range of forty feet. Are you with me so far, Clayton?"

Barth's eyes narrowed. "You'd need another murderer."

"Precisely." Englehardt took out the black revolver and held it like a pointer, speaking more rapidly. "Peter Carey as a murder victim reopens the question of the murderer. And yet, clearly, his existence leaves us quite vulnerable—particularly my operative and you, who are now both known to him." He began pacing beside his desk. "It's the gift of the superior intelligence officer, therefore, to be able to turn a plan on its axis to view it from a second angle. In itself, the notion of a suicide was lovely." Gently, Englehardt placed the revolver to

Barth's temple. "As the child of a suicide, I'm sure that you can appreciate the richness of it."

In one last terrible moment, Barth saw his father's face. *"No . . ."*

"So what would you do, Clayton?" Englehardt concluded, and pulled the trigger.

CHAPTER 17

Carey inched the stranger along the path he ran with Noelle.

They moved in darkness. Arc lights bathed the traverse in a swath of yellow running forty feet to their right; night wove the trees in front of them into a twisted maze, obscuring the lights of Central Park West. The night grew colder; the maze thinned; the stranger's footsteps plodded toward the lights. Carey aimed the revolver at his back.

"Keep moving..."

Cabs sped by on the traverse; headlights stabbed the trunks of trees and patches of dead grass; tires hummed and went and came again.

A car braked, squealing.

"I'm losing control..."

Carey could not turn: captor and imprisoned, he must always watch the stranger. Dull rhythmic pounding drove pain from his skull through his eyes and the cords of his neck, sapping strength from his legs. "Hurry up..."

"Faster, Daddy..."

Slivers of memory, a gift from Levy, exploded from his subconscious.

"Peter!"

Carey fought them; he must not be distracted.

Levy was dead.

He must always watch the stranger.

His palm was scraped raw; the gun rubbed sweat into it. He did not know if he could pull the trigger.

A prowl car cruised the corner of his eye; he tensed to shout.

"Go to the police, and he'll kill her..."

Its taillights vanished around a curve.

They kept walking.

The lights loomed higher and closer; the broad shoulders of the stranger moved toward them, catlike but too slow.

"Faster . . ."

His steps kept falling in the same deliberate beat.

"Faster, damn you . . ."

The man did not seem to hear.

The path rose; there were street sounds; the lights grew square and large. They passed beneath a bower of dead branches.

Carey watched his back.

The traffic noise grew nearer; the two men walked in tandem. Abruptly, the stranger wheeled on him.

Carey could not fire, shouted, *"Stop!"*

A streetlight caught the stranger's crooked smile of contempt. In a slurred voice, he said, "We can take the subway now."

Carey shot one look past him. The stone entrance to the park; the Aristocrat across the street; the doorman, waiting . . .

The stranger was pointing to the subway entrance on the corner of West 72nd Street.

Carey slid the gun into his overcoat pocket, gripping its butt. "We'll use a cab."

"So you can take me to the police?"

"I said I wouldn't do that."

The stranger shook his head. "I don't want some cabbie remembering my face, or writing where he dropped us. This way it's just the two of us, alone."

A woman in furs passed behind them on the sidewalk, walking a poodle. Under his breath, Carey asked, "Where are we going?"

The ugly man still smiled at him. "SoHo."

Englehardt despised Clayton Barth for his ugliness in death.

It upset him, altered his balance. He had never killed a man, and then looked into his face.

Barth's head lolled; his arms flopped on both sides of the chair. His eyes still stared at Englehardt with the shock of his betrayal.

Englehardt thought of Phillip. There was bile in his mouth.

His first instinct was to run.

Turning away, he breathed deeply. He could not leave Martin in the grasp of Peter Carey, for Martin knew his name.

He walked back to Barth, seized him by the hair, and gently laid his head on the desk. His hand trembled...

He would no longer see Barth's face.

He did not wish to see the face of Peter Carey, so much like his father's. But the circle of fate was closing fast...

He began pacing.

Once more he picked up the revolver he had used to murder Barth.

Walking around Barth's chair, he knelt, and took him by the hand.

Carefully, systematically, he put Barth's fingerprints on the barrel, stock and trigger, while his skin was still warm. The revolver would be Barth's alone: his own gloves would leave no trace.

Standing, he walked back past the desk, to the far side of the room.

There was a board of wall switches. One by one he flicked them off until a single overhead lamp cast a pool of light in front of the elevator. His desk was swathed in darkness.

He walked toward it.

The drawer was still open. At the rear, behind the second revolver, was a cassette recorder. Englehardt took the tape from his pocket and slipped it into the recorder. Punching the button marked "playback," he felt the first welcome rush of confidence: so carefully edited, the tape would serve him well.

Precisely, he angled the desk lamp away from his face, so that its streak of light ran across the blotter to illuminate the head of Clayton Barth.

He sat, closing the drawer.

For one final moment, he reviewed his plan; the ritual soothed him, like the fingering of rosary beads. By instinct, he reached into his right breast pocket, and touched the check with Phillip Carey's signature. Phillip...

He shut his eyes. Shooting him, Martin had smiled.

There could be no misstep now, no failure of his nerve. He must frighten Peter Carey, as he could not frighten his father, until Carey lost control.

His own control must be like iron.

Slowly, Englehardt forced himself to look across the desk, at the head of Clayton Barth.

Blood trickled onto the blotter.

Englehardt rose and left the room.

Noelle Ciano was past tears.

She had strained at the ropes that bound her, desperate for the sound of Peter's voice, until her wrists bled and her shoulders and the muscles of her stomach ached with the cramping pain that robbed her legs of feeling. She smelled urine and no longer cared. Her eyes and heart were dry.

The man would kill her now.

Perhaps she was dying for Peter's memory.

Time had slipped from her in the dark with the hope of living. She knew only pain and blackness; there was no daylight or the taste of wine, or the scent of Peter's skin.

She hoped he would not know the despair of becoming an animal.

Would he live, she wondered suddenly, and have a child? Would he reach for its mother in the darkness of the night?

Her throat caught; for one split second Peter Carey smiled in her mind, alive again.

Footsteps.

"Peter?"

She could not die now, just as she had found him.

A metallic scraping sound, the door opening . . .

Tears came to her eyes, and then a thin hand touched her.

Martin's hatred drew him on.

He led Carey up the steps from the subway, emerging in a trickle of passengers at the corner of Spring Street and Sixth Avenue. They stopped, facing a triangular park of brick and benches and bare trees; night made it stark and soulless, a piece of modern sculpture. No passengers looked up as they passed; unwitting and uncurious, they dispersed along dim cobblestones and the two men stood alone.

The gun dug into his back. "Move," Carey whispered.

Martin felt Carey breathing on his neck.

Slowly, he turned down Spring Street. Pain throbbed through his face and skull, nothing to the pain of his emasculation.

Perhaps she was already dead.

Martin was not sure; Englehardt killed through him alone, just as he himself had entered Noelle through Peter Carey, passion without risk. He did not know if Englehardt could murder whom he touched.

Martin's stomach twisted. He still wanted the woman; he would prove himself by taking Carey.

A flag flapped above them; Martin felt the gun jerk, heard the quick hiss of Carey's breath.

If she was still alive, he could take Carey as she watched.

He knew his weakness from the subway.

Deliberately, he had picked a local; head ringing and mouth trickling blood, he had staunched his hate by watching each new stop stretch Carey to the breaking point. The train squealed to a standstill, loaded and unloaded its meager burden, and then lurched forward again, flickering and half-empty, stopped as a few passengers trooped on and off, started and stopped, stopped and started, and still Carey faced him with the gun in his pocket, white knuckles grasping a center pole, so stiff and fearful of losing him that he lost track of where they were until they had arrived at SoHo, and Martin had smiled at the useless gun, saying, "We can get off now, Peter," as if to a stupid tourist.

Carey's eyes had never left his face.

Englehardt would not permit such concentration; he was bringing Peter Carey to be killed.

Englehardt could not let Carey have him.

Martin wondered what price the small man would exact for his failure, what wounds and psychic cruelties. There would surely be some penalty; in the matter of Phillip Carey, he had pushed Englehardt much too far.

He must show him that his skills had not eroded.

Crossing Wooster Street, he slowed.

Carey did not like these streets; Martin had learned this by watching him with the woman. She had stopped to read the poster; Carey had stared up at the tangle of fire escapes hanging over the narrow streets until Martin sensed the warehouses tumbling down on him. Martin would use this now, to drain Carey of the crazy energy that had sustained him in the park, replacing it with fear.

"Faster..."

Carey's voice was ragged. A couple passed them on the other side, hailing a taxi.

Martin slowed still more as they turned down Greene Street.

Bare and treeless, it was narrower than the others—only arc lamps, corrugated-iron doors and garbage bags, the metal signs of rag merchants. Fire escapes climbed seven-story buildings on both sides, blocking the sky.

The gun slid to his neck.

"Don't worry, Peter." Martin's voice was soothing. "We're getting close."

He wondered what Englehardt had waiting for Peter Carey.

There would be some final shock to snap his self-control; some playing with light and darkness, Carey's fears and nightmares. Perhaps the woman...

Martin would pause before he killed him, savoring the climax of their drama.

He stopped at the door to the gallery. "We're here," he said softly.

Carey stepped through the door.

Vague, frightening shapes receded toward the wall. He jerked up the revolver...

The shapes did not move.

The stranger walked between them. "Wait," Carey shouted. A coiled dragon appeared to his left.

Carey's eyes adjusted to the light.

Dark and vast, the room was filled with statuary that menaced from all angles. Shadows fell on other shadows until they took on a human aspect, and the stranger, now still, became one of them. There was no sound.

"Wait," Carey repeated softly.

Aiming the revolver at the stranger's back, he surveyed the room. It was widest to his left, cluttered with statues at odd distances. Ahead, an aisle had been cleared, leading straight to an open service elevator on the opposite wall, covered in burlap and pads.

The stranger began walking toward it.

Slowly, Carey followed him inside.

The elevator closed. "Hands on the door," Carey snapped. "And don't move."

The stranger leaned forward, the flat of each palm pressed above his head. Carey held the gun to his back.

Rumbling, the elevator started up. Carey heard the cables straining with its weight, thought of his faceless enemy, waiting.

The elevator kept rising.

Abruptly, it lurched. Carey's knees buckled, free hand catching his fall, and then the elevator came to a stop.

"Don't move," Carey repeated. His voice was taut.

The door opened.

They were splashed in yellow.

Blinking, Carey saw the stranger, framed in the door with his arms raised, crucified by light.

"Hello, Peter."

The voice echoed from some great distance. The stranger moved toward it.

Carey stepped from the elevator, and blinked.

He stood in a circle of light, staring into the massive outline of a loft, darkness so vast that for an instant it seemed they were outdoors on a starless night. A beam stabbed from the wall of black.

His eyes followed it to a small wooden desk.

Barth's head lay on it, facing Carey. Blood ran from the temple.

Noelle Ciano sat on the other side.

She was blindfolded. From the darkness, a gloved hand pointed a gun to her head.

It had no face or body.

From deep within him, Carey cried, *"Who are you?"*

The despair in Carey's voice crossed forty feet of darkness.

Englehardt no longer trusted his own: films and photographs had not prepared him for this presence, so close to Charles Carey that it seemed to replace memory with the impact of their meeting.

"That, Peter, you can never know."

His throat was dry. He saw Carey blindly pointing the revolver; Martin tensed in front of him; blood trickling down

Barth's face; the blindfolded woman leaning toward her lover's voice—a frieze of light and darkness. He could not think . . .

Carey called out, *"Noelle!"*

She tried to stand, hands tied behind her. Her mouth opened. Englehardt pressed the gun to her temple.

Carey stepped toward him.

"Wait." Englehardt reached for his normal tone. "Startle me in any way, and Miss Ciano will die in the reflex of my finger."

He saw Martin dip one shoulder, Carey's gun twitch back to him. Englehardt nerved himself on. "I hope to persuade you, Peter, that I need not harm Miss Ciano at all. What I'm about to propose is a rather complex trade. If you agree, I will simply take the man who brought you here, and vanish from your life."

Carey moved closer behind Martin. Englehardt paused to let Martin count the sound of each step; preparing to use the tape, this moment helped him plan. "Your intelligent consent demands that you appreciate the components of the trade, and time requires that I be blunt. To begin with, you no longer own the firm left you by your grandfather. You'll recognize, of course, the head of Clayton Barth. Last night, he purchased your firm from Phillip Carey for ten million dollars." His voice was sardonic. "His heirs own it now."

Carey stared at Barth's bloody face. "Where's Phillip?" he asked softly.

"I'm coming to that, with your indulgence. As you know, Barth's motive was more than love for publishing. Before you were born, his father killed himself when your grandfather refused to restore him to his salesman's position. The young Barth's hatred of John Carey became an adult obsession to own the firm which bore his name.

"He succeeded by blackmailing Phillip."

Carey looked drawn in the light. He did not speak.

"You must feel quite confused, Peter." He watched Martin's knees tense as he reached into the drawer. "Do you wish me to explain how Barth came to own your uncle?"

There was silence. Slowly, Carey nodded.

"Yes," Englehardt answered gently. "I think it's time you understood the hidden meaning of your life."

He switched on Pogostin's tape.

CHAPTER 18

"Daddy..."

Peter Carey heard himself screaming in the voice of a six-year-old.

"Go faster, Daddy..."

Pogostin's voice was soft. "What happened next?"

High-pitched and afraid, the child's answer came to Carey from the darkness. "Mommy doesn't want him to..."

"*Go faster, Daddy...*"

Carey shook his head.

"*Go faster, Daddy. Don't let him beat you...*"

"No," Carey cried out. "Stop!"

His father grinned, accelerating to catch Phillip. His mother reached back to zip Peter's windbreaker. She touched his cheek. "Then at least you won't catch cold."

Peter leaned forward, wind whipping his hair. Trees and houses and picket fences on both sides flashed like shadows at the corners of his eyes. The road grew steeper, dipped into a shady hollow, rose sharply in front of them. Peter began chuckling. The precipitous grade ahead, curving to the right, snapped in front of him like a photograph. His father took the curve, sped up the grade between green trees dappling it with light and darkness.

At the top of the grade, almost without warning, flashed an abrupt left curve.

Phillip took it, the mint-green car vanishing. Peter's laugh grew wilder. Clutching Dewey by the trunk, he shouted, "Catch him, Daddy."

His father stepped on the gas. Two hundred feet, a hundred. "Charles..." his mother entreated.

Peter grasped Dewey's trunk. "Faster, Daddy..."

343

His father braked abruptly, crying, "I've lost control," as the steering wheel spun like a toy in his hand and their car slid toward the cliff. In sickening freeze frames, Peter saw them jump the last rocks, trees and sky appearing in the windshield, his father turning to his mother, their eyes locking for one split second before his father whirled and threw him from the car.

Peter hit dirt, still clutching Dewey, falling, tumbling, air bursting from his lungs, rocks buffeting his skull and ribs. He glimpsed his father's car plummeting next to him in a hundred-foot deadfall of jagged rock, and then lost sight of it as he spun in punishing darkness on a long strip of grass and rolled until the speed of it threw him on his stomach at the bottom of the cliff and he saw, within ten feet of him, two red cars smashing into trees, his mother's necks snapping like two rag dolls, and then his vision fused, and a single car burst into flames, and his father screamed in animal torment as fire consumed his body and his face fell forward . . .

"Daddy!"

The tape kept playing. "Daddy . . . Daddy . . ."

"Tell me, Peter, is there any reason you might feel guilt over your father's death?"

Carey felt tears.

A door opened . . .

The room was a blur. Blindfolded, Noelle reached toward him. The voice of his enemy came from behind her. "You see, Peter, it was your *father* who saved you."

Noelle began rising.

Englehardt touched her shoulder.

"Wait," he said softly.

The scenes unfolded before him: Noelle blindly reaching; Carey stunned; Martin looking toward him for a signal. Englehardt held up one finger.

The tape played on.

"Let's go back," Pogostin was saying, "to the night before . . ."

"I don't want to . . ."

"Can you tell me about Dewey, Peter?"

Englehardt saw Martin lean slightly to the left.

"Do you remember?" Pogostin asked.

"I left him in the race car, in Uncle Phillip's garage." The child's speech became rapid, fearful. "Daddy kissed me good-night and said he'd get him for me."

"And did he?"

Martin's shoulder dipped.

"Peter?"

"No." Peter's voice turned cold. "He didn't."

"What happened?"

"I'm afraid." Pause. "Do I have to tell you?"

"Nothing you can tell me now will hurt you, Peter. I promise."

The voice grew smaller. "I woke up and Dewey wasn't there."

"What did you do?"

The tape spun silently.

"Just the first thing, Peter."

"I went downstairs to the kitchen."

"Why did you go there?"

"There was a door to the garage." The voice rose. "It was dark there. I was afraid."

"What did you do?"

"I touched the door."

"And?"

"I opened it."

Slowly, Peter opened the door.

Carey saw the garage.

A light was on.

Phillip turned from the wheel of his father's car.

"Peter!"

"Phillip!" Carey shook his head. "Oh my God, no!"

He heard a series of clicks; abruptly Pogostin asked, "Why didn't you tell your father what you saw?"

"I was scared to."

"Do you know why, Peter?"

The ugly man tensed. From the tape, the child Peter said: "Because of Uncle Phillip."

The door to his room opened. "Peter?"

"After I took Dewey back upstairs, he came to my room."

"Why don't we talk, Peter?"

"He promised not to tell Daddy I was spying on him. I saw them fighting; he knew Daddy didn't want me to..."

His father spotted Peter in the doorway; in a soft voice, he told him, "Sometimes even brothers need their privacy, all right?"

Recalling the naked woman, Peter looked away. "I'm sorry, Daddy."

"Grown-ups have secrets." The child sounded guilty, confused. "My Mommy got mad because I sneaked up to hug her and she broke the glass."

"Was that all?"

There was silence.

"Peter?"

"No..."

"What else?"

"In the library." The voice was barely audible. "I saw my Daddy with the dark-haired woman..."

"What did they do?"

Peter stopped, transfixed by naked arms and legs and bodies, a slim, dark woman he had never seen...

"She put her mouth on him." The child's voice shook. "Grown-ups do things I shouldn't see. Phillip promised..."

Phillip kissed his forehead, as his father had done. "Promise..."

"Then why are you mad at him, Peter?"

On the tape, Peter Carey started crying.

"Peter?"

"Phillip did something to the sports car." The child's voice choked, and then burst out, "I helped them kill my Daddy..."

Carey felt himself fuse with the child Peter. "No-o-o-o..."

The ugly man spun on him...

Englehardt saw Martin pivot, his good arm swinging, Carey jumping sideways. Englehardt jerked up the gun and fired.

The bullet echoed; Noelle cried out.

Martin's other arm flew up in the air.

A stain appeared on his back. He turned, staring through the darkness with a look of dumb amazement, reached out for Englehardt. Blood spread on his shirt front, began running from his mouth.

Englehardt watched him, silent; the ugly man had gone too far.

Martin's eyes rolled; he took two last staggering steps, and pitched forward.

Carey caught him, fell to his knees, pointing the gun toward Englehardt.

"Wait!" Englehardt stuck his revolver to Noelle's ear.

On the tape, Peter cried, "It was Uncle Phillip!" and then the tape clicked off.

Carey clung to the dead man, for cover.

"This time," Englehardt told him from the darkness, *"I saved your life."*

Carey clasped the dead weight, felt the warm blood through his shirt. Over one shoulder, he pointed his gun at the voice. "Consider it, Peter."

Noelle leaned straining across the desk. The revolver followed her. "Noelle," Carey called. "Don't move."

A second arm reached out to pull her back into the chair. She sat as if drugged. The arm was attached to a shadow with no face. Turned from it, the face of Clayton Barth stared blankly through the darkness at the man who had died in Carey's arms, seconds before.

The shadow spoke rapidly. "I could have killed you just as easily, Peter. Now this man's death becomes part of our deal. There's much more that I'll need."

Carey shook his head. "You have *me* now. Let her go."

"I need your informed understanding, Peter, and we haven't much time." The voice was thin, angry. "You can cling to that corpse if it helps you."

"I saved you . . ."

"What about Phillip?"

"That part's quite simple. Somehow Phillip obtained a copy of your grandfather's will, and discovered its humiliating terms. He meant to kill both you and your father by tampering with the steering mechanism—that was what you saw, the night before your father's death." The words slowed, became more gentle. "But Phillip was a tender murderer: impulsively, he saved you, perhaps hoping that a six-year-old would not connect the accident with what he'd seen in the garage. In the end,

his foolish act of pulling you away cost him dearly. For twenty-
three years he lived in mortal terror: from the time you were
six, he did everything in his power to keep you from remembering what had happened, and then making sense of it as an
adult. It was he who destroyed the elephant, of course." The
voice lowered. "You see, the faceless man was Phillip Carey . . ."

Leaping, Phillip rolled him from the car . . .

Carey saw Noelle weeping, tears running down her face
from eyes he could not see. "How do you know these things?"

"Barth told me: how he'd learned them I don't know—I
suppose through Phillip's analyst. But he *used* them to blackmail your uncle, and then hired the man whose body you're
holding to determine from Dr. Levy's files what dangers your
memory might pose, and what pressures might cause your will
to crumble. They chose Miss Ciano . . ."

"Noelle? Tell me, dammit—what's Barth got on you?"

"Retrieving the tape that I just played, the man encountered
Dr. Levy, and killed him. Once he'd heard the tape, Barth
became frightened that Phillip could be pressured by a murder
charge into exposing his blackmail and therefore connecting
him with Levy's death—after all, Phillip would have nothing
left to lose. So Barth ordered this man to kill *him*, too."

"It's not Barth."

"Is he? . . ."

"Oh yes, Peter. Phillip's quite dead—your memory killed
him. You've wreaked your revenge: on your uncle, on the man
who killed Levy, on Barth himself."

Carey could smell the intestines of the ugly stranger draining, feel his skin start turning cold. He remembered the recorder; instinctively his hand slid toward his pocket as the voice
continued. "You see, Barth planned to have this man kill Miss
Ciano, your only alibi, and then stage your death as a suicide,
with the gun he had already used to kill the others. Your
apparent guilt in two earlier killings would help satisfy the
police. You were to serve as the murderer of your analyst,
uncle and lover. But by capturing the killer you turned the gun
on Barth."

The gun was too close to her head, the voice too tight for
the calm it pretended. Carey's knees ached; one arm was heavy

from pointing the gun, the other from clasping the stranger. He tried to reason . . .

"I've been helping Barth on matters of security. He called in a panic, and told me what I've just told you. For the first time I saw the impact of his father's suicide, the depths of his hatred for you and your uncle—realized, truly, that he was insane. I said I could do nothing.

"Barth could not face the prospect of exposure. He killed himself with the revolver he had meant for you, leaving me to clean up the mess.

"I've done more than that, Peter—I've set you free." The voice became gentle. "All I ask now is that you do that much for me."

Englehardt watched Carey look from Noelle to the direction of his voice. "Now," he urged, "will you stand and talk with me?"

Seeing Carey hesitate, he fought the tension connecting his nerves to the memory of Charles. The father had seen through him . . .

Carey released the body.

Martin pitched face-forward to the cement. His head struck . . .

Wincing, Englehardt saw Carey snatch back his hand as if in horror, thrust it in his coat pocket for a moment, then seem to remember that the right hand held a gun. He pointed it, kneeling without shelter.

"That's better." Englehardt held Phillip's check to the light. "Now I have something for you.

"Barth wrote this check to Phillip. Unless I arrange for its deposit, the sale will fall through for lack of any payment, and you will regain from Barth's heirs what your grandfather left you—one half of what you seem to need so desperately.

"The other half is Miss Ciano.

"It would be ironic if she died, as did your father and uncle, as part of John Carey's terrible legacy. I doubt you could preserve your sanity, Peter."

Carey aimed at the sound of his voice. "How do I know you won't kill her now?"

"Peter, Peter—I could have let this man kill *you*, or shot you myself. Instead I've extended our balance of terror. You don't wish to die, and I've an incentive to avoid further gunfire. While it's unlikely that *you* could kill *me*, two extra bodies— even an extra bullet fired from a second gun—require more cerebration than I care for the police to give this. And, should you so much as wound me, whatever medical care I require might connect me to this scene.

"I don't propose to let that happen.

"What I propose is that we vanish, leaving Barth as the killer of your uncle, Levy and this man."

Carey gazed out from the circle of light. "How is that possible?"

Englehardt slowly drew the second revolver from the desk and pointed it at Noelle. Almost casually, he slid the gun he had been holding across the desk, so that it dropped at Barth's side. He spoke into the echo of its fall.

"That, Peter, is the same revolver which *Barth* used to kill all three men, and then himself. His fingerprints are even on it, and the man whose body lies in front of you will be discovered to have been on his payroll. So it's as good as done, really. All that *I* require is a graceful way to leave, and two million dollars of *your* money—a rebate, you might say."

Carey looked incredulous. "There's no way you can..."

"*We*, you mean?" Englehardt paused for effect. "Not one name or scrap of paper connects me to these men or to this place; neither of you knows my name or has even seen my face. I can utterly disappear, and there will be nothing but your word to say that I exist.

"You've no reason to insist on that.

"You've been avenged for your father's death, and your firm has been restored to you. By leaving, you can spare yourself involvement with tonight's untidy incident and let Barth solve your considerable problems with the police, all the while preparing to discharge your substantial debt of gratitude to me. As its measure, all that I require is the sum of two million dollars to help me continue my career elsewhere. As banking hours have passed, I'll accept your promise to pay me in cash, at a time and place of my choosing; retaining Barth's check as collateral. Upon receiving the money, I'll destroy the check for you, and the firm will be indubitably yours." Englehardt's voice chilled. "Most important, you'll both still be alive.

"With these two men dead, *you're* the only living witnesses who could conceivably link me to this time or place. By sparing you now, I leave you able to repay me. Any time you wonder who I am, consider keeping my two million dollars, or perceive some further reason to regret our deal, remember that I could find and kill you both with infinitely greater speed and certainty than you could ever help anyone find me. That expressly goes for Miss Ciano: the money I ask is little enough to pay for what she brings to you, let alone clear title to John Carey's firm. Now, Peter, I need your answer."

Carey did not speak.

As seconds passed, Englehardt felt the scene erode his calm: two men with revolvers, the first framed in light, the second cloaked in darkness, pointing a gun at the woman.

Carey stared at her. Her face sought the sound of his voice.

"Well, Peter?"

Carey stood, holding the gun, and looked back toward Englehardt with his father's cobalt eyes.

"Let her go first," he said.

CHAPTER 19

Englehardt wished that he could read Carey's eyes more closely. "What do you propose?"

"I want Noelle to leave here safely, now."

"You don't have that much leverage."

"*You* want to leave, and then be paid for it." Carey's voice was tight. "I'm giving you a way."

He stood behind Martin's crumpled body, aiming the gun. Englehardt gauged the distance between them. Still forty feet...

"How, exactly?"

Carey hesitated. "Is that a telephone on the desk?"

"Yes."

"Let her call a taxi."

The absurdity made him angry. "Peter, we're wasting time."

"Untie her hands—she won't turn around. As soon as she gets in the cab and drives away, you can leave."

Noelle leaned forward. Aiming at her head, Englehardt felt his arm grow weary. "How will we know when she's left?"

"She'll have the driver honk." Carey's gun had begun wavering. "We can hear it from the gallery."

"That's rather clever, Peter, in a self-serving way. With one of you free, you'd diminish the odds of my killing the one who remains."

"I thought you were trying to avoid killing anyone."

He even sounds like Charles Carey, Englehardt thought. He had meant the tape to destroy Peter's reason; instead, functioning on instinct, Peter had adapted—as if, like himself, Peter had some hidden agenda...

"If you have something further in mind, Peter, recall that I killed the man in front of you with just one shot."

"Untie her," Carey said. *"I'll stay with you until the end."*

352

* * *

The loft fell silent.

Slowly, the shadow vanished behind Noelle's chair. "Don't move," the voice said.

Carey watched. His gun arm ached. The stranger bled at his feet. As if in an eerie dream, Noelle's hands appeared in the light near Barth's head, and then the shadow rose, removing her blindfold.

She gasped at Barth. "Don't look," Carey called.

She turned to his voice, real again, a face . . .

"There's a telephone next to your right hand. Pick it up."

She looked back at him, an animal blinded by light. Her lips parted. The gun moved to her temple. "Pick it up," Carey repeated.

Turning slowly, she grasped the telephone..

"Call Yellow Cab. Don't think, just do it."

She hesitated, and then the shadow spoke a telephone number.

Stiffly, she dialed.

"Ask for a cab that's en route." Carey looked from Noelle toward the shadow, gun pointed. "We're at the corner of Greene Street and Broome. Get a taxi number and a description of the driver. Tell him ten minutes . . ."

Noelle began repeating his instructions into the telephone. Each word she spoke echoed through the loft. Carey kept watching the shadow.

He saw Noelle's hand move at the corner of his eye, heard the telephone click. "They'll be here?" he asked.

She nodded.

The voice came from behind her. "You've less than ten minutes, Peter. Tell me, how will you get us from here to the gallery."

Carey hesitated. "The elevator."

"I can't let you see me, Peter. It's time that I name my conditions. First, *you'll* go to the gallery, alone."

Carey looked at Noelle. "You'd kill her."

"You'll have to trust me, as I'm now trusting you to wait while I follow with Miss Ciano. When we arrive, you'll be standing by the door to the gallery. I'll release Miss Ciano. She will slowly walk from the elevator, toward the door. You can aim your revolver at me; mine will be pointed at the base of her spine. If you do nothing foolish, she will pass through the door, alive." The voice paused. "You've less than nine minutes, Peter."

Noelle stood. "Don't..."

The gun moved to her temple.

"Well, Peter?"

Carey's eyes locked with Noelle's. "How will you leave?" he asked the shadow softly.

"Upon hearing the taxi's horn, you're to step to the far side of the gallery. I'll begin edging through the statuary, toward the door. If you so much as move, I'll shoot you. If not, I'll leave as I came."

Carey stared through the darkness: at the man at his feet; at Barth's bloody head; at the faceless shadow, holding the gun to Noelle's temple.

"Seven minutes, Peter."

Carey felt Noelle's face, pleading and stunned, freeze in his memory.

"If she dies," he said quietly, "I'll kill you. You've got sixty seconds from the time I get down."

Seventeen...

Alone in the gallery, Carey watched the door to the elevator.

Twenty-one, twenty-two...

Each second, flashing on the luminous dial of his wristwatch, ticked in his brain.

Quickly, he glanced through the window behind him. The street was empty.

Twenty-seven, twenty-eight...

The elevator kept groaning upward: stepping out, he had pushed the button marked "three."

Thirty-one, thirty-two...

Reaching in his pocket, he touched a different button on the cassette recorder.

Thirty-six, thirty-seven...

The elevator stopped.

Crouching by the coiled dragon, Carey listened.

Forty-five...

The shadow could walk free. He had taken the psychiatrist's

tape from the drawer, wiping Noelle's fingerprints from the telephone as Carey backed to the elevator.

Silence.

Statues watched him, becoming shadows. Still he heard no sound.

Fifty-two, fifty-three...

"Phillip's quite dead—your memory killed him."

Sixty.

Noelle was dead.

He stood, starting toward the elevator.

Cables groaned above his head.

The elevator started down.

Backing up to the dragon, Carey heard the elevator coming closer.

The shadow, crouched and alone, would shoot him as its doors parted.

Carey knelt, aiming his revolver at the door.

The doors opened.

Noelle and the shadow appeared in a square of light.

Half rising, Carey crouched behind the dragon.

The shadow had no face. It stood close behind Noelle, gun angled to one side of her head. Its arms and shoulders framed hers in a double image. Her face concealed his.

"Well?" the voice asked.

Carey watched Noelle. Her face was white, immobile, as if in shock.

He stood. "Let her go."

The shadow nudged her two steps forward, and then the elevator closed behind them.

Noelle became a second shadow in the darkness, merging with the other as if in eclipse. "If you move," the voice said, "I'll shoot her in the spine. You do understand that?"

Carey nodded, then realized that his nod could not be seen. "Yes," he said softly.

Slowly, Noelle's shadow separated from the one standing behind her.

She took one step forward, then another, toward Carey.

The two men were still as the statues surrounding them. Only Noelle, crossing the thirty feet between them, moved. There was no sound beyond the creaking of her steps.

Carey could not see her face.

Each step was slow, measured. Carey looked past her at the shadow; its gun hand seemed to follow her...

Slowly, her shadow grew larger, clearer; blocking the other. Carey leaned slightly right, to see the stranger's shadow...

Floorboards groaned. He winced; the shadow stiffened, did not shoot...

Noelle became a form darker than the darkness which surrounded her, coming closer.

Carey heard the sound of rubber whining on the cobblestones, a car slowing. Noelle came nearer.

The car stopped...

Her face appeared, five feet away.

Her eyes were glistening. They looked not at the street, but at him.

He aimed the revolver past her head.

Her face moved slowly closer. Carey prayed that the taxi would not leave.

She reached him, began passing to his right. When she stopped their faces were so close that he could feel the softness of her breath. Their shoulders brushed.

"Keep going," he murmured.

She looked into his eyes.

Carey stared past her, aiming at the shadow.

Noelle began moving.

He could not see her now, only hear her close behind him, stepping toward the door. The shadow's arm moved with her.

Carey strained to hear the taxi.

The door clicked, opened...

Cold air hit Carey's neck. "Let her go," he whispered to the shadow. "Please, let her go."

He heard her footsteps stop, sliding, as if she had turned back. His jaw tightened.

The door clicked shut behind him.

Carey faced the shadow, arm raised to shoot.

The shadow's gun moved toward Carey. He forced himself to listen.

A door slammed in the street.

Carey closed his eyes.

There were two quick blasts of a horn. Wheels began moving, a motor roared and then slowly faded, and she was gone.

He and the shadow were alone.

"All right, Peter." The shadow's voice was quiet, almost tender. "It's become my turn to leave you."

They watched each other. Silent, Carey began backing from the door, and then the shadow started toward it.

Gun aimed at Carey, he glided among the statues in a half-crouch. Knees tensed, Carey backed from statue to statue; he felt them become two marionettes, moving across a puppet stage.

The shadow kept edging toward the door; Carey, along the window facing Greene Street, backing into a corner. The distance between them slowly widened until only the floor, creaking, told him that the shadow was still there.

Carey reached into his pocket.

In the dim light from the street, the shadow reappeared, ten feet from the door.

Carey felt the space behind him shrinking. Soon he would reach the corner between two windows; then the only movement possible would be to his left, in front of the second window.

The shadow, moving, passed the last shadow that was still.

Carey's back touched the corner.

Stepping to his left, he knelt behind the statue of a serpent. The shadow kept moving.

Carey took the cassette recorder from his pocket, resting it on the serpent's tail.

The shadow reached the door.

Carey clicked on the tape.

The door opened; the tape started spinning.

From it, the shadow's voice repeated, "Barth wrote this check to Phillip . . ."

The shadow stopped in the doorway.

Its voice kept speaking: "The other half is Miss Ciano."

Covered by the sound, Carey began sliding to the left.

The voice was thin and clear. "It would be ironic if she died, as did your father and uncle, as part of John Carey's terrible legacy. I doubt you could preserve your sanity."

The shadow knelt, listening to itself.

"Peter, Peter—I could have let this man kill *you*, or shot you myself. Instead, I've extended our balance of terror . . ."

Carey kept sliding behind parallel statues, toward the shelter of a massive warrior. Only the window was behind him.

"What I propose is that we vanish, leaving Barth as the killer of your uncle, Levy and this man . . ."

The shadow vanished.

Carey heard the soft creak of something moving, as if drawn to the sound of the voice. Reaching the warrior, he rose to his knees.

"Not one name or scrap of paper connects me to these men or to this place . . ."

Carey turned, aiming the revolver toward the sound of the tape. Disembodied, the voice seemed to issue from the serpent: "Neither of you knows my name or has even seen my face . . ."

The gun glinted in Carey's hand; the window behind him cast too much light . . .

"I can utterly disappear, and there will be nothing but your word to say that I exist . . ."

Carey no longer heard the shadow crawling, saw only shadows that did not move.

"By leaving, you can spare yourself involvement with tonight's untidy incident and let Barth solve your considerable problems with the police, all the while preparing to discharge your substantial debt of gratitude to me."

Sweeping the room with his revolver, Carey still saw nothing.

"Most important, you'll both still be alive . . ."

A sound: clothes brushing the floor. Carey could not place it.

"*You're* the only living witnesses who could conceivably link me to this time or place . . ."

The floor creaked, closer. Perhaps the shadow had chosen not to stalk the tape, but him.

"Any time you wonder who I am, consider keeping my two million dollars, or perceive some further reason to regret our deal, remember that I could find and kill you both with infinitely greater speed and certainty than you could ever help anyone find me."

He would have to guess.

"Now, Peter, I need your answer..."

Carey aimed his gun at the voice.

The voice stopped.

All at once, Carey heard the shadow.

He turned, looking up.

The shadow stood over the warrior statue, revolver aimed at Carey's head.

Carey froze, face turned toward the shadow, gun pointed uselessly toward the spinning, silent tape.

The shadow seemed to pause. "So much like your father," it said softly, leaning closer with the gun. The floor creaked...

The shadow started.

A hand reached out to grasp its arm; the gun twitched, fired...

Its bullet smashed the window. Carey jerked up his gun; the shadow wrenched his arm free from the hand which grasped it as its taped voice asked: "Well, Peter..."

Carey aimed at his head and fired.

He felt the gun recoil in his hand, heard someone scream.

The shadow tottered, gun extending toward Carey in eerie slow motion.

The gun dropped, shattering the statue of the warrior, and then the shadow fell sideways at Carey's feet.

His head rolled into the light.

His face was wizened, sallow as parchment. His eyes stared back at Carey.

There was a bullet hole in his forehead.

Carey reached out to touch his bow tie.

"Peter?"

It was Noelle who knelt beside them. Carey looked across the dead man, into her face.

"He was the faceless man," he said softly. "The one who killed my father..."

A light was on; Phillip turned from the wheel of his father's car.

"Peter!"

His uncle stood, mouth open. Peter stared at him.

"I came to get Dewey."

In the pale light, Phillip looked frightened. Peter's voice grew smaller. "I want my elephant."

Phillip did not answer. Fearful, Peter backed away, to find his father.

A second man stepped from behind the car.

Peter stopped, staring.

The man took Dewey from the front seat, and held him out. "Here, Peter, is this what you want?"

The man smiled.

Peter liked his bow tie . . .

PART III

MOUNT SNOW, VERMONT

MARCH 1983

CHAPTER 1

Noelle Carey cried out.

Peter was ten feet ahead, skiing for his life. Pines flashed past at the corners of her eyes and then the trail burst abruptly into a glistening sweep of white. Peter dug in his ski poles; snow rose like mist and melted on her face. She pushed to catch him.

Peter curled in a shell, heading breakneck for the marker.

Straining forward, Noelle tucked her ski poles in a last rush down the slope. Snow swept beneath and behind her in a shooting line; her knees were like springs; the marker raced at them. Peter's back drew closer.

She was three feet from him when he passed the stake.

He spun, grinning through a nimbus of powder. Noelle stopped next to him.

"Bastard," she repeated.

"Well," Peter grinned. "You're one year older now."

He looked so pleased with himself that she began laughing.

At first, she had wondered how they could go on.

Her nightmares of the ugly man were constant. Peter held her; in the morning light, his face would remind her of all the things she had learned in SoHo that she never wished to know.

Peter, who no longer dreamed, treated her with haunted kindness. He would not speak of how he felt. The police, probing the frightening and inscrutable, bled them of emotion; his apartment made them feel caged.

Gregorio had broken down the doorman.

Visiting, she would pace from room to room, imagining the moments she had valued as pictures stolen by a pervert. It became hard for her to work.

She began to wonder about leaving the city.

She had mentioned this one evening, sitting by the fireplace. For a long time, Peter simply looked at her, as if she should be listening to the sound of her own question. Finally, he said, "Then you'd be changing who you are, Noelle. I wonder if you want that."

She was silent. At last, she looked into his face.

"No," she told him softly. "That would be too much."

In April, on a fresh spring day, Carey called her at work.

"I've been thinking," he said. "Can you look at a house with me?"

There was a pause. "When?"

"Around five."

"I don't know, Peter." Carey could almost hear her thinking. "I'm really kind of tired."

"I'll buy you dinner afterwards, near your place." He felt curiously desperate. "Looking at houses is something new for me. I'd like your opinion."

Noelle hesitated. "Okay," she finally said.

They were in the subway before she asked where it was.

"Near you," Carey answered.

She looked surprised. "The Village?"

"Uh-huh. I'll show you when we get there."

A woman was standing in front of a town house on St. Luke's Place. "If there's anything that scares me," Carey murmured, "it's a realtor in furs."

Noelle had stopped, staring at the town house.

It was three stories of fresh-scrubbed brick in the middle of the block. Steps climbed between wrought-iron railings to an arched oak doorway; the door and railing ran in perfect symmetry with its neighbors' down the south side of the street. The street itself was cobblestoned and flanked by gaslights and parallel rows of trees, leaves touching in an arbor, high above Noelle. Carey turned to her. "Best block in Manhattan, Ruth says."

Noelle said nothing.

When the realtor unlocked the door, she disappeared inside.

The woman started after. "Let her go," Carey said.

Ahead of them, doors began opening and closing, rapid footsteps took the stairway to the second floor and then back down again. In the living room, Carey half-listened to the realtor's rhapsody of hardwood floors and intricate molding and exposed brick in the library. It didn't really matter; Carey had seen the house that morning.

"Noelle?" he called.

No one answered.

He found her standing in the middle of the street, hands on hips, grinning at the house.

"Buy it," she said.

The night he moved in, they made love for the first time since SoHo.

Afterwards, she told him, "I know how hard it's been—dealing with what happened, and then dealing with me."

Carey felt relief course through him. "Sometimes caring for you kept the other from crashing down on me—I can't face that yet, or really even talk it out. It's just that I got lonely . . ."

"It hurt me so much, Peter. Inside."

She wept in his arms.

Very close to morning, she spoke again. "There's this about it," she said softly. "I've got no reason to doubt you love me."

He touched her face. "Nor I."

In the morning, Noelle stayed, making coffee.

They sat in the kitchen. "The faceless man," she finally asked. "When did you remember him?"

Peter stirred his coffee. "At the end of the tape. I knew then that he had to be the man who played it. No one else could know so much."

For a moment, she watched him. "Is it okay now—with Pogostin?"

"Fine." Peter hesitated. "I miss Levy, though. Sometimes I miss him a lot."

"How long will you be going, do you think?"

"Awhile yet." He turned away. "If I'd told my father, none of this would have happened. It's hard to figure what to do with that."

"You were six, Peter. You couldn't know."

"I do now." He looked up at her. "Still, I suppose it's better dealing with a known."

"Phillip," she said gently. "You're dealing with Phillip."

* * *

Phillip's will left everything to Peter.

It was three months before he could bring himself to enter Phillip's town house, and when he did, Noelle went with him.

In an attic trunk, beneath a pile of Peter's baseball cards that Phillip had saved, he found a small stuffed elephant.

He stood staring down at the doll, cradled in both hands.

Finally, he looked at Noelle. Neither of them spoke.

Quietly, she gave Dewey to a friend's small son, to take with him to day care.

"You can keep avoiding Ruth forever," Noelle had told him. "Or you can remember the people you loved in common, and go on from there."

It was summer, and they were painting the living room. "Then why," Carey responded, "do you still have nightmares?"

She nodded. "I'm not saying you can change what happened, Peter. You can only change how you deal with her, now."

He was pensive. "It's not that I avoid her, really. It's just that she reminds me of my father: what I didn't tell him, why they killed her brother . . ."

"Then tell her that—part of it, anyhow." She paused. "The other part is not the fault of either one of you."

Carey frowned, and then cocked his head. "You're getting surer of yourself, aren't you?"

She glanced at the walls. "The paint I chose worked out . . ."

The next morning Carey poked his head around Ruth's door. "Have a moment?"

She reached for a cigarette. "Of course."

Carey closed the door behind him. "I'm worried about losing you."

Ruth lit the cigarette, eyes still fixed on him. "Why?"

"We both know that your brother died because he helped me. I feel as though you've had it with the Careys—including me."

"I'm rational enough to know who murdered Bill." She exhaled. "I remember you were kind that morning. What more can be said?"

"Between you and me?" His speech was quiet, tentative. "A little more than that, I think."

"Peter, please..."

"I'll remember your brother as long as I live." Carey paused, adding softly, "Just as you've never stopped loving my father."

Their gaze met.

"When my father died," he finished, "I was only six, and there was no one I could share it with. Now there is."

Her eyes filled with confusion. "You *saw*..."

"Now there is," he repeated gently. "Talk to me, Ruthie. Please."

The cigarette smoldered in her ashtray, ignored. "How long have you known?"

"Since the day I came here." She looked down. "It never mattered, Ruthie. I loved him, too."

There was silence. Finally, she gazed back at him. "I've been looking for something else, yes. This is *hard*, Peter—I think it's for the best."

"It isn't, though. Not for me."

Her mouth twisted. "Your father told me something like that—about twenty-five years ago."

"Then please give me a few more months." He waited a moment, to smile. "After all, I've got a publishing company to run."

Ruth took another puff on the cigarette, watching its smoke. "Two more months," she answered.

They started having lunch.

They seldom spoke of Levy, or his father. Instead, he asked her about publishing while he had the chance, using her advice to help run the firm. Their lunches became longer.

One Friday in July, during the summer doldrums which settle on Manhattan and publishing alike, their lunch hour stretched past three o'clock. "I wonder," he asked, "if it makes sense for me as publisher to also be editor-in-chief."

"Only if you have children." She shot him a sardonic glance. "Your grandfather kept both jobs to tease his sons. But our finances are so complex now that whoever serves as publisher has his hands full with just that."

Carey nodded. "That's why I'd like to split the two, with

Sometimes the two of them would sit up late, drinking brandy in his living room; Ruth would talk of Charles Carey, the things they had said or done together, the love he had for Peter. "He *did* leave you things," she said one evening. "You look more like him every day, and you're sensitive in the quirky way he had—he usually knew when *not* to talk, and what to say to me when he did. But your instinct for a dollar you got from Black Jack Carey." Smiling, she added, "Given that we're meeting with the banks tomorrow, that's probably just as well."

Carey looked at her. "I hope you don't mind remembering."

"Charles?" She shook her head. "I only mind that I don't have more than memories, as I do of Bill . . ."

Impulsively, Carey kissed her cheek, and then the talk turned to the meeting.

It ended early. Coming home, he encountered Noelle bounding upstairs from the darkroom, photographs in hand. The sense of his good fortune, wondrous and irrational, hit him with a rush . . .

"Marry me, okay?"

She stopped in her tracks, grinning.

"I mean it," Carey said. "You're precious to me."

Noelle put down the photographs.

"It's fine with me," she told him later. "But we're too old to stage some bogus event."

They did it quietly, at Christmas.

At the end of their last ski run, Peter stopped to watch a small boy with his father.

They stood at the bottom of the hill. The boy was quite young, no more than four, and his skis resembled slats. Noelle watched him, a small figure on small skis, legs spraddling in a precarious split. The boy's young father held his hand; laughing and patient, he looked as if no one else were as important, or ever would be. Peter smiled after them.

"Remind you of someone?" she asked.

"In a way." Still watching, he added, "What I remember is how good he was with me, when my mother couldn't be. I wonder how he understood so much."

Noelle turned to him. "You'd understand."

She took his hand, and they went back to the cabin.

In the warm darkness of their bedroom, they touched each other, gently and without haste, until at last their bodies lay skin to skin, and they moved, and then cried out, together.

Afterwards he held her, warm and drowsy in the night. They felt too close to speak.

That Sunday, they had breakfast at the lodge. Peter bought the *Times*.

They split it. On the first page of the Arts and Leisure section, Noelle found a photo of Natalia Makarova, dancing with Baryshnikov. The picture snapped with electricity: from the height of her leap, Makarova seemed to stare straight at them, all fire and ambition. The credit beneath it read, "Noelle Ciano Carey."

"That's her, all right." Peter turned the picture toward him, smiling as he read the credit. "I hope you don't mind."

"The name, you mean?"

"Uh-huh."

"Not really—I had a choice." She grinned. "Besides, it'll be less confusing for the kid."

Peter looked up from the photograph.

They laughed together.

NO SAFE PLACE
Richard North Patterson

YOU CAN RUN – BUT YOU CAN'T HIDE

Kerry Kilcannon's future looks golden, but in an election campaign seven days can be a dangerously long time.

NO SAFE PLACE is Kerry's story – an electrifying novel that follows the campaign trail, where death and the undying past haunt the most charismatic presidential candidate in a generation, where violence and scandal threaten to erupt, where public image and private life collide with explosive effect.

'Patterson has his finger on the pulse of contemporary America'
Cosmopolitan

EYES OF A CHILD

Richard North Patterson

'This was my first Patterson: I can't wait for another'
Time Out

First he was a defence lawyer. Now he needs a lawyer of his own . . .

Ricardo Arias is found dead in his apartment, the gun that killed him wedged into his mouth. The physical evidence might confirm suicide, but it also strongly suggests murder.

Chris Paget is the lover of the victim's estranged wife. Suddenly accused of the crime, he finds himself at the centre of a storm of emotion and conflict that threatens to tear his family apart forever. He has the motive – the dead man's accusations seem destined to put Paget's son on trial for abuse of Arias' daughter. Worse, his alibi is full of holes.

And only a six-year-old girl knows the truth.

'A chilling success . . . Patterson is one of the best in the business'
Time Magazine

'Patterson's new thriller is a miracle of agonizingly focused suspense'
Kirkus

THE FINAL JUDGEMENT

Richard North Patterson

On the very day Caroline Masters is offered a prestigious appointment to the US Court of Appeals, she receives a cry for help she cannot ignore, a cry that turns her world inside out.

Her niece Brett's boyfriend has been murdered. Brett herself is found naked, covered in blood, disoriented by drugs and alcohol. In her car, by her side, lie a blood-stained knife and her boyfriend's wallet. A conviction for murder seems inevitable.

As Caroline battles to protect Brett and discover the truth, secrets buried deep in her own past surface, threatening to tear her family apart and destroy her future.

'Destined for celebrity status alongside Scott Turow and John Grisham . . . He belongs among the élite'
Los Angeles Times

'Surprise upon surprise . . . the pages seem to turn themselves'
San Francisco Chronicle

SILENT WITNESS

Richard North Patterson

'Patterson is one of the best in the business'
Time

Two brutal murders. Two dead high school students. Two families bereaved. Two men suspected of killing their lovers . . .

Twenty-eight years separate the crimes that link Tony Lord and Sam Robb.

In 1967 Tony Lord is suspected of killing his girlfriend Alison, but the case never comes to trial, and Tony has never officially cleared his name in a cast that is still open.

In 1995, Tony is a successful San Francisco attorney and receives a desperate call from Sam's wife: Sam has been accused of the murder of one of his students. Reluctantly, but inevitably, Tony agrees to defend his boyhood friend.

At once, Tony is plunged into the unfinished business of his past. And in the merciless arena of the murder trial, he must face not only his fear that Sam is a killer, but also the dark, buried truths that surround Alison's death all those years earlier . . .

'Destined for celebrity status alongside Scott Turow and John Grisham'
Los Angeles Times

'Patterson has his finger on the pulse of contemporary America'
Cosmopolitan

OTHER BESTSELLING TITLES IN ARROW

☐	No Safe Place	Richard North Patterson	£ 5.99
☐	Silent Witness	Richard North Patterson	£ 5.99
☐	The Final Judgement	Richard North Patterson	£ 5.99
☐	Degree of Guilt	Richard North Patterson	£ 5.99
☐	Eyes of a Child	Richard North Patterson	£ 5.99
☐	Private Screening	Richard North Patterson	£ 5.99
☐	The Chamber	John Grisham	£ 6.99
☐	The Client	John Grisham	£ 6.99
☐	The Firm	John Grisham	£ 6.99
☐	The Pelican Brief	John Grisham	£ 5.99
☐	The Rainmaker	John Grisham	£ 6.99
☐	The Runaway Jury	John Grisham	£ 6.99
☐	A Time to Kill	John Grisham	£ 6.99

ALL ARROW BOOKS ARE AVAILABLE THROUGH MAIL ORDER OR FROM YOUR LOCAL BOOKSHOP AND NEWSAGENT.

PLEASE SEND CHEQUE, EUROCHEQUE, POSTAL ORDER (STERLING ONLY), ACCESS, VISA, MASTERCARD, DINERS CARD, SWITCH OR AMEX.

☐☐☐☐☐☐☐☐☐☐☐☐☐☐☐☐

EXPIRY DATE .... SIGNATURE ....

PLEASE ALLOW 75 PENCE PER BOOK FOR POST AND PACKING U.K.

OVERSEAS CUSTOMERS PLEASE ALLOW £1.00 PER COPY FOR POST AND PACKING.

ALL ORDERS TO:

ARROW BOOKS, BOOKS BY POST, TBS LIMITED, THE BOOK SERVICE, COLCHESTER ROAD, FRATING GREEN, COLCHESTER, ESSEX CO7 7DW.

TELEPHONE: (01206) 256 000
FAX: (01206) 255 914

NAME ....

ADDRESS ....

....

Please allow 28 days for delivery. Please tick box if you do not wish to receive any additional information ☐

Prices and availability subject to change without notice.